Acclaim For the W

MAX ALLAN

"Crime fiction aficionados are in for a treat...a neo-pulp noir classic."

—*Chicago Tribune*

"No one can twist you through a maze with as much intensity and suspense as Max Allan Collins."

—*Clive Cussler*

"Collins never misses a beat...All the stand-up pleasures of dime-store pulp with a beguiling level of complexity."

—*Booklist*

"Collins has an outwardly artless style that conceals a great deal of art."

—*New York Times Book Review*

"Max Allan Collins is the closest thing we have to a 21st-century Mickey Spillane and...will please any fan of old-school, hardboiled crime fiction."

—*This Week*

"A suspenseful, wild night's ride [from] one of the finest writers of crime fiction that the U.S. has produced."

—*Book Reporter*

"This book is about as perfect a page turner as you'll find."

—*Library Journal*

"Bristling with suspense and sexuality, this book is a welcome addition to the Hard Case Crime library."

—*Publishers Weekly*

“A total delight…fast, surprising, and well-told.”
—*Deadly Pleasures*

“Strong and compelling reading.”
—*Ellery Queen’s Mystery Magazine*

“Max Allan Collins [is] like no other writer.”
—*Andrew Vachss*

“Collins breaks out a really good one, knocking over the hard-boiled competition (Parker and Leonard for sure, maybe even Puzo) with a one-two punch: a feisty storyline told bittersweet and wry…nice and taut…the book is unputdownable. Never done better.”
—*Kirkus Reviews*

“Rippling with brutal violence and surprising sexuality…I savored every turn.”
—*Bookgasm*

“Masterful.”
—*Jeffery Deaver*

“Collins has a gift for creating low-life believable characters …a sharply focused action story that keeps the reader guessing till the slam-bang ending. A consummate thriller from one of the new masters of the genre.”
—*Atlanta Journal Constitution*

“For fans of the hardboiled crime novel…this is powerful and highly enjoyable reading, fast moving and very, very tough.”
—*Cleveland Plain Dealer*

“Nobody does it better than Max Allan Collins.”
—*John Lutz*

She looked at him strangely. She was a very pretty woman; striking eyes. She said, in a surprisingly kind voice, "What's a nice kid like you doing in a situation like this?"

When he'd researched other skyjackings, he'd found that his goal was different from most. Funny, too, because his would seem the most likely goal. But it wasn't. Many skyjackers did it for glory; he wanted none of that. True, the adventure of it had been appealing to him, but the publicity meant nothing. He had no desire to become a folk hero, à la Rafael Minichiello or D. B. Cooper; and he certainly didn't want to see his name in the papers! Some skyjacked out of death wish, suicidal tendency; if he had any of that, he didn't know it. Much skyjacking was political protest and/or the seeking of political asylum, the skyjackings to Cuba being the most obvious example of that. But there was no political motivation to his skyjacking, although a disillusionment with the American Dream had had something to do with it. He was no protester; he cared nothing for politics. His was an admittedly selfish goal he shared with few skyjackers; D. B. Cooper and a handful of others, that was all.

So, when the stewardess asked him for his reason, he was almost anxious to clarify himself.

"I need the money," he said....

HARD CASE CRIME BOOKS
BY MAX ALLAN COLLINS:

SKIM DEEP
TWO FOR THE MONEY
DOUBLE DOWN
TOUGH TENDER*
MAD MONEY*

QUARRY
QUARRY'S LIST
QUARRY'S DEAL
QUARRY'S CUT
QUARRY'S VOTE
THE LAST QUARRY
THE FIRST QUARRY
QUARRY IN THE MIDDLE
QUARRY'S EX
THE WRONG QUARRY
QUARRY'S CHOICE
QUARRY IN THE BLACK
QUARRY'S CLIMAX
QUARRY'S WAR *(graphic novel)*
KILLING QUARRY

DEADLY BELOVED
SEDUCTION OF THE INNOCENT

DEAD STREET *(with Mickey Spillane)*
THE CONSUMMATA *(with Mickey Spillane)*
MIKE HAMMER: THE NIGHT I DIED
(graphic novel with Mickey Spillane)

**coming soon*

Double DOWN

by **Max Allan Collins**

CRIME NOVEL

A HARD CASE CRIME BOOK
(HCC-149)
First Hard Case Crime edition: May 2021

Published by
Titan Books
A division of Titan Publishing Group Ltd
144 Southwark Street
London SE1 0UP
in collaboration with Winterfall LLC

Print edition ISBN 978-1-78909-141-0
E-book ISBN 978-1-78909-142-7

Design direction by Max Phillips
www.maxphillips.net

Typeset by Swordsmith Productions

Printed and bound by CPI Group (UK)Ltd, Croydon CR0 4YY

Visit us on the web at www.HardCaseCrime.com

Introduction

The Nolan novels, like most of my series, began with what was intended to be a one-shot novel, *Bait Money*, written in the late sixties and early seventies when I was at the Writers Workshop at the University of Iowa in Iowa City. I had grown up wanting to write "tough guy" fiction, very much in the thrall of Spillane, Hammett, Chandler, Cain and Thompson, but had recently discovered the Richard Stark-bylined "Parker" novels by Donald E. Westlake. Don became something of a mentor to me, and he said nice things about *Bait Money*, even though it was obviously in part an homage to his own series about a hard-bitten professional thief.

That book originally had Nolan dying at the conclusion—my thinking being that once is homage, twice is rip-off—but when the publisher, Curtis Books, asked for sequels, I said yes. (Don was kind enough to give his blessing, saying that the Jon character, Nolan's youthful sidekick, humanized both Nolan and the series itself in a way that was quite apart from his Stark novels.)

Blood Money was an outgrowth of dangling plot threads from *Bait Money*. Since Nolan had originally kicked the bucket in that book, at the hands of a former Family boss of his (the Family being my name for the Mob or the Outfit), plenty of loose ends awaited tying off.

So in a way, *Fly Paper* (which makes up the first half of the volume you are now holding) was the first true series entry. It was tricky because Nolan had retired from professional crime and was trying to go straight, in his jagged way. That meant to some degree all of the novels have, like *Blood Money*, grown from the previous ones. The series, in a way, is one long sprawling novel that resolves in *Spree*, and perhaps that's why I didn't write another until recently when Hard Case Crime editor Charles Ardai twisted my arm into writing a coda, *Skim Deep*.

The idea of the crook trying to go straight, and having his past come back at him in a bad karmic fashion, is the heart of these novels. Nolan is not a guy who has gotten religion, not hardly—he has always been a capitalist, a businessman chasing the American dream, and nothing grandiose, either.

Fly Paper grew out of the basic idea of, "What if a tough guy of Nolan's stripe had been on board when D. B. Cooper famously skyjacked a plane?" This also provided an opportunity to make the D. B. Cooper character sympathetic, and pursue what has been a recurring plot device in my work: sending two sympathetic, opposing forces up against each other, to fuck with the reader.

It also gave me the opportunity to create a new recurring source of opposition for Nolan, now that his score with the Chicago Family was more or less settled. The Comfort family (lowercase "f") became that new collective adversary for Nolan, and they are among my proudest creations, part Scraggs from *Li'l Abner*, with a dose of various characters Strother Martin played in '60s and '70s movies, and a big dollop of a real rural family of miscreants who used to love to come hear my band Crusin' play, back (as they say) in the day.

Fly Paper was written around 1973, and was unfortunate enough to go into publishing limbo when Curtis Books was bought up by Popular Library, who (despite assurances) never got around to publishing the four Nolan novels in their inventory. I didn't get the rights back until the early '80s, when all of the first six books (*Bait Money* through *Scratch Fever*) were purchased by Pinnacle Books. In the intervening almost-a-decade, security measures at airports had heightened and that required a minor rewrite. Now those updated security measures seem mild indeed.

Hush Money, the fourth Nolan novel, is among the four in the series that were written in the early '70s but not published till the early '80s. When Curtis Books, a lower-end paperback publisher despite its supposed relationship to the fabled *Saturday Evening Post*, got itself absorbed by Popular Library, those four Nolan novels (and the first two Mallorys) went into that dreaded publishing limbo called inventory.

My agent received periodic assurances that the books would be published, but that never happened—editors prefer to publish books they've discovered and bought themselves, not something that's a remainder from the overstock of some failed publishing house their firm swallowed up. Finally, however, the rights came back to us, and Pinnacle Books even ordered up two new novels. I don't believe I've ever had a six-book contract since.

I performed some minor rewriting on the first two, already-published books (*Bait Money* and *Blood Money*) and did some updating where necessary, in particular the skyjacking novel, *Fly Paper*. *Bait Money* came out in a spiffy, pulpy new Pinnacle edition and sold very well. Things were looking up.

The irony of *Hush Money* is that it touches upon the reason that Pinnacle wanted six books out of me and—had the future gone in the fashion it portended—probably would have wanted three to six a year thereafter. Pinnacle had recently lost its signature crime series, the Executioner, a break-up between publisher and author (Don Pendleton) that was as awash in bad blood, as, well...an Executioner novel.

I had read a few Executioner novels, because early on they

were a sort of updating of Mike Hammer, the creation of my literary "ideel" (as Li'l Abner would put it), Mickey Spillane. But they weren't my style—just too overtly pulp and over-the-top for my refined tastes. I was more a Richard Stark guy now, and of course the Nolan series was in that tradition. Some call the Nolans a pastiche of Stark's Parker novels, and there are overt influences—in particular, the strict points of view and switching back and forth between those points of view.

But I was at least as influenced by the Sand novels by an obscure author of '60s softcore porn, Ennis Willie. Willie didn't write softcore porn, but his publisher sold him that way. Really, the Sand novels were a skillful, unlikely melding of Spillane and W. R. Burnett, and for my money were far superior to Pendleton and his eventual ragtag army of imitators (a few exceptions there, particularly the Destroyer). Ennis Willie was an enigma in crime fiction fan circles for decades, until turning up a few years ago—two volumes of vintage Sand material are now available from Ramble House with introductions by me.

I had written my first Nolan—*Mourn the Living*, a book that didn't get published till many years later—in 1967, before the Executioner came along in 1969. The first Nolan novel to be published, *Bait Money*, got its first draft in 1968. *Hush Money* was just my way of showing what would happen to the Executioner in my world—Nolan's world, which is to say, nothing like Pendleton's. Not that there was anything mean-spirited about it—it was just my darkly satirical take on what was then a newly minted, very popular series. *Hush Money*, remember, was written around 1974 or '75.

I have no idea whether Pendleton was offended by *Hush Money*, when it was published in 1981. But he was offended overall by Nolan, which he said was "a silly syllable away from Bolan," his character. Ironically, Nolan had initially been called

Cord (in *Mourn*), which was changed to Logan in *Bait Money*; but because a long-forgotten paperback series had a hero called Logan around the time I was first sending *Bait Money* out to publishers, I changed the name to Nolan.

So there was nothing intentional about Nolan/Bolan. The packaging of the novels was similar, but all the series Pinnacle was publishing in that genre were similar. Nolan's save-his-ass "war" with the Chicago mob was nothing like Bolan's holy one. Nolan's world was violent but in a less cartoony fashion than that of the Executioner.

Nonetheless, Pendleton threatened a lawsuit (there was already a lawsuit on other issues between him and his erstwhile publisher), and despite impressive sales figures, the Nolan series was canceled. The last two books on the contract (*Hard Cash* and *Scratch Fever*) even had his name stripped from the covers.

Later, I exchanged letters with Pendleton and made it clear I had not imitated him—that in fact, the Nolan character predated Bolan. He was apologetic and very nice about it, but it was too late. Nolan was really dead this time.

Of course, I later got to revive him for a single novel, *Spree*, in 1987, and then to close the series off with *Skim Deep* in 2020.

But that's another story.

MAX ALLAN COLLINS

BOOK ONE

Fly Paper

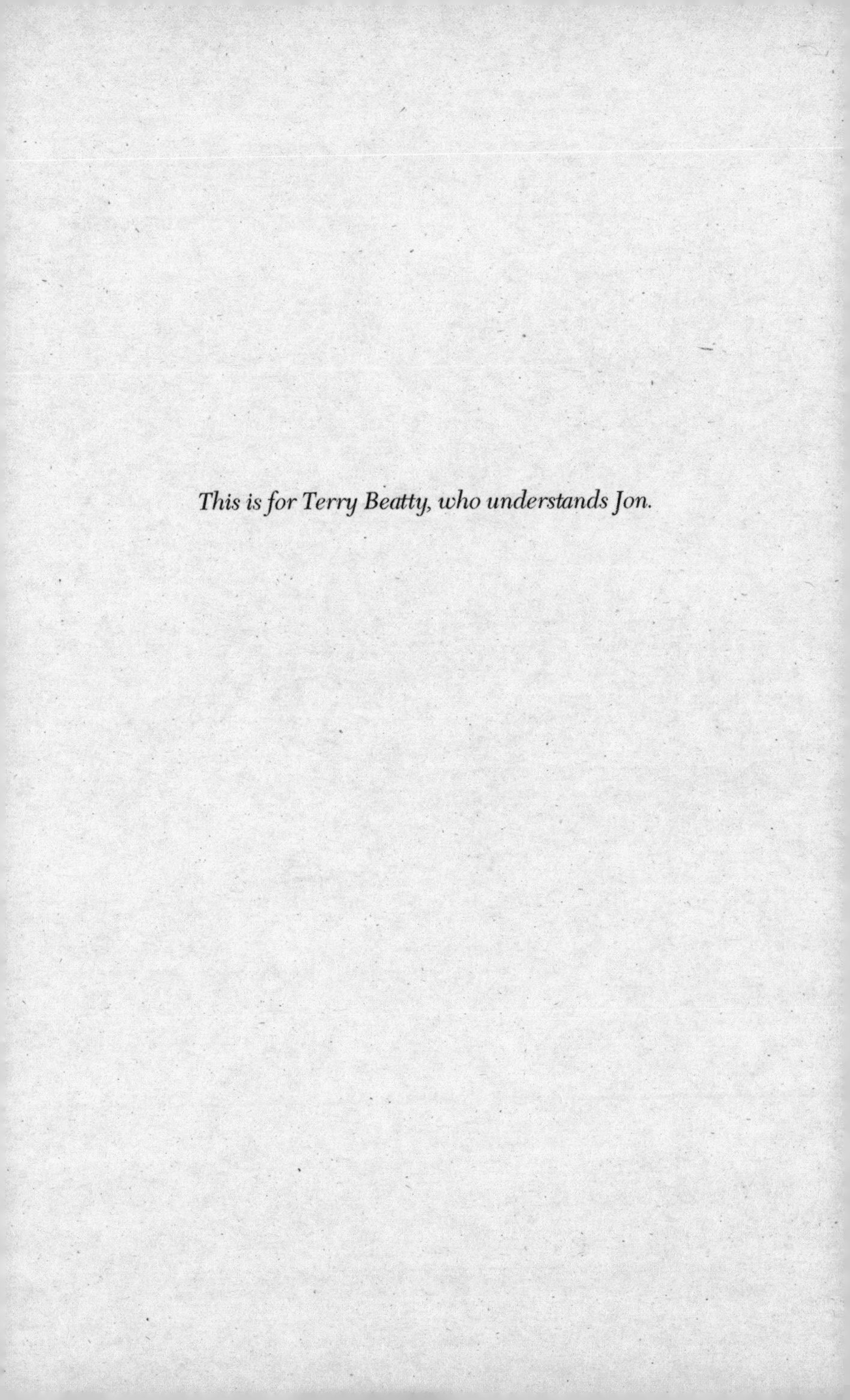

This is for Terry Beatty, who understands Jon.

"Sky piracy…involves the interests of every nation, the safety of every traveller, and the integrity of that structure of order on which a world community depends."

R. M. Nixon

"Take me to Mexico."

D. B. Cooper

Prologue:
Pre-Flight Check

The suitcase itself was a bomb. It would be harmless enough going through baggage check, and no matter how roughly it was tossed into the cargo hold, it wouldn't explode: all the jostle in the world couldn't do that. *Not till I arm it,* he thought. By remote control, when the plane is in the air. Even then, nothing could set it off. Except his finger, on the right button.

Not that he *wanted* to blow up a plane, killing all the people on board, himself included. He wanted no part of that. But it was a possibility, a calculated risk he had to take; high stakes, high risk, simple as that. A more desperate man wouldn't have twitched an eye at such a prospect, and his concern for his own life and the lives of others was proof positive that he was anything but a desperate man.

He was, rather, a man who'd made a decision. A difficult one at that, reached through calm, rational consideration. And as for the plane blowing up and people getting killed, well, that would be someone else's decision: the decision of the airline official or FBI agent or heroic crew member who might force upon him the pushing of that final button.

He'd decided, too, that only under the most extreme circumstances would he even consider pushing that button before all the passengers (except a handful of hostages) were off the plane. He was not a monster, after all: the killing of perhaps several hundred people was not something his conscience could easily bear, even if that killing was forced upon him. Of course if it came to that, his conscience would be blown to pieces along with everything and everybody else, wouldn't it?

But that was the most far-fetched of possibilities. That was not according to his plan. This is how it will go, he thought: after commandeering the plane, he would direct the pilot to a specific airport, at which the bulk of the passengers would be allowed to disembark. Remaining on the plane would be crew members (pilot, copilot and navigator), as well as a stewardess (a volunteer) and some passenger hostages (likewise volunteers). After the ransom money was delivered, the passenger hostages would be released, and the plane would again take off.

He felt no moral responsibility toward the lives of any of these people. The crew members were, after all, professionals highly paid to bear the hazards of flying, including that of skyjacking. And likewise, he couldn't be expected to feel concerned about the passengers who volunteered to stay on as hostages. They would be volunteers, who'd made their own decision to stay on the plane, wouldn't they? He was not responsible.

He was twenty-six years old and looked eighteen, with an eternally boyish face, like Johnny Carson. His hair was fair and short, neatly trimmed, neatly combed; he was freckled and blue-eyed. Despite the sloppiness of his surroundings, he was dressed in conservative, tidy work clothes: a deep brown sweatshirt with the words "Greystoke Teacher's College" spelled out in white, light brown jeans, brown Hush Puppies and dark socks. His was the type of appearance many fathers long for in their sons; he was just what the recruiting officer was looking for: he was clean-cut.

He was hunched over the workbench in a basement that looked like a warehouse of a small electronics firm after a rather untidy burglary. While the workbench itself was well ordered, the room surrounding was chaos: supplies, abandoned projects, empty cartons, stacks of Radio Shack and other electronics catalogs, all were scattered about like so much refuse.

Still, mess or no mess, he knew where to find whatever he needed, whenever he needed. To the uninitiated, the basement was a mess; to him it was a filing system.

The basement also held the artifacts of a childhood not entirely given up: a table with an electric train, still functioning, though one would have had to do a ballet around the boxes and unfinished projects to get to the control; a go-cart, mostly disassembled, awaiting the mood to strike its owner to put Humpty Dumpty back together; a guitar amplifier he'd half finished back in early high school, when he'd thought for a while he might take up that instrument; a motorcycle from that same era, a lightweight Honda, also still functioning, or almost—as soon as he got the engine put back together it would be; and off in one corner, stacks of science fiction comic books and pulp digests, as well as an overflowing box of tattered Big Little Books, space stuff mostly (*Buck Rogers*, *Flash Gordon*, *Brick Bradford*), old junk left from his older brother's childhood but also a fond part of his. The yellowed pages of those little books, as well as the sf comics and pulps he'd bought himself, stirred his sense of adventure as much in their way as the go-cart and Honda had in theirs.

Upstairs, his wife kept things orderly. When they'd moved to this modest but cozy house from their small apartment (which had been more his workshop than their apartment, every room but the bath looking not unlike this basement), she had asked him if he could limit his projects and such to the downstairs. Though he could have overridden her if he'd wanted to, he'd deferred to her wishes. After all, she was his wife and deserved a nice home, didn't she? He stayed downstairs.

Now he was rechecking all his leads, making doubly sure they were firmly soldered to the various solid-state chips that made up his remote control system. He was good at this sort of thing. He was an all-around handyman, good at anything mechanical—no electronics genius, maybe, but he knew what he was doing. There were guys with degrees in chemistry and biophysics and the like (his degree was in business) who had the knowledge, sure, but not the knack, not the knack for putting things together, making them work. He could make something out of nothing. Give him a pile of junk and a little time, and he would provide the sweat and imagination and come up with something special. The suitcase/bomb, for instance. He'd made that from, well, he'd made it from crap. Literally. Fertilizer, that is, nitrate-based fertilizer purchased at a local farm supply outlet. The nitrates were the key, and utilizing a variation on standard industrial "cook-book" recipes, he'd had no trouble processing the nitrate-based fertilizer into 10 x 4 x 3-inch blocks of plastic explosive, which looked like nothing more than six loaves of unbaked rye bread.

Next to the suitcase on the workbench were three items of great importance.

The first was a light, compact, but serviceable parachute, one he'd used when skydiving was a hobby of his several years ago, an emergency chute, worn strapped to the stomach.

Next was a portable citizen's band radio, sender/receiver, about the size of a small hardcover book; this would provide communications when he hit the ground, so that his wife could come pick him up (she'd be receiving and sending on a C.B. in the car). The C.B. had a black, slightly padded case with a clip that would slip over his belt.

And, finally, there was the pocket calculator, an inconspicuous block of black plastic with numbered push-button face, not much bigger or thicker than a deck of playing cards. In this case, however, the deck was decidedly stacked: he had wired in several special functions in addition to the calculator's usual ones.

Except for a chip of circuitry that ran the calculator (whose bulk was primarily due to the panel of push buttons, and the window that displayed the answer to whatever mathematical question you might ask via those buttons) the inside was hollow, and there'd been plenty of space for the extra wiring. He'd wired in a signal, using a frequency higher than the regular broadcast band, one that would penetrate sufficiently into the cargo hold of the plane. This high frequency would be diffracted throughout the entire compartment, seeking out the suitcase, whereas a lower frequency would be blocked out by the metal of the plane. Four times four would arm the suitcase/bomb. Four times four times four would detonate.

"Honey!"

His wife. Carol. He covered the suitcase with some newspapers and went upstairs to her, before she could come down.

She was in the kitchen, sitting at the yellow formica-top table, stirring cream and sugar into a cup of coffee. She'd been crying again. Crying made most girls less attractive; ran their mascara and everything. His wife was different. Crying didn't spoil her looks at all: she was a natural beauty, wore practically no makeup, just a touch of pale pink lip gloss. She had long, cascading blonde hair. Natural. Her eyes were cornflower blue. While her nose was a trifle large, it was nicely formed, and she had a nice white smile, too, though she wasn't showing it now. Only on the occasional times when he stopped and studied her like this did he realize how really beautiful she was, and how good it was to have her around.

Like her hair, the kitchen was yellow, except for the white appliances that Carol kept so highly polished that when morning sun came in the window and reflected off them, it was almost blinding. Right now, however, the kitchen was dark, gloomy dark. It was the middle of the evening, and the window next to the table, curtain drawn back, let in nothing but moonless night. She'd left windows open all around the house, and though it was late October, the breeze was just cool, nothing more. No sounds came from outside: the night sounds in Canker, Missouri, population 12,000, ran to little more than the sporadic squealing of a teenager's tires. What little light there was in the kitchen came from the living room where the TV was going, unattended; a comedy show was on, volume low, but every now and then a rumble of canned laughter would break the stillness. Carol's face was pale. Expressionless.

"What's wrong, Carol?"

"I don't want you to do it."

"Carol."

"Ken. Honey. I don't want you to go through with it."

"And I don't want to discuss that anymore. I already made up my mind. This is one project I'm going to finish."

"Sit down, will you? And talk to me?"

He sat down, but he didn't say anything.

"What are you working on downstairs?"

"You know. What I told you."

"Why's it taking so long to put together? I mean, if it's a fake bomb, why's it taking so long?"

"I explained that. It has to look realistic. It'll help me if they have to waste a lot of hours defusing what they think is a bomb." That didn't really make much sense, but fortunately, she hadn't questioned the logic of it.

"Ken?"

"Yes?"

"I don't understand you."

"Sure you do."

"I don't. I don't understand any of this. It seems so unnecessary..."

"Carol. Look at my face. It's got lines in it. I'm a kid and I got lines in my face." It was something that was bothering him lately. Not that he was vain, but he did like to think of himself as young, and damn it, he *was* young. But his features, while boyish as ever and always would be, had grown tight these few years past; crow's feet at the eyes, deep lines in his face from frowning too much and from smiling too much, too. He'd been a salesman these last three years, and excessive frowning (to himself, in private) and smiling (at prospective buyers, in public) were inescapable hazards of the trade. It came, as they said, with the territory.

"Still, honey," Carol was saying, "you're not old. Really. Would it be so hard to start over?"

"It sure would. You want me to die of a heart attack by thirty? I mean, look at my face, the lines. Jeez."

Tears were welling up in her eyes. Even in the dark he could see that. Out in the living room, the TV was laughing.

"Come on, Carol. Knock it off. It's going to work out okay."

"Ken?"

"What?"

"You wouldn't hurt anybody, would you, honey?"

"You know me better than that, don't you? Jeez, Carol. How can you even say that."

She touched his hand, stroked it. "You want some coffee?"

"Okay. Then I got to get back downstairs and finish up."

One

1

Somebody was banging at the side door. Jon ignored it for a while, focusing his attention on the late movie he was watching—the original 1933 *King Kong*. But the banging was insistent and finally, reluctantly, Jon pulled away from the TV and headed downstairs to see what inconsiderate S.O.B. had the crazy idea something was important enough to go around bothering people in the middle of *King Kong*. *Better be pretty damn earthshaking,* Jon thought, *pisses me off,* and yanked open the door and saw a heavyset man leaning against the side of the building, his shirt and hands covered with blood. The guy had blood on his face, too, and looked at Jon and rasped, "Who…who the hell are you?"

Which took the words right out of Jon's mouth.

Up until then, it had been a normal day. He'd risen around noon, showered, got dressed, thrown some juice down, and gone out front to the box to see if he'd gotten any comic books in the mail. Jon was a comics freak, a dedicated collector of comic art in all its forms, and did a lot of mail-order buying and trading with other buffs around the country.

He was also an aspiring comics artist himself (as yet unpublished), and while he was disappointed to find no letters of acceptance for any of the artwork he'd sent off, so too was he relieved to find no rejections.

Jon was twenty-one years old, a short but powerfully built kid (he was such a comics nut that he'd actually sent in for that Charles Atlas course advertised on the back of the books) with a full head of curly brown hair and intense blue eyes. He also had a turned-up nose that he despised and that girls, thankfully, found cute. His dress ran to worn jeans and T-shirts picturing various comic strip heroes, everything from Wonder Warthog of the underground comics to Captain Marvel (Shazam!) of the forties "Golden Age" of comics. Today he had a Flash Gordon short-sleeve sweatshirt; the artwork (a full-figure shot of Flash with cape) was by Alex Raymond, the late creator of Flash. Jon would accept no substitutes.

You see, comics were Jon's life.

Take his room, for example. When his uncle had first given it to him, this room was a dreary storeroom in the back of the antique shop, a cement-floored, gray-wood-walled cubicle about as cheerful as a Death Row cell. Now it was a bright reflection of Jon's love for comic art. The walls were literally papered with colorful posters depicting such heroes as Dick Tracy, Batman, Buck Rogers, and the aforementioned Flash Gordon, all drawn by Jon himself in pen and ink and watercolored, and were uncanny recreations of the characters, drawn in their original style. (That was both a skill and a problem of Jon's: while his eye for copying technique was first-rate, he had no real style of his own. "Give me time," Jon would say to the invisible critics, "give me time.") Shag throw rugs covered the floors in splashes of cartoon color, and the walls were lined three deep with the boxes containing his voluminous collection of plastic-bagged and filed comic books, a file cabinet in one corner the keeper of the more precious of his pop artifacts. A drawing easel with swivel chair was against the wall, a brimming wastebasket next to it, and sheets of drawing paper and Zip-a-Tone backing lay at the easel's feet like oversize dandruff. And the two pieces of antique walnut furniture his uncle had given him were not exempt from comics influence, either: the chest of drawers had bright underground comics decals stuck all over its rich wood surface (Zippy, the Freak Brothers, Mr. Natural), and on top

Jon's pencils, pens, brushes, and bottles of ink were scattered among the cans of deodorant and shave cream and other necessities. Even the finely carved headboard of his bed was spotted with taped-on scraps of Jon's artwork, cartoonish sketches of this and that, mostly character studies of his girl, Karen, and Nolan, and his Uncle Planner.

His Uncle Planner. Still hard to think of Planner as being dead. Just a few months since it happened, and though Jon was almost used to the absence of the old man, he still didn't like living alone in the big, dusty old antique shop. Soon he'd be getting around to contacting some people to come in and appraise and bid on the merchandise in the store. Planner's collection of antique political buttons alone would bring a pretty penny. Of course the stuff in the front of the store, the long, narrow "showroom" of supposed antiques, was junk, crap Planner had picked up at yard sales and flea markets just to keep the shop sufficiently stocked; the good stuff was in the back rooms, because when Planner had run across actual antiques, he'd crated them up carefully and packed them away. Jon's uncle had had real respect for real antiques, and felt it was silly to sell them, as their value was sure to increase day by day. Jon, however, had no hesitation about selling those back-room treasures, though he'd do his best to find a buyer who'd haul away the junk as well as the jewels.

Mostly, of course, the shop had been a front for Jon's uncle. Planner had been just what his name implied: he planned things—specifically, jobs for professional thieves. He'd traveled around on "buying trips" and, in the role of cantankerous old antique dealer, had gathered the information necessary to put together successful "packages" for professional heist men like Nolan. Planner's packages were detailed and precise, at times even including blueprints of the target, and he'd charged a fee plus percentage of the take. Two years ago, with the guidance of his uncle, Jon had participated in the execution of one of those packages, a bank robbery headed by Nolan (whom Planner rated as perhaps the best in a dying craft), and some three quarters of a million dollars from that robbery had rested in Planner's safe since then—until this summer, when two men with guns came into the antique shop and shot Planner dead and took the money.

Jon and Nolan had gone after the two men and the money, and caught the two men, all right, but the money was lost. And so was Jon's dream of owning a comic book shop, a mecca for collectors like himself—as were his hopes for having enough money to support himself for as long as it took to break into the comic art field. All of that—up in smoke.

But not really. As Planner's sole heir, he was now owner of the shop, which he could conceivably convert into his comic book mecca, even if its location (Iowa City, Iowa) was a bit off the beaten track. And he had those two back rooms full of valuable antiques to turn into cash. And, too, Nolan had told him that the next time something came together, Jon was the first man he'd call. So things weren't so awfully bleak, really.

Jon returned to his room with the mail (not much—just some bills and the latest issue of *The Buyer's Guide for Comics Fandom*) and flopped on the bed, his eye catching the poster of Lee Van Cleef on the wall over his easel. The Van Cleef poster was one of a few posters in the room that were photographic and not his own drawings. Van Cleef was in his "man-in-black" gunfighter stance and, it seemed to Jon, resembled Nolan a great deal: they shared the same narrow eyes, mustache, high cheekbones and genuinely hard, hawkish look, though Nolan could get an even surlier look going, if that was possible.

He wondered for a moment if Nolan was just being nice when he'd promised to contact Jon when something came up.

No.

Jon was sure Nolan had been telling the truth. He knew that Nolan felt responsible for the loss of their money, and that sooner or later Nolan would come to Jon with a plan to get them both back on their financial feet again.

Karen had once suggested to Jon that he was using Nolan as a father substitute, a bullshit idea that embarrassed and irritated Jon; why, he wouldn't even talk about it, it was such dime-store bullshit psychology. He'd never needed his real parents; why the fuck should he need a fake one? His father was just some guy his mother knew before Jon was born; and his mother was just a fourth-rate saloon singer who was on the road all the time, leaving him to shuttle back and forth between one relative or another, none of them particularly grateful for an extra mouth to feed. A few years ago, his mother had died in an automobile mishap, and he hadn't even shed a tear; he simply hadn't known her that well. Early on he'd developed a capacity for amusing himself, for losing himself in the four-color fantasy of the funnies, for being a self-sufficient loner. And, in fact, when he moved to Iowa City to attend the university (briefly, as it turned out), he'd taken a cubbyhole apartment for himself rather than move in with a relative again, even if that relative was Planner, the most pleasant of the lot. Only after the robbery last year, when Nolan had stayed at Planner's, healing from gunshot wounds, only then had Jon moved in with his uncle. And that was to help his uncle help Nolan.

His life since meeting Nolan had been hectic but exciting, tragic but exhilarating. Nolan's reality put the fantasy of Jon's comic book superheroes to shame. Reality was harsh—in fantasy, Planner would still be alive, and last year's bank job wouldn't have erupted into insanity and blood—but, as Nolan might have said, jerking off is less trouble than screwing but it's nowhere near as rewarding.

The Van Cleef poster seemed to be squinting skeptically over at Flash Gordon, as if knowing how ridiculous it was of Jon to equate Nolan with comic book heroes. Ridiculous to think of Nolan as any kind of hero. But Jon did. Even though Nolan was a thief. The way Jon saw it, heroism had nothing to do with morality, or just causes, or politics, or anything else. Heroism had to do with courage; derring-do; a personal code; a steel eye and cool head. And all of these Nolan had. Plenty of.

Jon thumbed through *The Buyer's Guide* (a weekly newspaper of comics-related ads and articles) and saw some photos of a comics convention held out on the West Coast. He wished for a moment he'd gone to Detroit for the convention there this coming weekend; today was Thursday and the start of the con. He'd attended the New York Comic Con several years running, but hadn't been to too many of the countless other such fandom gatherings. Seemed a pity with a con located here in the Midwest, for a change, that he hadn't been able to go.

But this weekend was Karen's birthday, and he had to be here. She would be justifiably hurt if he chose comics over her. And this would be a traumatic birthday for her: Karen would be turning thirty-one, and the ten-year difference in their ages would be shoved to the front of her awareness. It was something that didn't bother Jon in the least, but Karen was somewhat paranoid about it. The only thing Jon didn't like about Karen being older than he was (and divorced) was her ten-year-old freckle-faced brat, Larry, a red-headed refugee from a Keane painting, who was the best argument for birth control Jon could think of.

Which was something he was very much conscious of when, an hour-and-a-half later, he was having a late lunch with Karen at the Hamburg Inn; now that school was started again, he could enjoy her lunchtime company minus Larry. Bliss.

Jon and Karen had been semi-shacked-up for six months now. *Semi*-shacked because Jon hadn't really moved in with Karen (and vice versa) for the simple reason that Jon and Larry didn't get along, and besides, Karen thought it might be bad for Larry if Mommy's boyfriend lived with them. A quaint idea in these loose days, Jon thought, but he didn't bitch: he liked his moments of privacy, and no way was he going to have his comic book collection and Larry under the same roof. It was a pleasant enough relationship as it was, and Karen was happy receiving the healthy alimony/child support check from her lawyer ex-husband (which would stop, of course, if she and Jon were to marry), and Jon had promised himself he wouldn't consider marriage with Karen until Larry was either old enough to send to military school or got hit by a truck.

Still, Jon *had* toyed with the idea of asking Karen to move in with him—even if Larry *did* have to come along. Karen ran the Candle Corner, a downtown Iowa City gift shop with head-shop overtones: hash pipes, Zig-Zag papers, posters, water beds, and the rack of underground comics that had brought Jon into Karen's shop in the first place. He'd considered asking her to help him convert Planner's antique shop into a larger version of her shop downtown, with more emphasis on water beds and apartment furnishings, and he would restrict his "comic book mecca" idea to a mail-order business out of one of the back rooms. She'd have no trouble interesting someone in taking over her long-term lease on that three-story building downtown that housed her shop, her apartment, and another to let above; and she and (ugh) Larry could move in with Jon, since the whole upstairs of the antique shop was a nicely remodeled five-room living quarters that Planner had used. So far, however, Jon had stayed in his room downstairs, only using the upstairs for its kitchen facilities and the living room's color TV, and that last only lately: it had taken Jon weeks to get used to the idea of Planner being dead and longer to lose the creepy feeling the upstairs gave him.

Anyway, he was considering that—asking Karen to move in, to become his business partner. But he hesitated, and when he'd put in a long-distance call to Nolan (who had met Karen), to ask his opinion of the idea, the following advice had come from Nolan: "Never mix bed partners and business partners, kid—you get fucked both ways." And since Nolan tended to be right about such things, Jon was, for the present, holding off asking Karen.

He spent the afternoon drawing, working up rough pencil layouts for a science fiction story he was hoping to sell to *Heavy Metal* magazine. It was to be somewhat in the style of the old EC *Weird Fantasy* and *Weird Science*, two great but long-dead comics, casualties of the bloody war waged upon comic books by parental groups and psychiatrists back in the early fifties. Jon's script was two Ray Bradbury stories put together and all switched around, and for the art he was combining elements of the underground's Corben and EC's Wally Wood in hopes of disguising his own lack of style with a weird mixture.

At four o'clock he watched a *Star Trek* rerun.

At five he went across the street to the Dairy Queen for supper—a tenderloin and hot fudge sundae. He usually ate with Karen, but she was at a Tupperware party, for Christ's sake. ("You're going to a *Tupperware* party, Karen? What kind of free spirit are you, anyway? Hash pipes, water beds, and Tupperware!" "Jonny, she's a friend of mine. She's one of my best friends and she invited me; I have to go. If you're not busy ...could you sit with Larry?" "Anything but that, Kare. Let me pay for the damn sitter myself. Anything.")

At six-thirty he got out a stack of comic books he hadn't gotten around to yet and started reading.

At ten he went upstairs and turned on the TV and got himself a bottle of Coke and some potato chips and got settled down for the showing of *King Kong* on the educational channel at ten-thirty.

At eleven-thirty somebody knocked on the back door.

The man with bloody hands and shirt.

2

The night after Sherry left, Nolan was consumed with boredom and hostility, and felt he had to get away from the motel for an evening or he'd go fucking crazy. The motel was called the Tropical, and Nolan had been managing the place for some syndicate people out of Chicago for months now, but it was a job he'd grown tired of lately, and he had to let off steam. Since he didn't care to embarrass or anger his employers, he took the time to drive some fifty miles to a little town where nobody knew him and, dressed in the grubbiest old clothes he could dig up, spent the evening in a tawdry little pool hall with the village's "rougher element," people who would have been born on the wrong side of the tracks had the town been big enough to have tracks.

Nolan was good at shooting pool. He was hustler-good, but chose to shoot by himself, and did so undisturbed for two solid hours, drinking beer and doing his best to run the balls as rapidly as possible. Tonight he was off a little, as his mind was busy with Sherry and the job at the Tropical and ways of changing what was becoming a tiresome life.

He was fifty years old, even if he didn't look it, a tall, rawboned man with just a little gut from several months of overly easy, overly soft living. His hair was black, widow's-peaked, with considerable gray working its way in along his sideburns; he wore a down-curving mustache that made his mouth take on an even more sour expression than it naturally wore; he had high cheekbones, and his face had a chiseled look, like something turned out by a sculptor in a black mood.

He had been a professional thief for almost twenty years, an organizer and leader of robberies, mostly institutional (banks, jewelry stores, armored cars, and the like) and his was the best track record in the business: there was not and never had been a single member of a Nolan heist behind bars—though some were in jail for other, non-Nolan jobs they'd been in on, and a few did die in double-cross attempts Nolan squelched.

Before that, when he was just a kid, really, Nolan had worked for the Family in Chicago, as a nightclub manager, utilizing those same organizational abilities of his. He turned a Rush Street dive into a legitimate (if Syndicate-owned) money-maker, partially from the local color he provided by serving as his own bouncer. Trouble was, his reputation for being a hardcase fed back into the Family hierarchy and gave some of the top boys the wrong idea: they tried to get Nolan to leave their Rush Street saloon and come in with them, for grooming as a young exec, so to speak, wanting him to start at the bottom in an enforcer capacity. He had balked at the suggestion, and the dispute that caused with the local Family underboss eventually got bloody, and Nolan had to drop out of the Family's sight for a while. "For a while" being almost twenty years, during which he'd turned to heisting. Only recently, when a long-overdue change of regime hit the Chicago Family, had Nolan come into Syndicate good graces. Through a lawyer named Felix (the Family *consigliere*), Nolan had been invited in, in the capacity he'd originally sought—nightclub manager—and part-owner as well. The Family offered Nolan a choice of several multimillion-dollar operations (including a well-known resort and a posh nightclub-cum-restaurant) on the stipulation that he buy in as a partner. That was fine with Nolan, because he had some $400,000 in his friend Planner's safe, his share from the Port City bank job, and this would make an excellent investment for putting the money to use.

Unfortunately, while he was still negotiating with Felix, Nolan's money was stolen and eventually lost, and Nolan was unable to uphold his half of the Family bargain.

And so the Tropical.

The Tropical was a modest operation in comparison with those other places the Family had offered him and, in fact, was used as a trial-run spot for people being considered for top managerial positions in the countless hotels, resorts, niteries and other such establishments owned by the powerful Chicago syndicate. The Tropical was a motel, consisting of four buildings with sixteen units each; two heated swimming pools, one indoor, one out; and a central building housing a restaurant and bar, both of which sported a pseudo-Caribbean decor meant to justify the motel's name. It was located ten miles outside of Sycamore, Illinois, and was devoted to serving honeymooning couples, some of whom were actually married. Lots of legit businessmen out of Chicago, as well as Family people, used it as a trysting ground, and so, accordingly, the Tropical made damn good money for its size.

Nolan himself had been serving a trial run at the Tropical before his money was stolen; now he was there on a more permanent basis, to observe the progress of others undergoing trial runs, doing little more than watching, really—just some mental note-taking and reporting back to Felix on the behavior and capability of the temporary managers. He would break in each new man (whose stay would range from three to six months) and see to it that a sense of continuity was maintained in between these pro tempore managers.

Which meant he mostly sat around.

And considering the salary he was drawing, that didn't make for such a bad setup. At least, not when Sherry was around.

Sherry was young, almost obscenely young, a pretty blonde child who spent most of her time in and out of bikinis. She had applied for a waitress job at the beginning of Nolan's stay at the Tropical, but she couldn't keep the food and coffee out of customer laps, and rather than fire her, Nolan found a place for her. The place was between the sheets of his bed, and when she wasn't there, she was adding to the Tropical's already erotic atmosphere by sunning in her hint of a bikini around the outdoor pool. She was not a brilliant girl, nor was she an empty-headed one, and if she did talk a trifle much, he'd gotten used to it quickly; anyway, her voice was melodious and soothing, so if you didn't listen to the words, it was no trouble at all.

Now she was gone.

The summer was over and there was no sun for her to lie under. She'd begun to get itchy at the tail end of September, and yesterday, when she got the call from her father saying her mother was sick, she'd decided to go back to Ohio and help out her folks. She and Nolan had had their most emotional night last night: she crying and Nolan making an honest effort to be cheerful and kind about the whole thing. She swore she'd come back the next summer; Nolan didn't mention that he hoped to be long gone from the Tropical by then. He just nodded and eased back up on top of her again.

He tried to bank the one ball in and missed. He said, "Shit," and chalked up his cue.

"Want some company?"

"No," Nolan said. He shot again; this time the ball went in.

"Hey. I said, want some company?"

"No," Nolan said.

The kid doing the asking was maybe eighteen, skinny, with long, greasy hair and a complexion like a runny pizza. A fat kid, older by a couple years probably, came sliding up to the table like a hog to slaughter. The skinny kid had on jeans and a gray work shirt with a white patch on the breast pocket that identified the shirt's origin as Ron's Skelly Station and the kid's name as Rick; the fat kid had on a yellow short-sleeve shirt with grease stains and massive underarm sweat-circles, and the buttons over his belly couldn't button.

"Hey, Chub," Rick said to his friend. They were like two balloons, one with the air let out, the other inflated to bursting. "You know what feeling I got about this guy, Chub? I got this awful feeling he's some kind of prick or something." There was emphasis on the word "prick."

Chub, however, said nothing. He just stood there, shifting his weight, from foot to foot and looking Nolan over.

Rick went on. "I mean, I ask him does he want some company and he says, 'shit no.' He's some kind of antisocial bastard, I think. What do you think, Chub?"

Chub, apparently, didn't know what to think. He'd come over to have a laugh with ol' Rick, but now that he was here and had a look at Nolan, he wasn't sure he liked what he saw. After a moment he tapped his skinny friend on the shoulder and gave him a flick of the head that said, come on, don't mess with this dude.

But then reinforcements arrived: two older guys, looking like something out of a fifties hot rod movie, came up from the other end of the hall to see what was the hassle. One of them actually had on a T-shirt with the sleeves rolled up and a cigarette pack stuffed in at the shoulder; he was an emaciated sort with pipe-cleaner arms down under the rolled sleeves, who made the skinny Rick look healthy. His cohort, however, was more genuinely menacing: a sandy-haired, greasy-haired, wide-shouldered bear with close-set, glittering eyes; he wore jeans and a T-shirt under a black cotton vest, and had biceps the size of California grapefruit.

"Okay," Nolan said. "Who wants to play some eightball?"

He played once with Rick and lost. His mind was still elsewhere. But the crowd around began making snide remarks about his shooting, and it brought his mind into focus. When he played the fat kid, for a five, he broke and didn't sink any; then next time his turn came around, he sank all the little-numbered balls and the eight, leaving Chub's stripes scattered all over the table. A murmur went through the small crowd, and pipe-cleaner arms stepped up, and Nolan took five from him the same way. He did it to all of them, except that most times he was running the balls right from the break.

He was good at pool; he was, in fact, good at most games. He'd been playing in a low-stakes poker game regularly with some Sycamore businessmen and had found it an enjoyable enough time killer. Good as he was at games, he was not a gambler. He was interested in pool and card playing for the chance to exercise his mind and to hone his skill; he didn't like to play with pros, because they had their life in the game, and you don't want to screw around with people in something they make a living at. The best amateur doesn't want to play the worst pro, because the game is a lark to the amateur, whereas the pro is deadly serious, and sometime you'll find yourself with a broken head and stuffed in a garbage can if you fuck with the pros and win.

Also, Nolan never hustled. Pool or cards or anything. He could go into a pool hall like this one and almost always clean the place out, if he felt like it; same with lots of small-town, high-stakes card games. But you made enemies that way. Same as when you diddled the pros, the amateur who thinks he's a pro can get pretty mad himself.

Like this crowd around him was now.

"Some kind of smart-ass hustler, buddy? That what you are?" It was the first kid, Rick—skinny Rick with the bad complexion. "Come in here and shoot real shitty and say you don't want to play, and then when we beg you, you say okay and wipe our butts, is that it?"

The bear with the close-set eyes, who seemed to be the leader of this small-time pack, said, "Just lay our money on the table, hustler. Just lay what you stole from us on the table, and you can walk out of here with your ass."

Nolan glanced over toward the proprietor, who was standing by the counter where he served up beers. The proprietor was an elderly guy with a flannel shirt and baggy pants and apron on. He was aware of what was going on, but knew he couldn't do anything about it; these were his usual customers, and he was looking the other way, toward some tables down at the other end of the room, which nobody was using right now.

Nolan picked up the cue ball and threw it at the bear and hit him in the middle of his forehead and knocked him on his back, knocked him out. He used the butt of the cue on Rick's stomach, and Rick promptly crawled away and threw up for a while. The rest of them just stood there and looked at Nolan. Nolan was smiling. And then he saw in their eyes that they realized he wanted them to continue the brawl.

Because Nolan was bored, and hostile, and it was something to do.

Disgusted with himself, Nolan threw the cue down across the table, said, "Fuck it," and walked out of the place. In an hour he was back in his room at the Tropical, fixing himself a shot of Scotch over ice and turning on the news to catch the sports.

At eleven, he was taking a shower and the phone rang.

"Logan?"

It was Sherry. The image of her face flashed through his mind: gentle, little-girl features framed by arcs of blonde-frosted brunette hair.

"Where you calling from, Sherry?"

"Home. Ohio. I miss you."

"Yeah. I'm stir-crazy myself, in this room alone."

"My mother's real sick, Logan."

Logan was the name she knew him by, the one he was using at the Tropical.

"Logan?" she said again. He'd been quiet for a moment, his mind full of her naked: her skin coppery from all that summer sun, except for the stark white where the bikini had half-heartedly covered the best parts, the breasts tipped as deep a copper as the sun-tanned skin; the light brunette triangle forming a similar contrast below...

"Yeah, I'm here," he said. "I'm sorry to hear your mother's sick."

"She's going to be bedridden a long time."

"I'm sorry."

"I got a job today."

"What kind?"

"Waitress."

"Oh, Christ."

She laughed. "I'll be careful. I haven't scalded anybody's nuts with hot-coffee-in-the-lap yet."

"Oh, then all your customers were women today, huh?"

She laughed some more and then said, "I miss you."

"You said that."

"I know. I want to see you again, Logan."

"Sure. Next summer."

"I don't think you'll still be there. At the Tropical, I mean. You been restless lately."

"Well."

"Let me give you my address. Come and see me when you can. Tell me where you end up, if you end up anywhere."

"I'd like that, Sherry."

She gave him the address, and he wrote it down.

"Logan?"

"Yeah?"

"Take care of yourself. Be happy."

"You too, kid."

They hung up.

Nolan sat there, dripping wet from the shower, getting the bed damp, feeling pissed off and, dammit, lonely. He couldn't understand it, because he'd been self-sufficient for a lot of years, hadn't ever been one to shack up with a broad for more than a day or two.

But he was fifty, and this goddamn life at the Tropical was goddamn getting him down.

He sat there a while and the phone rang again. It was Jon. Calling long-distance from Iowa City.

"Nolan? You got to come here, right away."

Life pumped into his veins; he didn't know what Jon wanted, but whatever it was, Nolan was game.

3

Breen never thought it would come to this. Stealing nickels and dimes. Christ! He pulled into the driveway of the little farmhouse where old Sam Comfort and his son Billy were waiting. At least this would end it, he thought. He would be glad to be done with this one; it certainly hadn't been the normal sort of heist he worked. In fact, it hadn't been one heist at all, but a series of thousands of little ones, infinitesimal heists, nickel-and-dime stuff. Literally. Because Breen had been helping the Comforts heist parking meters.

He was a stocky guy of forty-two, black hair cut military-short, his fleshy cheeks covered with a perpetual five o'clock shadow. His eyes were wide-set and dark blue, his nose bumpy and squat in the middle of a rough but intelligent face. Right now, as he sat in his battered green Mustang in the farmhouse drive, Breen's often intense features were softened in pleasant anticipation of severing the alliance with the Comforts.

He guessed he'd been lucky till now. Before this, he'd worked with only the best people; never before had he stooped to the level of the Comforts. He was spoiled, he supposed, from years of working with guys the caliber of Nolan. Used to be, Breen would work at least one job a year with Nolan, picking up one or two more with somebody else reliable. But Jack Taylor and a whole string of good men got busted two summers ago heisting an art gallery, and last year Laughlin and three others were killed after that Georgia armored-car job went sour and they'd been caught between state and local cops in a back-roads chase that turned fucking tragic. Worst of all, about two years ago this time, Breen had been in Chicago with Nolan and several others, planning a bank heist, when some syndicate guy shot the job right out from under them. Word got out later that though Nolan wasn't dead after all (surprising, as that syndicate guy nailed him a couple times; Breen had seen it happen), the Chicago Family was definitely declaring open season on Nolan. Which made it less than healthy to keep company with the man. So what was a guy to do? You had to work with somebody. And if you were desperate enough, you worked with the likes of the Comforts.

Old Sam Comfort's reputation was bad; it went back years before Breen had gotten into the business, and he'd never heard any specific stories about the old man, just that Sam Comfort was not to be trusted. In recent years Sam had worked strictly with his two sons, Billy and Terry, but last year Terry drew a short term for statutory rape, and the Comforts had been lacking a man on their string. And according to Morris (a pawn shop fence in Detroit, whom Breen used as a sort of underworld messenger service), the Comforts had a racket going that required a minimum of three, and they'd been using a fill-in man for Terry Comfort but weren't satisfied with him. Morris suggested that Breen go see the Comforts.

Breen would've dropped the whole thing right there, would've read the handwriting on the wall and just got the hell out of heisting, but he needed the money too bad. Breen was from Indianapolis, where he had a little bar he owned and operated with the help of his wife and brother-in-law. He would've made a good enough living with just the bar, but he was a horseplayer; Breen played the horses like an alcoholic drinks and a nymphomaniac screws: in dead earnest, with little joy and less success. He was trying to give it up, but he was into his bookie for four gee's worth of markers, and there was the alimony and child support for his first wife, that blood-sucking bitch; he was way behind on that, and wouldn't it be shit if *that* was the way he finally ended up in stir.

So he'd left the bar in the hands of his wife and brother-in-law and gone to see the Comforts. It was almost a whirlwind trip: when Sam explained they were heisting parking meters, Breen damn near left without sitting down.

But the parking meter deal wasn't as ridiculous as it first sounded. Old Sam had done his homework, no question about it. He'd put together a route: Des Moines, Cedar Rapids, and the

Quad Cities, all linked by Interstate 80. He'd spent time in each town tracking prowl car runs, and pinpointed the most untraveled, poorly lit streets, and such prime targets as waterfront parking lots and parking ramps, with thousands of meters for the picking, virtually unattended in the pre-dawn morning hours. He had keys to open the meters, and son Billy (decked out in olive-green uniform with the words "Meter Maintenance" stitched across the back) would go about draining the meters, while Sam stayed around the corner in the car, motor going, Citizen Band radio on to monitor the cops. Breen's role was to empty each bucket of coins that Billy brought him and hand him back a fresh one; Breen would pour the coins into a large, rubber-lined metal tray built down in the floor of the trunk. A lid flopped down over the tray when the night's work was done, a false bottom that made this trunk look like any other in a Buick Electra. No one questioned the maintenance man working the meters (traffic was slow in the wee hours), and most people probably just went by muttering, "Always wondered when they emptied those damn things."

Even with cities as small as those that comprised the Iowa-Illinois Quad Cities, they could pick up several thousand a night, easy, and that was playing it Sam's safe, cagey way, leaving enough coins in each meter to fool the actual maintenance people. That way they could go back for more periodically, and no one would be the wiser, not till the monthly tally for meter earnings came in. Even then, the city might not figure it out: maybe meter revenue was just down that month, who could say?

Sam and Billy rented a house on the outskirts of Iowa City, because it was midway along their Interstate 80 route, but Breen didn't choose to join them. The old man was a boozer and the kid blew grass all the time, and Breen preferred his own company. He chose to stay in Cedar Rapids, where he found an apartment and, before long, a young cocktail waitress to shack up with.

Working with the Comforts had been a royal pain. Not only had the work been hard and tedious, hitting a different city six nights a week for a solid month, but the Comforts had personalities that put a burr up Breen's ass. Billy was an introspective, cynical type, and his old man was an egotistical, egocentric loudmouth, and Breen was glad that most of the time he spent with them was on the job, where keeping quiet was a necessity. Listening to Billy's occasional sarcasm and Sam's constant bullshit was trouble enough on the ride down from Iowa City; at least when the team worked Cedar Rapids, he didn't have to ride in the car with them.

But he had to hand it to old Sam. He'd underestimated the crafty old coot. Sam had the operation down pat, slicker than shit. The Comforts had worked the parking meter scam for a straight year now, alternating between six routes Sam worked out, never staying in one area longer than a month, keeping the local authorities confused. Sam had an account in a bank in each area he hit, but not in any city on the route (he had an account in Iowa City, for example) and used a fictitious name and fictitious business, of course, to keep the bank free of suspicion regarding the heavy amount of coin involved. In Iowa City, Sam posed as the owner of a pinball rental outfit, so the tellers were used to seeing him haul in sacks of coin for deposit. This was canny: others might have fenced the coin at a loss; not old Sam.

Also, Sam had told Breen that he closed out a route after hitting an area a certain number of times; this was the third go-round for the Iowa Interstate 80 route, and it would not be used again, not for several years, anyway. He would develop a new route in untapped territory and add it to his list. And he would be closing out his account at the local bank. This time, the month of meter lootings had tallied $47,000; he had another $110,000 in the Iowa City bank from the other two times he'd hit the area.

Tonight was the payoff. Breen would receive just under twelve thou for his month of hardass work. The $47,000 would be split four ways, with Sam taking a double cut because the package had been put together by the old man. That was fair, Breen thought, and though $12,000 was hardly the best he'd ever done in a heist, it would be enough to get him out of the woods with his bookie and his alimony-hungry ex-wife. Now, if he could just stay away from the damn nags.

He approached the farmhouse, a ramshackle clapboard the Comforts had picked up for cheap rent, not unlike the equally run-down farmhouse outside Detroit, where the Comforts actually lived, a sprawling shack filled with luxurious possessions bought with the spoils of Comfort heisting. Bunch of slobs, Breen thought, glad tonight would be the end of 'em.

"Come on in, Breen," Sam said, standing in the doorway, framed in light. "Come get your cut." The white-haired, pot-bellied old sot was wearing a green cotton sportcoat with patched elbows over a T-shirt showing the brown suspender straps holding up the baggy brown pants; the old man needed a shave and stood there scratching his ass in the doorway. Fucking slob, Breen thought. Somewhere in the house, the kid would be sitting in his underwear sucking up weed. Nice family.

Breen approached Sam, bracing himself for the blast of whiskey breath, heading up the slanted cement walk toward the house and saying, "After tonight, I'm out, Sam. I've had it; this meter bit is not my bag. You're going to have to add somebody different to the string after tonight."

"Fine with me," Sam said, jovial. "Terry'll be out of stir next month, and we were going to ask you out anyway." They were about ten feet apart. Sam's hand moved out from behind him, where he'd seemed to be scratching his ass, and something glittered in the light coming from inside the house.

Gun metal.

Breen rolled to the left, tumbling on the grass, but old Sam's shot caught him anyway. More gunfire broke the solitude of the Iowa country evening, explosions as terrifying to Breen as nuclear war. Breen was almost back to his car when another slug caught him in the leg. No matter. He scrambled behind the wheel anyway, ignoring the gunfire behind, ignoring the pain. The back windshield shattered into a sudden spiderweb with a hole punched in its middle, and he felt one of the back tires sag flat.

But he made it out of there. He drove the half-mile into Iowa City, not even looking behind him to see if the Comforts were following. He knew he could lose them; he'd been in Iowa City before and could wind through streets and confuse them. He did that, though he had no idea if they were back there or not. He was getting delirious. He looked down at himself and he was all bloody.

Then he remembered Planner.

That was why he'd been to Iowa City before. To see Planner, that old guy at the antique shop who put together most of Nolan's packages. He could go there for help. He could go see Planner.

He got there, somehow, and stumbled up to the side of the shop and slammed his fist against the door, slammed his fist against the wood again and again, hard as hell, as much to stay awake and keep some sensation going in his body as to rouse somebody inside.

Finally somebody answered. A wild-haired hippie kid, and Breen's hopes sunk in his chest. He mumbled something, like who the hell was this kid, and dropped to the floor just inside the door.

4

This was one of those rare times when all the Charles Atlas muscle-building came in handy. Jon was carrying the bleeding man like an absurdly oversize babe in arms. The guy was heavier than Jon and a shade taller too, and so made quite a load. Jon hauled the fleshy freight to his room in the rear of the shop, hoping that following his impulse to help the guy wasn't some gross error in judgment. Anytime something like this came up, Jon wished he had Nolan around to check with, to consult.

But Nolan isn't here, Jon thought, *so screw wishful thinking*.

As he carried the man, Jon looked him over carefully, trying to get past that first impression of a guy covered with blood. The man was in his early forties, Jon estimated; he had short dark hair, and wore a light blue sportshirt, bloodstained on the lower right side, and summery white slacks, also stained with blood down the left lower leg. The blood on his face apparently had gotten there when a hand had touched one or both of the wounds, and speckles and smears of blood were spread variously around his clothing in spots other than those immediately around the wounds. Jon eased him onto the bed, went upstairs, and came back down with some bandage makings, a bottle of hydrogen peroxide, a basin of water, and several washcloths.

The wounds weren't bad, really. Not near as bad as he'd at first thought, from the shock of the blood-soaked clothes; it was the light colors that made the red stand out so, the light blue shirt and white pants, and the guy must've run after he was shot, scattering blood around on his clothes. Jon was relieved to find the leg just nicked, and the side wound showed evidence of the bullet going through clean, nothing important having been hit. Or that was Jon's guess, anyway; if the slug had caught an artery there'd be blood gushing everywhere, but the bleeding here wasn't severe at all. Jon washed the wounds clean and applied bandages that were tight, but not tourniquet-tight.

The guy came around just as Jon was finishing.

He said, "Who...who the hell are you?"

"You asked that before," Jon said. "Suppose you tell me who the hell you are, and we'll see about who I am afterwards."

"Where's Planner?"

Jon's suspicions were confirmed: this was an associate of his late uncle, someone who'd run into trouble on a heist or something and had come here for help. That had been Jon's first guess, and as he'd been in a similar boat that time with Nolan, his instinct had been to help this man.

"I said, where's Planner, kid? You do know who I'm talking about?"

"I know who you're talking about," Jon said. Then, after a moment, "Planner was my uncle."

"Was?"

"He's dead. Few months now."

"Jesus." The guy propped himself up on his elbows and spoke, almost to himself. "Jesus Christ, these days everybody good's either dead or in jail, seems like....Jesus H. Christ. How'd it happen, anyway?"

Jon started to hesitate again, but those last comments from the guy sounded right, so he said, "My uncle was keeping money in his safe for some people. Two men came in and took the money and killed him."

"Shit! Is that right? Shit. Somebody ought to find those guys and..."

"Somebody did. You feeling okay? You look kind of pale. You better lay back and take it easy."

"I feel okay."

"Yeah, well, I don't think your wounds are too serious, but you better lay back and take it easy just the same."

"I appreciate this, kid, you taking me in, patching me up like this."

"If you appreciate it so damn much, you might tell me who you are and what's going on."

"Well, I'm in the business your uncle was in. You know what sort of business your uncle was in, don't you, kid?"

"I do. I'm in that line of work myself."

"Antiques, you mean? Like all this old comic book bullshit you got in here?"

"You know what I mean."

"Okay, then. So who have you worked with, if that's the line of work you're in."

"Nolan. He's the only one so far. Him and some people you wouldn't know."

"I thought Nolan had Family troubles."

"Not anymore."

"You worked with Nolan? What, on your first job? What'd he want to screw around with a goddamn kid like you for? No offense."

"Because big-deal pros like you wouldn't come near him. No offense. That Family trouble, remember?"

The guy was convinced. He said, "My name is Breen," and held out his hand, which Jon shook; for a guy just shot, Breen had a hell of a grip. "An old whoremonger named Sam Comfort and his pothead kid Billy just pulled a double-cross, with me on the shitty end of the stick. I wouldn't be talking about it right now if the senile old fart hadn't been half crocked when he started shooting."

Jon had never heard of the Comforts. He said so.

"Well, you're lucky. They aren't a family, they're a social disease." He sat up again, quickly. "Hell! Listen, you better move my car. I left it outside, and the Comforts know about Planner and might figure I came here. You got a gun? I don't carry one, goddamn it, or I might've stayed there and shot it out with the fuckheads. But you better get a gun and go out there and move that goddamn car of mine, the windshield's shot to shit, and if nothing else, you don't want some cop spotting it and asking questions."

"Okay," Jon said.

"*Do* you have a gun, kid?"

"I got a couple."

"Maybe I ought to back you up. Maybe you ought to help me out of this bed, and I'll stand at the window or something and back you up..."

"Look. Lean back and shut up. For a guy just got shot, you're sure lively. If you don't talk yourself to death, you'll do it to me."

"Say," Breen said. "You do know Nolan, don't you?"

Jon grinned, told the guy to shut up and rest, and left him.

Back upstairs, Jon stuck one of his uncle's .32 automatics in his waistband, threw on a windbreaker, and went down to move the car. First he drove his own car, an old Chevy II he'd had for some time, out of the garage in the rear and replaced it with Breen's Mustang. Then he shut the garage door and pulled the nose of the Chevy II up just close to touching. The door had no windows, and the way the garage was built into the shop's back end, it had windows on the left side only, and those were opaque and grilled, with no way for anyone to see whether or not the Mustang was in there, short of breaking in. Not that breaking in didn't sound like something the Comforts were easily capable of.

He was just inside the door when light came shooting through one of the side windows in the shop, the lights from the front beams of a car pulling in. The Comforts had come calling. He took the windbreaker off and stuck the .32 in his belt behind his back, leaving right hand on hip for easy access.

The knock came soon enough, and Jon sucked in wind. He told himself to be calm, damn it, calm, and wondered if once, just once, he could pull off something without Nolan holding his hand. There was a night latch on the door, which Jon left bolted, cracking open the door to stare into a gray-eyed, wrinkled old face that had to belong to Sam Comfort. It was the sort of face that looked kind, superficially, but actually was full of the smile-lines that come from a sadistic sense of humor. Sixty-some years ago, you would've found this man a child, pulling the wings off butterflies.

"Who the hell are you?" Sam Comfort asked.

Jon was getting tired of that question. On top of his case of nerves, it was especially irritating, and he moved his right hand further back on his hip, closer to the .32, rubbing the sweat off his palm as he did. He said, "It's after midnight, mister. We're closed."

Comfort's boozy breath was overpowering, but the gray eyes were not unclear; he was the type of man who could drink you under the table and not feel it himself.

He said, "I'm not a customer."

"That makes us even," Jon said, "because I'm not selling anything."

"I'm an old friend of Planner's."

"I don't care what you are," Jon said, and started to close the door.

Thick, strong fingers curled around the door's edge and held it open. “I said I’m a friend of Planner’s. Tell him an old friend’s here to see him.”

“Let go of the door.”

Comfort did, tentatively.

Jon said, “My uncle—Planner—is dead.”

“Oh, I’m sorry. Sorry. I hadn’t heard. How did it happen, boy?”

“Heart attack.” Which was what the death certificate had said, anyway, and an expensive damn piece of paper that was, too.

“And you’re his nephew, then? Taking over the business, are you?”

“No. I got no interest in antiques, and I’m going to sell all the stock at once, soon as a good buyer turns up, and will you please get out of here and let me get some sleep?”

The gray eyes narrowed, then eased up. “Well, I’m sorry to see you so hostile to an old friend of your uncle’s, and I’m sorry to hear the news about his untimely end. Please accept my condolences.”

“Sure. Sorry if I was short.”

“Understandable. Say, what you keep in that garage of yours?”

“If it was a garage, I’d keep my car in it. But it isn’t, it’s a storeroom. Good night.”

And he pushed the door shut and locked it, and stepped to one side in case any bullets should come flying through. Several heartbeats later, he crept to the side window and looked out to see the old man join a long-haired kid, leaning up against their Buick Electra. They shared a few moments of heated conversation, most of the heat coming from the old man, as the kid was a spacey type. Then both men shrugged. The old man got behind the wheel, the kid next to him, and they drove away.

When he rejoined Breen, the man was asleep and snoring. Jon was at first relieved that he wouldn’t have to listen to any more of the talkative man's ramblings, but then he thought better of it, shook the guy awake, and told him about the brush with the Comforts.

"You're okay, kid," Breen said, grinning. "You handled old Sam beautiful, sounds like."

"Why don't you show your gratitude," Jon said, "by telling me what all this is about."

Breen did. He told Jon he'd been working a month of parking meter heists ("Small potatoes, kid, but over the long haul, she adds up!"); told him old man Comfort had over a hundred and fifty gees, cash, from several such runs of meter heisting in the area, and had tried to kill Breen less than an hour earlier, to avoid paying Breen's $12,000 share.

"Listen," Jon said. "I'm going to call Nolan. I think maybe he'll have some ideas concerning the Comforts."

Breen thought that was fine.

Jon went out to the phone that sat on the long counter behind which Planner had constantly sat puffing expensive cigars. Jon sat on the counter, dialing the phone, thinking of his uncle's violent death, wondering if he was being a fool to follow in those bloody footsteps. But he forgot that when he heard Nolan's, "Yeah?"

"Nolan? You got to come here, right away."

"What's the problem, kid?" Nolan's voice was calm, but Jon seemed to detect a note of enthusiasm in it.

"You know a guy named Breen?"

"I do."

Jon filled Nolan in on what had happened to Breen, and how he'd come bleeding up to Jon's doorstep.

"What about a doctor?"

"I bandaged him up, Nolan. He'll last okay. Maybe tomorrow we can get Doc Ainsworth in for a look at him. So far, I been more concerned about the Comforts than anything."

"Rightly so. And you were right not bringing in a doctor,

because the Comforts might be watching. You locked the doors, of course? And moved Breen's car?"

"Of course. And the Comforts have already come around once." He'd held that back to shock Nolan with—saved it for effect.

But he should have known better with Nolan, who just said an emotionless, "Well?"

And Jon told him about the run-in with Sam Comfort.

"You're doing better all the time, kid. In fact, what do you need me for there? You got things under control."

"Well, for one thing, these damn Comforts got me sweating. They're unpredictable, judging from what Breen says, and from what I saw of them."

"Did you fool old Sam, you think?"

"I got an idea what was going on in that head. He could come barging in with a gun right now and I wouldn't be surprised. You know the Comforts pretty well, Nolan?"

"I worked a job with that crusty old son of a bitch, years ago. He didn't cross me, because I didn't give him the opening. But if my back had been to him, he'd have put the knife in, no doubt about it. Breen was stupid to work with him in the first place. Everybody knows Sam is as crazy as he is unreliable."

"Well, Nolan, what do you think?"

"I'll come, yeah."

"It's not that I need help, exactly…"

"I know, kid. You just like having me around."

"That's part of it."

"And that hundred and fifty thousand of Comfort's is another."

"Right."

"We're about due, Jon. Maybe we can help my old buddy Breen and do ourselves a favor, too."

Jon grinned into the phone. "Right."

Two

5

The riots could have been last week, the way this neighborhood looked. Buildings stood black and gutted from flames; no one had even bothered boarding up the broken-out, blown-out windows, which stared from the buildings like the empty sockets of gouged-out eyes. Other blocks had fared better, their buildings untouched by flame, some stores none the worse for wear, open for business. But even these more fortunate blocks showed the scars of violence, their wounds no less ugly for the pus being dried up and crusted over. The sites of many small businesses were vacant now, abandoned by their white proprietors in the wake of black unrest, leaving behind storefront windows broken out and never replaced, nothing remaining but jagged edges of glass, like teeth in the mouth of a screaming man. Outrage had fired this violence, from which had come further outrage: one emigrant had boarded up his storefront window and written, in an angry red scrawl: "AFTER 20 YRS. SERVICE, CHASED FROM OUR HOME," a Star of David beneath the words like a signature. Passing by the boarded-up store was a thin black woman in a pale, worn, green dress, trudging along like a parody of a weary darkie, pulling a child's wagon filled with groceries, and her face told the whole story: she'd had to walk blocks and blocks to a grocery store, and hoped like hell nothing spoiled. She seemed to shake her head a little as she moved along past her neighborhood corner grocery, which was an empty, burned-out shell.

Nolan sat in the back of the taxi cab, listening to the meter tick his money away, and half listening to the cabbie, who'd been pointing out the sights like a cynical tour guide. The cabbie had grown up in this part of Detroit himself and was saddened and somewhat pissed off about what had happened here since he'd left it for a better neighborhood.

Back at the airport, Nolan had chosen this black cabbie over a white one, because he wasn't sure if the white cabbie would've wanted to drive him into this neighborhood. Matter of fact, Nolan was a little ill at ease himself; he'd feel a hell of a lot better armed, but he hadn't been able to carry heat on the plane because of skyjacking precautions. He'd brought a gun along, of course, a pair of them in fact: two S & W .38s with four-inch barrels. But they were packed away in his suitcase (no sweat from airport security on that—only hand-carried bags routinely got checked), and a .38 nestling between his fresh socks and change of underwear wouldn't do him much good down here. The suitcase, and Jon, ought to be at the hotel by now; this taxi ride had been one that Nolan felt better taken alone, so he'd sent the kid on ahead with the luggage on the airport-to-hotel shuttle bus.

Which was considerably cheaper than this damn taxi, but then, you didn't find a shuttle running from airport to ghetto and had to expect to pay the price. The price in this case was double stiff: the tinny racket of that disembodied mechanical head hooked to the dash, wolfing down Nolan's money, was depressing enough, let alone having to put up with the cabbie's gloomy line of patter.

The cabbie was a thickset, very black man with white hair and white mustache, and was maybe a year or two older than Nolan. "Yessir," the cabbie was saying (*why couldn't I get a sullen one,* Nolan thought, *or at least one of those mumble-mouths you can't make heads or tails of*), "this neighborhood was hit super-bad, rioting and lootings and snipings and you name it. Bad hit as any place in the country."

Nolan grunted, to show he was paying attention. He glanced at the meter and winced: attention wasn't all he was paying—fourteen bucks and climbing. Christ!

The cabbie rambled on. "Martin Luther King weren't the only thing got killed, that time. This whole neighborhood went down with him. Look at it. You ever seen a place so tore-up?"

"No," Nolan said, though it wasn't true. Berlin had been like this, after the war.

"You know, where I'm taking you, it's about the only business in the area didn't get hurt. All them cars, and not even a antenna busted off. And a white fella runs it, can you beat that?"

"No."

"Huh?"

"No, I can't beat that."

Nolan's lack of interest finally dawned on the guy, and shut him up. Which was no big deal, as they were within a block of Bernie's Used Auto Sales anyway.

Bernie's was indeed a white man's business that had gone untouched in the rioting, and with half a block of cars sitting out in the open like that, it was a wonder. The big garage next to the lot had gone untouched as well, not even a broken pane of glass. It was not hard to figure: Bernie's business was not one the neighborhood would like to lose. A grocery store was expendable, but not Bernie's.

Nolan got out of the taxi, looked at the meter, which read "$15.50." He handed the cabbie a twenty and waited for change, but the guy just grinned, said "Thanks," and roared off. Nolan now understood how the cabbie had made it to a better neighborhood.

Immediately, a salesman approached Nolan, saying, "What can we do for you, my man?" His words were mild enough, but his tone and expression said, *What the fuck you doin' here, whitey?* He was a lanky, chocolate-colored guy who couldn't keep still. Nolan hated goddamn funky butts like this; he liked people who didn't move anything but their mouths when they talked, and not much of that. This guy was a fluid son of a bitch poured into a white-stitched black suit and a wide-brimmed gangster hat. The band was wide and black, the hat itself white, and Nolan had seen George Raft in a similar one, years ago. It looked better on Raft.

"Tell Bernie I'm here."

The guy stopped dancing, narrowed his eyes on Nolan. "Uh, like who should I say..."

"Tell him Nolan."

"He's not..."

"He's expecting me. Didn't he tell you? No, I don't suppose he would. Tell him."

The guy's eyes filled with something, and it wasn't love. "Okay," he said. "Wait here till I see if it's cool with the man."

"Okay."

The salesman strode off, but his butt seemed slightly less funky now. His reaction to Nolan had been a natural one, as most of Bernie's white customers never showed their faces around here, making arrangements to see Bern at his suburban home or at one of his junkyards. Nolan walked around the lot while he waited, taking a look at Bernie's stock.

The lot was packed with cars, of recent vintage mostly, every make and model from Volks to Mercedes, Pinto to Caddy. An impressive selection, but to the casual observer, nothing unusual. Nolan was not a casual observer, and he was smiling, thinking of the one thing that separated Bernie's from your run-of-the-mill used-car lot: virtually every car on the well-stocked lot was a stolen one.

But the skill and workmanship of Bernie and staff saw to it

that every car sold off the lot was not only untraceable, but offered to the public at bargain pricing and with full warranty. This was why Bernie's had been an oasis in a desert of rioting: nobody kills the golden goose, and Bernie was him, Bernie was the goose who'd provided this neighborhood with countless golden eggs. Rip off a car in the morning, and by early afternoon Bern's cash was in your pocket, and Bern was cool, he paid off fair, no hassle, no shuck. And on top of being where you could unload the car you stole for ready cash, Bernie's was a mother of a cheap place to buy wheels. If there was one white dude in the neighborhood who deserved being called brother, it was Bern, baby, Bern.

Nolan wasn't precisely sure how Bernie worked this gig, but he did know that Bernie had been a jump-title expert for years. Last Nolan knew, Bernie owned a chain of junkyards all over the Detroit area and, by matching up stolen cars with junked cars of the same make, he simply spot-welded the junker's serial numbers onto the stolen job—under the hood, inside the door and, when possible, on the frame— and presto, a "new" car ready for titling. Legislation had, in recent years, crippled jump-title rackets badly, especially on the large scale that Bernie worked; but fortunately, a southern state notorious for its lax titling laws was glad to have Bernie's trade, and the particular county Bernie did his business through even went so far as to service him by mail-order. Sounded far-fetched, but Nolan remembered the time in Alabama, not so very long ago, when he'd stolen a car and, with no proof of ownership whatever, driven up to the courthouse, got the auto titled, and driven it away.

"Yer fat!"

Nolan turned, and Bernie was standing there, a short, massively muscled man with not an ounce of flab on him; he had a round face with round eyes and round nose and, when he spoke, a round mouth. If he hadn't had a full head of curly brown hair, he'd have looked like a talking cueball. He was wearing the world's dirtiest coveralls, with "Bernie's" emblazoned over one breast pocket "How'd you get so goddamn fat?"

"I'm an old man, Bernie. I live a soft life these days."

"Soft life, my ass. Come on, Nolan, let's go in the back and have some beer."

Why Bernie didn't have a potbelly from constant beer guzzling was one of the mysteries of life Nolan would never understand. Maybe the man just worked hard enough to offset all those suds: Bernie, never content to live high on the carloads of cash his business brought him, spent most of his time in there doing the drudge work—painting the cars, doing body work, replacing parts, everything. It was obvious that Bernie didn't need to do illegal work to make a good living; but the illegal route had led to his own shop, his own operation, and freedom was always worth a little risk. One thing was for sure, Nolan thought: Bernie ran the most efficient automotive firm in Detroit. And probably the most honest.

The back room was a cubbyhole with a small desk and a large cooler of beer. The desk was cluttered with car manuals, the Red and Blue Books of this and many a year, bills and receipts, and so on. Nolan knew the reason for the mess: Bernie kept good books, but felt that overly neat records made the IRS unduly suspicious. Besides, he got a kick out of making them come in and dig. If they wanted to come and look for ways to screw you, cross your legs and make 'em work their asses off getting in.

Bernie popped a top and handed a foaming beer to Nolan, did the same for himself. "So yer fat, and you ain't dead."

"Yes I'm fat, no I'm not dead."

"You already told me why you're fat. Now tell me why you ain't dead."

"Didn't you hear about the change of regime in Chicago?"

"No. I got no Family ties, never did have. I'm an independent and like to stay clear of that shit. You know me, Nolan. So what, the people that wanted you dead, those Family people, are out? And what, the new people love you?"

"Something like that."

"What are you up to now?"

Nolan told Bernie about the Tropical.

"Sounds boring."

"It is. But it's a good deal, for the immediate present, and I don't want to blow it."

"How could you blow it?"

"Well, you see, Bernie, I'm here on business. Detroit's never been my idea of a place to vacation."

"So?"

"The Family people I'm fronting for don't want me straying from the straight and narrow. They got a name and background set up for me, so I can front the Tropical with no static from the law or anybody. Somebody runs a check on me, I sound like the president of the goddamn Chamber of Commerce. Hell, I'm even a college graduate, would you believe that?"

"I believe you can pass for one," Bernie said, getting a fresh beer. "I joined this country club, and it's full of those Phi Beta crappers. They're some of the dumbest, most boring assholes I ever hung around with. If Thelma didn't insist we belong, I'd get the hell out."

Bernie's social-climbing wife, and the indignities he suffered because of her, was a topic Nolan could do without, so he steered around it, saying, "Anyway, Bern, my point is, there are certain of my former activities the Family doesn't want me engaging in."

"Shit, you're even starting to *sound* like a damn college man. Okay, so you're here for a heist. And you want the lid kept on it."

"Right, Bern."

"What do you need, a car? You can have a car as long as you're in town, Nolan. On the house. Course, if you wreck it, I'll expect you to buy the thing. That's only fair, I mean."

"More than fair. But you could help me another way."

"Whatever it is, I'll do what I can."

"I need some supplies for the job. And I figure the less people I talk to, better off I am. Can you get me what I need?"

"Think so. Anything short of a tank, anyway. What is it you want?"

Nolan told him.

"What the hell you need those for?"

"I don't want the guys I'm heisting to see me. If they see me, I'll have to shoot them."

"Getting soft, Nolan? Ain't fat bad enough?"

"I never been one to kill without reason, Bernie." That was true enough, but Nolan didn't go into the rest of it—that his main reason was, he didn't want to subject Jon to violence that extreme. If he could help it.

"Well, okay, Nolan. You always known what you was doing. Sit and have another beer—there's plenty in the cooler. I'll go get a man to rustle that crazy shit up for you. Run you about twenty-five bucks per. What you want, a couple?"

Nolan nodded.

"Okay, good as done. But I were you, I'd remember those toys're no substitute for firepower. You can't beat a gun, no way."

"Oh, I'll have a gun, Bern. I may be getting soft and fat, but I'm not crazy."

6

The ballroom was filled with long tables, tables stacked with the wares of dozens of individual dealers, and hundreds of kids-of-all-ages were filing past the tables, stopping to examine those wares. The dealers ranged from small-time local collectors getting rid of their duplicates to big-time operators who'd come from either coast in vans loaded with boxes and boxes of rare material. The goods of both were scrutinized with equal suspicion by prospective buyers, who slipped the books from their plastic bags to make sure each was properly graded, fairly priced, going over each yellowing artifact like a jeweler looking for flaws in a diamond. A generally cordial mood reigned, however, and the horse-trading, the bickering over an item's monetary worth, was considerably more amiable than what you might run into at a pawnbroker's, say, or an antique shop. Jon, in his jeans and sweatshirt, fit in well with this crowd, who hardly looked prosperous, unless you noticed that greenbacks of just about every denomination were clutched in the countless hot little hands like so much paper. Though the throng included kids below teen-level, as well as men into middle age and beyond, most were closer to Jon's age, and ran to type: male; glasses; skin problems; skinny (or fat) or short (or tall); ultra-long hair (or ultra-short); T-shirts with super-heroes on them. If Nolan were here, he'd look at this crowd and figure them for the bums of tomorrow—hell, bums of *today*—but in reality these were highly intelligent, if slightly screwball young adults, potential Supermen even if they did look more like offbeat Clark Kents.

What was going on was a comic book convention. This ballroom in a downtown Detroit hotel had been converted into

"Hucksters' Hall," and Jon, like all the scruffy fans wandering through the room in search of pulp-paper dreams, was dropping money like a reckless Monopoly player: in his first twenty minutes, Jon passed GO, spent his $200. This is what he purchased: three Big Little Books, two Flash Gordon, one Buck Rogers; one *Weird Fantasy* comic with a story by Wood; and two *Famous Funnies* comics with old Buck Rogers strips inside and covers by Frazetta. All of it was the comic book version of science fiction; that is, pirates in outer space: Killer Kane hijacking Buck's rocket ship; Ming the Merciless holding Dale Arden captive to lure Flash into a trap; pirates flying the skull-and-crossbones in the sea of outer space. Great stuff.

So why was he so damn unhappy?

Not about the prices he'd had to pay—he'd done all right on the items he picked up so far, by shrewd if halfhearted haggling—and not in disappointment at the size of this convention, though it really didn't compare to the New York Cons, whose Huckster rooms were breathtaking, both in scope and prices. This convention was not, after all, totally devoted to comics, being the Detroit Three-Way Fan-Fare, a joint gathering of comics freaks, science-fiction enthusiasts and old-movie buffs. Since Jon fell into each category, he naturally was more than pleased with the arrangement.

But right now he was feeling low, an exceptional state of affairs considering he was now in the middle of the atmosphere that most nearly fit his conception of heaven: namely, a room full of comic books. Not unhappy exactly, more like unnerved. Moody. Jumpy. Ill at ease.

Tonight—the prospect of tonight—was scaring the bejesus out of him.

When Nolan had suggested going to Detroit and ripping off old man Comfort, the convention came immediately to Jon's mind; but he decided to wait for the right moment to spring the idea on Nolan. When Jon did ask if it was okay if they stayed at this particular hotel, Nolan's left eyebrow had raised and he'd said, "Comic books. It has something to do with comic books...I don't know how in hell it can, but it does."

Jon admitted as much, pointing out, "The convention'll get my mind off the job—I won't get all fumble-ass nervous about the thing. You can do your setup work, getting the car and the other stuff, and I can spend the afternoon looking at old comic books. It'll keep my mind from dwelling too much on tonight."

They'd been sitting on the plane at the time, having driven to the Quad City Airport in Moline for a Friday morning flight to Detroit. They hadn't phoned ahead any hotel reservations, as it was Nolan's intention to find a cheap motel once they got there. He'd made the intention known to Jon, who hadn't been surprised by it, considering that right then they'd been sitting in the plane's tourist section, another of Nolan's money-saving tactics. Their conversation had to be couched in euphemisms, as they took up only two of three adjoining seats, the window seat being occupied by a conservatively dressed businessman who might be offended by discussion of the armed robbery pending.

Jon had discovered, through experience, that Nolan was something of a cheapskate. While Nolan had earned some half-million dollars in his fifteen years as a professional thief, he'd kept the bulk of it salted away in banks, while living a painfully spartan existence. Nolan had been satisfied with modest apartments and secondhand Fords because he lived for tomorrow—that is, had planned an early retirement from the heist game, a retirement that would include a nightclub Nolan wanted to own and operate through his "twilight years."

But now that Nolan had been wiped out of his half-million nest egg, not once but *twice* (Jon's along with it, the second time) you'd think the guy would've learned you might as well enjoy yourself today since a safe's liable to fall on you tomorrow.

But no. With Nolan it was tourist-class seats and cheap motels and, Jon supposed, a hamburger joint for supper.

So when Nolan didn't seem to be buying the argument about the hotel with the comics con being a way to keep Jon's mind off the job, Jon mentioned the special room rate; if thrift didn't win Nolan over, nothing would. "We can have a double room for twenty bucks, Nolan. That's less than half price. People attending the convention get the rooms less than half price."

"Okay, kid. Whatever you want."

It pleased him he was finally beginning to find the means to occasionally come out on top with Nolan.

Not that Jon didn't still admire the man. But Nolan's cheapness was at least a chink in the armor; it was nice to know the guy wasn't perfect, that he was human in a few ways, at least. Nicer still was knowing that in the ways that counted—survival, for instance—Nolan was a rock. Jon liked to cling to that rock.

He could've used that rock right now.

Because the convention wasn't proving to have the distracting effect he'd thought it would.

That old man, Sam Comfort, with his spooky gray eyes and sadism-lined face, was a constantly recurring image in Jon's mind, a strong, chilling image that could crowd out even the four-color fantasies strewn out along the dealers' tables in Hucksters' Hall. Tonight. Tonight Jon and Nolan would be going up against that crazy, *crazy* old man, and if all went well, they'd come away with a strongbox full of that senile old bastard's money. Which was dandy, only they hadn't done the thing yet; it lay ahead to be done, tonight.

And Jon was scared shitless at the thought.

He'd been eager at the prospect, sure; he was hot to get back some of that money he'd lost a month and a half ago, and when

Nolan outlined the plan to rip off Sam Comfort and Son, it had sounded good to him, and still did. But that was back in Iowa City, in homey, security-lined surroundings, where planning a robbery was like plotting the story of a new comic strip. The execution of the plan seemed light-years away, the hazy end result of a sharp but abstract concept. And this, this was Detroit, they were *here* already, and a few hours from now Jon would be laying his ass on the line.

He'd done it before, of course, laid his ass on the line in one of Nolan's potentially violent undertakings (hell of an unpleasant word, that—undertaking, Jesus!) but that didn't make things any easier. Last year, he'd gone into that first robbery with a very naive sort of attitude, an out-of-focus view, a comic-book idea of action and adventure and derring-do. Then, when everything had turned to shit, guns blasting into people and throwing blood around and turning human beings into limp and lifeless meat, Jon had suddenly realized that Nolan's life was not capes and bullets-bouncing-off, it was the real goddamn thing. The bullets went through you, and blood and bone and stuff came flying out the other side, and afterward, Jon would've been glad to take Nolan's advice to "let this cure you of living out your half-ass fantasies." But no sooner had Nolan got out those words, than the situation erupted into violence once again, and Jon had to respond in kind, had to pull Nolan's ass out of the fire, and get him to where he maybe could be kept alive.

When the cordite fumes had lifted from the situation, when the blood had been cleaned up and the people buried, when the bank robbery and its gory aftermath had fuzzed over in his mind and become just an exciting memory, Jon had been lulled into thinking it had been sort of fun and, after all, he'd come out of it with not a scratch. So he'd fallen into the trap again, equating Nolan's life with goddamn Batman or something, only to be reminded, the hard way, that the game Nolan played was for high stakes, the highest—life or death—not to mention those lesser gambles, getting maimed, maybe, or jailed. He'd been reminded of that when those guys shot his uncle and stole the money and got him back in the thick again. And now, with that nightmare just beginning to fade in his mind, he was suckering himself back into Nolan's precarious lifestyle once more, hopefully to recoup some of the money they'd both lost last go-round.

Not so many hours ago, Jon'd had a talk with Breen, and that talk was lingering in the back of Jon's head, nagging him as much as the image of old man Comfort. Nolan had arrived around two-thirty in the morning and, after a talk with Breen, had driven out to the house on Iowa City's outskirts to see if the Comforts were still around. Nolan figured they wouldn't be, but felt it best to check, and had Jon stay with Breen at the antique shop, armed, in case the Comforts attacked while Nolan was gone.

During that time, while they waited for Nolan's return, Jon and Breen had talked. Breen's first question was, "Are you related to Nolan or something? His fucking bastard kid or something?" Breen seemed slightly irritated.

Jon was taken aback by the question. "Not that I know of. What the hell makes you come up with an idea like that?"

"I don't know," Breen said, shaking his head. "I known Nolan a long time, and I never seen him act like this."

"Like what?"

"He's goddamn pampering you, kid. Isn't like him. You know what he said to me?"

"No." Which was true. Jon had not been a party to Breen and Nolan's conversation.

"He said he had to be careful old man Comfort didn't see who was robbing him! Can you imagine?"

Jon said, "What's wrong with that? Comfort and Nolan know each other, and so of course Nolan doesn't want him to know who's pulling the job."

"Don't you see it? He's puttin' on the kid gloves when he ought be bare-knuckle punchin'. This kind of thing, when you heist another heister, you got to kill the guy. You don't leave people like that alive after ripping 'em off. Not people like Sam Comfort, you don't. Or he'll come around and cut off your dick and feed it to you."

Jon swallowed at that not particularly appetizing thought. "So what?" he said, straining to sound flip. "That just means Nolan is right—you got to keep Comfort from knowing who it is, otherwise you got a lot of…you know, bloodshed on your hands."

Breen sat up in bed, groaning just a little from his gunshot wounds. "Now, I'll admit," he said through tight lips, "I'll admit that Nolan's always been one to avoid killing when he could, but not in a case like this. You got to lance a boil like the Comforts. It's safer all around, just to go in and blow those bastards' heads off and call it a night."

"Big talk, Breen. And you don't even carry a gun."

"Right, *I* don't, but Nolan *does*. I wouldn't go for killing the Comforts or anybody, but I wouldn't think of ripping them off, either, not for revenge or nothing. I'm lucky to be out of it with my ass. I'm a coward. Ask Nolan. I ran out on him that time in Chicago, when those syndicate boys shot him up. And that's another reason this thing puzzles me. Nolan says he's going to give me a share of the take, like he's going after the Comforts as a favor to me. What for? He owes me nothing. I'm lucky he doesn't kick my fuckin' butt in for running the hell out on him that time. So what is it with him? Why's he jumpin' on this like it's his golden opportunity? Why's he a goddamn humanitarian where the Comforts are concerned?"

And at this stage Jon had realized what lay behind Breen's point of view. After the robbery, the Comforts might naturally figure that Breen had had a hand in it, to get back at them for their double-cross and get his due from the parking meter heisting. So of course Breen wanted the Comforts dead; of course he was uneasy about Nolan sparing the lives of that miserable family. Breen himself was the one most likely to (gulp) get his dick cut off and fed to him.

But what Breen said did bother Jon. Was Nolan taking undue risks, to spare Jon? Was Nolan avoiding violence with the Comforts to keep things from getting too rough for Jon? Was Breen right—with people like the Comforts, were you better off just killing them? That final concept was one Jon didn't really think he could stomach. Did Nolan know that, too, Jon wondered?

After spending another hundred bucks, Jon left the Hucksters' Hall and went upstairs to the room he and Nolan would share. It was a dreary cubicle, despite the hotel's lavish lobby, dining area, and bar, and was robbery even at convention rates. He undressed, had a cold shower, and got dressed again and went down to the bar, to have a drink and fog his mind if not clear it.

It was an off-time right now: the bar was part of a big nightclub setup, with stage and arena of tables over to the right, and the room was almost as big as the ballroom where the comic dealing was going on, only this was as empty of people as Hucksters' Hall was full. Up at the bar was a pretty woman with short brown pixie hair. She was wearing slacks and a sweater over a blouse—casual clothes but very stylish, in dark, soft colors: blues, browns. She was thin as a model, but full-breasted. Jon supposed she was in her early thirties, close to Karen's age.

Why did he have to think of Karen at a moment like this? Now, along with all those other bad vibes running through him—fear and depression and edginess—now he felt *guilty*, too. Because he was thinking of going up and sitting next to that woman at the bar, pinning his hopes on the improbable possibility of his picking her up, thinking that maybe a little sex game (even if conversation was as far as it got) would drain off his tension. But, no—just thinking of it made things worse; now he felt guilty for possibly betraying Karen.

Fortunately he was able to brush the guilt quickly from his mind. He just thought about this morning, when he'd called Karen to tell her as tactfully as possible that he would be attending the comics convention, and she'd gone into a fury, a goddamn rage about him missing her birthday for a stupid bunch of comic books. She'd given him no chance to explain (and he couldn't have—Karen knew of Nolan and disapproved of Nolan-sponsored activities even more than she did comic books), and she'd really been quite unreasonable.

So, conscience clear, he sat down next to the pretty brunette and smiled and built a strategy. And when the bartender came around, Jon ordered a Scotch on the rocks for himself (he hated Scotch, but it sounded rugged), and as he turned to her to ask what she'd have, damn if the bartender didn't card him!

His outline for seduction erased itself on his mental blackboard and, as he looked at the beautiful, dark-haired, full-breasted woman in her early thirties sitting next to him, with her finely chiseled features and a smile turning from invitation to condescension, Jon decided not even to bother digging his I.D. out of his wallet, just forgot the Scotch and the woman and got the hell out of there.

He went back up to the cubicle, had another cold shower, and got dressed again and went down and spent another hundred on comic books. It killed the time till he was supposed to meet Nolan in the coffee shop downstairs.

7

Nolan stepped onto the elevator and was all alone, except for a girl with sharply pointed ears and skin tinted a dark green. She was wearing a silver sarong that made her look as though she'd been wrapped in aluminum foil, like a sandwich. She was young, probably sixteen, a chunky but not unattractive girl—considering she was green and had pointed ears.

It was Nolan's sincere hope that she would not be going all fifteen floors down to the lobby, as he was. He'd just come from the hotel room, where he'd found evidence that Jon was developing a cleanliness fetish—the boy apparently had had at least a couple of showers already, as all the towels were used up and the floor was wet. All of which was only in keeping with this nuthouse hotel, this asylum populated by kids so weird they made Jon seem normal.

Like, for instance, this green, pointy-eared girl with whom he shared the elevator. Nolan hoped she'd get off soon so he wouldn't have to say anything to her. Strangers were always a pain to talk to, let alone green ones. She would ask him if he wondered why she was made up this way, and he would say no, but it would be too late: they would be talking, and this was a particularly slow elevator that could make a fifteen-floor ride seem a lifetime. Besides, he figured he already knew why she was dressed this way: there was going to be a full moon tonight, and she was just getting an early start.

"I bet you're wondering why I'm dressed like this," she said, in a squeaky voice.

Nolan said nothing, but he did manage a smile. Sort of.

"Normally I wouldn't be wearing this."

"Oh?"

"At least, not till tomorrow night. There's a convention going on, you know, comic books and *Star Trek* and things, and the costume ball isn't till tomorrow night."

"Oh."

"This is just for the press conference. Some of us were asked to dress up now for the press conference. Some newspaper and TV people are here, doing interviews and stuff about the con. If you watch the six o'clock news, you just may see me."

The elevator was now at ballroom level, just a floor above the lobby. The doors slid open and crowded in front of the ballroom entrance were maybe a hundred and fifty people, mostly kids five years either side of Jon in age, some in strange getups, and cameramen and reporters and newsmen shuffling around, jockeying various equipment and holding mikes up to some people standing under klieg lights a shade brighter than the aurora borealis.

Nolan stepped to the rear of the elevator; he did not want to be on the six o'clock news.

The green girl shouted, "Scotty!" and ran out of the elevator and into the crowd, toward a red-cheeked, roughly handsome dark-haired guy who looked familiar to Nolan; some television actor, he guessed. He caught the actor's eye and smiled sympathetically and the actor shook his head, as if to say, "I wish I was going down to the bar like you, my friend." The poor actor was swamped by girls and reporters, and Nolan wondered how anybody could ever stand going into a business as hair-raising as that.

The doors slid shut and Nolan got out at the lobby. He quickly went into the bar and had a Scotch, as much for that put-upon actor as himself.

Sitting on the stool next to him was a very pretty girl with short brown hair, wearing a chic pants outfit. Nolan gave her a look that asked if he could buy her one, and she gave him back a look that said he could.

"Gin and tonic," she said, in a voice designed to order gin and tonics.

Nolan glanced at his watch. He was running early. He hadn't really expected his buddy Bernie to be able to supply him with everything he needed, and so quickly. It was a good hour and a half till he was supposed to meet Jon in the coffee shop, and he decided to kill some time.

He examined the girl's delicate but distinct features (her eyes were a hazel-green color you don't run into that often) and asked, "Model?"

She shook her head. "Flight attendant."

"Stewardess, you mean."

She gave him a firm little smile. "Flight attendant," she said. "Don't worry."

"Don't worry what?"

"I don't believe what I read in paperbacks."

She laughed, and the bartender brought her the gin and tonic. She looked at him, examining him in much the same way he had her. "Gangster?"

"Right the first time."

"Don't worry."

"Don't worry what?"

"I don't believe what I read in paperbacks, either."

They both laughed, and in her room on the tenth floor, forty-five minutes later, she kissed his cheek and played with the salt-and-pepper hair on his chest and said, "No, really, what are you?"

"I told you downstairs. Gangster, like you guessed."

"Come on."

"Very specialized gangster, though."

"Oh?"

"Yeah. All I do is see to it nobody gives Sinatra a bad time." She laughed again, and the covers fell down around her waist, and he got a long look at her breasts. They were full, very, too full for her otherwise slender body, but he didn't mind. The nipples were small, which made the breasts look even bigger. They were coral color, her nipples, and he liked them. He leaned over and nibbled one.

"Hey!" she said. "You're a horny S.O.B., aren't you? Don't be a glutton."

"Lady," he said, between nibbles, "I'll take all the servings I can get. I don't often eat at restaurants this nice."

"Quit it," she giggled, in a tone that said go ahead. Ahead was where he went, and they had a good time, their second. Nolan believed in going twice whenever possible, because the second time can be done slow and lovingly, without the urgency that makes the first round so good but so frantic. She had an ass as nice as her breasts, not skinny like the rest of her; something soft and fleshy and fun to fill his hands with.

She was doing him a lot of good: his bridges with Sherry were getting burned a bit faster than he had anticipated, and that was a relief. He realized his separation from Sherry had been a little heavy on his mind, and though he hated to admit it, even to himself, he missed the girl, damn it; and he didn't like going into a heist with that sort of emotional preoccupation working on him.

So sex this afternoon was a real lucky break for him. Made him feel purged. Made him feel great, like a fucking kid.

"Don't get the wrong idea," she said, sitting up again, her breasts hanging loose now, sagging just a little, as though tuckered out.

"Wrong idea about you?" he said. "Or about stewardesses?"

She grinned; a good grin, the sort many pretty girls avoid. "Either one. Want a smoke?"

"No. Gave 'em up."

"How come?"

"Not healthy. Man gets to be my age, he better watch his ass."

"What do you mean 'your age'? How old are you, anyway?"

"Forty-eight," Nolan lied.

"That's not so old. I'm thirty-five, which is kind of old for a flight attendant."

At least thirty-five, Nolan thought, saying, "You look like twenty, kid." He stroked a breast. Kissed her neck.

"Hey, give me a break…enough's enough. For right now, anyway. So tell me, what is your racket? What are you doing in Detroit?"

"I manage a nightclub, Chicago area," he said. (Which was semi-true, after all: the Tropical did use entertainment in their bar setup.) He told her that a friend of his, an old army buddy, had a little talent agency up here, and he'd promised to check out some of the guy's new clients.

"Oh really? You done that already?"

"No. Tonight. Going out to his place tonight and see what he has to offer."

"Sounds like fun. Care for some company?"

"Naw…it'll be a drag. This guy's agency is really small-time, I'm just looking at these acts out of friendship. Or pity. You'd fall asleep, the acts'll be so bad."

She made a face. "Well, looks like another rip-snorter of an evening for old coffee-tea-or-me," she said, apparently feeling brushed off. "Suppose I'll just catch another movie tonight, and if I'm lucky maybe get molested walking back to the hotel."

"Don't give me that," he said. "I can't picture you sitting home alone unless you wanted to."

"I thought you said you didn't believe what you read in paperbacks? My life isn't any swinging party. This is the first time I've gotten any in weeks."

"Bullshit."

"No, really. I been a lousy *nun* lately. Ever since my marriage broke up, last year."

"You were married? I thought a stewardess had to be single."

"Haven't you heard of Women's Lib and equal rights and all? The airlines can't pull much of that crap these days, though God knows they'd like to. And in my case, maybe I'd be better off, at least as far as the old anti-wedlock rule goes. The marriage, it just didn't work out, with my being a flight attendant and gone days at a time. My husband was balling some secretary at his office, some mousy little twerp with boobs like ping pong balls."

Nolan shrugged. "Then losing him should be no great loss. He's obviously an idiot. But there's plenty of other guys in the world."

"Yeah, and plenty of other idiots, too. Like there's this pilot who's been chasing me, but he's married, and he's obnoxious as hell too, so I been ducking him. I have had a fling or two, tiny ones, with some interesting passengers I've met on longer flights. But those guys also are married, usually, and I come out of an afternoon like this one feeling like a whore or something. How about you?"

"I never feel like a whore."

"I mean, are you married? Don't be a prick." She said "prick" in a nice way, with affection.

"Not married. Never have been. It's an institution that holds little appeal to me."

"After a two-year marriage that was just slightly less successful than the war in Vietnam, I tend to agree with you. Hey, you know something?"

"What?"

"I sort of like you. Your personality is a little on the sour side, but I like it. And your sexual enthusiasm, especially considering you think of yourself as an old man, has me somewhat winded, I'll admit, but I like that too. Let me make you a proposition. Why don't you come back tonight and see me, when you're through hearing those auditions? Then we can resume our conversation…and whatever else you'd care to resume."

"It could be late."

"I'll give you the spare key. Let yourself in and crawl under the covers with me. How does that sound to you?"

Nolan smiled. "That sounds fine."

They chatted for a while longer, and she mentioned that she had a flight tomorrow, and he mentioned he'd be taking a flight tomorrow himself, and it turned out to be the same one. That was a happy coincidence, and Nolan felt unnaturally pleased that this afternoon's encounter would be continued tonight and, in a way, on the plane tomorrow. In his younger days, he preferred light involvement with his women, in-and-out situations; but he found, as he grew older, that he liked something more—not much more, maybe, but something.

He got dressed, and as he went to the door, he turned and said, "Hey! Your name. What the hell is it?"

"Hazel."

"Like your eyes," he said.

"Like the fat maid in the funnies," she said, squinching her nose.

"Well, you're in the right hotel for that."

"Yeah, I noticed. Comic book fans all over the place, kids in costumes, kids wearing T-shirts with cartoon characters on them. A kid with a T-shirt like that tried to pick me up in the bar, just before you showed, would you believe it?"

"Sure, woodwork's full of 'em. Listen, I got to get going. I'll see you tonight"

"Okay. Hey!"

"What?"

"Your name? What's your name?"

He hesitated for a moment; he better not use the Logan name. He was registered as Ryan, but for some reason he wanted to give her the name he himself felt most comfortable with. So he said, "Nolan," and to hell with it.

"Is that a first name," she asked, "or a last?"

"Whatever you want," he said, and went out.

This time he had the elevator to himself, and damn glad of it.

Jon was in the coffee shop, working on a Coke.

Nolan joined him at the counter, said, "How much you blow on funny-books so far?"

The kid grinned. "Four hundred and thirty-five bucks and feeling no pain."

Nolan had no criticism of that. It was a harmless enough indulgence. Besides, he remembered Jon showing him a copy of a comic book, two years ago when he first met the kid; the comic had cost Jon two hundred bucks, which had seemed insane to Nolan, but just recently he had seen an article about an eighteen-year-old kid who'd paid eighteen hundred dollars for that same comic. Nolan asked Jon about it at the time, and Jon had said, rather bitterly, "That stupid clod...with him shelling out all that dough, and with all the news coverage he got, shit, prices'll inflate like crazy again. That comic wasn't worth any eighteen hundred bucks. Why, it wasn't worth a penny more than a grand."

Considering the interest Jon had made on his two-hundred-buck investment, Nolan was impressed, and no longer ridiculed his young friend's hobby. In fact, he counted himself a sucker, because he too had owned that comic book (bought it off the stands, when he was a kid) and after reading it had thrown his dime investment in the trash.

"How'd it go, Nolan?"

"We have wheels. No problem."

"Good. Rest of the stuff, too?"

"Rest of the stuff, too."

"What about the farmhouse?"

"Drove out there, had a look around. No, nobody saw me. I drew up a layout of the farm and all. We can go over it later, up in the room."

"Fine."

"Nervous?"

"Yes."

"Thought the funny-books would distract you."

"Me too. No soap. Tried to pick up a woman in the bar to see if *that* would distract me. But it fizzled too."

Nolan glanced at Jon's Wonder Warthog T-shirt, and wondered if—but no, that was ridiculous.

"Look, kid, there's one thing I want you to do for me."

"What's that?"

"Go buy some hose."

"Sure. Go buy some hose? Like rubber hose?"

"Like nylon hose. The kind women stick their legs in."

"Stockings? What the hell for, Nolan?"

"I thought we'd pose as Avon ladies."

"Oh. You mean masks. We'll pull 'em over our heads, you mean."

"Just buy them."

"Why didn't you?"

"I don't want to go in buying hose. What're you, crazy?"

"Too embarrassing?" Jon smiled.

"Hell yes. Why don't *you* want to?"

"Too embarrassing," Jon admitted.

"Right, and I'm in charge, you're my flunky, and when I say buy hose, goddammit, you buy hose."

"Well, they'll probably take me for some kind of pervert or something."

"Probably." Nolan grinned. He was in a good mood.

"What are you so happy about?"

"It's going to be clockwork, kid. We're going to fill our pockets with Sam Comfort's ill-gotten gains, and he won't be the wiser."

Now Jon was grinning too. "You make me feel better. I don't think I'm nervous anymore. I don't even mind buying the hose. If the salesgirl asks me what I want nylons for, I'll just tell her I want 'em 'cause they'll go so good with my black lace garter belt."

"That's the spirit, kid. Here, I'll even pay for your damn Coke."

8

It was Friday evening, eight-fifteen. The country was calm and quiet tonight, the traffic along this gravel back road seemingly nonexistent. Across the way was a two-story gray frame farmhouse, beginning to sag, whose paint was peeling like an overbaked sunbather. It was a slovenly, ramshackle structure, a shack got out of hand; it sat in a big yard overgrown with big weeds, its location remote even for the country, the lights of neighboring farmhouses barely within view. The place was, in effect, isolated from civilization, which suited the people who lived there. And it suited Nolan and Jon's purpose, as well.

Jon had been studying the hovel the Comfort clan called home. He shook his head. "Dogpatch," he muttered.

"What?" Nolan said.

They were sitting in the dark blue, year-old Ford Nolan had leased from Bernie that afternoon. The motor was off, lights too; the car was parked in a cornfield across the road from the Comfort homestead. They were a good half-block down from the house, the nose of the car approaching but not edging onto the dirt access inlet that bridged ditch and gravel road. They had entered a similar access inlet to cross the corner of the field, having cut their lights as they drove down the road that eventually would have intersected the one running past the Comfort house. They'd rumbled slowly across the recently harvested ground, like some prehistoric beast lumbering after its prey at a snail's pace. The only sound had been that of corn husks cracking under the wheels, but the stillness of the night and the insecurity of the situation had magnified that husk-cracking in Jon's perception, unsettling him. The moon seemed to Jon a huge searchlight illuminating the field, making him feel naked, exposed, unsettling him further. But nothing had happened, and now they sat in the car, in the cornfield, getting ready. They were dressed for their work, in black: Nolan in knit slacks and turtleneck sweater; Jon in jeans and sweatshirt (the latter worn inside-out because the other side bore a fluorescent Batman insignia). The clothes were heavy, warm, which was good, as the night was a cool, almost cold one. Both wore guns in holsters on their hips, police-style: .38 Colt revolvers with four-inch barrels, butts facing out. Between them on the seat were two olive-drab canisters, looking much like beer cans, but with military markings in place of brand names, and levers connecting to pin mechanisms. Also on the seat was a package of nylon stockings, unopened.

Jon let his Dogpatch remark lie; he'd just been thinking aloud, and though Nolan had been very tolerant lately about Jon's comics hobby, now was no time to put that tolerance to a test by going into the resemblance the Comfort place held to something Al Capp might have drawn.

Nolan said, "You want me to go over it once more?"

"No," Jon said.

"Okay." Nolan was sitting back in the seat, loose, apparently relaxed, but Jon thought he sensed an uncharacteristic tightness in the man's voice, perhaps brought on by concern over Jon's relative inexperience in matters of potential violence.

They'd been over the plan several times, first at the hotel, in their room, and again on the way here, in the car. Nolan would come up behind the Comfort farmhouse, through the pasture in back; the ground was open, open as hell, but there were trees along the property line, and also a barn, and those would provide whatever cover Nolan needed. Jon would allow Nolan five minutes, during which time Nolan would jimmy the basement window open, crawl inside, deposit his calling card, and crawl out. After those five minutes were up, Jon would initiate phase two of the plan, in that weed-encroached front yard.

Jon felt sure everything would go without a hitch, but he wished he could also be sure Nolan felt the same way. Jon's own confidence was undercut somewhat by the lack of confidence he suspected in Nolan, an attitude that stemmed back to that discussion they'd had about firearms, back at the hotel.

"I don't exactly understand," Jon had said, "how we're going to subdue these dudes—I mean, what do we do, brain 'em with the butts of our guns, or what?"

"For Chrissake, kid," Nolan had answered, eyes narrowed

even more than usual, "never go swinging a gun butt around. You got the barrel pointing at you, and you can end up with a hole in your chest big as the one in your damn head. Why do you think I prefer a long-barreled gun?"

"Better aim, you said."

"Yeah, that. And this too—with a long-barreled gun you can put a guy to sleep without firing a shot."

"So, what then? We brain 'em with the gun barrels?"

"You would if it was called for. But it isn't. I told you what the plan was, and you didn't hear any part where you go slugging people with a gun, did you? All right, then. You just leave the subduing to me—and leave the gun in its holster, dig?"

"Look, I'm capable of using it if I have to, Nolan."

"Maybe, but don't act like it's something to look forward to. By now, you been through enough shit like this to tell the difference between what we're about to do and some goddamn comic-book fairy tale. If we get in a totally desperate situation, sure, use the gun. That's what it's there for. But since we got the element of surprise working for us, I don't see that happening."

Jon was determined now to make a good showing tonight, to regain Nolan's confidence by behaving like a cold, hard-ass professional, not like some naive kid. Next to him, Nolan was opening the package of nylons, and Jon listened to the crackle of cellophane and waited for Nolan to hand him one of the stockings.

But instead there was a long moment of silence, and even in darkness Jon had no trouble making out the stunned look on Nolan's face.

"Kid."

"Yeah?"

"I think we're going to have to make a change of plan."

"Oh?"

"Yeah. I don't think we're going to be able to split up. You're going to have to follow along pretty close behind me."

"Why's that?"

Nolan held up the nylons.

Pantyhose.

"Pantyhose," Nolan said.

Jon started to sputter. "Nolan, shit, I mean, that's all the girls are wearing these days. I should've checked to make sure they were the old-fashioned kind. I mean…"

Nolan dug in his pocket and got out his knife.

"Nolan—what're you doing?"

A grin flashed under Nolan's mustache, a grin so wide and out of character, it startled Jon. "I'm not going to kill you, kid," he said, "I just got to perform some hasty surgery."

Nolan separated the siamese twins; he handed one amputated leg to Jon and kept the other. "You know, kid," Nolan said, "this is a hell of a lot of trouble to go to, just to get your way."

"Get my way?"

"Yeah. But you win. From now on, I buy all the nylons."

They both grinned this time, and enthusiasm ran through Jon like a drug. "I won't let you down, Nolan."

"I know you won't."

Nolan pulled the stocking over his head, immediately disfiguring himself. "Five minutes, Jon."

"Five minutes, Nolan."

And Nolan was gone.

Five minutes? Five hours was what it seemed. Jon made a concerted effort not to study his watch, not to follow the second hand around. But he did, of course, and the time was excruciatingly slow in passing, the seconds pelting him like the liquid pellets of the Chinese water torture; the ticking of his watch seemed abnormally loud, as if in an echo chamber, and he wondered how the hell a relic like that (a Dick Tracy watch, circa late '30s) could put out such a racket.

He thought he saw something moving across the road, over in the Comfort yard, but it was only the tall weeds getting pushed around by the wind. That brought his attention to the farmhouse, which was what he was supposed to be doing anyway—watching the house, keeping alert for anything out of order that might be going on over there. The Comforts couldn't be expected to stick to Nolan and Jon's game plan, after all; and as Nolan had said more than once, you never can tell when the human element might enter in and knock a well-conceived plan on its well-conceived ass.

Jon sat studying the old gray two-story, and thought back to the verbal tour of the place Breen had given him last night. Though from the run-down exterior you'd never guess it, the Comfort castle was, according to Breen, expensively furnished and equipped with modern appliances and gadgetry galore. Its shabby appearance was no doubt partially purposeful at least; as a thief himself, old Sam Comfort would have an unnaturally suspicious and devious mind, certainly capable of devising a defense of this sort: that is, living in a house that looked like a junk heap on the outside, but was a palace on the inside. Crafty as hell, because judging from what he could see, Jon could hardly imagine a less likely prospect for a robbery. Looting a place like that—why, you'd be lucky to come away with a six-pack of beer and a handful of food stamps.

Not that they had in mind stealing any of the possessions the Comforts had acquired through years of applied larceny; the creature comforts the Comfort creatures had assembled for themselves were of no interest to Jon and Nolan. There was only one thing in that house that interested them: the strongbox of cash kept somewhere within those deceptively decayed walls. Breen had reported that old Sam kept a minimum of fifty thousand in that box at all times, and there was a good chance the Comforts (having just returned from Iowa City) hadn't yet banked their latest parking meter bonanza. Which meant, in all probability, that some two hundred grand was locked up within that metal box.

He checked his watch.

Thirty seconds shy of five minutes.

He withdrew the gun from the holster, hefted it, put it back. Took a deep breath. Another. The butterflies in his stomach began to disperse.

Ten seconds.

He pulled the nylon mask down over his face. It didn't impair his vision particularly, though he could feel it contorting his features, feel it tight on his face. It was a strange feeling, like pressing your face against a window.

Five minutes, and he left the Ford, got down in the ditch, and walked till he was across from the house, then crawled across the gravel road, moved up and over the opposite ditch, and into the high weeds of the Comforts' front yard. The weeds were more than sufficient cover; he traveled on his hands and knees and couldn't be seen. He was within a few yards of the house when he heard a muffled pop, and after a moment smoke began to fill the air. Nolan had said the smoke would penetrate, and penetrate it did, in spades. The smoke was curling out through openings the house didn't know it had, from around windows and between paint-peeling boards and from every damn where—gray, creeping smoke—and if Jon didn't know better, he'd have sworn the house was on fire.

Which was, of course, the idea.

To convince the Comforts their house was burning.

To panic the old man into grabbing his treasure box of loot and abandoning his ship.

By this time, Jon was right up by the cement steps that rose to the front door, and he pulled the pin on his little olive-drab can, which made it pop and sprayed out smoke, blowtorch fashion, to the accompaniment of a loud hissing sound. As he retreated to the tall weeds, Jon wondered how so much smoke could fit into one little can. Earlier, he'd asked Nolan about the canisters; why, he'd wanted to know, was the top of the can gray and the rest green? Because, Nolan explained, the green was for camouflage purposes, while the top of the can was marked the color of smoke it made. Jon almost wished they'd used one green smoke bomb and one red one; it wouldn't have looked like a fire, but it sure would've freaked out that pothead Billy Comfort. The poor burned-out bastard would've thought he was hallucinating.

Nolan should be coming around the house any time now. The smoke was thickening, but Jon wasn't having too much trouble maintaining a reasonable level of vision, even with the nylon mask. A figure was coming around from the left of the house. Must be Nolan, Jon thought, but then he saw the outline of the figure's head: it was a head with a bushy mane of hair, Afro-bushy.

It was Billy Comfort, speak of the goddamn devil.

The shaggy-haired figure was moving toward Jon, and Jon ducked behind the cement steps. Billy was carrying a pole of some sort, and though he apparently hadn't spotted Jon, he was heading straight for the smoke grenade, which was still spewing its gray guts out, hissing away like a big sick snake. As Billy approached, Jon suppressed a cough, covering his already nylon-covered mouth, wondering where the hell Nolan was, or, for that matter, old man Comfort.

Billy knelt beside the smoke grenade, fanning the fumes away with his free hand. He nudged the blisteringly hot canister with one foot, like a Neanderthal trying to figure out what fire was. Finally, he said, “Far fuckin’ out,” and began to laugh and cough simultaneously.

Jon’s hand touched the butt of the .38 lightly. Nolan had said leave the subduing to me, but Nolan wasn’t around. Somebody had to subdue Billy Comfort, and right now, before Billy went screaming out the truth of the deception to his old man.

So Jon did what he thought best.

He tackled Billy, burying his head in Billy’s balls.

Billy yelped accordingly, and his foot connected with the smoking can and he slipped on it, like a contestant taking a fall in a log-rolling contest, and he went down hard, the air escaping from him in a big whoosh. Jon clasped a hand over Billy’s mouth and grinned in what proved to be a premature victory, because Billy managed to swing something around that caught Jon on the side of the head and blacked him out.

When Jon awoke, seconds later, he saw right away what it was that had put him to sleep: the handle of that pole Billy was carrying, only it was more than just a pole: it was the wooden shaft of a five-pronged pitchfork. And Jon looked up through the smoke-and-nylon haze and saw in Billy’s eyes a haze of another sort: a druggy haze. Billy was high, and Billy was on to the game. Maybe he’d even witnessed Jon and/or Nolan planting the smoke bombs; perhaps he’d been back in that barn, smoking or snorting or doing God-knows-what sort of dope, when he’d spied suspicious things going on up by the house, and had grabbed a pitchfork as a make-do weapon and come rushing to the rescue of home and hearth.

So that’s how it stood: Billy with one foot on Jon’s chest, smoke floating around them like a choking fog, Billy raising the pitchfork to impale Jon and put him to sleep again.

Permanently.

9

Nolan crossed the gravel road in a crouch, hopped down into the ditch. It must have rained here recently, as the ditch was damp and got his shoes muddy. When he was safely within the sheltering trees that divided the Comfort land from the neighboring spread, Nolan cleaned his shoes off on the trunk of one of the clustered evergreens.

He was uncomfortable in the nylon mask; the thing was hot, even on a cool night like this. He pulled it off and stuffed it in his pants pocket. He'd put it back on when he got up by the house. Right now, he preferred having his vision completely unimpaired; enjoyed having the clear, crisp country air fill his lungs without a damn nylon filter.

Pantyhose, he thought, and grinned momentarily.

In his left hand was the olive-drab canister, the U.S. Army smoke grenade identical to the one he'd left with Jon. With his right hand he withdrew the long-barreled .38 from the police holster; it was going to be necessary to rap a head or two, and perhaps do more than that, should something go out of kilter, despite what he'd told Jon about going easy with the firearms. He'd taught him well, but Jon's experience under fire was more than limited; if push came to shove, Jon would be armed, would be able to respond, but Nolan didn't want that kid waving a .38 around frivolously.

He stayed within the thick evergreens, got up parallel to the big gray barn and, crouching again, crossed half a block's worth of pasture and then flattened himself against the barn's back side. He could hear cattle or something stirring around in there, but not a Comfort, surely; the Comforts owned this land, according to Breen, but leased both pasture and barn to a farmer whose own property adjoined the Comforts' in back. Which made the Comforts a part of the landed gentry, Nolan supposed, which was a hell of a thought.

The house was maybe a hundred yards from the barn, maybe a shade more than that. Open ground and, with the moon full and the house fairly well lit up, not easily crossed unseen. He got on his hands and knees and began to crawl, like a commando training under the machine-gun fire of some square-jaw sergeant.

He crawled two feet, and his hand—the one with the gun in it—sank into something soft which, on closer examination, proved to be cow dung. Nolan wasn't happy about having gunk all over his hand, or his gun either, and wiped both clean on the grass. Holstering the .38, he swore to himself and crawled on. But the pasture was a cow-pattie minefield and, several feet later, the same hand ran into the same substance, a bit drier this time but no less irritating. So he said a mental "Fuck it," got back up in a crouch, and moved on. What the hell, he thought, it wasn't like the Comforts were out watching for him, and you can't expect a city boy to go crawling through cow shit, not for anybody or anything.

A barbed-wire fence separated the Comforts' yard from the pasture, and Nolan squeezed under the fence without so much as snagging his sweater—a much more successful enterprise than his aborted attempt at crawling across the cow-pattie beachhead. The weeds were waist high in the yard and, keeping in his low crouch, he proceeded until the weeds ended and the gravel drive, which circled the place, took over. The family Buick was parked alongside the house on the left, which meant it would be a toss-up which door Sam would head for—front or back—when the "fire" broke out. Before he left the high weeds to cross the drive, Nolan got out the nylon mask, pulled it on, and drew the .38 again. Down to business, cow shit or no cow shit.

The house had many windows, and lights were on in most of the rooms, but all the window shades were drawn. This was frustrating, because Nolan had to make sure both father and son were present in the house, and where. The shade of one window on the right side of the house allowed an inch or two clearance at the bottom to peer through, and since Breen had given him a full layout of the house, it didn't surprise Nolan to find that the room beyond the window was the living room. He was, however, slightly surprised to find that Breen's description of the Comfort place had not been an exaggeration: the house really was as lavishly—and tastelessly—furnished as Breen had said. The living room had wall-to-wall red shag carpeting and a sofa and reclining chair covered in a yellowish leather; there were any number of heavy, expensive wood pieces of various and totally nonmatching styles, as well as a couple of clear plastic scoop-seated chairs. Everything in the room was of high quality, but was slapped together like a furniture store's warehouse sale. Drab, old, pale wallpaper, faded and peeling, was a backdrop to all this expensive but oddly coupled furniture, and the high point of the room was the Hamms beer sign over the sofa, lit from within, displaying a shifting panorama of shimmering "sky blue waters." Lying on the sofa, sipping a Hamms, basking in the glow of a color television console the size of a foreign car, was Sam Comfort—a skinny old man with a potbelly, wearing gray longjohns, the buttons open halfway down his chest. He was watching *Hee-Haw*.

None of the other, shaded windows around the house afforded Nolan any view, though from Breen's description he knew where everything was: adjacent to the living room was a kitchen (with space-age refrigerator, of course—stick a glass in a hole in the door and you get ice water) and Sam's bedroom, which were side by side and together took up the same space as the rather large living room; in there somewhere was a toilet—Nolan didn't remember exactly where—unless the Comforts still went the outhouse route, or maybe the cows weren't the only ones crapping in the pasture. According to Breen, the old man's room was unlike the others in the house, as it alone did not show signs of acquired affluence; the master bedroom was as empty and functional as the old man's mind. Upstairs was a bedroom for Terry (the statutory rapist presently being rehabilitated) and another for Billy—also an office affair Sam used for planning sessions and the like. Nolan could see colored lights flashing behind the shade on Billy's window; Breen said Billy's room was a pot freak's retreat, water bed and strobe lights and black-light posters and tons of stereo equipment, enough wattage in the latter to power a fair-size radio station. He could hear the faint throb of rock music coming from that upper floor room, and he would have to make the hopefully safe assumption that Billy was mind-tripping up there, as was the boy's usual practice.

Satisfied that he'd pinpointed both Comforts, Nolan went to work on the basement window in back of the house. The window came open easily, soundlessly, with the proper prying from his knife. He climbed down inside the Comforts' lowest level, a washing machine right below the window serving as a step down for him, making his entry a quiet one.

He used a pen-flash to examine the room. This end of the long basement was the laundry room; the other was being converted into a bar and recreation area. This was the first remodeling the Comforts had undertaken, and they were apparently doing the work themselves, as it was pretty slipshod: boards, cans of paint, various building bullshit lying around.

Which was good, because this was the makings of a fire hazard; this made a logical reason for a basement fire, and should help to con Sam as he quickly tried to make some logic out of a fire breaking out in his house. The remodeling was almost finished, but not quite: the bar was in and linoleum was on the floor, but the ceiling wasn't tiled, which was also good: those open ceiling beams would insure the effectiveness of the smoke bomb's penetration.

Nolan knelt with the canister, pulled the lever, heard its *pop*, left it on the floor, mid-basement, turning his head away even before he'd let go of the can, as already its stream of smoke was shooting out like water from a firehose. The can hissed as it dispersed its contents, and Nolan headed toward the laundry end of the basement, then hopped up onto the washing machine and out the window.

He immediately returned to his view of Sam Comfort relaxing in the living room. A smile formed under the nylon mask as Nolan watched bewilderment grow on Sam's face, first as Sam sniffed smoke, then as he *saw* smoke. After a slapstick double-take, the old clown jumped from the couch as if goosed and ran upstairs via the stairwell opening in the far corner of the room. The positioning of those stairs was a break for Nolan; with this view of the action, he'd be able to key on whether or not Sam opted for the front door, here in the living room, or the back door, out in the kitchen. Sam was only gone half a minute, then came tumbling out of the stairwell, a man who'd all but fallen down the stairs, coughing from the ever-thickening smoke, showing signs of panic, shaking in his damn underwear. As Sam came into clearer view in that smoke-clogged receptacle of a room, Nolan could see plainly under one of Sam's arms an oversize green metal strongbox—*Bingo!*—while slung over Sam's other arm was a double-barreled shotgun. He's panicked all right, Nolan thought, but the old coot's as suspicious and crafty as ever.

A sound—*pop!*—turned Nolan's head, in reflex, before he realized the sound was only Jon's smoke grenade going off, meaning things were running to plan. When he turned back, the old man was no longer in sight.

Shit! The room was pretty well dense with smoke now, and Nolan couldn't tell if the front door was slightly ajar, which would have indicated whether Sam had gone out that way. Damn it, there was nothing to do but circle behind the house, and if Sam wasn't back there, come on around and catch him out the front. Damn!

Nolan ran.

Sam wasn't in back, nor was the back door ajar. Alongside the house, where the Buick was, no sign of Sam there, either.

And what about Billy? An ugly chain of deduction was forming in Nolan's mind. Sam had gone upstairs for three reasons, hadn't he? To get the strongbox; to grab the shotgun; to warn his boy Billy. But Sam hadn't been up there very long, barely long enough to do all those things. Why hadn't Billy been following along on his daddy's heels, down those steps? Why hadn't Sam yelled "Fire!" when smoke first began trailing into the room, to warn Billy immediately? Shouldn't that have been Sam's natural reaction?

If, then, Billy hadn't been upstairs, where had he been?

And more important, where the hell was he now?

Once around the front of the house, Nolan knew the answer to that. Nolan's questions about Billy were, for the most part, anyway, answered: Billy had not been in the house; Billy had been outside, Christ knows why or where. And Billy was onto the "burning house" trick. In fact, Billy was right next to the smoke grenade Jon had planted.

And Billy was grinning. The smoke was just as thick out here as in the house, but Nolan could see that Billy was grinning. Billy was laughing, or was doing something like laughing, a combination of rasping smoke-cough and sick snickering. Billy was stoned out of his head, and Billy was standing with one foot on Jon's chest, getting ready to heave one mother of a pitchfork down into Jon, punching steel teeth through the kid, pinning him to the earth like a scarecrow.

Nolan was still running, a slow but steady jog, and he bumped into Sam, who'd come out the front door, and the two men came face to face and for just a moment. Nylon mask or no, Nolan felt he could sense recognition in Sam's flat gray eyes.

Nolan slapped the old man across the side of the face with the .38 and Sam said, "Unggh!" and toppled, colliding with Nolan. Nolan hit the ground and was on his feet again within the same second, and he brought up the .38 and fired twice.

The shots broke the country calm like cracks of thunder. The bullets hit Billy Comfort in the chest and rocked him, shook him like a naughty child, exploded through him, blood squirting from the front of him, a spatter of bone and organs and more blood bursting out his back. He pitched backward, gurgling, dying.

Jon was awake now and rolling to one side as Billy Comfort's last effort in life—the hurling of the pitchfork—came to no account: the fork quivered in the ground, right next to Jon, but not, thankfully, in him.

Nolan looked at Jon and, with their stocking-distorted features, they exchanged a look that had in it any number of things—relief and shock and frustration among them, perhaps regret as well—and suddenly Jon's face distorted further under the mask, as he yelled, "Nolan! The old man!"

And as he remembered Sam Comfort, whom he'd merely cuffed out of the way so he could take care of more important business, as he recalled the crazy old man with a shotgun, Nolan heard the country calm shatter a second time in gunfire.

Interim:
Takeoff

10

Carol said, "I wish I was going with you."

Ken made a face at her in the bedroom mirror, as if to say, *Don't be ridiculous*, and went on strapping the emergency parachute to his stomach, over his black cotton pullover. On the bed, closed, locked, was the suitcase with the fake bomb in it. The suitcase was a cheap, tan overnight bag they'd picked up at a discount department store. "Picked up" was literally right: Ken had shoplifted the suitcase, much to Carol's discomfort, and the thought of that afternoon, several weeks ago, still gave her something of a chill.

Ken had said he didn't want to leave anything behind that could be traced to him, and he felt purchasing any such items locally would be dangerous. Carol didn't agree: the items he had in mind (the suitcase, some clothes, a wig) could be purchased at any large chain store and should be virtually untraceable. How could you tell, for example, which of the hundreds of thousands of stores an overnight bag had been purchased from?

But Ken had poured out a stream of double-talk, saying many items were code-marked for certain distribution areas, and skyjacking was a federal offense of the most serious nature, and those FBI men can trace a piece of string to the shirt on your back and blah blah blah. Carol didn't believe any of it, but realized that Ken probably didn't either. There was some secret reason he hadn't divulged to her yet for his going one hundred miles to a discount department store to purchase the items: he was going to shoplift them—a bit of news he saved for Carol until they were parked in the discount store's huge parking lot.

"You will cover for me," he said. "Make sure none of the floor-walkers or sales people see me."

"But Ken…this is crazy."

She looked across the sea of cars—it was Saturday, and the only parking space they'd found was at the rear of the endless lot—and even from this distance the store looked gigantic, some grotesque national monument to commercialism. Though the massive building was a pinkish brick, its face was primarily steel-trimmed glass, topped with enormous neon letters that said BARGAIN CITY. She knew, without ever having been in there, that those rows and rows of doors would open onto an entryway big enough to put their house in, an entryway lined with bubble gum machines and armed guards.

Wasn't Saturday the worst possible day to go shoplifting? All those people? All those people were precisely why Saturday was ideal, Ken said; there'd be too many people for store personnel to keep track of. Carol didn't quite buy that line of reasoning, either, but she went along with Ken. When push came to shove, she always went along with Ken.

She realized it wasn't stylish these days to let your husband—or any man—control your life. But she wasn't a liberated woman, and had no desire to be one. That point of view came from being the last of six children, she supposed, all the rest of whom were boys. She'd been the little sis, and she and her mother had lived in the shadow of her father and his five sons. And it hadn't been so bad. Being the only sister of five brothers had plenty of advantages, and she was the baby of the family besides and accordingly was awarded extra attention: on a holiday, she'd get more gifts, more kisses, than anyone.

Still, a big part of her childhood had been learning to keep her place. As the youngest child, you learned that anyway, and as the youngest and a girl, you got used to having your life controlled for you; your decisions made for you; your thinking done for you. You got used to having men dominate your world.

Ken had been just the kind of man she was used to. They'd met at a junior college in their hometown, in downstate Missouri, and he had been the firm but gentle sort of guy she'd been looking for, always. It hadn't been hard to grab him; she was aware of her good looks, and Ken was a loner whose nonconformist ways had turned off most of the girls he'd dated—he'd rather spend Friday night working on some electronics project than at a movie, say, or a dance. He had a quiet strength she liked, and he was cute, and while he wasn't thoughtful, he certainly wasn't cruel. Besides, she was used to having self-centered men around her. Wasn't that the way of all men? The ones worth having, anyway.

There was a side to Ken that bothered her, when she got to know him better; but she'd cherished the flaw in him, rather than rejected him because of it. By the time she noticed his weak spot, she was already hopelessly in love with him, so her reaction was positive: the flaw in Ken was something she could, in her quiet way, help him with; she could give him the encouragement to overcome his one weakness.

His weakness was that he had a tendency not to finish things. He had a fine mind, brilliant, really; he could do most anything. But his mind moved so quickly, his enthusiasm shifted so rapidly, that he often did not complete what he'd started. He'd flunked out of the junior college, primarily because he had no interest in the subjects he was taking, and one just doesn't flunk out of J.C.—J.C. is where a person goes 'cause he might flunk out (or already *had*) someplace else.

After they were married, Ken had gone to Greystoke Teacher's College, while Carol worked as a secretary and helped put him through, and he finally graduated after an extra semester.

Greystoke was an expensive school that ate up much of what Ken's parents had left him, not to mention most of Carol's weekly paycheck; but Greystoke was a special sort of college, a school for students who hadn't hacked it elsewhere, an educational court of last resort, guaranteed to graduate its enrollees. Mostly rich kids from back east made use of Greystoke, just so they could pick up a token degree. Some years it was accredited, others it was not. Fortunately for Ken, his was one of the accredited years, though with the school's poor reputation, it hardly mattered. Not that the odds of landing a good job with a Greystoke degree were bad; why, they were excellent—provided you were the son of some tycoon.

So she'd watched, reluctantly, while Ken took the salesman job, selling Florida real estate with a pitch that included a free meal and the showing of a film. Ken would go into towns of medium size, mostly, with the dinner invitations already sent out, and proceed with his routine. He didn't know where the company got its mailing lists, but the prospects who attended the dinners were excellent, couples nearing retirement who were ripe for a good land offer. It was a lucrative field, though Carol was bothered by the fact that the company sales pitch sounded uncomfortably like a con game. Ken assured her it was on the up and up. And she'd finally been convinced, because after all, hadn't the sales executive invited them to Florida to give Ken a first-hand look at the land he was selling? And they'd gone, they'd seen it; it was gorgeous land; they'd bought a chunk of it themselves.

Of course, that had been part of the deal: Ken had to invest in a lot of his own and become a stockholder, purchasing a specified minimum number of shares. That had taken the last of the money his parents had left him—just over ten thousand dollars. But what better investment was there than land?

This time Ken hadn't been a quitter, and Carol had been so proud of him. For three years he sold the lots, and he and Carol racked up quite a savings—as one of the company's top salesmen, Ken was regularly offered stock options, and they fed over half of Ken's earnings into Dream-Land. And they'd bought the house in Canker with a bank loan, choosing the quiet little town so they could be close enough to Carol's family to make visiting easy, but far enough away to enjoy privacy. Ken's plan was to keep selling for another three years, and then they'd have amassed enough stock for him to borrow against and open up a small TV and radio repair shop, which would be ideal for him and for Carol, too, who didn't like sharing her husband with the road.

Ken's investment of his time and money had assured Carol that her husband's flaw—that tendency not to finish what he started, which came from a certain immaturity—was now a thing of the past, a wound healed over, with not even a sign of scar tissue.

But wounds can open up after the longest time, if enough pressure is applied to them. And pressure in this instance emerged in the form of Ken's aptly named parent company, Florida Dream-Land Realtors.

Part of Ken's pitch had included pointing out that, while the cash outlay for a piece of Dream-Land land was amazingly low, that low price was made possible by holding off actual development of the land, actual building of homes, until 70 percent of the lots had been sold. Of course, a buyer couldn't be expected to wait forever for his home and his land, so a projected date (five years hence, from Dream-Land's first sale) was set for development to begin. This was guaranteed; either said development began, or the buyer's money would be returned, with the buyer retaining full ownership of his lot.

All of which sounded swell, both to salesmen like Ken and to prospective buyers, most of whom were far enough away from retirement that waiting a few years for their dream land was no problem. Five years wasn't so long.

But long enough for a swindle.

Plenty long enough for that. Oh, the land was down there, all right; everybody who bought a lot owned a slice of Florida land. But not the land in the film Ken had shown to the people at the invitation-only dinners; not the land the sales exec had pointed out to Ken and Carol on their trip down there. The land in the film, the land the exec pointed out, belonged to somebody else.

Dream-Land was Florida land, too.

Swampland.

Uninhabitable damn swampland that could gag an alligator; dream land that was a nightmare. And Ken and all the other salesmen and the folks they'd sold the land to, all of them, were stuck in that swamp up to their rears.

The only happy aspect was that Ken himself, and most of the other salesmen, were in no way liable for the fraud perpetrated; they, like everybody in it (except the Dream-Land wheels) were the butt of the joke.

So there they sat, in Canker, Missouri, with over three years of their lives wasted, no savings, not a damn thing—except a mortgaged house and plans that had fizzled into nothing.

But you can always make new plans, and Ken came up with one. Carol hadn't liked it from the outset, but what could she say? Ken was, after all, the man of the house.

But sometimes bowing to every wish of the "man of the house" could go too far. She shouldn't be expected to do something she would hate herself for doing. Like helping him on this crazy skyjacking thing. Even aiding and abetting his silly, stupid shoplifting. There just wasn't any sane *reason* for it; no logic to it. And besides, she didn't for the life of her see how he was going to get the shoplifting done. He had picked the suitcase up first, actually just tucked it under his arm, then strolled around the store, and while she kept an eye peeled, he'd slipped the various items in: curly brown wig, some sunglasses, green corduroy shirt, and some jeans.

"How are you going to get past the registers?" she asked him.

"Just watch," he said, and headed to the front of the store. There was a coffee shop up on the right, off to one side of the rows of check-out counters. They sat in a booth in the shop, and Ken carefully drew a folded-up sack from his pocket, a large sack with the discount store's name on it. He put the suitcase inside. When that was done, she followed as he slid past the check-out counters, mixing in with the shoppers pouring out of them, and with the suitcase-in-sack snugly under his arm, went out the door.

Past several armed guards who were standing by that door for the express purpose of nabbing shoplifters. No one questioned him. Nothing.

In the car, she found she was panting. Sweat was rolling down her cheeks, though the day was a cool, overcast one. "What would you have done," she managed to ask, "if someone stopped you?"

"I was prepared for that," he said, the tone of his voice implying he'd almost been hoping for that as well. "I had a story ready."

"What kind of story?"

"That I'd seen a lady drop this package in the coffee shop and was going out into the lot after her, to give her her package."

"But there would be no sales slip in the sack."

"So what? It was her package, not mine."

"Do you think they would have believed you, Ken? Do you honestly think they would've believed you?"

"Been interesting to find out, wouldn't it?"

They drove fifty miles and then Ken stopped for lunch, but Carol didn't order anything. Her stomach was still jumping. All the while, sitting in the car, she'd been expecting a highway patrol car to come screaming up behind them. The heavyset Broderick Crawford cop would say, "Okay kids, let's have a look at that suitcase there in the back seat." He had never shown up, of course, but he was there in her mind, the cop and his car and siren and gun.

Finally, she consented to a grilled cheese sandwich, which she nibbled at. She said, "I never stole anything before, Ken."

And Ken looked at her, and there was something in his eyes, a damn twinkling in his eyes. He grinned and said, "Me neither."

There it was: the reason. The secret purpose of the trip. The skyjacking he'd been planning, this new, obscenely dangerous project, this terrifyingly large-scale *crime* he was going to commit, was the first time he'd ever even contemplated breaking the rules.

Ken. Conservative Ken. Arrow-straight Ken. It was quite a leap from shoplifter to skyjacker, but an even bigger one from Eagle Scout to skyjacker. She understood that now.

She understood that in a crazy way the shoplifting had been a trial run, as well as an absurd ritual of self-initiation; that had Ken been caught and been unable to bluff his way out of the situation, he would have taken it as, well, a *sign*, an indication from somewhere that he was in way over his head. That this should be another project left unfinished.

But he hadn't been caught, and here they were, weeks later, the skyjack plan finally going into effect.

Ken seemed very calm, the late afternoon sunlight filtering through the filmy pink curtains of the bedroom window and bathing him in a golden, contented glow; he seemed almost peaceful, as he neatly assembled himself, climbing into the green shirt, which fit over the chute as though he had a paunch. It was as if he was assembling the components of one of his electronics gadgets. *Could he really be so cool?* Carol wondered. *Did that silly afternoon of shoplifting free him so from worry?*

She wouldn't be free from worry, not until she had him back again, in their house, in this bed. Her only consolation was that the bomb in the stolen suitcase was a dummy. Carol wondered for a moment why Ken would have spent so much time building a mock bomb into the suitcase. This, like his shoplifting escapade, was an almost eccentric aspect to the "project" that Carol would never completely understand. She just took comfort in knowing that her Ken could never really hurt anybody, let alone blow up a planeload of people.

She touched his shoulder, caught his eyes in the mirror, and held them. "Maybe something will happen. Something you haven't thought of. Maybe…maybe we won't ever see each other again."

This time he *really* made a face. This time he said it out loud: "Don't be ridiculous."

And he looked away.

Fifteen minutes later, they were in the car, and she was driving him the eight miles to a town where no one knew them, where he could catch the bus to Detroit. She felt uncomfortable in the driver's seat.

Three

11

Like all airport restaurants, this one was lousy. The $2 hamburger was cold, the potato chips stale, the Coke flat and mostly ice. Jon looked out the window. The sky was overcast. Right in front of him, some men in coveralls were stuffing the belly of a 727 with luggage; behind them stretched an endless concrete sea of runway, planes taxiing around as if wandering aimlessly. It was a gray day. Jon's was a gray mood.

The Detroit airport was a cold, monolithic assemblage that didn't exactly cheer Jon up, its overall design a vaguely modernistic absence of personality, heavy on dreary, neutral-color stone, and its infinite intersecting halls converging on a toweringly high-ceilinged lobby in what might have been intended as a tribute to confusion. The only thing he liked about the place was that, compared to Chicago's O'Hare, there were fewer people and, consequently, not as much frantic rushing around. But the less hectic pace didn't do Jon any good, really; it only gave him time to reflect on things that were better left alone. It gave him time for a gray mood.

And he was tired. He'd been up all night practically, watching movies—not on the tube, but in a ballroom at the hotel, with hundreds of other voluntary insomniacs. The showing of old films ("from eight till dawn") was a traditional part of a comic book convention, and when he got back to the hotel after the Comfort bloodbath, he figured he might as well enjoy himself, he wouldn't be getting much sleep that night, anyway. Not after what happened.

He'd made a point of not sitting with anyone he knew and,

despite the common interests he shared with those around him, avoided conversation, and struck up no new acquaintances among his fellow fans. His hope was that he'd lose himself in the flickering fantasy up on the screen, and so he sat watching, all but numb, leaning back in the uncomfortable steel folding chair and letting the Marx Brothers and Buster Crabbe as Flash Gordon and any number of monster movies roll over him in a celluloid tide. Jon and the rest of the crowd followed the films through most of the night; the feature set for a 4:30 A.M. screening was worth staying for: the original 1933 *King Kong*, and Jon thought to himself, *This is where I came in.*

After that, the crowd had thinned, even the diehards throwing in the towel in the face of an especially dreadful Japanese monster epic, and Jon finally headed up to the room, where he grabbed a couple hours of restless sleep.

Only now was the shock beginning to subside.

Only now was he able to begin exploring the significance of what had happened last night. Last night, afterwards, he had tried to squeeze what had happened out of his mind, filling his head instead with the harmless, distracting images of old movies. Now, the next morning, Saturday, he sat by the window at the airport, watching the ground crew scurry around a Boeing 727, sipping his flat Coke and replaying the events of the night before on the movie screen of his mind. Jon remembered waking up after being struck by Billy Comfort with a pole of some kind, and remembered looking up at Billy and realizing that the pole was the handle of a pitchfork, a pitchfork Billy was a second away from jamming into Jon. He knew he should roll out of the way, but Billy's foot was pressed down on his chest, holding him there, firm, for the pitchfork's downstroke....

And then a shot, and another, and Jon had seen two thin streams of blood squirt from Billy's chest, and Billy was knocked off his feet, allowing Jon to roll clear, which he did, the pitchfork sinking into the earth next to him. For a moment, both Jon and the pitchfork trembled. Meanwhile, Billy had flopped on his back and died.

Jon got to his knees, turned, and saw Nolan. They looked at each other, a look that had a lot in it.

Then Jon saw Sam Comfort, whom Nolan had evidently knocked down but not out, rearing his head above the high weeds that had hidden him from Jon's vision, and Sam Comfort had a great big goddamn gun in his arms, a *shotgun*, and was lifting its twin barrels to fire them into Nolan, and Jon yelled, "Nolan! The old man!"

And instinctively Jon clawed for the .38, yanked the gun from its holster, and wrapped both hands around the stock and aimed and squeezed the trigger. Just as Nolan taught him.

The shot was an explosion that tore the night open.

And Sam Comfort.

Old Sam caught it in the chest, high in the chest, about where one of the bullets had struck his son, and fell over on his back, much as his son had.

Jon got to his feet, but didn't go over to where Sam was. Nolan was already leaning down to examine the man.

Jon said, "Is he?..."

"Not yet," Nolan said.

"What should we do?"

"We should get the hell out of here."

"And...leave him...to bleed to death?"

"Yes."

"Jesus, Nolan."

"Listen, what is it you think we're doing here? Playing tag-you're-fucking-It? We've robbed these people, Jon, and killed them. Now what do you think we should do?"

"Get the hell out of here," Jon said.

So now, having spent a shocked, pretty much sleepless night, Jon tried to begin facing up to the fact that he'd—damn it!—that he'd killed a man. Every time he admitted that to himself, every time the phrase *killed a man* ran through his mind, his stomach began to quiver, like that pitchfork in the ground.

Sure, the prospect had always been there, ever since he first teamed up with Nolan, on that bank job. And yes, there'd been blood before; people around them had died, violently—his uncle Planner for one. Bloody brush fires like that could spring up around a man like Nolan at just about any time. But reacting to such brush fires was one thing, and starting them something else again. Nolan had introduced Jon to a world of potential violence, but together they had never initiated violence. Never before, anyway. This time—pitchfork or no pitchfork, shotgun or no shotgun—this time, Jon and Nolan had invaded someone else's home territory, had initiated violence, and people had died. This they had known, these thoughts Jon and Nolan had shared in that look they exchanged after Billy's death; a loss of innocence for Jon, for their relationship, that they could recognize even through the smoke and nylon masks.

That the Comforts were perhaps bad people, evil people, was weak justification at best, rationalization of the most half-assed sort, and made Jon wonder just how he and Nolan were any different from Sam and Billy Comfort.

It all came down to this: Jon had killed a man.

And it made him sick to think it.

"Sorry I took so long," Nolan said, sitting down across from Jon at the window table. He took a bite of his sandwich, a hamburger identical to Jon's. "Damn thing's cold. Was I gone *that* long?"

"It was cold when they brought it."

"Goddamn airports. I told you we should've just grabbed a hot dog at one of those stand-up lunch counters."

"I hate those things, Nolan. Standing at those lousy little tables, getting your elbow in somebody's relish..."

"Yeah, but the food's hot, isn't it? And not so goddamn expensive."

Jon had to smile at Nolan's consistently penny-pinching attitude. Here they'd picked up, what? Over $200,000 from the Comforts' strongbox last night, and the man is worried about nickels and dimes. Jon could figure why Nolan had taken so long in the can, too: he'd waited till the non-pay toilet was vacant.

Nolan noticed Jon's smile, weak as it was, and said, "You feeling better, kid?"

"I'm feeling all right."

They really hadn't talked about it yet, but it was there.

"You can't let this get you down."

"Nolan, I'm all right. Really."

"I believe you."

They were silent for a while, each nibbling at his cold, lousy hamburger as if it were a penance.

Jon glanced around to make sure a waitress wasn't handy to overhear, then said, "Are you sure the money's going to be okay?"

"Sure."

"What about the..." Jon gestured, meaning the two guns, which along with the money were in one of Nolan's suitcases.

"Don't worry," Nolan said. "The baggage goes through unopened, I told you."

"Don't they have an X-ray thing they can run the baggage through?"

"That's just for carry-on luggage. Shut up. Eat."

Neither one of them finished their hamburgers. Nolan left no tip. When Nolan wasn't looking, Jon left fifty cents. After all, the waitress wasn't necessarily to blame for the hamburgers being cold.

Fifteen minutes later, boarding passes in hand, they were standing in line while a pair of female security guards, armed, took all carry-on luggage, right down to the ladies' handbags, and passed it through the massive X-ray scanner. Ahead of them in line a few paces was a college-age kid with curly brown hair, similar to Jon's, wearing jeans and a green corduroy shirt tucked in over a premature paunch, carrying a Radio Shack sack.

"Hey, Nolan," Jon whispered.

"What."

"That kid up there."

The kid was presently handing the Radio Shack sack to the security guards and being checked through with no trouble.

"What about him?"

"Isn't that a wig he's wearing? Take a look. That isn't his hair, is it?"

"Maybe not," Nolan admitted. "So what?"

"Well, it just seems strange to me, a young guy like that, wearing a wig."

Nolan shrugged.

So Jon shrugged it off, too; maybe the kid was prematurely bald or something. Like the paunch. Weird, though—young guy with no fat on him elsewhere, no hint of a double-chin, and here he has a gut on him.

Jon stepped up and smiled at the two security guards, both of whom were pretty and blonde, and allowed his brown briefcase to be slid into the X-ray. Then he and Nolan stepped through the doorlike framework that was the metal detector.

On the other side Jon picked up his briefcase of comics, wondering offhand if X-rays had a negative effect on pulp paper.

They climbed the covered umbilical ramp to the plane, boarded, and were met by the flight attendant Nolan had met at the hotel. She was a knockout brunette who, for some reason, looked vaguely familiar to Jon. She gave him a brief, similar where-have-I-seen-you-before look, and then she and Nolan traded longer looks of a different sort, Nolan saying, "Morning, Hazel."

"Good morning, Mr. Ryan," she said, and she and Nolan made eyes for a second. It was damn near embarrassing.

They passed through the forward, first-class compartment and past the central galley, where the fourth and final flight attendant (a dishwater blonde not quite as attractive as the others) was already fussing with filling plastic cups with ice. They continued on into the tourist cabin, where they took the very last seats in the rear of the plane, near the tail. Only a few people were on board as yet, but Jon and Nolan had been toward the front of the metal-detector line, and the plane was going to be close to capacity.

Jon was having problems with the briefcase: it was so jammed full of comics and stuff, he hadn't been able to get it shut again, since the security guard checked it. He was struggling with it in his seat, and it got away from him and flopped out into the aisle, in the path of another passenger.

It was the kid in the wig, still lugging his Radio Shack sack.

The contents of Jon's case were scattered in the aisle, and Jon and the guy in the wig bent over and began picking the books up.

"I've got some of these," the guy said, holding up a Buck Rogers Big Little Book. He had a soft voice, or at least was speaking in a soft voice. He seemed almost shy.

"Really? You a collector, too?"

"No. I read them as a kid."

"You don't look that old."

"They were my older brother's."

"Oh. Well, thanks for the help."

"Hope I didn't damage them or anything."

"Never mind. My stupid fault."

The guy in the wig smiled a little—a very little—and went on toward the rest rooms in back of Jon and Nolan's seat. He stepped inside the first one.

"Must be nervous," Jon said. "Plane isn't even off the ground and he's going to the can already."

Nolan hadn't been paying much attention. "Maybe it's his first flight," he said.

12

Nolan looked out the double-paned window as the Detroit airport flowed by, the plane beginning to make its move down the taxiway. Above him, the little air vent was blowing its stale, recycled air down into his face and, as he looked up to turn it away from him, he noticed the FASTEN SEATBELTS and NO SMOKING signs flash on in red letters, and he buckled up. About that time, Hazel's voice came over the tinny intercom and reminded anyone who hadn't yet complied with those two requests that now was the time.

He didn't really like planes that much, didn't care for flying. He didn't feel in control on a plane and preferred traveling by car, where he himself could be behind the wheel. Years ago, he had traveled by train fairly often, but train service in this country had gone to hell, and buses were a pain in the ass and slower than walking. So he was adjusting, finally, to the jet age, despite his firm belief that if God had wanted men to fly, he'd have given them parachutes.

They had the three-abreast seat to themselves, though the unused third was presently being taken up by the briefcase of comic book crap that Jon had lugged aboard. Right now, the cabin pressure was making its abrupt increase, and Jon was making faces, swallowing as he popped his ears. Nolan did the same, with less facial contortion.

Hazel's voice came on the intercom again, while two of the other flight attendants stood, one at the front of the tourist compartment and the other halfway down the aisle, going through the oxygen-mask-and-emergency-exit ballet to the accompaniment of Hazel's narration. When that was over, one of the flight attendants came walking down, checking to see if all smokes were out and seat belts fastened, and when she came to Jon and Nolan, she asked Jon to please put his briefcase under the seat in front of him. Jon explained that it wouldn't fit under there, and she took it away from him, paying no heed to his protests, and put it in a closet compartment opposite the rest rooms that were right behind them.

For a while, Jon sat there, looking like a kid whose favorite toy got taken away. Then he said, "Nolan."

"What."

"Get a load of that."

The kid who'd collided with Jon's briefcase of comic books a few minutes before, the same kid Jon had noticed was wearing a wig, had come out of the john from behind them and was now heading back up the aisle.

"Get a load of what, Jon?"

"That kid in the green shirt."

"What about him?"

"That isn't his stomach."

"What?"

"He's got something under his shirt."

"No kidding."

"No, really, Nolan, something bugs me about that guy. Why's he playing dress-up? Wearing that wig. Carrying something under his shirt."

"Maybe it's old comic books."

"You can laugh if you want to, but that's a weird kid, take it from me…and don't say 'takes one to know one.' "

"Would I say that?"

"You'd think it."

"You got me there."

The plane had stopped now, having reached the end of the taxiway, and out the window Nolan watched a DC-8 land, bouncing twice on its motionless tires, making blue smoke as rubber met concrete, and then settling down. The soft throb of the 727 jets began to build as the plane started to move, picking up speed fast, shoving Nolan and Jon back in their seats. The nose of the plane lifted, and they headed for the gray sky, Detroit slipping away rapidly under them.

The seat belt and no-smoking sign soon winked off, and Nolan loosened his seat belt but left it buckled. The captain's voice came out of the intercom and went into the standard flying-at-assigned-altitude-and-estimated-time-of-arrival spiel. According to the captain, the overcast day would be turning into rain here and there up ahead, but he anticipated smooth flying nevertheless. Sure.

On the whole Nolan was pleased with the way things had worked out at the Comforts. Maybe *pleased* wasn't the word—more like *satisfied*. The take had been over two hundred thousand (he hadn't counted it, except for a fast shuffle through the strongbox of cash), and they'd got out with their asses intact, in spite of the foul-up. What more could he ask?

It was, of course, unfortunate that Jon had had to shoot a man; but something like that was bound to happen sooner or later, and the kid had been exposed to the rough side of the business before, so it wasn't like he'd been a complete virgin. Last night, what had happened had left Jon silent and shocked, but today he was as talkative as ever, and seemed only slightly depressed. And sleepy. Nolan would bet his share of the take that the kid hadn't slept more than a couple hours, at most.

If he had his way, it wouldn't have happened. He'd sure as shit tried to plan around any overt violence. But what the hell, you can't shelter a kid forever; if you do, he's going to suffocate. He figured Jon would get over it. There'd be a scar, but Jon would get over it.

Yes, the kid would have a rocky conscience for a while, Nolan knew, but that was the way it should be. It wasn't healthy to feel good about killing a man, even a man the likes of Sam Comfort. When killing gets easy, a man is less than human, in Nolan's opinion, and a man who likes killing isn't a man at all. Besides, it's bad for business. Society and its law-enforcement agencies take a much dimmer view of killers than they do of thieves, possibly because most of society fits into that latter category, to one degree or another.

Anyway, it was over and done, and they were sitting pretty: pretty rich, and pretty lucky to be alive, and pretty sure nothing could fuck up at this late date. Nolan did feel a little bad about holding onto the two guns. Normally, he'd have got rid of them immediately, since they'd been fired on a job—especially when they'd been fired and killed somebody on a job—which these guns had. And he would get rid of them when he got back, after he had seen to it Jon and the two hundred thousand were returned safely to that antique shop in Iowa City. He would've asked Bernie for a fresh gun when he returned the Ford early that morning, but Bernie wasn't there yet, so he'd decided to risk holding onto the .38s for a short while. But it was not good policy to do so, and it grated on him even now, thinking of those two guns down in the suitcase in the hold, nestled next to all that cash. Even Jon, over their mid-morning brunch (two bucks for a goddamn stinking *cold* hamburger!) had expressed concern about the guns, which had pleased him because it showed that Jon was getting more perceptive about things that counted, and irritated him because the kid had spotted a flaw in Nolan's supposed perfection.

Hazel was coming down the aisle, looking very nice in the tailored flight attendant outfit, with its soft, light colors. She stood beside their seat, leaned down, and asked, "Can I get you gentlemen something to drink?"

"I thought you were working first class," Nolan said.

"I was, but since you were riding tourist, I traded off with one of the other girls."

"Can you do that?"

"If you're senior flight attendant, you can."

"Oh, you got rank, huh?"

"It's called age. But it was kind of silly for me to do."

"How's that?"

"Well, this junket's such a short hop, I'm not going to have much of a chance to do anything besides serve a few drinks and pick up the empty cups."

"Yeah, but anything, just so you can be close to me, right?"

Hazel said to Jon, "I see why you need all three seats. One for you, one for him, and one for his ego."

Jon said, "He's just talking big so nobody notices he's airsick. If he had his way, we'd be traveling by covered wagon."

Hazel laughed, and Nolan did too, a little. Nolan ordered a Scotch and Jon a Coke, and let Hazel go.

"She's a nice lady," Jon said.

"Yeah. She lives in Chicago. One of those high-rises on the lake. Has lots of days off, she says. Maybe I'll be able to get in and see her now and then."

"Chicago isn't much of a drive from the Tropical, is it?"

"An hour, if the traffic is bad. Only, I hope I won't be at the Tropical much longer."

"With half of last night's take in your sock, you shouldn't have to be."

Nolan nodded, then said, "Say, kid."

"What?"

"I, uh, never really, you know, thanked you for last night."

"Thanked me?"

"Yes, goddammit. You did save my fucking ass, you know."

"Well, you saved mine. So what?"

"Yeah. So what."

They both sat back and tried to look gruff. Nolan was better at it than Jon.

"Hey, Nolan."

"What?"

"That kid. The one with the wig."

"I don't want to hear about it."

"He's headed up toward the front going up through the first-class compartment."

Nolan had no comment.

"I don't know, Nolan, something weird about him, I tell you. Something's going on with that kid."

"Aw, shut up. Go to sleep for half an hour, or go get one of your funny-books and read it or something."

They sat in silence. Five minutes went by, and then the dull little bell sounded that signaled the intercom coming on.

The captain again.

"We'll be having a little change in course this morning, ladies and gentlemen. We'll be rerouting our plane directly to the Quad City Airport at Moline. Those of you who were headed there anyway shouldn't mind this little detour as much as the others."

The captain's lame attempt at humor had the reverse of its intended effect: it was easy to see past his superficially light, joking tone and tell something was wrong, very wrong, and the murmur of passenger concern swept through the plane like a flash flood.

He continued, "Now, I don't want anyone to panic. Everything is in control." The captain hesitated. "But I feel you should be aware that we have a man with a bomb aboard…and he's just chartered himself a plane."

13

Like all flight attendants, Hazel knew she might one day be involved in a skyjacking, but she wasn't overwhelmed with fear by the prospect. At one time she would have been: at one time she'd been deathly afraid of flying itself.

Fifteen years ago, when she'd first applied for a job with the airlines, she'd requested ground duty. Then, when she got into the program, she'd begun a gradual change of mind, even after that grueling week of intensive training under emergency conditions, in which she'd had to overcome some of her fears, anyway, just to live through the damn thing. The advantages a flight attendant had over girls on the ground were many, with fewer hours of work for the same amount of pay perhaps the biggest lure of all, and oh, those gorgeous travel possibilities! Factors like that had whittled away at her flying fears, and the statistics had helped, too. Knowing that a plane was safer than a car, for instance, if for no other reason than that the man behind the controls was a professional, not a sloppy amateur like most motorists. That if an engine went out, there were three more to take its place. That practically every little town in the world had some sort of airstrip, so a landing spot was always close at hand.

Of course, there were accidents, and air accidents have few—if any—survivors. A flight attendant friend of hers (not a close friend, but more than an acquaintance) had been on a plane that was struck by lightning and went crashing to the ground, providing a fiery death for the friend and fifty-some other people aboard. Don't think Hazel didn't have a sleepless night or two over that.

But every profession had its risks, and for a woman, being a flight attendant was pleasant, even glamorous, no matter what Women's Lib had to say about it. In fact, liberation of the sexes had only gone to show what a good job the flight attendant had: males had begun clamoring for the jobs, and many a tired businessman had recently had the disappointment of looking forward to a bouncy blonde stewardess and getting instead a brawny blond steward.

Skyjacking was one risk, however, Hazel hadn't had to consider fifteen years ago; during the first years of her career the term hadn't even been coined. The hijacking of a commercial airliner was so infrequent that the industry, from board of directors down to flight attendants, thought of it as some bizarre, freak occurrence, an incomprehensible and frightening crime, but certainly no large-scale threat to air travel itself. The 1968 rash of hijackings—twenty-one in all—changed that attitude quickly enough, and skyjacking became a major worry in the minds of all airlines personnel. Hazel included.

She'd seen the public's reaction turn from amusement and titillation to terror and rage. Early on, the skyjackings (usually to Cuba) seemed a free vacation of sorts; even *Time* magazine urged skyjacked passengers to "enjoy the experience" and "make the most of your side trip by doing a little shopping," telling them of the "magnificent" Cuban beach, and noting that "the food is excellent, too." Was it any wonder she'd overheard a passenger wistfully wishing for a skyjacking experience to brighten the boredom of a business trip? She'd winced as one federal aviation official had gone so far as to announce that skyjacking "sure takes the blahs out of air travel."

And then violence had changed the amusement to terror: a pilot shot in the stomach by a skyjacker angry because the ransom money delivered to him was short of what he'd asked; a black militant beating crew members about the head with a revolver, threatening passengers with similar abuse; a prisoner being transported by plane finding a discarded razor in the john and, holding that razor to a flight attendant's throat, demanding his own Cuban "side trip"; and, of course, the chaotic violence of the Arab-Israeli airline war, the world witnessing the destruction of a $23 million aircraft, a Pan Am 747 melted to junk by exploding dynamite charges.

With a feeling of disappointment verging on despair, Hazel and other flight attendants had watched as the FAA tried desperately to find means of fighting skyjacking, most of those means proving ineffective at best, ludicrous at worst. A bulletproof shield protecting the pilot was one FAA official's suggestion, as well as barring the cockpit door. Just how this would dissuade a skyjacker, who'd have plenty of unprotected hostages aboard to choose from, was not explained, unless Hazel and her sisters were to wear bulletproof bras and issue bulletproof shields to each passenger. The FAA then distributed to ticket-sales personnel a "psychological profile" of the "typical" skyjacker, but skyjackers seemed able to get past ticket counters without hassle despite the "profile," which was general to the point of silliness, anyway, the most solid "fact" being that "the average skyjacker is a man between sixteen and thirty-five years of age." The FAA's next move was to create a system of armed guards for planes, in response to a request heard repeatedly from the public, and the Sky Marshal Program was the result. This particular concept terrified Hazel from the start: the idea of a shoot-out at 30,000 feet was enough to terrify anybody. The "unwritten directive" of the sky marshal was well known among flight attendants: "If a skyjacker uses a flight attendant as a hostage, shoot the flight attendant to reach the skyjacker." Swell. In actual practice, however, the sky marshals were little threat to either skyjackers or flight attendants. Typical of their ineffectiveness was the successful skyjacking of a jumbo jet to Cuba, though three sky marshals were present on the plane, as well as an FBI agent. The Sky Marshal Program was discontinued some time ago, but the recent rash of skyjackings by Cuban refugees and other social outcasts had prompted the FAA to reinstate it. This Hazel saw as more of a gesture than an anti-skyjack measure.

The only way to effectively deal with a skyjacker was to stop him before he got on a plane. She remembered when the first real step was taken: the search of carry-on luggage before passengers boarded the plane. Suddenly guns and knives were commonly found dumped in waste cans in airport johns. Then metal detectors came into use, and X-ray of carry-on luggage, and skyjacking again became an exception, not a rule. Still, skyjackings had been pulled off by men using "guns" that turned out to be plastic ball-point pens and combs; one skyjacker proclaimed himself a human bomb, while his "explosives" turned out to be rolls of candy mints strapped to his body. The most hair-raising of the boomerang effects caused by the use of metal detectors was the switch skyjackers had made to non-metallic devices such as homemade bombs. Hazel shuddered at the thought of that. Though neither situation exactly appealed to her, she would much prefer facing a man with a gun than a man with some unstable, patchwork homemade explosive device.

And now she was doing just that.

A young man of perhaps twenty years of age was aboard with what appeared to be a pocket calculator in his hand—claiming he was prepared to blow up the plane if his demands were not met.

JoAnne, the youngest of the other three attendants on board, had come to Hazel with a look of stark panic in her eyes. Hazel was in the galley section, which was between the first-class and tourist cabins, getting drinks ready. JoAnne said, "He says he wants to talk to the head stewardess. That's you, Hazel."

"Who says what?"

"A kid. He says he's got a bomb. He wants to talk to you."

"All right. Now, JoAnne. Listen to me. Keep your head on. Are you all right?"

"Yes."

"Where is he? Up forward?"

"Yes."

"Okay. Are you all right, JoAnne?"

"Yes."

"Okay. You stay right here. Don't say a word to anybody. I see him up there. Green corduroy shirt and jeans? With a beer belly?"

"Yes."

"Okay, then. You stay here. You might finish getting these drinks ready for me."

"Yes."

He was just a boy, really. A kid. With damn freckles, yet. He was wearing mirror-type sunglasses, which she didn't believe he'd been wearing when he came aboard, and he was wearing a wig. Why hadn't she noticed that wig before? Damn.

"Are you the head stewardess?"

"I'm the senior flight attendant, yes."

"Hazel?" he said, reading her name off the badge on her breast pocket. "Your name is Hazel?"

"Yes, it is."

"Hazel, I have just now pressed some buttons that have armed a bomb that is on this plane, in my suitcase in the cargo hold of the plane. If my fingers touch this—" he indicated the black plastic calculator— "just so, the bomb will explode and all of us won't be here anymore."

"Do you want to see the captain?"

"Yes. You tell him to come out here."

She entered the cockpit, the greenish glow of the instrument panel brighter than the overcast sky out the forward windows.

Captain McIntire, a handsome gray-templed man in his early forties, a married man with two kids, and a confirmed letch who'd tried a hundred times to get in Hazel's pants (unsuccessfully), turned in the left-hand seat and grinned wolfishly, saying, "How's tricks, Hazel?"

Beside him, the copilot, Willis, suppressed a groan. He was a thin guy with a pockmarked complexion and short brown hair, in his late thirties. He hated McIntire, and it showed sometimes. Behind McIntire was the navigator, Reed, a balding, fleshy, middle-aged man with no discernible personality, as far as Hazel knew—an invisible man as gray as that sky out there.

Hazel did not play it cute. No, Captain, tricks are not good, she thought, and said, "We have a skyjacker aboard. He's just outside the cockpit here."

The three men traded expressions of disgust that masked fear.

McIntire cleared his throat, but his first words came out a squeak, anyway. "Send him in, damn it."

"He wants you to come see him."

Reed said, "Whoever heard of hijacking a plane out of Detroit?"

Willis said, "We did. Now."

The captain turned over the controls to his copilot and rose from his seat. He wasn't grinning anymore.

Hazel stood next to the captain while the boy told him about the bomb. He spoke in a voice that was soft and seemingly calm but had a faint tremor in it. Then he made his demands. He said, "Two hundred thousand dollars in cash. This is how I want it: ten thousand twenty-dollar bills. Radio ahead and have the cash delivered to the Quad City Airport at Moline. We will, naturally, fly directly to the Quad City Airport. Then we'll fly somewhere else."

The captain stood there for a moment, waiting.

Then the boy said, "That's all I want. Go back and fly your plane. Tell your passengers the situation."

Which the captain did.

The skyjacker asked Hazel, "I believe you're working in the tourist-class section, aren't you?"

"Yes, I am."

"My seat is in tourist. I'll walk back with you."

So now she was serving drinks, the skyjacker sitting among the chattering, fidgeting passengers like just another victim, giving no indication to anyone he was the villain of the piece.

But when she served Nolan his Scotch, he said, whispering, "It's the kid in the wig, isn't it?"

Surprised, Hazel nodded.

"What's the airline's policy in a skyjacking?"

"Do what the man says, what else?"

"How does the kid claim he'll detonate his bomb?"

"He's got a pocket calculator wired to do it, he says."

Nolan thought a moment, then said, "I think he's bluffing. I don't think he has any bomb on board."

"We have to assume otherwise," Hazel said.

"You do," Nolan said. "But I don't."

And a chill ran up her spine. For a moment, for reasons she didn't wholly understand, she was afraid of her last-afternoon-and-night's bed partner. For a moment this man calling himself Nolan—though he was flying under the name Ryan, for "business purposes," he'd told her last night—frightened her far worse than the young skyjacker sitting a few feet away.

14

By the time the plane landed at the Quad City Airport, most of the passengers were smashed. Common practice during a skyjacking was for flight attendants to serve free drinks to anyone who wanted one, and that included just about everybody on board; the exceptions were sitting in front of Jon and Nolan: a trio of nuns, who looked like they could use a good, stiff drink, at that.

The booze had had its intended calming effect on the passengers, creating an atmosphere not nearly as tense as it might have been. Other factors had also helped lessen the tension, the main one being that the skyjacker had remained anonymous to his fellow travelers, and had not gone about waving a gun and shouting obscenities and generally reminding everybody they were sitting on a flying powder keg. Of course, the tension was there, underneath it all, and if the atmosphere was strangely like a party, it was a less than jolly affair—a going-away party, perhaps, or a bankrupt company's last Christmas fling.

Even Jon had fallen prey to the free-flowing liquor; he wasn't much for hard booze, but the role of skyjacking victim was upsetting enough to his nerves for him to gladly switch from Coke to Bourbon and Coke and its soothing, analgesic powers. Jon had downed only two of them so far, but he was feeling the glow. He and Nolan hadn't spoken much since the news of the plane's enforced change of destination, and now he glanced at Nolan and regarded his older friend's expressionless, tight-jawed demeanor. He figured Nolan's stern countenance meant one of the following: either Nolan was pissed off, or he was putting together a scheme of some sort, or both.

Anyway, Jon thought, something was wrong. Nolan hadn't had anything to drink since that first Scotch, which he'd barely finished. That wasn't like Nolan, turning down free drinks. Turning down free anything.

For some reason, Nolan was taking this skyjack thing very, very hard, and it puzzled Jon.

"Hey," Jon said, whispering. "This'll work out all right. What's the harm? I mean, it got us home quicker, didn't it?"

Nolan said nothing.

"I agree with you," Jon continued, "about the kid in the wig. I don't think he put a bomb on board, either. Or anyway, if he did, I don't think he's the type to set it off."

Nolan was shaking his head now. He looked disappointed.

"Nolan, what's wrong?"

They were speaking low anyway, because of the holy trio in

the seat ahead, but now they lowered their voices to less than whispers, reading each other's lips, really, a communication just this side of telepathy.

"Don't you get it?" Nolan said. "Don't you see it yet?"

"Get what? See what?"

"We're screwed."

"Huh?"

"Your pal in the wig, Jon. He's screwed us. Shoved it in and broke it off."

"What d'you mean? How are we worse off than anybody else on the plane?"

Nolan took Jon's almost-empty glass of Bourbon and Coke away from him, set it on the floor, said, "You better stick to straight Coke in the future, kid. You aren't thinking too clear."

"I don't..."

"Okay, Jon. We're on a skyjacked plane. Now, what's the best we can hope for? What's the best thing that can happen in this particular situation?"

"Well, I suppose the best thing that could happen would be for somebody to take that supposedly rewired calculator away from the skyjacker. That would put the plane back in the hands of the good guys, right?"

"Okay. Then what."

"Everybody rides off into the sunset, I guess. Except for the skyjacker. He goes straight to jail, do not pass Go, do not collect two hundred thousand dollars. Right?"

"Half right. The skyjacker isn't the only one who goes straight to jail and doesn't collect two hundred thousand dollars."

"What?" The clouds began to lift inside Jon's head. "Oh. Oh Jesus."

"Yeah. Oh Jesus. Even if they could grab this guy before he's done any damage, the 'good guys,' as you call them, would still have to assume there's a bomb on the plane. Which means the bomb squad'll be called in and…"

"They'll fluoroscope all the luggage. Shit. Oh shit. And all our money? All our beautiful money?…"

"We'll just have to forget it. Best we can hope for is to leave the airport fast as possible, before people start asking embarrassing questions. Hope to Christ they don't trace the luggage to us. My phony name'll lead them nowhere, that's one good thing. You're using your right name, but your luggage has nothing suspicious in it. I just hope nobody remembers we were traveling together. I hope Hazel'll cover for us—a little, anyway. I hope a hell of a lot of things, frankly."

"Jesus, Nolan. We can't just let all that money go…."

"We have to. I been trying to figure a way to save it, but I can't find one. That money isn't the only thing in that damn suitcase, don't forget."

"I haven't forgotten, Nolan. I wish I could, but I haven't."

The guns, Jon thought, the goddamn guns.

The two .38s they'd used at the Comforts'. The two .38s they'd used to *kill* the Comforts. Bad enough to have to try and explain two hundred grand in cash, but two hundred grand in cash and two revolvers, both of which might be traceable to a multiple killing and robbery…

Jon didn't want to think about it.

"And," Nolan was saying, "that's what happens in the best of all possible worlds. The other possibilities are even more depressing. Such as, maybe there is a bomb on board, and the skyjacker gets rattled, and we all get blown to hell, in which case we won't sweat the money. Or, the guy lets some of us off the plane and keeps some hostages, and then gets rattled, and our money gets blown up. Or the goddamn skyjacking is a success, and the guy gets away, and the bomb squad moves in to work on the plane and…well, it goes on like that. No matter how you figure it, Jon…"

"We're screwed."

Hazel was coming down the aisle. She stopped beside them and said, "Now that we've landed, he's having me ask among the passengers for volunteers to be hostages. He's going to keep ten people on the plane and let the rest go."

"Then what?" Nolan said.

"He says he'll let the hostages go when the ransom's delivered. When we take off again, just the pilot and copilot and navigator and yours truly'll be aboard. And the skyjacker, of course."

"Has he made any more demands?"

"He wants two parachutes."

"Why two?" Jon asked.

Nolan grinned. "Because he's smart. He learned that trick from the best skyjacker of 'em all, of D. B. Cooper. Asking for more than one insures him that the chutes won't be sabotaged."

"Why?" Hazel wanted to know.

"Because with two parachutes, he might make somebody else jump along with him."

Hazel still didn't understand. "Certainly not the pilot or copilot or navigator," she said.

Nolan nodded. "Certainly not."

Hazel swallowed. "Let's hope the powers that be don't consider us flight attendants expendable."

"Any other demands?"

"Just that we aren't to reveal his identity to the other passengers. As you said, he's smart. He figures the fewer people that get a good, long look at him, the better. This way, he'll just blend into the crowd."

Jon said, "I don't know, he looks pretty obvious to me, with the wig and sunglasses and everything."

"Not really," Nolan said. "Most of the passengers on this plane are businessmen. They just figure him for some hippie kid or something; a fairly likely suspect, maybe, but not much more so than anybody else."

"D. B. Cooper," Hazel said, "was dressed like a businessman. Suit and tie, topcoat oxfords. Like most of the people around you."

Nolan asked, "Has he told you where you'll be flying yet?"

"No. Mexico, though, don't you suppose? Parachute out into some flat area, where somebody'll be waiting to pick him up?"

"Maybe."

"I'm supposed to be asking for volunteers right now. But I'm not asking you. I don't want you. Understand? We'll have plenty of volunteer hostages, and I don't want you two to be part of them. Especially you, Nolan or Ryan or whoever you are. I get the feeling you're the hero type, and I don't want you grandstand-playing me into getting blown to pieces."

"I'm telling you, Hazel," Nolan said, "that kid doesn't have any damn bomb on board. Take it from me, I'm a judge of character if there ever was one. That kid just doesn't have the balls for it."

They'd been keeping their voices down anyway, but she leaned over and whispered, so as not to take any chance of ruffling the feathers of the nearby nuns, and said, "It doesn't take balls to blow up a plane, dummy. Just a little dynamite." And she headed back up the aisle, skirt flashing over those fine, long legs of hers.

"So what are we going to do, Nolan?"

"I'm glad Hazel gave us an out. A hostage is one thing we don't want to be. We can't afford to stay. Or you can't, anyway. Now, soon as you get off this plane, you get your ass back to Iowa City, got me?"

"You got an idea, Nolan?"

"I might have."

"What is it?"

"You just let me do the thinking, and do as I say."

"Yeah, I know, I know, mine is not to reason why. You're the mastermind and I'm the flunky."

"Think of yourself as second in command, if it softens the blow."

Thirty seconds later, the captain's voice came over the intercom: He instructed all the passengers, except those who had volunteered to stay on board, to come forward and disembark. Everyone but the hostages began to rise from their seats, the businessmen straightening their ties, grabbing their briefcases; women fussing with their hair, tidying themselves in preparation for the photographers who'd be waiting out there; even the three nuns were smoothing out their habits. Everyone but the hostages, and the skyjacker of course, began to move forward.

Except Nolan.

Who slipped into the nearest of the two johns around the corner from their seat and, giving Jon a look that said, "Keep quiet and do as I told you," sealed himself inside the cubicle.

And now Jon stood alone, at the rear of the aisle, everyone else trailing on up toward the front, excluding the handful staying behind; Jon began up the aisle, hesitantly, wondering what the hell to do.

He could almost identify with the skyjacker; they were about the same age, after all, and had both got in over their heads in daring, potentially violent endeavors in pursuit of riches. And Nolan stowing away like this meant one thing to Jon: the skyjacker was in for it. Nolan was going to do God-knows-what to that poor kid, and Jon didn't know who to be more worried for, Nolan or that dumb-ass skyjacker.

And then a realization hit Jon, a short, hard jab that almost knocked him down: Nolan was wrong!

Nolan's assumption that the skyjacker had not planted a bomb on the plane was clearly false. Otherwise, why would the skyjacker take the trouble to let the bulk of the passengers disembark here at the Quad Cities? The kid evidently had a conscience of sorts, and didn't want to blow any more people to smithereens than he absolutely had to! The stupid fucking hypocrite.

Jon didn't know what to do. Should he warn Nolan? Go back and tell him, explain the logic of it, pull him out of that damn can and fuck the money, just get the hell out of here? What good was Nolan going to do jumping the kid, anyway? *Nolan!* he screamed in his brain. *There* is *a bomb on this goddamn plane!*

But it was too late to go back. He was passing beside the seat where the young skyjacker was sitting calmly, just another brave volunteer hostage, as far as anyone could tell. A sudden rush of indignation ran through Jon. He wanted to grab that little shit by the shoulders and shake him till his wig fell off. What kind of fucking monster could do a thing like this? Didn't the bastard have any respect for human life at all? How could the son of a bitch coldly plant a bomb on a plane and treat life and death like some casual goddamn thing?

Jon glared at the skyjacker as he passed him, but in the reflecting mirror-sunglasses, he saw only himself.

15

He looked out at the airport. It was a modest affair, two creamy-brown brick buildings joining a central tower, some hangars off to the side. You could set this airport down in the lobby at O'Hare and no one would notice. Its relative smallness was one reason he'd picked it. He'd chosen Detroit as takeoff point and the Quad Cities as ransom drop, partially because neither airport had been involved in a skyjacking before; the Quad City Airport was especially poorly equipped for such a contingency. He realized the money would probably have to be flown in from Chicago, but that was just a twenty-minute flight, and since he'd had the pilot call the demand ahead, the money could almost beat them there. Here at the Quad Cities, a skyjacking would be more than the local enforcement agencies could handle, and the people flown in on the spur of the moment from Chicago would be disoriented and, in teaming with local people, disorganized; by the time anyone was at all prepared to deal with him, he would be gone. But had he chosen O'Hare, for example, he'd have had to face a damn anti-skyjack task force.

He was more than aware of the harsh fate dealt out to others who'd engaged in this particular crime: there were so many instances of FBI snipers dropping skyjackers, he couldn't keep them all straight in his mind, though one recent episode was vividly clear to him: a skyjacker had been cut in half, literally, by the close-range blast of an FBI agent's shotgun. Consideration of such facts had led him to the choice of a relatively "small-town" airport, but even then, he knew that overconfidence was insanity. For that reason, he had sent the stewardess out to pick up the money. He was not about to stick his head outside the plane and get it blown off his shoulders by an FBI marksman.

He watched as the attractive brunette flight attendant walked out on the runway, per his instructions (the transfer of money was to be made in full sight of the plane, in broad daylight), while a heavyset, sour-faced probable FBI man in a brown suit, carrying an attaché case and two parachutes, walked out from the airport complex and met her. He handed her the case of money so reluctantly, you'd have thought it was his, then gave her the chutes and headed back. She returned to the plane. No apparent attempt at trickery.

He smiled, sat back in the seat.

The flight attendant, Hazel, brought him the attaché case.

"Sit across the aisle," he told her, "and open the case."

"You want *me* to open it?"

"Yes. I'm sorry, but it might be sabotaged. I might snap it open and release a gas or something. I have to be careful, you can understand that."

"Of course," she said.

She sat across from him, opened the case.

There was no gas, no explosion.

There was, however, a lot of money. Rows and rows, stacks and stacks, of green packets, packets of cash still in their Chicago bank wrappers.

"Shall I count it?" she said.

"Please. There should be ten thousand twenty-dollar bills."

It took a while.

"All there," she said.

"Thank you. Close the case, please."

She did, and handed it to him. He laid it on the seat beside him, next to the tape recorder.

She looked at him strangely. She was a very pretty woman; striking eyes, the color of her name. She looked something like Carol, as a matter of fact, only brunette instead of blonde. She said, in a surprisingly kind voice, "What's a nice kid like you doing in a situation like this?"

When he'd researched other skyjackings, he'd found that his goal was different from most. Funny, too, because his would *seem* the most likely goal. But it wasn't. Many skyjackers did it for glory; he wanted none of that. True, the adventure of it had been appealing to him, but the publicity meant nothing. He had no desire to become a folk hero, à la Rafael Minichiello or D. B. Cooper; and he certainly didn't want to see his name in the papers! Some skyjacked out of death wish, suicidal tendency; if he had any of that, he didn't know it. Much skyjacking was political protest and/or the seeking of political asylum, the skyjackings to Cuba being the most obvious example of that. But there was no political motivation to his skyjacking, although a disillusionment with the American Dream had had something to do with his transition from straight, conservative citizen to air pirate. But who was not a pirate, after all, when the Establishment reeked corruption, from the White House on down? And he'd seen how the great capitalist system worked, hadn't he? The protestant work ethic he'd obeyed so religiously, only to be swindled and squeezed and screwed out of his savings and his youth and his ideals by those good capitalists at Dream-Land Realtors. Still, he was no protester; he cared nothing for politics. His was an admittedly selfish goal he shared with few skyjackers; D. B. Cooper and a handful of others, that was all.

So, when the stewardess asked him for his reason, he was almost anxious to clarify himself.

"I need the money," he said.

And she smiled—couldn't help herself—and nodded, almost sympathetically. "I know what you mean," she said.

He wanted to tell her that he didn't want to hurt her, but he knew it would sound silly, hypocritical to the point of absurdity. But he really didn't. And he didn't want to hurt himself, either, but if they forced him to, he knew he'd have to consign this plane and the pretty stewardess and himself and all his hopes and dreams to a fiery hell. The only consolation was, it would be over in an instant. Like turning off a TV. Press the button, and boom. No pain.

He told her, Hazel, to let the hostages off the plane, and she made the announcement over the intercom, as the hostages were scattered all about the plane, having remained in their own seats, at his request. He'd felt it best not to let them huddle together, as people in such situations often do; that type of thing could lead to an uprising or some other sort of half-assed heroism, which he could do without.

He was glad to see the hostages go. Relieved. He'd felt the same earlier, when he watched the other passengers leave. It was as if a great weight on him was gradually being lessened. Now, with just the crew and the single stewardess left aboard, he felt almost at ease. The pilot, copilot, and navigator—and the stewardess, too, for that matter, much as he liked her—were the equivalent of military personnel who had taken on a risk-prone job and were prepared, to some degree, anyway, to die in the line of duty. His conscience was taxed far less by their presence than by that of the passengers. Having the passengers around him had proved much more disturbing than he'd expected. The possibility of pressing some buttons on that specially wired calculator and destroying the plane and people on it had been just that: a possibility, a hopefully unlikely eventuality that Those-in-Authority might force him to, if they were foolish. The responsibility would not be his. But once on the plane, with faces all around him, lives all around him, his emotionless, laboratory theorizing blew up in his face like a misjudged experiment; his rationalizations strained at the seams, as the faceless ciphers of his game plan turned out to be flesh-and-blood human beings, people, not pawns. And this hand had trembled around the plastic case of the calculator.

Now, though, the passengers were gone, the last remainder of them trickling out at the stewardess' guidance, and the hand around the calculator no longer trembled—even if its palm was a trifle sweaty.

With the hostages safely off the plane, the stewardess came to him for further instructions. He told her to inform the captain to take off immediately.

And they did. The stewardess remained in the cockpit, and he strapped himself into his seat while the plane taxied down the runway and lifted its nose in the air. Once the plane had leveled out again, he unbuckled and, taking along only the calculator, left his seat and went forward and knocked on the cockpit door.

The stewardess answered, and he told her to tell the captain to come out and talk to him.

He didn't want to go in there, in the cockpit. He didn't want to be contained in that small area with those three probably very capable men. And he wanted to show them, the captain especially, that he, the skyjacker, was in command now; when he told the captain to come, the captain damn well better come.

The captain came.

And said, "What's our destination?"

"I think we'll be going to Mexico," he said.

"We'll need fuel for that."

"I know. You can refuel at St. Louis." The captain nodded.

"I would like all of you," he said, and he nodded toward the stewardess, "to remain in the cockpit throughout the rest of the flight. Understood?"

They indicated they understood.

"Captain, I want you to fly this plane at low altitude and low speed, from here on out."

"How low?"

"Five thousand to six thousand feet, speed one hundred and twenty-five knots. Fly a straight course to St. Louis. I know the terrain. I'll know where we are. No stunt flying, please."

"You intend to jump?" the captain asked. "I thought you said Mexico...."

"Maybe. That's my concern. I think you can understand that it's to my benefit to keep you, as well as the people you'll be in constant contact with on the radio, in doubt as to exactly what my intentions are. By the way, you'll notice very soon that the rear ramp exit is down. I'll be lowering that ramp as soon as you return to the cockpit."

The captain got a knowing look in his eye; what he knew was this: the ramp was ideal for use by a parachutist. Only 727s and DC-9s had such ramps.

"Do not assume, captain, that I'm going to jump immediately. Maybe I will. Maybe I won't. But I am aware that a warning light on your panel lights up when the ramp is lowered, so I am lowering the ramp now, so that you will not be able to pinpoint when or if I've jumped. If I haven't knocked on the door by the time we approach St. Louis, you'll know I'm gone."

"Which airport in St. Louis?"

"It doesn't matter. The FBI will be at whatever place I pick. Tell you what. Feel free to select the one you like best. You're the captain, after all."

The captain's eyes tightened, while the stewardess seemed almost to enjoy the put-down, and when the captain returned to the cockpit, she remained in the doorway to say something to the skyjacker. What she said was, "It's a little late to be saying this, but try not to do anything you'll regret."

He smiled. "It is a little late for that."

"Well. Enjoy your money, anyway."

"Thank you. I'll do my best."

She disappeared into the cockpit.

He went back to his seat and waited while the pilot brought

the plane to a lower altitude; then he walked to the rear of the plane to let down the ramp. Seats the flight attendants used during takeoff were folded against the door, and above that was the handle, which he pushed all the way to the left, pulling the door in; just outside the door, on the left, was the stair release control, a little box with a lever in it, which he pushed outward. The ramp lowered. There was an immediate suction effect, which he'd anticipated, and he braced himself accordingly. The wind noise and jet roar were deafening, but there was no pressurization problem at this altitude. Ears aching, face whipped by gusting air flow, he smiled out at the ramp, the little mini-flight of stairs that would allow him to jump from the plane with ease.

He went back to his seat, where the attaché case of cash waited. He took off the wig, the sunglasses. He stripped off the green corduroy shirt; beneath it he wore a thin black cotton pullover, long-sleeved, and the single emergency chute, strapped to his stomach. He wasn't about to use the two chutes he'd asked for. He knew they would be bugged; they would be hastily but well armed with homing devices that could lead the FBI and everybody right to him. He would wait a while, and, one at a time, throw those chutes out, to send the posse on a wild goose chase or two.

He settled back in the seat and, breathing easily for the first time in hours, began to relax. The project was going well. Flawlessly. Admittedly, it had been harder to execute than to plan—well, not harder, really, but more taxing emotionally. It was one thing to coolly plot, to engage in deliberated planning, to rehearse his lines in his head, and quite another thing to carry out all of that in a plane filled not with Xs on a diagram, but human beings.

And that was the element he couldn't plan for, the human

element, and it had worried him, both at home and on the plane. Blueprints were fine for building houses; diagrams were great for putting together electrical systems. But human beings weren't as dependable as diodes, and he realized something could go haywire, despite his thorough engineering; he knew some human could throw a wrench in the works.

In fact, he had thought he'd spotted someone who might be just the person who would throw that wrench. Sitting next to that kid, that curly-haired guy with the Big Little Books and comics, was a rock-faced man with dark hair and mustache and narrow eyes that had an almost Oriental cast to them; he'd felt those eyes on him, boring into him, and had noticed the stewardess, Hazel, talking to the guy more than was perhaps natural. He'd almost decided the guy was an FBI man or sky marshal or something, but to his relief the guy hadn't stayed around as a hostage, which would have been a good indication that he was a law enforcement agent of some kind who'd happened to be on the flight. He hadn't banked on having someone like that aboard, and was glad to find his suspicions were groundless.

Some time passed, and he went back to the noisy aperture and tossed out the first of the parachutes.

He went back to his seat, the calculator still in hand but not so firmly now, and he sat and watched the land go by. He'd told the pilot to fly a straight course, not wanting to be overly specific about precisely what course he wanted (since that would alert everyone that he indeed did intend to jump soon) but knowing that if the pilot wasn't pulling something, Highway 67 should be in constant sight. It was. It was important for Highway 67 to be within reasonable walking distance when he jumped, in order for Carol to pick him up as planned. He checked his watch; time was working out okay. All was running smooth, then.

A few minutes passed, and he went back to the ramp and threw out the second parachute.

He sat down again, looked out the double-paned window. Missouri was rolling by. Some of it was hilly, but most was relatively flat farmland, which was what he was after. Soon he should spot the landmark he was looking for and make his jump. He prepared himself, checked out the chute; got the C.B. out of the Radio Shack sack, which had been under the seat in front of him; he set it on his lap, atop the attaché case. He still had the calculator in hand, and hadn't decided whether to take it along or not; probably wasn't wise to leave anything behind he didn't have to, but maybe there was some freak chance of the thing detonating the bomb on the plane, with the impact of his fall.

He watched out the window, the familiar landscape gliding by. And then he saw the landmark—a red barn whose slanting roof bore white letters advertising MIRACLE CAVERNS—and he got up. He clipped the C.B. onto his belt, tucked the attaché case under his arm.

Now was the time.

He walked down the aisle, toward the ramp at the rear of the plane; the opening beckoned him, a gateway to freedom, to a new start for Carol and him. And as he walked by the rest rooms, a hand reached out and clamped onto him by the wrist, shook the calculator from his hand. Then a fist crashed into his jaw, damn near breaking it, knocking him back on his butt.

His mind reeled: *Someone sneaked on the plane at Moline*, he thought, *damned FBI sneaked someone aboard!*

Then he looked up and saw who it was.

That hard-faced S.O.B. with the mustache.

Who was now on the floor, in the aisle, scrambling after the calculator, which had flipped between some seats. The guy had a look of pain on that scowling face of his, from the mingled wind-noise and jet-screech coming from the open ramp door, a harsh, grating sound that was working on the guy's eardrums.

The skyjacker was used to the sound, as the ramp door had been open some time now; but the guy with the mustache had been hidden away in the rest room, apparently, where the sound had been muffled. Which meant the guy was somewhat incapacitated, but the skyjacker was still hesitant about retaliation: the guy was big, and looked mean as hell, and was probably armed.

He knew he was close enough to that door to make a successful jump, no problem; he had the money. Why not go for it?

But the guy with the mustache had seen him, sans wig, sans sunglasses, sans any disguise; and would be able to report exactly where he'd jumped. Which meant one thing: the skyjacker would be caught.

He'd never considered the possibility of capture, really; he'd always thought it was either/or, heaven or hell—a bundle of money and make a new life, or no life at all. Now, with capture, he'd have prison to face; life imprisonment, perhaps, and the same for Carol....

In the three seconds it had taken the skyjacker to make these realizations, the guy with the mustache had retrieved the calculator from between the seats, though he was still on his hands and knees. He looked up with an expression of annoyance; he was a mean-looking S.O.B., all right, like an Indian with a grudge.

The skyjacker swung his attaché case and caught the guy on the chin, throwing him back, on his back, apparently unconscious. The skyjacker went to retrieve the calculator from the man's hand—best not leave that behind....

But the guy reached out a big hand and grabbed him by the ankle, and yanked, and he fell on his ass in the aisle, hard, and the attaché case of money went skittering out of his hands, landing a few feet away from the open ramp door. With that suction effect, the case would get pulled outside in a second if he didn't reach it first, and on his hands and knees he crawled after it, like a grossly oversize infant. He got his hands on the case, the suction of the open door tugging at the skin on his face, the wind slapping him, and he felt something come down hard on his back.

A foot.

And then the guy said something; he had to yell, scream it really, to get his voice above the jet roar and wind. He said, "If I let you up, will you behave?"

Now it was the skyjacker's turn to yell. "Yes!"

"I shouldn't," the guy said, still screaming, "I should kick your goddamn ass out of this plane."

But the pressure subsided; the foot went away.

He got to his feet and looked at the guy. He had expected the guy to be fuming, but he still seemed more annoyed than enraged. And another surprise: he had no gun, at least not in sight.

And that gave the skyjacker a burst of courage.

He knew he was close enough to that door to make a successful jump, no problem. He had the attaché case in his hands. Why turn the money over to this guy when there wasn't even a gun pointed at him? Why give up now, after working so hard and coming so close?

He lurched forward, shoved a hand into the guy's chest, pushing into him, knocking him off balance.

But it wasn't enough.

The guy with the mustache lashed out with a fist as big as a softball, and the skyjacker tumbled back, head spinning, knocking against the edge of the open ramp door; then the suction got hold of him and he was gone, unconscious or damn near but somehow instinctively clutching the attaché case to him, falling down those steps into the gray sky.

Four

16

Someone dropped something in the kitchen and woke Jon.

He sat up in bed, startled by the sound, and found the room around him dark, which startled him too. When he lay down late this afternoon, it was still light outside—or as light as an overcast day can be—but now it was pitch black. He'd fallen asleep and now, as he checked his watch, he found he'd slept well into the night.

Damn, he thought. He'd only meant to rest for a moment, just lie down and relax a while, really. Not fall asleep. He hadn't even had a chance to call Karen yet, to tell her he was back in Iowa City. Too late for that now. Damn. How could he fall asleep, with Nolan literally up in the air like that? What the hell was wrong with him?

Another sound.

Someone was moving around out in the kitchen.

Breen, Jon thought. Just Breen, up having a post-midnight snack.

They had left Breen at the antique shop while they went to Detroit for the Comfort heist; Breen hadn't felt like traveling right away, with his wound and all, and besides, his car windshield was shot out, so they'd left him to mind the store.

When Jon got back late this afternoon, Breen had been full of questions.

And complaints.

"You might've called," Breen had said, "and let me know how the goddamn thing came out. I had a stake in it, too, you know."

And Jon had said, "Well, you know Nolan. He couldn't see

wasting a long-distance call when we were coming right back, anyway."

Breen had mumbled something about what a cheap-ass Nolan was, and then went on to ask, well, what the hell happened at the Comforts, anyway? What Jon told him sounded like a good news/bad news joke. First the good news: they had successfully stolen over $200,000—even the part about the Comforts dying was good news to Breen, who was glad to see them go. Then came the bad news: the skyjacking.

And Breen had started to moan and groan—such a terrible thing, losing all that money. Jon was in no mood to listen to him bitch, and went upstairs and fixed himself a ham and cheese sandwich. Breen came up and ate half of Jon's sandwich and asked Jon if he could recommend some place to get a new windshield put in his car. Jon told him where he could get that done, then went into his uncle Planner's bedroom and lay down for a short rest.

So now it was the middle of the night and he was awake, finally, and someone was moving around out there, in the kitchen. Probably Breen, but Jon wasn't sure; he was nervous, not having heard from Nolan yet, and he wondered if it could be an intruder of some sort out there. He pulled open the nightstand drawer by the bed and got out one of his uncle's .32 automatics.

He stalked through the pine paneled living room and slowly edged toward the archway that led into the kitchen. The lights were on in there, bright and white. Breen, probably; but he kept the .32 leveled out in front of him, just the same.

He lunged through the archway and into the kitchen, and Nolan was sitting at the kitchen table, eating some breakfast cereal.

"Don't shoot, kid," Nolan said, holding up his hands, one of them with a spoon in it, dripping milk down on the table.

"Nolan!"

"Quiet," he said. He put down his hands. "You want to wake up Breen? He's down sleeping like a baby in your bed, and I don't want that talkative son of a bitch waking up and making me explain things all night."

"Nolan," Jon said, incredulous. He sat down at the table with him, set the .32 next to the box of breakfast cereal. "Where'd you come from?"

"Caught a bus at St. Louis. Where's the goddamn sugar? These fucking Grape Nuts are supposed to be naturally sweet, but they taste like wood shavings to me. Get me the damn sugar."

Jon got him the sugar, rejoined him at the table.

"Well, Jesus, Nolan."

"Jesus what?"

"What happened? What happened?"

"I caught a bus at St. Louis, I told you." He ate some cereal and grinned at Jon as he chewed.

"Oh, for Christ's sake, Nolan, quit being so goddamn cute. I can't stand it. Tell me what happened!"

"Say, have you been listening to the news, kid?"

"No, I fell asleep, damn it."

"I'd like to know what they're saying on the news. I'd like to know what they're saying about our money, which ought to've been found by now. Turn on that radio on the counter. The news'll be on in five minutes."

"I'll turn it on in five minutes. How'd you get in here, Nolan? The doors were locked and you don't have a key."

"I don't need a key to get in a house. So you were sleeping, huh, kid? Your concern for me's overwhelming."

"Yeah, well, Nolan, I'm sorry I fell asleep, but could you please tell me what happened?"

"Not much to tell. I stayed in the can. Nobody caught on I was in there, least of all the skyjacker. I waited till all the hostages were off the plane, waited for that stupid kid to make his move to jump, and then I took that calculator away from him. Didn't want him blowing me up, whether by accident or not, and that wasn't unlikely with him jumping with a damn detonator in his hand. So I took it away."

"Then you decided he *did* have a bomb on the plane?"

"Yes," Nolan said, and he ran through the same chain of logic, proving the bomb's existence, as had Jon. Which would have given Jon a certain sense of satisfaction, if he hadn't been so confused about so much else.

"But I don't get it, Nolan. Why'd you even bother staying on the plane? Certainly not just to take the calculator away from the guy, to save the airlines their plane. You're not the knight-in-white-armor type."

"I had my reasons." And he grinned again, chomping cereal. "I got a surprise for you, kid."

"Surprise? What do you mean, surprise?"

"Well, just before the plane got to St. Louis, I knocked on the cockpit door and told Hazel and the pilot and everybody what I'd done. That I'd taken that thing away from the skyjacker, before he jumped. And I was a hero. They were so grateful they could shit. When we landed and were getting off the plane, I asked Hazel if she would go get that briefcase of funny-books out of that closet across from the john, because if I left that behind, my young nephew—that's you—would never forgive me. She obliged, and before the FBI or anybody could ask me a thing, the hero of the hour, briefcase tucked under his arm, excused himself to go to the can and instead went out and caught a cab and went straight to the bus station. After all the time I'd spent boxed up in that crapper in the plane, you'd think it would occur to those jokers I'd already had ample opportunity to relieve myself. But it didn't."

"Now let me get this straight," Jon said, not understanding at all. "You mean you went to the trouble of asking for that briefcase, just to be nice to me? That doesn't sound like you, Nolan. No offense, but you're not the most thoughtful man I ever met. I mean, it's a nice surprise, but..."

"That's not the surprise," Nolan said. He reached down and brought the briefcase up from the floor beside him; he put it on the table.

"Hey," Jon said, "that's not my briefcase."

"No, it isn't."

"It looks something like it, but that's not it."

"Open it. Go ahead."

Jon snapped the case open.

"Jesus," he said.

The case was full of money.

Crammed with packets of money; packets of $20 bills, in bank wrappers. Thousands and thousands of green dollars.

"The skyjacker's money," Jon said. Awestruck. "You switched on him!"

"Yeah," Nolan said. "Easy as pie. He went forward to boss the pilot around, and I just sneaked out of the can, switched his briefcase with yours, and sneaked back again."

"Damn, you switched on him! You switched on him. Nolan, you're a genius. And an even trade, at that. We hardly lost a cent on the deal."

"I wouldn't say that, kid. Every serial number on every bill in that briefcase was recorded by the feds before they let it go, you can bet on it. We'll have to peddle it to a fence, at a loss."

"But we'll still come out okay, won't we?"

"We'll come out okay."

"What about *our* money? The money in your suitcase? Who gets that?"

"I'm not really sure. It's confiscated, of course, so I suppose the government ends up with it. Don't they always?"

"Nolan…how in hell could you know the money would come in a briefcase so similar to mine?"

"I didn't. That was dumb luck. The way I had it figured was I'd have to switch the contents of the two briefcases, and that would've been tougher. But possible. Maybe I would've had to tangle with the skyjacker sooner that way, and that could've been risky."

"What happened to the skyjacker, then? Did he make his jump or what?"

"Well, we had a little scuffle. I hit him pretty hard and he fell out of the plane. His chute opened, late, but it opened. I told the pilot later that the kid waited till we were almost to St. Louis before jumping, which I said to throw them off, since it's to our benefit if he gets away, with everybody assuming he has the money. I suppose he's alive."

"I kind of hope so."

"Yeah, me too, but only because it helps us if he is. Otherwise, after what he put us through, he could break his goddamn neck and be okay with me."

"He's just another kind of thief, Nolan. Like you. And me."

"No. There's a difference. He's an amateur. I…we…are professionals."

Jon smiled. "I don't think I'm much of a pro, but thanks anyway, Nolan. There's only one thing I regret…."

"What's that? You still brooding about killing old Sam Comfort? Don't. You couldn't have shot a more deserving soul."

"Oh, not that. That does bother me, don't think it doesn't. But that wasn't what I meant."

"What did you mean?"

Jon leaned forward and spread his hands. "Well, it's great you got the money, and I don't want you to take this wrong, but if you'd have just told me what you had in mind, I could've emptied the briefcase and taken my comic books with me. Do you have any idea what those things are worth? How hard they are to find? Do you know that…"

Nolan put some more sugar on his cereal.

Epilogue: Crash Landing

Epilogue
Crash Landing

[illegible]

[illegible] the [illegible] [illegible]

[illegible] ow the [illegible] or something. [illegible]
the money back [illegible] that [illegible]
[illegible] look [illegible] Okay?

17

Carol found him in the high grass off to the side of the highway, behind a billboard advertising a bank savings plan. She was relieved she'd had so little trouble finding him; he'd told her, over the C.B., that he'd overshot their target area just a little, but that he could still make it to Highway 67, and when he had, he'd told her of the billboard and she'd found it—and him—with ease.

He was a mess. He was as pale as a cadaver, the black pullover and jeans streaked with the mud from the farmer's field he'd landed in, and probably from stumbling and falling in the miles of other fields he'd trudged through to get to the highway. His discomfort was obvious: he was curled up in a crumpled ball, like a wad of paper littered along the road; he was clinging to the brown attaché case like a drowning man clutching something buoyant.

Still, he was in one piece, and it could have been worse. She'd expected it to be worse. If he'd been bloody and twisted, she wouldn't have been surprised; she knew his jump had been a bad one, that he'd hit hard and wrong, even if he hadn't said so, because even over the C.B., the pain was evident in his voice, no matter how he tried not to show it.

"Baby," she said, "how bad is it?"

"Not so bad," he said. "Collar bone's broken, I think."

"Oh baby…"

"It can wait till we get home."

"Can't we…?"

"No. We can go to the hospital at Canker, soon as we get back. We'll say I fell down the stairs or something. Here. Take the money back to the car. Do that first, then come help me. It'll look less suspicious. Okay?"

"Okay."

She returned to the car and opened the trunk. Cars were whizzing by, but no one was paying any attention to her. She put the attaché case in and started to close the trunk lid, then stopped. She was curious. She wanted to see what $200,000 looked like. She wanted to see what they'd gone through hell for. So she snapped open the case, for a quick peek....

Bright four-color covers in plastic wrappers flashed up at her: pirates in outer space, ray guns, and rocket ships.

She shut it again, quickly, as if maybe she hadn't really seen what she'd seen.

She didn't know why, or how, but the elaborate plan, the "project," had gone wrong. Dreadfully, disastrously, absurdly wrong. A practical joke turned back on the joker. And, like all good jokes, it was funny, or would be: in their old age, perhaps, they could reflect on this foolish episode and its ironic result with some amusement. Yes, she thought, Ken and I might laugh about this someday.

But not right away.

Not today.

She closed the trunk, wondering what to do. It was obvious Ken didn't know anything had gone wrong; that he still thought he'd got off the plane with an attaché case full of money. And now was certainly not the time to tell him any different.

Now was a time to go back and put her arm around her husband's waist and help him to the car and get him to a hospital. Later would be a time for mending wounds, for putting pieces back together.

She got Ken settled in the back seat, and he was asleep almost at once.

Now was a time for going home. Alive and free, and going home, Carol thought. That in itself was a lot, wasn't it?

She got behind the wheel.

BOOK TWO
Hush Money

This is for CWO2 John W. McRae,
pride of the USMC, who was there.

A thief is anybody who gets out and works for his living, like robbing a bank, or breaking into a place and stealing stuff.... He really gives some effort to it. A hoodlum is a pretty lousy kind of scum. He works for gangsters and bumps off guys after they've been put on the spot. Why, after I'd made my rep, some of the Chicago Syndicate wanted me to go to work for them as a hood—you know, handling a machine gun. They offered me two hundred and fifty dollars a week and all the protection I needed. I was on the lam at the time, and not able to work at my regular line. But I wouldn't consider it. "I'm a thief," I said, "I'm no lousy hoodlum."

ALVIN KARPIS, IN 1936 CONVERSATION
WITH J. EDGAR HOOVER,
WHO DIDN'T UNDERSTAND

One:
Thursday Afternoon

I

One of the two men approaching the golf tee was being studied in the crosshairs of an assassin's sniperscope. The two men were riding in a red and mostly white golf cart that was putt-putting across the brown grass toward the first tee of the back nine. One of them would soon fold in half as a .460 Magnum blew his intestines and much of his spine and a good deal of blood out of the back of him. But that would not happen immediately. The man in the assassin's crosshairs had almost five minutes to live.

The driver was a tall man, well over six feet and in obvious good shape, a man with smooth, seemingly unused and handsome features that gave him the look of a twenty-five-year-old when he was in fact forty. His hair was brown and wavy, no gray, his chin deep-dimpled, cheeks too, eyes the color of Paul Newman's. The passenger was of medium height and build, with a sagging middle that helped to make him look every one of his fifty-four years. His face was spade-shaped, deeply lined, and his brown hair was thinning on top, getting white at the temples. Wire frame glasses nestled on the bridge of a slightly bulbous nose and magnified his colorless gray eyes.

Their cart ascended the slope of the mound from which they'd begin their second nine. They got out of the cart.

They were men as strikingly different in appearance as in background. The smaller man, the one in the more conservative attire—gray golf sweater, light blue Banlon shirt, gray slacks—was Carl H. Reed, former minority leader of the Iowa state legislature, recently retired from that position, recently appointed state highway commissioner. The big man, in the bright red sweater with dyed leather trim, deep blue Banlon shirt and white slacks, the tanned blue-eyed man who had the bearing of a professional athlete, was Joseph P. DiPreta, youngest of the three DiPreta brothers and perhaps foremost amateur golfer in the state, one of the best amateur golfers in the nation.

Excluding the sniper, who lay some distance away in the rough, the two men had the course to themselves on this cool and overcast autumn afternoon. It was late enough in the month—October—for even the most diehard of golf addicts to have hung up their shoes and stowed away their clubs for the season; but Joey DiPreta was more dedicated to the game than most and often played well into November, weather permitting. Today, however, Joey had other reasons for going out on the course: business reasons. Getting in a round or two of golf was a decidedly secondary concern; far more important to get Carl Reed out here on the course this afternoon, alone.

Carl Reed was delighted, almost honored, to have been invited to share an afternoon of golf with Des Moines' most colorful and celebrated amateur athlete. Carl was a sports nut who took an interest in everything from the World Series and the Super Bowl to log-rolling contests and pro wrestling. He admired and came close to envying guys who pursued athletics as a way of life, and he could especially identify with a Joey DiPreta, since golf, of all sports, meant most to Carl. Golf was the game that let him come down out of the bleachers and onto the playing field, a game that got his mind off the pressures of politics and business. Not that golf was merely a pastime for Carl, an escape valve he could turn when psychological steam built up inside him. No. He was, in his way, as dedicated to the game as was Joey DiPreta.

Carl was aware, of course, of the DiPreta family's less than wholesome reputation. Their present-day interests, which included a construction company and a Midwestern chain of discount stores, among many others, were not so much in question as were the origins of the DiPreta wealth, which, according to rumor, dated back to the days of bootlegging and worse. As a kid he'd heard stories of the DiPretas and protection rackets and loan-sharking. During the war the name DiPreta always seemed to come up when the black market was being discussed. Some said they had never totally severed their ties with organized crime, and just last year there had been accusations of stock swindle leveled at Vincent DiPreta, Joey's eldest brother. Nevertheless, Carl had lived in the Des Moines area all his life, holding for over twenty years positions of financial and political responsibility and, yes, power; and in all that time he'd seen no hard evidence to substantiate allegations relative to the DiPretas being a Mafia-style crime family. Nothing at all to turn ugly rumor into ugly fact.

Still, Carl was sensitive to its being a somewhat risky proposition for him to have contact with even a possible mob associate. He'd fought long and hard to build and then maintain a good name in a field that had become more and more tainted in recent years. It was with considerable sadness that he'd come to hear his own college-age children using the word "politician" as if it were spelled with four letters.

Joey could sense the other man's uneasiness, had sensed it immediately on meeting Carl at the clubhouse. For that reason he'd cooled it on the first nine, not even hinting at the real purpose of the afternoon, just breaking the ice with the guy, whose nervousness, Joey soon decided, must have come from rubbing shoulders with a local superstar. Joey took advantage of Carl's admiration, using it as an excuse to get overly chummy, to try to become an instant close friend of Carl's. It seemed to be working.

Funny thing is, Joey thought, watching the skinny but pot-bellied Carl select a wood, *that awkward looking son of a bitch shoots a pretty fair game*. The afternoon had been damn near an even match, and Joey was maybe going to get beaten. And he surely wasn't doing that on purpose. He wanted to win the clown over, but he wasn't about to throw the match for it—some things were just against Joey's principles.

Carl shoved a wooden tee into the hard ground, and Joey said, "Whoa! Hey, hold on a second. How about we catch our breath a minute, Carl? Got some beer in a little cooler in back of the cart. What do you say?"

Carl hadn't wanted to admit being winded, but he sure was, and a beer sounded good. He'd been playing hard, and though he knew he was outclassed, he'd somehow been managing to hold his own; he hoped Joey hadn't been just going easy on him. He told Joey a beer was fine with him and Joey went and got the beer and they sat in the cart for a while and drank and talked. Joey complimented Carl on holing out on the last green, said that was really some show of putting, and Carl said thanks, his luck was running good today.

"Luck, my ass," Joey said. "That was a hell of a round you just shot, my friend."

"I guess you must've inspired me," Carl said with a grin.

Joey, who was grinning too, his teeth as white as fresh white paint. "Don't you politicians ever let up laying on the bullshit?"

"No, I mean it, Joey. This is really a pleasure, playing with someone of your standing. I can't tell you how I appreciate your inviting me to join you this afternoon."

"You think it's easy finding somebody else crazy enough to want to come out in the dead of winter and knock a little white ball around the ground?"

"Now who's laying on the bullshit?" Carl swigged his beer.

"Look, I saw you on TV last year, when the guy at KRNT interviewed you. He asked you why you played so late in the season, after most of us've given up the ghost, and you said—"

"And I said I liked having the course to myself, because I could concentrate better. Well, that's true, I guess, but a guy's got to have *some* friends, right? Can't be a goddamn hermit all the time. Tell you the truth, though, Carl, I did have sort of an ulterior motive for getting together with you."

"Oh?"

Joey noticed the crow's-feet pulling in tight around Carl's eyes. *Careful*, Joey thought, *don't blow it now*. "Yeah, well, I mean I've wanted to meet you for a long time. Admired you, you know? You got quite a reputation yourself."

"Come on now, Joey."

"No, really. I'm a Democrat too, you know. That's pretty rare around these parts." Joey forced a laugh, and Carl laughed a little, too. But just a little. Joey had a sinking feeling. He'd appraised Carl Reed as a pushover, a mark, judging from the hero-worshipping attitude the man had displayed earlier; but now Joey had his doubts about being able to pull this thing off, and he just had to. It wasn't that often his brothers entrusted him with something this important; it wasn't that often he helped out with business at all. Damn.

"Joey, if you have something on your mind..."

"Hey, remember that junket to Vegas last year? We had some kind of good time on that one, huh?"

Carl nodded. He'd first met Joey DiPreta on that trip, had spoken to him casually on the plane, talked about golf, sports in general.

"That wasn't your first Vegas hop, was it, Carl?"

"No, it wasn't. I went a couple other times. What's your point, Joey?"

The junket was a weekend trip to Las Vegas that Carl and many others in his social circle—doctors, lawyers, executives—had gone on every year now three years running; it was a husband and wife affair, $1500 for the whole trip for both, including hotel room and plane fare and five hundred dollars in casino chips.

"I don't think you were aware of it at the time, Carl, but my family owns the travel agency that sponsored that junket—in fact all the junkets you've been on. Just one of a number of gambling trips we sponsor. To Vegas, the Caribbean, England."

Carl shrugged, sipped his beer, wondered where this conversation was going and said, "Joey, you're right…I wasn't aware your family owned that travel agency. But I'm not particularly surprised, either. I'm aware the DiPreta interests extend to many areas."

"That's for sure, Carl. We got lots of interests. We own a sand and gravel company, for instance. And a construction firm. And some other businesses that you might run into now and then, Carl, in your position as state highway commissioner."

Carl Reed leaned forward and looked at Joey DiPreta straight on. The eyes behind the wire frame glasses were as hard and cold as any Joey had seen. Carl spoke through his teeth: "Wait just one moment, Mr. DiPreta, while I make something clear to you…"

"Hold on, hold on, hold on. I know what you're thinking."

"Do you? Then I see no reason to continue this discussion."

"I know what you're thinking and I'm not going to suggest anything of the kind. We know you. We know all about you, what sort of man you are. I said I knew your reputation, remember? You're a man of character, with a name like goddamn sterling silver. So we aren't about to suggest anything, uh, out of line to you. No. No under-the-table stuff. No kickbacks. Nothing. We'll bid for jobs, sure, but if our bid isn't lowest and best, to hell with us."

"Then what's this about?"

Joey lifted his hands palms out in a you-know-how-it-is gesture. "Some people aren't as incorruptible as you, Carl. Your predecessor, for example."

"My predecessor?"

"We had dealings with him. A lot of dealings. I guess you could call them extra-legal dealings. You see, it was a family thing. Mr. Grayson, your predecessor, was married to a cousin of ours and, well, a thing worked out where he sent some business our way and we kicked back some money to him."

"Why in God's name are you telling me this?"

"Because you're going to find out anyway. You're going to know. When you get settled down in Grayson's chair and start examining his records, and then in about a year when those roads we laid down start cracking up like plaster of Paris, you're going to know what was going on all right."

"And I'm going to have the makings of a large-scale political scandal. Not to mention possible indictments against members of the DiPreta family."

"Not to mention that."

"Well. Thank you for the nine holes, Joey." Carl rose. "And thank you for the information."

"Sit down, Carl," Joey said, pulling him back down to the cart seat with some force, though his voice stayed friendly and pleasant. "I'll get you another beer."

"I haven't finished this one and I'm not about to. Let go of my arm."

"Listen to me. All we want of you is silence. We will have no dealings with you whatsoever during your term of office, other than this one instance. My family is legitimate these days. This stuff with Grayson all took place back four, five years ago when Papa was still alive. My brothers and me are moving the DiPreta concerns into aboveboard areas completely."

Carl said nothing.

"Look. The publicity alone could kill us. And like you said, it's possible indictments could come out of it, and if indictments're possible, so are prison terms, for Christ's sake, and more investigations. So all we're asking of you is this: Just look the other way. You'd be surprised how much it can pay, doing nothing. That's what they call a deal like this: something for nothing."

"It's also called a payoff. It's called paying hush money, Joey, cover-up money."

"You can call it whatever you want."

"How much, Joey? How much are the DiPretas willing to pay to hush me up?"

"You're a wealthy man, Carl. You're a banker. Your wife has money—her family does, I mean. Land holdings. It would take a lot to impress you."

"Yes, it would."

"I want you to keep in mind that an investigation would bring out your own contacts with the DiPreta family. We've been seen together this afternoon, for one thing, you and me. And those yearly Las Vegas junkets, on the last of which you and me were seen together..."

"You're really reaching, Joey. Tell me, how much to cover it up? What's the offer I can't refuse?"

Joey leaned close and whispered with great melodramatic effect: "Fifty. Thousand. Dollars."

Carl was silent for a moment. "That's a lot of money. Could have been more, but it's a lot of money."

"A very lot, Carl. Especially when the IRS doesn't have to know about it."

"Let me ask you something, Joey."

"Sure, Carl. Anything."

"Where do we stand on our golf scores?"

"What? What are you..."

"Humor me. How many strokes down am I right now?"

"Well, uh, one stroke, Carl. I'm leading you by one, you know that."

"Good. That way you're going to be able to quit while you're ahead, Joey. Because this game is over."

Carl got up and out of the cart and began walking away.

"Carl!"

Without turning, Carl said, "Thank you for an interesting afternoon, Mr. DiPreta."

"Carl, today you were offered money. Tomorrow it could be...something else. Something unpleasant."

Carl kept walking.

Joey hopped out of the cart and said, almost shouting, "You know that term you used, Carl—hush money? That's a good term, hush money. I like that. There's two different kinds of hush money, you know—the kind you pay to a guy so he'll keep quiet and the kind you pay to have a guy made quiet. Permanently quiet."

Carl felt the heat rising to his face. Unable to contain his anger any longer, he whirled around, ready to deliver one final verbal burst, pointing his finger at Joey DiPreta like a gun.

And Joey DiPreta doubled over, as if shot, as if somehow a metaphysical bullet had been fired from the finger Carl was pointing; or at least that was Carl's immediate impression.

Within a split-second the sound of the high-power rifle fire caught up with the .460 Magnum missile that had passed through

Joey DiPreta like a cheap Mexican dinner, tossing him in the air and knocking him off the mound and out of sight before Carl really understood what he'd just witnessed; before he really understood that he'd just seen a high-power bullet bore through a man and lift him up and send him tumbling lifelessly off the hillock.

Carl drew back the pointing finger and hit the deck, finally, rolled off the hill himself, to get out of the line of any further fire.

But there was none.

The assassin had hit his mark and fled, satisfied with his score for the afternoon, and why not? As one of Des Moines' finest would later caustically point out, it isn't every day somebody shoots a hole in one.

2

His name was Steven Bruce McCracken, but nobody called him any of those names. His friends called him Mac. His sister called him Stevie. His mother, when she was alive, called him Steve. His father, when he was alive, called him Butch. His crew had called him Sarge. The VC had called him a lot of things.

His reputation, it was said, was considerable among the Vietcong. That was what he'd heard from ARVN personnel, who themselves seemed a little in awe of him. To his own way of thinking, he'd never done anything so out of the ordinary; he was just one of many gunners, just another crew chief doing his job. As crew chief one of his responsibilities was to provide cover fire as men (usually wounded, since the bulk of his missions were Medivacs) were hustled aboard the helicopter. He would stand in the doorway, or outside of it, firing his contraband Thompson submachine gun (which he'd latched onto early in the game, picking it off a Cong corpse) and shouting obscenities in three languages at the usually unseen enemy, unflinching as return fire was sent his way, as if daring those gooks to hit him. Personally, he didn't see how any of that could build him any special reputation among the enemy or anyone else. He always suspected those damn ARVN were putting him on about it—he had trouble understanding them half the time anyway, his Vietnamese lingo consisting mostly of bar talk and their English being no better—but later G-2 had confirmed that he did indeed have a name in Charlie's camp. He supposed his appearance must've had something to do with whatever reputation he may have had. He stood out among the Americans, who, to the gooks, all looked alike, and he made a bigger target than most, which must've been frustrating as hell to the little bastards, missing a target so big. He was six-two and powerfully built—his body strung with holstered handguns and belts of ammunition and hand grenades—his white-blond hair and white-blond mustache (a slight, military-trim mustache that still managed a gunfighter's droop on either side), showing up vividly against his deeply tanned skin.

His appearance today, a month out of service, was little different, even if he wasn't wearing guns and ammo and grenades. True, the hair was already longer than the Marines would have liked, but other than that he looked much the same. His physical condition was outstanding; even his limp had lessened, seemed almost to have disappeared. A chunk of flesh along the inside of his right thigh had been blown away in the helicopter crash, just some fat and some not particularly valuable meat, leaving a hole six inches long by three inches wide, a purplish canyon that at its greatest depth was two inches. There was still some shrapnel in that hole, and pieces worked their way out now and then; he could feel them moving. Nothing to be worried about, really. He'd never look good in a bathing suit again, but what the hell? He was lucky. A few inches higher and he could've spent the rest of his life pissing through a tube and trying to remember what sex was like.

He'd been sole survivor of the crash. They'd been coming down into a clearing for a Medivac, and some fucking brush-hugging gook shot the hydraulic system out of the plane (they never called it a helicopter, always a plane) and made their landing premature and murderous. Coming down, they caught another shell, a big one, and at hover level the plane blew up and killed most of the men they'd been coming to save. He himself had been the only one on the scene who got off with relatively light injuries. The pilot lasted an hour, died just minutes before another plane came in to pick up survivors, which was him and two badly wounded ARVNs, one of them a lieutenant who died on the way back.

He had learned at the beginning not to form too close a friendship with any of his fellow crew members, because he'd had a whole goddamn crew shot from under him the first goddamn month. The damn mortality rate was just too fucking high for friendship.

But sometimes you can't avoid it.

The pilot had been a friend. A friend he'd talked with and laughed with. A friend he'd gone on R and R with in Bangkok. A friend he'd shared smokes and booze and women with. A friend he'd held in his arms while a sucking chest wound took care of the future.

His own wound, the wound in his thigh, was nothing. Nothing compared to the wound left by the loss of his friend. Trauma, it's called. At the hospital the powers that be decided he needed some visits with the staff psychiatrist, and by the time he was patched up again, mentally and physically, he was told that because of the trauma of losing the pilot and rest of the crew, because of that and his shot-up leg, he was being sent home.

That had been fine with him at the time, but soon the trauma had faded, as far as he was concerned, and the leg felt better, and he demanded to be sent back; he'd re-upped specifically because he *liked* combat. But barely into his first tour of his reenlistment, he was stuck stateside. He was told he would not be sent back to Vietnam, because *no* one was being sent back: the gradual withdrawal of troops was underway, with the Marines among the first in line to leave.

He had no regrets about Vietnam, other than not getting his fill of it. He would've liked to have had another crack at the gooks; losing another crew had only made him more eager to wade in and fight. But now, finally, he was glad to be out of the Corps. His last two years and some months had been spent at glorious Quantico, Virginia, which was the sort of base that made Vietnam seem like a pleasant memory. Stateside duty bored the ass off him; he preferred the war: that was where a soldier was meant to be, goddamn it, and besides, the pay was better. Sometimes he wished he had signed on as a mercenary, with Air America, instead of reenlisting in the Marines. As a mercenary he could've picked up a minimum of twelve thousand a year and be more than a damn toy soldier, playing damn war-games in the backwoods of Virginny.

But now that he was a civilian again—on the surface, anyway—he was glad he hadn't gone the Air America route. He might have been killed as a mercenary, which was a risk he wouldn't have minded taking before, and still didn't, but not for money. The money a mercenary could make, which had once looked so attractive to him, seemed meaningless now. Dying wasn't a disturbing concept to him, really; in fact sometimes it damn near appealed to him. What disturbed him was the thought of dying for no reason, without purpose. If he lost his life in pursuit of his private war, well, okay; at least he'd have died pursuing a worthwhile cause. You could argue the pros and cons of a Vietnam, but not this war, not *his* war. Anyone who knew the facts would agree—even the damn knee-jerk liberals, he'd wager.

Since parting company with Uncle Sugar, he'd been living alone in an apartment but spending some time with his sister and her small daughter. He didn't have a job, or, rather, he didn't have an employer. He told his sister he was planning to go to college starting second semester and actually had filled out applications for Drake, Simpson, and a couple of two-year schools in the area. Hell, he might even attend one of them, when his war was over; he had GI, he had it coming.

Not that he was thinking that far ahead. That was a fairy-tale happy ending, off in the fuzzy and distant future of a month from now, and he wasn't thinking any further ahead than the days his war would last. Yes, days. With a war as limited as this one, a few days should be enough, considering no further reconnaissance would be necessary, to seek out and destroy the enemy. He'd been over and over the legacy of tapes, documents, committing them to memory, all but word for word, and he now knew the patterns, the lifestyle of the DiPreta family like he knew his own. A few days of ambush, of psychological warfare, and the score would be settled, the war would be won. He might even survive to go to college and become a useful member of society as his sister wanted. Who could say.

It was 4:47 P.M. when he arrived at the two-story white clapboard house, the basement of which was his apartment. The neighborhood was middle to lower-middle class, the house located on East Walnut between East 14th and 15th Streets, two main drags cutting through Des Moines, 14th a one-way south, 15th a one-way north. His apartment's location was a strategically good one. Fourteenth and 15th provided access to any place in the city, with the east/west freeway, 235, a few blocks north; and he was within walking distance of the core of the DiPreta family's most blatantly corrupt activities. A short walk west on Walnut (he would have to circle the massive, impressively beautiful Capitol building, its golden dome shining even on a dull, overcast afternoon like this one) and he'd find the so-called East Side, the rundown collection of secondhand stores, seedy bars, garish nightclubs, greasy spoons and porno movie houses that crowded the capitol steps like a protest rally. The occasional wholly reputable business concern seemed out of place in this ever-deteriorating neighborhood, as if put there by accident, or as a practical joke. At one time the East Side had been the hub of Des Moines, the business district, the center of everything; now it was the center of nothing, except of some of the more squalid activities in the capital city.

Location wasn't the only nice thing about his living quarters; nicer yet was the privacy. He had his own entrance around back, four little cement steps leading down to the doorway. The apartment was one large room that took up all of the basement except for a walled-off laundry room, which he was free to use. He also had his own bathroom with toilet and shower, though he did have to go through the laundry room to get to it. Otherwise his apartment was absolutely private and he had no one bothering him; he saw the Parkers (the family he rented from) hardly at all. He had a refrigerator, a stove, and a formica-top table that took up one corner of the room as a make-do kitchenette. A day bed that in its couch identity was a dark green went well with the light-green-painted cement walls. There was also an empty bookcase he hadn't gotten around to filling yet, though some gun magazines and *Penthouse*s were stacked on the bottom shelf (he'd given up *Playboy* while in Nam, as he didn't care for its political slant), and a big double-door pine wardrobe for his clothes and such, which he kept locked.

The wardrobe was where he stowed the Weatherby, which he'd brought into the house carried casually under and over his arm. It was zipped up in a tan-and-black vinyl pouch, with foam padding and fleece lining, and he'd made no pretense about what he was carrying. He'd already explained to the Parkers that shooting was his hobby. Luckily, Mr. Parker was not a hunter or a gun buff, or he might've asked embarrassing questions. Someone who knew what he was talking about might have looked at the Weatherby and asked, "What you planning to shoot, lad? Big game?"

And he would've had to say, "That's exactly right."

He laid the Weatherby Mark V in the bottom of the wardrobe, alongside the rest of the small but substantial arsenal he'd assembled for his war: a Browning 9-millimeter automatic with checkered walnut grips, blue finish, fixed sights, and thirteen-shot magazine, in brown leather shoulder holster rig; a Colt Python revolver, blue, .357 Magnum with four-inch barrel, wide hammer spur and adjustable rear sight, in black leather hip holster; a Thompson submachine gun, .45 caliber, black metal, brown wood; boxes of the appropriate ammunition; and half a dozen pineapple-type hand grenades, which he'd made himself, buying empty shell casings, filling them with gunpowder, providing primers.

He closed the wardrobe but left it unlocked.

He felt fine. Not jumpy at all. He sniffed under his arms. Nothing, not a scent; this afternoon had been literally no sweat.

That was good to know, after some years away from actual combat. Good to know he hadn't lost his edge. And that the helicopter crash hadn't left him squeamish: that was good to know, too. Very.

But he took a shower anyway. The hot needles of water melted him; he dialed the faucet tight, so that the water pressure would stay as high as possible. If he told himself there was *no* tension in him, he'd be lying, he knew. He needed to relax, unwind. He'd stayed cool today, yes, but nobody stays *that* cool.

The phone rang and he cut his shower short, running bare-ass out to answer it, hopping from throw rug to throw rug to avoid the cold cement of a basement floor that was otherwise as naked as he was.

"Yes?" he said.

"Stevie, where've you been? I been trying to get you."

It was his sister, Diane. She was a year or two older than he, around thirty or so, but she played the older sister act to the hilt. It was even worse now, with their parents dead.

"I was out, Di."

"I won't ask where. I'm not going to pry."

"Good, Di."

"Well, I just thought you'd maybe like to come over tonight for supper, that's all. I came home over lunch hour and put a casserole in, and it'll be too much for just Joni and me."

Joni was her six-year-old daughter. Diane was divorced, but she hadn't gotten out of the habit of cooking for a family, and consequently he'd been eating at her place several nights a week this last month. Which was fine, as his specialty was canned soup and TV dinners.

"I'd like that, Di."

"Besides, I want to talk to you."

"About school, I suppose."

"About school, yes, and some other things. I'm your sister and interested in what you're doing. Is that so terrible?"

"Well, not a lot has changed since you saw me yesterday, Di."

"I give you free meals, you give me a hard time. Is that what you call a fair exchange?"

"Hey, I appreciate it, Sis. I even love you part of the time."

"When I put the plate of food down in front of you, especially."

"Yeah, especially then."

"Look, I got to get back to my desk. See you at six?"

"That'll be fine. What's for dinner? Casserole, you said."

"Oh, you're really going to love me tonight, little brother. Made one of your favorites."

"Oh yeah? What?"

"Lasagna."

Appropriate, he thought to himself, smiling a little.

"Stevie? Are you still there?"

"I'm still here, Di. See you at six."

3

Every day, both going to and coming from work, Diane would turn her head away as she drove by the little white clapboard house where her mother had been murdered. Across the way was a junk dealer's lot, a graveyard for smashed-up and broken-down automobiles, which she would shift her attention to to avoid looking at the house. The junkyard was hardly a pleasant landscape to gaze upon and even had its metaphorical suggestion of the very thing she wanted not to think about: death, destruction, mortality. But she would look at it every day, twice a day, rather than look at the house.

She would have avoided the whole road if that were possible, but there seemed to be no way to avoid this particular stretch of concrete. East 14th Street seemed to run through her life like her own personal interstate, complete with all the rest stops and exits of her life, significant and insignificant alike, everything from the insurance company where she worked to shopping centers, restaurants, movie theaters. Her mother's house, of course, was on East 14th; so was the Travelers Inn Motor Lodge, where her father had been manager and where, in his private suite of rooms, he had died. Her brother lived in an apartment on Walnut, just off East 14th, while she herself lived in an apartment house on the outskirts of Des Moines, where East 14th turns into Highway 65, the highway along which the DiPretas, her father's employers for so many years, lived each in their individual homes, enjoying the expanse of Iowa farm country between Des Moines and its small-town neighbor, Indianola.

It was a street that rolled up and down and over hills that seemed surprised to have a city on them. On her drive home, once past certain landmarks—the skyscraper outline of the Des Moines downtown, the awesome Capitol building, the bridge spanning the railroad yard—East 14th turned into an odd mélange of small businesses and middle-class homes, with random pockets of forest-type trees as a reminder of what had to be carved away to put a city here. It was an interesting drive, an interesting street, and she liked having access to all her needs on one easy route. But today, as every day, she averted her eyes as she drove by that little white clapboard house where her mother had been shot to death.

Diane didn't look at the house, just as she didn't look at the loss of her parents. She ignored both, because recognizing either would emotionally overwhelm her. She hid the pain away in some attic of her mind and went on with her life as though none of it had happened. She'd cried only twice during the course of the whole affair: first, on receiving the news of her mother's murder, and second, on hearing of her father's suicide. Both times she had cried until she hurt; until her chest hurt, her eyes hurt, until nothing hurt; until emptiness set in and she could feel nothing at all. After that, after crying those two times, she didn't cry any more. Not a tear. Even at the funeral she hadn't wept. People congratulated her on her strength, found it remarkable she'd been able to face the tragedy head on as she had. But they were wrong; she hadn't faced a thing, head on or otherwise. Facing it would have ripped her apart, left her emotions frayed and her mental state a shambles. So she faced nothing; she blocked off everything.

And she knew it. She knew that repressing emotion, letting the pressure build up behind some closed door in her head, was probably an unhealthy attitude. Sometimes she wished she *could* cry again, wished she *would* cry again. Sometimes she wished she could get it out, all of it. She'd lie in bed, consciously forcing the thoughts from her mind, feeling emotion churning in her stomach like something she couldn't digest. Wishing that were the case, wishing it were that simple, wishing she could stick a finger down her throat and make herself heave all of that bile out of her system.

Her husband, Jerry, used to try to make her talk about it; talk it out, get rid of it. It wasn't that Jerry was a particularly sensitive individual, Christ no. She smiled bitterly at the thought. Jerry just wanted in her pants all the time; that was Jerry's only concern. After her parents died she lost interest in sex, which had of course bruised Jerry's overinflated ego. She didn't know why, but she just felt cold toward Jerry as far as sex was concerned. Nothing stirred in her, no matter what he tried.

And try he did. Before, he'd never been particularly sex-oriented during their marriage; after the first year, it had been a three-times-a-week affair: Friday, Saturday, Wednesday, a passionless, clockwork ritual. She used to feel slightly rejected because of that, since she'd always been told she was sexy and sexy-looking, had always been sought after by guys and liked to think of herself as cute. Sure, maybe her boobs weren't so big, but how often did a guy meet up with a girl with natural platinum blonde hair and the blue eyes to go with it? She *was* cute, goddamnit, and knew it, and was proud of it. She'd always *liked* sex, had *fun* with it; that had been a lot of what she'd liked about Jerry, though Jerry the Tiger had turned tame after a marriage license made it legal. That was Jerry, all right: back-seat stud, mattress dud. But when he found out about her newly acquired sexual reluctance, Christ, then he was waving a damn erection in her face every time she looked at him. Which was as seldom as she could help it.

"You're frigid," he'd tell her, and she wouldn't say anything. After all, she didn't turn him away; she just wasn't particularly responsive. And how the hell could she help that? How the hell could she help how she *felt*? You don't turn love and sex on like tap water, Jerry. "If you didn't think about your parents all the time, we wouldn't have this problem," he would say. I am *not* thinking about my parents, she'd say. "Oh, but you are. You're thinking about *not* thinking about them." That doesn't make sense, Jerry. "It makes more sense than you, you frigid goddamn bitch." And she would say, all right, Jerry, do it to me if you want, Jerry, you will anyway. And he would. And she would feel nothing.

Nothing except contempt for her husband, which blossomed into the divorce, which as yet was not final, as the law's ninety-day wait (to allow opportunity for reconciliation) wasn't quite up. But the marriage was over, no doubt of that. Diane was aware that even before the divorce thing arose Jerry had been seeing other girls; and mutual friends had told her recently that Jerry had already narrowed his field to one girl, who oddly enough was also a platinum blonde (not natural, she'd wager) and who had a more than superficial resemblance to somebody named Diane. Which seemed to her a sick, perverse damn thing for the son of a bitch to do.

She thought back to what he'd said to her the night their marriage exploded into mutual demands for divorce. He'd said, "You're cold, Diane. Maybe not frigid, but cold. You got yourself so frozen over inside you don't feel a goddamn fucking thing for or about anybody."

It was a blow that had struck home at the time, a game point Jerry had won but a thought she'd discarded later, after some reflection. She wasn't cold inside. She could still feel. She could still love. She loved little Joni more than anything in the world. She was filled with the warmth of love every time she held her daughter in her arms, and she was having trouble, frankly, not spoiling the child because of that.

And there was Stevie. She loved her "little" brother, damn near as much as her little girl. She worried about him, hoped his life would take on some direction, hoped there wasn't an emotional time bomb in him, ticking inside him, because he too had shown no outward emotional response to the deaths of their mother and father.

And why wasn't Stevie going out with any girls? It wasn't right, wasn't like Stevie, who was a notorious pussy-chaser. She hoped he hadn't contracted some weird jungle strain of VD over there and couldn't have normal relations because of it. She asked him what was wrong, why wasn't he dating or anything, and he explained he wanted "no extra baggage right now." That was unhealthy. A man needed a good sex life.

True, she was hardly the one to talk, hardly the one to be

dispensing advice to the sexually lovelorn. She hadn't seen any men since breaking with Jerry, hadn't gone out once. Hadn't had sex, hadn't been close to having sex, since Jerry's last rape attempt almost eight months ago. Hadn't had any desire for it.

Her social life was limited and anything but sexy, but she enjoyed it. She spent her evenings with her daughter, watching television, playing games, sometimes going to movies, when she could find one rated G. If Joni wanted to stay overnight with her friend Sally, downstairs, well, that was fine; Diane could catch another, more adult film with one of the girls from the office. And now with brother Stevie home from service, she could have him over and cook for him and have him join their diminutive family circle and add some needed masculine authority.

She was just a few blocks from the apartment house now. She glanced at the clock on the Pontiac's instrument panel and switched on the radio to catch the news. The newscaster was in the middle of a story about a shooting that had taken place earlier that afternoon. She didn't catch the name of the victim, but she heard enough of the story to tell it was a ghastly affair, a piece of butchery out of a bad dream. Some psychopath sniper was loose, had cut a man down with a high-power rifle in broad daylight, on the golf course of an exclusive local country club. She shivered and switched off the radio. That was just the sort of thing she *didn't* need to hear about.

She pulled into the apartment-housing parking lot. She saw her brother's car in the lot and smiled. Christ, it was good to have Stevie home.

4

Vincent DiPreta was known, in his earlier, more colorful days, as Vince the Burner—even though he himself rarely set fire to anything outside of his Havana cigars. The name grew out of Vincent's pet racket, which was bust-outs. A bust-out is setting up a business specifically with arson in mind, and it works something like this: You set yourself up in an old building or store picked up for peanuts; you build a good credit rating by finding some legitimate citizen looking for a fast buck and willing to front for you; you use that credit to stockpile merchandise, which will be moved out the back door for fencing just prior to the "accidental" fire; you burn the place down, collect the insurance on the building and its contents, and declare bankruptcy. A torch artist out of Omaha did the burning for Vincent; theirs was an association that dated back to the forties and lasted well into the seventies. Vincent was dabbling in bust-outs long after he and the rest of his family had otherwise moved into less combustible and (superficially, at least) more respectable areas of business.

In fact, during the course of his bust-out career, Vincent was so brazen as to burn two of his own places, right there in Des Moines. Even for Vince the Burner that took gall. "You don't shit where you eat, Vince," he was told the first time; but nobody said anything the second go-around, as the sheer fucking balls of the act was goddamn awe inspiring. First he'd burned one of his two plush, high-overhead key clubs. Both had been big money-makers for years, but when liquor by the drink passed in Iowa and made the key-club idea a thing of the past, he decided to convert one of the clubs into a straight bar/nightclub and put the torch to the other. Then, a few years later, he'd burned DiPreta's Italian Restaurant on East 14th, because he was planning to remodel the place anyway, so what the hell? And besides, most of the money had gone to the Church, who deserved it more than some goddamn insurance company, for Christ's sake.

Vincent was a good Catholic, or at least his own version of one. His wife went to Mass every Sunday, and his money did too, though he himself stayed home. In recent years, when his teenage son, Vince Jr., had contracted leukemia, Vincent had upped his already generous contributions to the Church in response to their priest's suggestion that the son's illness was repayment for wrongdoings committed by the DiPreta family over the years. Vince Jr.'s illness was a classic example of the son paying for the sins of the father, the priest suggested, and a monetary show of faith might help even the score. This sounded worth a try to Vince Sr.—maybe a healthy donation to the Church would work as a sort of miracle drug for Vince Jr.—and Vincent promptly got in touch with his torch-artist friend in Omaha for one last fling. DiPreta's Italian Restaurant burned, got remodeled and was now doing as good as ever—no use busting out a money-maker, after all.

But it hadn't done much good for Vince Jr., who died anyway, despite massive injections of cash into the local diocese coffers. And even though their priest had been on a nice DiPreta-paid trip to Rome when Vince Jr. passed away, Vincent bore no bitterness toward the Church. No promises had been made, no miracles guaranteed. Secretly, however, he couldn't help wishing his and his son's salvation was in more reliable hands, though he said just the opposite to his wife Anna.

It was no secret, though, to Anna or anyone else, how hard

Vincent took the death of his son, his only son. Vince the Burner had always been a fat man, the stereotype of a jolly, heavyset patriarchal Italian. But after his son died, Vincent began to lose weight. He immersed himself in his work as never before, pushing harder when age dictated slowing down, but at the same time seeming to care less about his work than ever before. He developed a bleeding ulcer, which required several operations and a restricted diet that made his weight drop like a car going off a cliff. The expression "shadow of his former self" was never more apt. The six-foot Vincent dropped from two hundred and fifty-five pounds to one hundred and sixty-three pounds in a year's time.

Vincent had been a handsome fat man, a round, jovial, eminently likable man. As a skinny man, Vincent was something else again. The flesh hung on him like a droopy suit, loose and stretched from years of carrying all that weight around; the firmly packed jowls of fat Vincent were jolly, while the sacklike jowls of skinny Vincent were repulsive. His face took on a melancholy look, his small dark eyes hidden in a face of layered, pizza-dough flesh. It was as though a large man's face had been transposed to a smaller man's smaller skull. The features seemed slack, almost as if they were about to slide off his face like shifting, melting wax.

If, these last seven years since the death of his son, Vincent DiPreta's countenance seemed a melancholy one, then on this evening that countenance could only be described as one of tragic proportions. He sat in a small meeting room at a table the size of two card tables stuck together and wept silently, pausing now and then to dab his eyes with an increasingly dampening handkerchief. There was a phone on the table, which he glanced at from time to time, and a bottle of Scotch whisky and a glass, which Vincent had been making use of, his restricted diet for the moment set aside. He was smoking a cigar—or at least one resided in the ashtray before him, trails of smoke winding toward air vents in the cubicle-size meeting room—and it seemed a strange reminder of Vincent DiPreta's former "fat man" image. When he would take it from the ashtray and hold it in his fingers, the cigar seemed almost ready to slip away, as if expecting the pudgy fingers of seven years ago.

Vincent had been sitting alone in the room for an hour now. He had heard the news of his brother's death on the car radio on his way home from his office at Middle America Builders. But he hadn't gone home; he couldn't face Anna and the deluge of tears she'd have to offer him over the loss of Joey. He'd called her on the phone and soothed her, as if Joey had been *her* damn brother (Anna had always had a special fondness for Joe—but then so had everybody in the family) and he had come here, to the new DiPreta's Italian Restaurant, for privacy, for a booth to hide in in a moment or two of solitary mourning. The restaurant was closed when he got there (it was six now; they were just opening upstairs), and he'd walked through the darkened dining room, where the manager and hostess mumbled words of condolence—"We're so very sorry, Mr. DiPreta," "We'll miss him, Mr. DiPreta"—and he headed downstairs to one of many small conference rooms. The whole lower floor was, in fact, a maze of such rooms, used by the DiPretas and any visiting mob personae, whenever unofficial official business needed to be discussed.

Many high-level mob meetings had taken place on DiPreta turf these past five or six years or so, even though the DiPretas themselves did little more than host the meets. There were several reasons for Des Moines being the site of meetings of such importance. For one thing, many older members of the Chicago Family, the aging elder statesmen, had chosen Des

Moines as a place to retire to, since Chicago was going to hell and the blacks, and the Iowa capital city was possessed of a low crime rate and a metropolitan but nonfrantic atmosphere that reminded them of Chicago in its better days. Whenever the Family needed to consult these retired overlords, which they did both out of respect and to seek the good counsel the old men could provide, a meeting place would be furnished by the DiPretas. And the DiPretas would do the same whenever the Family wanted to confab with other crime families, such as Kansas City and Detroit, for example, because Des Moines made a convenient meeting place, pleasantly free of the federal surveillance afflicting the Chicago home base. Until not long ago, meetings were divided pretty evenly between the restaurant and the Traveler's Lodge Motel, with the nod going to the latter most often; but then the McCracken problem arose, and both the DiPretas and the Family had quickly gotten out of the habit of utilizing the Traveler's Lodge facilities. Even with Jack McCracken gone, a bad taste lingered.

The door opened. Frank DiPreta joined his brother in the small conference room. Frank was a thin man but a naturally thin one, a dark and coldly handsome man with a pencil-line mustache. At fifty-three he was an older version of the deceased Joey but without Joey's blue eyes. Frank's eyes were dark, cloudy and, at the moment, slightly reddened. He wore a black suit, which was not his custom, and a .38 revolver in a shoulder holster, which was. He alone of the DiPreta brothers had continued carrying heat these past ten or twelve years, and he'd been alternately teased and scolded for the practice by Joey and Vince, who'd insisted "those days" were long over. Eventually he would say, "I told you so." Now was not the time. He joined his brother at the table.

Vincent studied his brother. Frank's face was set in its typical stoic expression and betrayed no hint of emotional strain. His eyes were a little red, but there was no other indication. Still, there seemed to be waves of tension coming from the normally calm Frank that were just enough to worry Vincent. Six years ago, when Frank's wife had been killed in an automobile accident, Frank had tried to maintain his standard hard-guy stance; but gradually cracks had formed in Frank's personal wall, and the emotional strain, the pain, the anger began to show through. And, ultimately, Frank had responded to the situation with an act of violence. Vincent studied his brother's seemingly emotionless expression, wondering if that would happen again.

"Vince, you shouldn't drink."

"Frank, I know. Have you taken care of everything?"

"Yes."

"The services?"

"Saturday morning."

"Who will say the Mass?"

"Father DeMarco."

"Good. He's a good man."

"Well I like him better than that son of a bitch you sent to Rome."

Vincent nodded.

Frank looked at the ceiling awhile, then suddenly he said, "The funeral parlor guy says the casket should stay shut."

"I see."

"He says he can't make Joey look like Joey."

"I see."

"You don't see shit, Vince. You want to see something, go down and see Joey. Go down and see goddamn meat with a twisted-up expression on its goddamn face."

The wall was cracking already.

"Then the casket will be shut, Frank. It'll be all right."

"All right? All right shit. Vince, do you know the size of the slug it was Joey caught?"

"Four-sixty Magnum. You told me on the phone."

"Hell, he didn't even *catch* it, it went straight fucking through him. Jesus. You could kill a fucking rhino with that. What kind of sick son of a bitch would do a thing like that?"

"I don't know, Frank. It's all very confusing to me."

"Well, I don't see what's confusing about it. Some son of a bitch killed our brother. Okay. Now we find out who and kill the fucker."

"But why was Joey killed? That's the question I can't get out of my mind. Why?"

Frank, realizing he'd slipped into emotional high gear, eased back behind his wall, shrugged and said, "We're in the kind of business that makes you unpopular sometimes, Vince."

"Even if I agreed with that, I don't see it applying to Joey. He was the least involved in family business of all of us."

"Maybe he was messing with something married. You know Joey and his women, Vince. You know what a crazy lad Joey was."

"He was a man. He was forty years old."

"He was a kid. He'll always be a kid."

And Frank touched the bridge of his nose with two fingers and swallowed hard.

His wall wasn't holding up very well at all.

"Frank, could it have anything to do with that politician Joey was talking to today?"

"Who, Carl Reed? No. I don't think Joe had even made the pitch to the guy yet, about paying him off to keep quiet about Grayson's kickbacks and all, remember? At least I know Reed hasn't said anything to the cops about anything. I talked to Cummins, and he interrogated Reed himself, Cummins and that nigger partner of his. Cummins says Reed didn't have much to say, outside of how horrified about the shooting he was, bullshit like that. Listen, Vince, what about Chicago?"

"No. Not yet. Only as a last resort, Frank. We can handle this ourselves."

"Maybe they know of some hit man who goes in for big guns or something. You could just ask them."

"No, I don't even want to call them and tell them about it."

"Hell, Vince, they'll find out soon enough, probably know already, thanks to the Family retirement village we got going in this town. At least one of those old Family guys has heard it on the news and called Chicago by now, you know that."

"I'm not going to call them. I'm not going to encourage them. I don't want them sending in one of those damn headhunters of theirs."

Frank thought for a moment, then nodded. "You're right. This is family, not Family. We'll handle it ourselves."

"The last time they sent anyone around, you know what happened."

"The McCracken fuck-up." Frank shook his head. "Seemed like we were tripping over dead bodies for a week."

"They got no finesse. Their example makes me glad we're getting to be mostly legitimate nowadays."

"Well and good, Vince, but if Papa was alive..."

"He isn't."

"If he was, he'd say this is a matter of blood, and we got to forget our goddamn business ethics and civic image and that bullshit. We got Joey's death to even up for, Vince, and we're going to even up, goddamnit. Not slop-ass, like the Chicago wise guys'd handle it. No way. We just find the guy and whack him out, clean and simple, and it's not even going to be *remotely* connected up to us."

Vincent studied his brother. Inside Frank's cool shell was a hothead wanting to get out. Frank was prone to violence anyway, as for example, his carrying a gun all the time, even though that part of the business had faded into the past long ago. This situation, Vincent thought, could prove to be a bad one for Frank, as bad or worse than when his wife died. This situation could open the door on all the bad things in the secret closets of Frank's mind; it could tear down Frank's wall once and for all.

Vince touched his brother's arm. "Let's sleep on this, let our emotions settle. We'll take care of whoever killed Joey. We'll choose a course of action on that tomorrow. But first we got a brother to bury."

Frank nodded and fell silent for a moment. Then something occurred to him, and he reached inside his sports coat to get at the inner pocket and withdrew an envelope. "Tell me what you make of this, Vince." He handed the envelope to Vincent.

Vincent looked at the outer envelope. It was typewritten, addressed to Joseph DiPreta, no return address. Judging from the postmark, it had been delivered yesterday, mailed locally. Inside the envelope was a playing card. An ace of spades.

"Hmmm," Vincent said.

"What the hell is that, anyway? Who sends a goddamn playing card in the mail, and for what?"

Vincent shrugged. "For one thing, the ace of spades signifies death."

"That thought ran through my mind, don't think it didn't. So what the hell's it mean? Is it a warning that was sent to Joey? Or maybe a promise."

Vincent withdrew a similar envelope from his own inside pocket. "Maybe it's a declaration of war," he said.

He opened the envelope and revealed the playing card inside —also an ace of spades—to his brother.

"I received this at the office, Frank, in the mail. This morning."

Two:
Thursday Night

5

Nolan didn't know what to think. The situation was ideal, really, but he wasn't sure how the Family would react to his wanting out.

It wasn't as if he were someone important in the Family; in fact, it wasn't as if he were someone in the Family at all. He was a minor employee who was probably more bother to them than he was worth, and he certainly wasn't involved in anything important enough to make it matter whether or not he stayed.

Years ago it had been different. Years ago he'd left the Family and all hell had broken loose. He had been in a position then not so very different from the one he was in now. He'd been managing a nightclub on Rush Street for mob backers; today he was doing the same thing, essentially, with a motel and supper-club arrangement out in the Illinois countryside, sixty or seventy miles out of Chicago. But today, at least, they were leaving him alone, not trying to involve him in any of their bloodletting and bone-breaking bullshit. Fifteen, sixteen years ago they had asked him to leave his club on Rush Street and move into head-crushing, a field that didn't particularly appeal to him.

He supposed his reputation for being a hard-nose, which had developed from his doing his own bouncing in that Rush Street joint, had convinced the Family high-ups that he'd make a good enforcer and that because of his administrative background in managing clubs he'd therefore have the potential to move up in the organization, a young exec who could start at the bottom and work up.

Except up was one place Nolan had no desire to go. Not in the Family, anyway. There were few things in life Nolan wouldn't do for money, but killing people was one of them. Later on, when he'd become involved in full-scale, big-time heists, an occasional innocent bystander might get in the way of a bullet, sure. A cop, a nightwatchman could go down; that was part of his job and theirs. A fellow heister with ideas of double-cross on his mind might get blown away—fine. That was a hazard of war; he could live with that. Going up to some poor guy in a parking lot and putting a .45 behind his ear and blasting—that was something else again. That was psycho stuff, that was for the ice-water-in-the-veins boys, the animals, and he wanted no fucking part of it.

But the Family had decided that that was the way they wanted him to go, and to start him off, to make him a "made man," they asked him to knock off a friend of his who worked with him at the club. This friend had evidently been messing around with some Family guy's prize pussy and had earned himself a place on the shittiest shit list in town. Nolan said no on general principles, and besides, he couldn't see knocking off a piece was worth knocking off a guy over and told them so. Told them he was going to tell his friend all about it if the hit wasn't called off. And he was assured it would be. The next day his friend was found swimming in the river. And a couple of gallons of the river was found swimming in his friend.

So Nolan resigned from the Family. This is how Nolan resigned: he went to the office of the guy who'd ordered the hit—the same stupid goddamn guy who'd been trying so hard to get Nolan to kill people for money—and Nolan shot him through the head. For free. Or almost for free. Afterward Nolan and twenty thou from the Family till disappeared.

An open contract went out.

The open contract stayed open for a long time. Something like sixteen years, during which time Nolan moved into heisting. He'd shown a natural ability for organization, running that club for the Family (getting Rush Street's perennial loser into the black in his first three months), and that same ability worked even more profitably for him as a professional thief. Nolan organized and led institutional robberies (banks, jewelry stores, armored cars, mail trucks) and had a flawless record: a minimum of violence, a maximum of dollars. A Nolan heist was as precise and perfect as a well-performed ballet, as regimented and timed to the split-second as a military operation, with every option covered, every possibility of human error considered. It was the old Dillinger/Karpis school of professional robbery, with refinements, and it still worked good as ever. Perhaps better. No member of a Nolan heist had ever spent an hour behind bars—at least not in conjunction with anything Nolan had engineered.

A couple of years ago Nolan had heard that his Family troubles had cooled off. His source seemed reliable, and after all, it was into the second decade since all that happened, so why *shouldn't* things cool off? He loosened up some of his precautions (the major one being to stay out of the Chicago area altogether) and had been doing preliminary work in Cicero on a bank job when some Family muscle spotted him and guns started going off. It took over a month to recover from that, and when he came out of hiding, recuperated, but weak and tired of getting shot at, he arranged a sitdown with the Family to negotiate an end to the goddamn war.

The sitdown hadn't worked. There'd been more gunfire and more months of recuperating from Family-induced bullet wounds. But then something had happened. A change in regime in Chicago, a relatively bloodless Family coup, turned everything around. One day Nolan woke up and his Family enemies were gone and in their place was the new regime, who viewed Nolan, enemy of the former ruling class, as a comrade in arms.

As a reward of sorts, Nolan had been set up at the Tropical, a motel with four buildings (sixteen units each), two heated swimming pools (one outdoor, one in) and another central building that housed the supper club whose pseudo-Caribbean decor gave the place its name. Actually, the Tropical was a trial-run center where potential managers for similar but bigger Family operations were given a try. Nolan had been in the midst of just such a trial run when nearly half a million bucks of his (with which he was set to buy into one of those bigger Family operations) was stolen and eventually went up in smoke. Since his agreement with the Family had been to buy in and since he no longer could, Nolan was asked by Felix—the Family lawyer through whom Nolan had been doing all of his Family dealings of late—to stay on at the Tropical and supervise other trial runs, sort of manage the managers.

It was a terrific deal as far as workload compared to salary went. Pretty good money for sitting around bored, only Nolan didn't like sitting around bored. In his opinion sitting around bored was boring as hell, and his ass got sweaty besides. He guessed maybe he'd been part of the active side too long to chuck it completely, even if he did find the prospect of no longer having to duck Family bullets a nice one.

Earlier this month Nolan had struck out in response to the boredom of the Tropical. The nephew of an old business partner of his had been tagging along with Nolan lately, and he and this kid, Jon, had pulled a heist in Detroit just last week that had run into some snags but eventually came out okay, resulting in a good chunk of change ($200,000—in marked bills, unfortunately, but easily fenced at seventy cents on the dollar), and now Nolan was again in a position to buy in.

Only not with the Family. Because a condition of Nolan's present employment with the Family was that he was not to engage in heists anymore. The Family had gone to great lengths to build a new identity for him, an identity that had everything from credit cards to college education, and they did not like their employees (those involved in the legitimate side of their operations, anyway) risking everything by doing something stupid.

Like pulling a heist.

So Nolan was frustrated. He had money again, but no place to spend it. He had a job again, managing a supper club and motel, which was ideal, but the job was numbing and thankless and paid okay but not really enough to suit him. He had his freedom again, with no one in particular trying to kill him, but it was an empty freedom. He was on a desert island with Raquel Welch and he couldn't get it up.

He was sitting in the basement of Wagner's house. The basement was remodeled. There was a bar at the end opposite the couch Nolan was sitting on. Between the bar and the couch most of the space was taken up by a big, regulation-size pool table. The lighting was dim, but there was a Tiffany-shade hanging lamp over the pool table you could turn on if need be. There was a dartboard, a poker table, a central circular metallic fireplace, all of which was to Nolan's right. It was obviously a bachelor's retreat, in this case an aging bachelor. Wagner had been married once but just for a short time, and that was a lot of years ago. There were framed prints of naked sexy women on the dark blue stucco walls: Vargas, Petty, Earl Moran. Good paintings, but very dated: Betty Grable-style women, Dorothy Lamour-style women. The fantasy of a generation that grew up without *Playboy*, let alone *Penthouse*; the fantasy of a generation that masturbated to pictures of girls in bathing suits. The fantasy of Wagner's generation, an old man's generation.

Nolan's generation.

Nolan was fifty years old and pissed off about it. Wagner was his friend, but Wagner irritated him, because Wagner was only a few years older than Nolan and was an old fucking man. Wagner was going on his third heart attack. Wagner's doctor had told him to quit smoking. Wagner's doctor had told him to quit drinking. Wagner had done neither, and was on his way to his third heart attack.

Wagner was down at the bar end of the room, building drinks. He was a small, thin, intense man who was trying intensely not to be intense anymore. He had the pallor of a man who just got out of prison, though it had been maybe twenty-five years since his one prison term. Wagner was lucky he hadn't spent more time in stir than that, the way Nolan saw it. Wagner had been a box-man, a professional safecracker, and, what's more, he'd been the best and, as such, in demand; but instead of picking only the plums, Wagner had taken everything he could, every goddamn job that came his way. That was stupid, Nolan knew. You take only a few jobs a year and only the ones that smell absolutely 100 percent right. Otherwise you find yourself in the middle of a job as sloppy as Fibber McGee's closet and afterward in a jail cell about as big. Otherwise you find yourself with a bunch of punks who afterward shoot you behind the ear rather than give you your split.

Of course Wagner's skill contributed to keeping even the most ill-advised scores from being sloppy, and that same skill made him worth having around, so perhaps, Nolan conceded, perhaps Wagner had some assurance of not being crossed, even by punks. But none of that had mattered a damn to Wagner. Wagner had been the intense sort of guy who had to work, had to work all the time, much as possible, and Nolan knew the little man was lucky he was alive and out of stir. Lucky as hell.

Another thing about Wagner, he'd saved his money. Wagner had dreamed of retiring early and getting into something legitimate, more or less. It was a dream Nolan could understand; he had it himself. The difference was Nolan's fifteen-year savings turned to so much air when a carefully built cover got blown, making it impossible for him to go near the bank accounts where even now that money was making tens of thousands of dollars interest every year.

Wagner had been lucky. He got out early (age fifty) and with a nest egg so big Godzilla might've laid it. He bought the old Elks Club in Iowa City and turned it into a restaurant and nightclub combined. The old Elks building was three floors, counting the remodeled lower level, which Wagner converted into a nightclub below, supper-club above, and banquet room above that. It was Nolan's dream come true, only Wagner'd made it work where Nolan hadn't.

But Wagner'd made it work too well. Wagner went after the restaurant business with the same vengeance he had heisting. And at fifty-two he'd had his first heart attack. Slow down, the doctor said, among other things. At fifty-three he'd had his second heart attack. Slow *down*, goddamn it, the doctor said, among other things. And now, at fifty-four, he was on his way to his third and had, on the spur of the moment, invited his old friend Nolan over to ask him if he wanted to buy in and be his partner and take some of the load off and help him avoid that third and no doubt fatal heart attack.

Wagner looked relaxed, anyway. He was wearing a yellow sports shirt with pale gray slacks, like his complexion, only healthier. Nolan was dressed almost identically, though his sports shirt was blue and his pants brown.

Their clothes began and ended the similarity of the two men's appearances. Wagner was white-haired, cut very short but lying down, like a butch that surrendered. His face was flat: his nose barely stuck out at all. It was a nebbish face, saved only by a giving, sincere smile. Nolan's face, on the other hand, seemed uncomfortable when it smiled, as if smiling were against its nature. He was a tall man, lean but muscular and with a slight paunch from easy days of Tropical non-work. He had a hawkish look, high cheekbones and narrow eyes; perhaps an American Indian was in his ancestry somewhere. His hair was shaggy and black and widow's peaked, with graying sideburns. He wore a mustache, a droopy, gunfighter mustache that underlined his naturally sour expression. Nolan did have a sense of humor, but he didn't want it getting around.

Wagner skirted the pool table, almost bumping into it, bringing the drinks back from the bar too fast.

"Take it easy, Wag," Nolan said, taking the Scotch from his friend. "I'm out of breath just watching you."

"Shit, I'm just excited to see you again after so long. Didn't Planner ever mention I was in town?"

"I guess maybe he did once. But it slipped my mind."

Wagner and Nolan had run into each other on the street this afternoon, in Iowa City. Planner was the business associate of Nolan's, dead now, whose nephew Jon had been Nolan's companion on his last three "adventures," as Jon might put it.

"I'm sorry as hell about Planner. I guess I was the only one at his funeral from the old days. The only one there who knew him before he retired."

Planner, too, had been active in professional thievery and had retired—or semi-retired—twenty years ago. In his remaining years, Planner (as his name would imply) had continued to help Nolan and other pros in the planning of jobs, using his Iowa City antique shop as a front.

"I never did get the story on how Planner got it, Nolan. I mean, I don't buy him dying of old age, for Christ's sake. He was too tough an old bird for that. I wish I had his ticker."

"Well, he didn't exactly pass away in his sleep."

"That's how it sounded in the paper."

"It better have, considering what I paid out to Doc Ainsworth for the death certificate."

"What really happened?"

"He was watching some money for me, and some guys came in and shot him and took it."

"Jesus. Did you find those guys? And your money?"

"The guys are dead. Or one of them is, anyway. The other one was what you might call an unwitting accomplice, and I let him go. I'm getting soft in my old age."

"What about the money?"

"Gone. Irretrievable."

"Well, what money was it? I mean, from one job or what?"

"It was all of my money, Wag. Everything I had."

Wagner stroked his thin gray face, and Nolan could see embarrassment flickering nervously in the man's eyes. Embarrassment because Wagner had earlier, on impulse, proposed to Nolan that he join with Wagner in the restaurant business—but that proposal had been made on Wagner's assumption that Nolan would have a healthy nest egg of his own.

Nolan took him off the hook. "I'm not broke, Wag, if that's what your latest heart attack's about."

Wagner grinned. "Jesus, Nolan, I'm sorry if I..."

"Fuck it. Money, I got. Not as much as I'd like, but enough to buy in, I think. I think I can muster seventy grand."

"Oh, well, no sweat, then."

"If I bought in, I'd want it rigged so I could eventually take over the entire ownership. I want my own place, Wag."

"I know. That's how I used to think. It's how I still think, but

I got to slow down, Nolan, you know that. I'm thinking maybe I'll spend the winters in Florida, or something. You lay some heavy money on me and I can go buy me a condominium and stay down there half the year or something, you know? I got to slow down."

Wagner said all that in about five seconds, which indicated to Nolan how much chance there was of Wagner slowing down. He could picture the little guy running along the shore in Florida grabbing up seashells like a son of a bitch.

"Look, Wag, this appeals to me. You don't know how this appeals to me. But I got a funny situation going with Chicago."

"I thought you said..."

"Yeah. Everything's straight. All the guys who wanted me dead are dead themselves. But I'm in with these guys, the new ones, and they been treating me pretty good. I got a not bad set-up with them as it is. And there's some complications you don't know about that I can't tell you about."

"But you will think about it."

"Sure I will."

"I'd like to have you aboard, Nolan."

"I know you would. I'd like to be aboard, Wag. The only thing I don't like about you, Wag, is it makes me so fucking tired watching you take it easy."

"Well, I *am* taking it easy, Nolan, damnit."

"Then what are you shaking your goddamn foot for, Wag?"

Wagner's legs were crossed and he was shaking his foot. He stopped. He grinned at Nolan. "You buy in and I'll take it easy. You'll see."

"Well, I want to be sole owner of the place, Wag, but I'd rather buy you out eventually than have you die on me and leave me the damn place in your will. So quit running life like it's the goddamn four-minute mile or something, will you?"

"Jesus, Nolan. Now you're a philosopher."

"It's just my arteries hardening. It goes with senility."

"How old are you, anyway?"

"Fifty."

"You look younger. You look like you always did."

"Not with my clothes off I don't. I mean, I'm not going to show you, but take my word for it. I got enough scars you could chart a map on me."

"Hey, you want to check my books over, Nolan, look into how I been running the place?"

"Let's think about it first. If I seriously think I'll want to buy in, then we'll go into that. How about getting me another Scotch?"

"Sure!"

"But take your fucking time, Wag. Nobody's holding a stopwatch over you."

While Wagner was building new drinks, the phone rang. Fortunately it was on the bar, otherwise, Nolan supposed, Wag would've gone running after it like a fireman responding to the bell.

"For you," Wagner said. "It's that lad, Planner's nephew."

Nolan went to the phone. "What is it, Jon?"

"I'm sorry to bother you, Nolan, but you better get over here right away. There's some guy with a gun here who wants to talk to you."

"Christ, kid, what the hell's happening? You okay?"

"Yeah, I got things in control, I guess. But I'll feel better about it with you here."

"I'm on my way."

He slammed the phone down, said, "Got to be going, Wag, catch you later," and headed up the stairs two at a time.

From down below him Wagner said, "Hey, Nolan! What's the rush?"

6

The floor was covered with comic strips. Old Sunday pages from the thirties, forties, early fifties, spread across the floor of his room like a four-color, pulp-paper carpet, but God help anybody who dared walk across that carpet; Jon'd kill 'em. Hell, some of the pages were so brittle, around the edges anyway, that heavy breathing was enough to turn precious paper into worthless flakes.

In fact, that was a problem Jon was doing his best to take care of now. He was sitting in the middle of the strip-covered floor, sitting like an Indian waiting for the pipe to be passed to him, and was painstakingly trimming the yellowed edges of the pages with barber shears, returning each strip, when properly trimmed, to its respective stack. He had already cut the pages up and sorted them, stacking each character individually—Li'l Abner, Terry and the Pirates, Joe Palooka, Alley Oop, dozens of others. Later, on another day, he would tackle the oppressive job of arranging them chronologically. Even a diehard comics freak like Jon had his breaking point, after all.

Jon was twenty-one years old. He was short—barely over five and a half feet tall—but with the build of a fullback in miniature; he'd worked his tail off to get in shape, through Charles Atlas muscle-building courses (anytime a bully wanted to kick sand in Jon's face, Jon was ready) and continued on with isometrics and lifting weights. His hair was brown and curly—a white man's Afro—his eyes blue, his nose turned up in a manner he considered piggish but most girls, thank God, found it cute. He was wearing his usual apparel: worn jeans, tennis shoes,

T-shirt with satirical superhero Wonder Warthog on the front.

His life was wrapped up in comic art. He was an aspiring cartoonist himself and a devoted collector of comic books and strips and related memorabilia. He had no profession, outside of comics, having dropped out of college several years ago because of a lack of funds. He'd intended to go back when he got the cash, but when he finally did get it (from that bank robbery he'd been a part of, with Nolan) he'd had so much money that going back to school seemed irrelevant.

The comic-strip "carpet" Jon was presently in the midst of was a fitting accompaniment to the rest of the room. The walls were all but papered with posters of famous comics characters, which Jon had drawn himself: Dick Tracy, Flash Gordon, Tarzan, Buck Rogers, Batman, recreated in pen and ink and watercolor, uncanny facsimiles of their original artists' style. The room was a bright and colorful shrine to comic art, and had come a long way from when Jon's uncle Planner had first turned it over to him, a dreary, dusty storeroom in the back of the antique shop, its gray walls and cement floor straight out of a penal colony bunkhouse. Jon had changed all that, first with his homemade posters, then with some throw rugs, circles of cartoony color splashed across the cold cement floor; and his uncle had donated a genuine antique walnut chest of drawers and almost-matching bed with finely carved headboard, neither of which Jon had spared from the comic art motif: bright decals of Zippy the Pinhead and the Freak Brothers, and taped-on examples of Jon's own comic art, clung to the fancy wood irreverently. Boxes of comics, each book plastic-bagged and properly filed, stood three-deep hugging the walls, and a file cabinet in one corner was a vault that guarded his most precious comic artifacts.

On the wall next to his drawing easel was one of the few non-comic art posters in the room: Lee Van Cleef decked out in his "man in black" spaghetti western regalia, staring across the room with slanty, malevolent eyes. Jon felt the resemblance between Van Cleef and Nolan was almost spooky, though Nolan himself was unimpressed. Nolan was, in many ways, a fantasy of Jon's come to life: a tough guy in the Van Cleef or Clint Eastwood tradition and a personification of the all-knowing, indestructible superheroes of the comic books as well.

Initially Jon had been almost awestruck in Nolan's presence. It was like coming face to face with a figment of his imagination and was unnerving as hell. Now, however, after two years of on-and-off close contact with the man, Jon realized Nolan was just another human being, an interesting and singular human being, yes, but a human being, imperfect, complete with human frailties and peculiarities. Take Nolan's tightness for example. Monetary tightness, that is, not alcoholic. Nolan was a penny pincher, a money hoarder whose Scrooge-like habits were too ingrained to be thrown off even when on two separate damn occasions his miser's life savings had been completely wiped out.

But the man was tough, no denying that. Jon knew of twice when Nolan had pulled through when he had enough bullets in him to provide ammunition for a banana-republic revolution. That alone was proof of the man's toughness and perhaps indicated a certain shopworn indestructibility.

Nolan was in Iowa City, but Jon hadn't seen him yet. He'd called Jon in the early afternoon to say that he was in town and that he'd stopped at the Hamburg Inn to grab a sandwich, where he'd run into an old friend named Wagner, with whom he was now spending the evening. Tomorrow Jon and Nolan would be driving in to Des Moines to sell some hot money to a fence—the money from the Detroit heist, which was all in marked bills.

Jon was getting a little groggy. The images of Li'l Abner, Alley Oop and company were starting to swim in front of his eyes, and maybe it was time he took a break and sacked out a few hours.

He checked his watch (early 1930s Dick Tracy), and it was almost nine-thirty. He'd been at this since just after lunch. He'd driven out to the country this morning to pick up the strips from an old farmer named Larson who had boxes of funnies up in his attic, stored there since the childhood of his two long since grown daughters and forgotten till Jon's ad, seeking old comic books and strips, came out in the local tabloid shopper. Jon had all but stolen the pages—there were thousands of them, easily worth a quarter to a buck per page—and felt almost guilty about it. But the old guy seemed tickled as sin to get fifty bucks in return for a bunch of yellowing old funny papers, so what the hell? As soon as he had finished a quick lunch at the Dairy Queen across the street from the antique shop, Jon had gone to work, cutting up the pages and stacking them for future, more thorough sorting.

There was a reason, he knew, for his going at the project with such manic intensity. Every time something went haywire in his life, he turned to his hobby, to comics, spending more than he should, both time and money. Collecting old comic books was no kiddie game; it was a rich man's hobby, roughly similar to the restoration of old automobiles but potentially more expensive. He'd gotten in the habit as a kid, when he was living with first one relative and then another, while his mother (who liked to call herself a chanteuse) toured around playing piano and singing in cheap bars. He'd never lived in one town long enough to make any friends to speak of. The relatives he stayed with, for the most part, provided hostile quarters where his was just one more mouth to feed and not a mouth that rated high on the priority list either. So he'd gotten into comics, a cheap ticket to worlds of fantasy infinitely more pleasant than the drab soap opera of his reality. Ever since then, he had turned to comics for escape. He was, in a way, a comic-book junkie. He needed his daily dose of four-color fantasy just as a heroin addict needs his hit of smack and for similar reasons. And prices.

But who could put a price tag on escape, anyway? To Jon, comics were the only happiness money could buy, a physically harmless "upper" he could pop to his heart's content.

Take yesterday, for example. He'd gone over to see Karen. Karen was the thirty-one-year-old divorcee he'd been screwing for going on two years now. She had brown hair (lots of it—wild and flowing and fun to get lost in) and the sort of firm, bountiful boobs Jon had always hoped to get to know firsthand. She was great company, both in and out of bed, and looked and acted perhaps ten years younger than her age, while at the same time being very together, very mature, mature enough to run a business (a candle shop below her downtown Iowa City apartment) that was making her disgustingly wealthy. Sounds terrific, right? A rich, fantastic-looking woman, with a beautiful body and a mind to match, as faithful and devoted to Jon as John Wayne was to the flag, a woman absolutely without a fault.

Or almost.

She did have one fault. The fault's name was Larry.

Larry was her ten-year-old, red-haired, freckled-face pride and joy. Larry was the one thing about Karen that Jon didn't like. Jon hated Larry in fact. Larry was a forty-year-old man hiding out in a ten-year-old's body. Larry schemed and manipulated and did everything in his considerable power to break up his mommy and Jon.

And yesterday he had damn near succeeded.

Yesterday Larry had been sitting across the room in Karen's apartment, staring at Jon with those shit-eating brown eyes, saucer-size brown eyes like the waifs in those godawful Keane paintings, and he gave Jon the finger. The goddamn kid just sat there and out of the blue thrust his middle finger in the air and waved it at Jon with a brazen defiance only ten-year-olds and Nazis can muster. Karen was in the other room making lunch. Jon glanced toward the kitchen to make sure Karen wasn't looking. He got up and went over and grabbed the finger in his fist and whispered, "Don't ever finger me again, you little turd, or I'll break your goddamn finger off and feed it to you." Jon let all that sink in, then released Larry's finger and returned to his position on the couch, proud of himself; he'd handled the situation well. Nolan would've approved.

Suddenly Larry began to cry.

Suddenly Larry began to scream.

And Karen came rushing in, saying, what's the matter, honey? "He hurt me! He hurt me! He hurt my hand and called me a little turd, Mommy! He said he'd break my goddamn arm, Mommy!"

Well, Jon had insisted that he hadn't said he'd break Larry's goddamn arm, that he'd said he'd break Larry's goddamn finger, and he had tried to explain his side of the story, but Karen hadn't believed him; she'd gotten teary-eyed and indignant and ordered Jon out of the apartment, and that was yesterday and he hadn't heard from her since. He had tried to call her, but every time he did he got Larry and Larry would hang up on him. So Jon had decided to let the scene cool, and he'd patch things up later.

For right now, he'd decided, the best thing to do was drown his sorrows in the comics. Escape to a brighter, more simple world. And so he found himself floating in a sea of Sunday funnies, his fingers dark with their ink, his butt cramped from sitting so long, his back aching from bending over so much, and it was time to get up and have something to eat and sack out awhile.

He made his way out of the room and into the larger outer room of the antique shop. It was getting dusty out there, and he would have to get around to cleaning up a little. He'd kept the shop closed since his uncle's death a few months ago, and as he had no intention of maintaining his uncle's antique-selling front, had been meaning to contact some buyers to sell out his uncle's stock. But he hadn't got around to that, either. In time, in time.

He went upstairs, to the remodeled upper floor and its pine-panelled walls and thick carpeting. ("I work all day downstairs with the old," his Uncle Planner used to say, "so I live at night around the new." Planner had remodeled the apartment-like upper floor four times in fifteen years.) It had taken Jon a while to be able to get some enjoyment out of the pleasant, all but plush upper floor. These rooms had been his uncle's living quarters, and ever since his uncle's murder he'd had a creepy feeling, a ghoulish sort of feeling, whenever he spent any time upstairs. But he was pretty much over that now. He went to the refrigerator, got a Coke and the makings of a boiled-ham sandwich, went into the living room and sat in front of the TV and watched and ate.

But TV was lousy, some phony cop show, so when he finished his sandwich and Coke, he switched off the set and stretched out on the couch and drifted off to sleep in a matter of seconds. He dreamed he was sorting and cutting and stacking comic strips, and pretty soon somebody nudged him awake.

"Uh, Nolan?" he said.

But it wasn't Nolan.

Jon's eyes came into slow focus, and he saw a mousy little guy with a mousy little mustache, wearing an expensive dark-blue suit that was a shade too big for him, tailor-made or not. The guy's eyes were so wide set you had to look at one at a time, and his nose was long, skinny, and slightly off-center. The extensive pockmarks on his ash-colored, sunken cheeks were like craters on the surface of the moon, and his teeth were cigarette-stained and looked like a sloppy shuffle. Jon put that all together and it spelled ugly, but it was more than that. It was frighteningly ugly, a strange, sullen, scary face that more than offset the guy's lack of size, a face calculated to give a gargoyle the shakes.

"I ain't Nolan," the guy said. "Where is Nolan?"

The guy's suitcoat was open, and Jon looked in and saw that one of the reasons the suit was too big for the guy was that the guy didn't want the bulge of the gun under his arm showing. It was a revolver—a long-barrel .38, like Nolan always carried—and it was in a brown leather shoulder holster that was hand-tooled, Western-style.

"Wake up, kid. I said, where's Nolan?"

Jon hit the guy in the nose. He hit the guy in the nose with his forehead. That was a trick Nolan had taught him. Nolan had said that one thing people don't expect to get hit with is a head. Nolan had pointed out that your head—your forehead, anyway—is hard as hell, a great natural weapon, and it doesn't hurt you much to use it as a bludgeon, and if you strike your opponent's weak spots, like the bridge of the nose or one of the temples, you can mess him up bad before he knows what hit him.

The guy toppled backward, one hand clutching his nose, the other grabbing for the holstered gun. Jon was still only half awake, but he lurched at the guy and fumbled toward that holstered gun himself, still not entirely convinced he wasn't dreaming all this.

The sleepiness beat him. Jon was still fumbling after the gun when he felt something cold and round and hard jam into his Adam's apple. His hand was down in the empty holster before he realized the guy was jamming the gun barrel in his throat.

"Get offa me, you little fucker," the guy said. "Get the fuck off!"

Jon got off.

"I got a fuckin' nosebleed, thanks to you, you little cocksucker. Get me some fuckin' Kleenex, for Christ's sake."

Jon was scared, but he knew enough not to let it show, thanks again to Nolan. He said, not without some difficulty as the gun barrel was still prodding his throat. "Try not to bleed on my carpet, will you? Try not to make a mess."

The guy shoved Jon away and stepped back. "Fuck you, you little brat. Get me a Kleenex before I blow your fuckin' balls off."

"The Kleenex is in the bathroom."

"Yeah, okay, I'll be following you, you fuckin' little shit."

Jon led the guy into the bathroom, withdrew some Kleenex from the box on the john and handed them over. The guy held them to his nose and, with an orgasmic sigh of pleasure, of relief, lowered his guard just enough to give Jon an opening, which he used to do two things in quick succession. First, he reached up and latched onto the shower curtain rod and brought the whole works down around the little guy. Second, he brought a knee up and smashed the guy in the balls.

That was something else Nolan had advised him to do. When you fight somebody, Nolan had said more than once, you can't beat hitting 'em in the balls—assuming, of course, they aren't women.

This guy was no woman. He was on the floor tangled up with the shower curtain and rod doing an agonized dance, screaming to beat the band. The gun was loose and mixed up in the curtain somewhere, and Jon found it and retreated to the stool, where he sat and waited for the guy to get over it. It took a while.

The guy's nose was still bleeding, blood getting all over everything, the curtain, floor, the expensive blue suit. Jon tossed him some Kleenex, but the guy thought Jon was trying to be a smart-ass and grabbed for Jon's leg. Jon kicked him in the head. Not hard. Just enough.

When he woke up, the guy put hand on forehead as if

checking for a fever and said, "Jesus shit. What makes a fuckin' little punk like you such a hard-ass, is what I wanna know?"

Jon shrugged, enjoying the tough-guy role to an extent, but not completely past being scared.

The guy sat up, rearranged himself, got the shower curtain pushed off to one side and said, "Look, kid. I didn't come lookin' for no fuckin' trouble."

And Jon laughed. "Oh, you didn't come looking for trouble. Well, I didn't understand that before. Could you explain one detail for me? Could you explain why you didn't just knock instead of breaking in and scaring the piss out of me?"

"Listen, I came to talk to Nolan, not some fuck-ass punk kid."

"You should've thought of that before you let the fuck-ass punk kid take your gun away from you. Now why do you want to see Nolan? What do you want him for?"

"I don't even know who the fuck you are, kid. What's Nolan to you, anyway?"

"I'm a friend of his. What's he to you?"

The guy shrugged. "He ain't jack-shit to me, kid. I never met the guy."

"So why do you want him?"

"Somebody sent me to get him."

"Get him?"

"Fetch him, I mean. Jesus. Hey, give me some more Kleenex. This fuckin' nose is still bleedin'."

Jon did, then said, "So who sent you?"

The guy hesitated, thought a moment; his mouth puckered under the mousy mustache, like an asshole.

"Who?" Jon repeated, giving emphasis with a motion of the .38.

"Take it easy with that fuckin' thing! You wanna kill somebody? Felix sent me."

"Felix," Jon said. "Felix, that lawyer for the Family?"

"That's right."

"Then we're back around to my first question: Why the hell didn't you just knock?"

"I knocked but you didn't fuckin' answer, that's why! I saw the light upstairs and used a credit card to trip the lock and get in, and all of a sudden you're hitting me in the fuckin' nose with your fuckin' head! Jesus."

"Well, Nolan's not here right now."

"I got to see him. Felix's got to see him."

"Something urgent? You want Nolan to go to Chicago right away, then?"

"More urgent than that, kid. Felix came himself. He's waitin' out at the Howard Johnson's. Something's come up that can't fuckin' wait, kid, so shake it, will you?"

"I know where Nolan is. I can call him."

"Then call him, for Christ's sake."

"Okay. You can get up now, if you want. If you can."

"Don't worry about me. I can get up, all right. You ain't that fuckin' tough, you little punk."

"I thought we were on friendly terms now. I thought you weren't looking for trouble."

"Friendly terms, my fuckin' ass. You best keep your balls covered when you see me comin', kid. I like to even my scores."

"Then you better not forget to give me a nosebleed, too, while you're at it."

"Fuck you. Give me my gun, why don't you, before you shoot your dick off or something?"

"When Nolan gets here. Let's go out and call him. Come on, get up. This time I'll be following you, remember."

And Jon, gun in hand, followed the guy into the living room, deposited him on the couch. Jon pulled a chair up opposite the guy so he could face him, keep an eye on him, and used the phone on the coffee table between them. Jon's hand trembled around the receiver. He was acting tough, as Nolan would've wanted him to. He'd handled himself well, he knew that. But he was trembling just the same.

7

Nolan pulled the Eldorado in next to a Lincoln Continental and got out, confused.

The Eldorado, which was gold, and the Continental, which was dark blue, took up all three of the slantwise spaces alongside the antique shop. Nolan's Eldorado was actually the Tropical's. His ever owning a Cadillac was unlikely, because he saw them as the automotive equivalent of an alcoholic, swilling gas with no thought of tomorrow. As far as he was concerned, a Cadillac was just a Pontiac with gland trouble. Still, being behind the wheel of one for the past couple of months had given him a feeling of—what?—prestige he guessed, and seeing the Lincoln Continental was somehow a sobering experience.

Neither car made much sense in the context of the old antique shop, which was a two-story white clapboard structure bordering on the rundown, whose junk-filled showcase windows wouldn't seem likely to attract even the most eccentric of wealthy collectors. In fact the shop looked more like a big old house than a place of business, which was only right because, other than the Dairy Queen and grade school across the way and the gas station next door, this was a residential neighborhood, a quiet, middle-class Iowa City street lined with trees still thick with red and copper leaves. The inhabitants of this shady lane would've been shocked to know of the different sort of shadiness attached to various activities centered for some years now in the harmless-looking old shop. This thought occurred to Nolan as he opened the trunk of the Eldorado, reaching behind the spare tire for the holstered Smith & Wesson .38 stowed there. Not that the thought worried him. It was late now, approaching midnight, the street was empty, no one at all who might notice him. Even the gas station across the alley was closed. He shut the trunk, slung on the shoulder holster, grabbed his sports coat out of the back seat, slipped into the coat.

He'd immediately recognized the Lincoln Continental as Felix's, but that only served to confuse him further. What in hell was Felix doing in Iowa City? The answer to that was obvious enough: he was here to see Nolan. But why? No obvious answer there.

No pleasant one, anyway.

The side door to the shop wasn't locked. Nolan withdrew the .38 and went in, cautious to the point of paranoia. There was always the chance that Jon had lost control of the situation since calling or, worse yet, that Jon had been forced to make the call in the first place. Nolan doubted the latter, as he felt pretty sure Jon would've sneaked a warning into his words somewhere, *some* indication, implication of trouble, and Nolan had been over Jon's words and their inflections a dozen times in the course of the ten-minute drive from Wagner's house out on the edge of town.

But being careful never hurt, and when the footing wasn't sure, Nolan was the most careful man alive. Because alive was how he intended to stay.

"Nolan?" Jon called from upstairs. "Is that you, Nolan?"

"It's me."

"Come on up."

Nolan leaned against the wall at the bottom of the stairwell. He said, "How you hanging, kid?"

"Loose, Nolan. Nice and easy and loose. Come on up."

That convinced him. Jon's voice had nothing in it but relief Nolan was there.

And once upstairs he found that Jon did indeed have things well in hand. Sitting on the couch was a rat-faced little mustached man, his blue suit cut large in the coat to accommodate shoulder holster and gun, though the latter was presently being trained on its owner by Jon, and the way the suit was rumpled it was apparent the guy had been on the floor a couple of times lately and not making love, either. Also the guy was holding some Kleenex to his nose and had a generally battered look about him. Nolan put his gun away and Jon said hello.

"You're getting better all the time, kid," Nolan said, unable to repress a grin. "I got to learn to stop underestimating you."

Jon, too, was unable to suppress his reaction, getting an aw-shucks look, which faded quickly as he said, "I'm not so sure you did underestimate me, Nolan. The first time I fouled up. I hit him in the nose—" Jon bobbed his head forward to indicate what he'd hit the guy with—"but he bounced back and it wasn't till I kicked him in the balls that I finally got him."

Nolan nodded. "That'll do it."

The rat-faced guy lowered the Kleenex and said, "You two fuckers gonna gloat all night, or can we get over to the Howard Johnson's and see Felix? He's been waiting half an hour. What do you say?"

"Felix sent you?" Nolan said, acting surprised. "I don't believe it. And you say he's waiting to see me out at the Howard Johnson's? I don't believe that, either."

"I wouldn't fuck around, I were you," the guy said. "You think Felix came all the way from Chicago just to check out the fuckin' Howard Johnson's."

"Maybe he likes the clams," Nolan said.

"I'm laughin'," the guy said. "I were you, Nolan, I'd shake a fuckin' leg."

"Don't call me Nolan," Nolan said.

"Oh? Why the fuck not?"

"Because," Nolan said, "I don't know you and you don't know me, and it's an arrangement that's worked fine till now, so leave it alone."

Jon said, "Nolan, I had no idea he works for that Felix character. I mean, the guy broke in the house and came up on me when I was asleep, and I saw his gun and..."

"You did the right thing. It's just a little surprising Felix would send such low-caliber help around. I didn't know the Family was hurting so bad."

"Hey, Nolan," the guy said, "tell you what. How 'bout you suck my dick and choke on it?"

Nolan went over and grabbed the guy's ear and twisted. "Be polite," he said.

"Christ! Awright, awright! Christ almighty, let go my fuckin' ear! Here on out, I'm Emily fuckin' Post!"

"Okay," Nolan said and let go of the ear.

The guy sat with one hand on his ear and the other covering his nose and eyes with Kleenex; if he'd had another hand to cover his mouth, he could've been all three monkeys.

Nolan reached over and picked the phone off the coffee table and tossed it on the guy's lap.

"Make a call," Nolan said. "I want to talk to Felix."

"Call him yourself, motherfucker!"

"I thought I told you to be polite."

"Okay, okay! Shit. Jesus." The guy stopped to look at the Kleenex and decided his nose was no longer bleeding. He composed himself. He dialed the phone and when he got the desk clerk he asked for Felix's room.

"This is Cotter," the guy said. "Well, I'm here with Nolan now is where I am.... Yeah, at the antique shop.... Well, I had a little trouble.... No, just a little trouble. I guess you might say I didn't handle this the best I could.... Yeah, I guess you could say that too. Look, Nolan wants to talk to you." Cotter covered the mouthpiece and said, "Hey, I was supposed to bring you out to see him right away, and now I'm calling up and you're wanting to talk to him and it's making me look bad. Give me a goddamn break and don't go into the, you know, little hassles we been havin'. I mean I come out on the shitty end of the stick anyway, right? A fuckin' half-hour nosebleed, you twistin' my fuckin' ear off my head, and I'm sittin' here with my balls needin' a fuckin' ice pack or something, so give me a goddamn break, what do you say?"

"Sure," Nolan said and took the phone.

"Nolan?" Felix said. "What's going on there?"

"Hello, Felix," Nolan said. "Say, are you missing an incompetent asshole? One turned up here."

"Nolan, I apologize," Felix said. "I don't know what's been happening there, but you have my apologies. This was a rather hastily contrived affair and I regret its being so rough around the edges."

"What the hell's that supposed to mean, Felix?"

"I have a room here at the motel, Nolan. This is a very important matter I've come to discuss with you, a matter of utmost urgency. Can you come out here straight away so we can put our heads together?"

"Well, I tell you, Felix. We put our heads together maybe four or five times so far this year and each time it's in a motel room. Every damn time I see you it's in a motel room. I start feeling like some cheap whore meeting a businessman on his lunch hour."

Felix laughed at that, trying to keep the laugh from sounding nervous, and came back jokingly, "Now how can you compare yourself to a whore, Nolan, with the kind of money you make?"

"Call girl, then. What's in a name? Either way you get screwed."

"Nolan…"

One nice thing about Felix was that he was afraid of Nolan. Nolan had learned early on that intimidation was his most effective means of dealing with Felix, which was one of the big advantages of going through a middleman lawyer instead of dealing with the Family direct.

"Felix, maybe you don't think it's important, maybe you don't think it's worth talking about, but when you send a guy around who breaks into my friend's house and sticks a gun in my friend's face, I guess I get a little—I don't know—perturbed, you could say. So I don't think I want to come see you at Howard Johnson's, Felix, whether you come all the way from Chicago to see me or China or where. You come here and we'll talk, if I'm over being perturbed by that time."

"Nolan, I don't even have the car here."

"Take a cab, Felix. Hitchhike. Walk. Do what you want."

Nolan hung up.

Cotter said, "Thanks a whole fuckin' bunch, pal. Now I'm really gonna get my fuckin' ass fried. Thanks, fucker, thanks for—"

"Jon, take that Kleenex he's been bleeding in and stick it in his mouth, will you? I'm tired of listening to him."

"Hey," Cotter said. "Here on out, I'm a deaf mute." And he covered his mouth.

Nolan dragged a chair over by the window and had Cotter sit in it.

"You watch for Felix," he told him. "And let us know when he's here."

So Cotter sat by the window and Nolan and Jon sat at the table in the kitchen, from which they could see Cotter plainly through the open archway.

Jon asked Nolan if he wanted a beer, and Nolan said no, he'd been drinking Scotch all night and maybe he ought to have some coffee before Felix got there. Jon fixed instant coffee and had a cup himself. They didn't say much for the next few minutes, just sitting and drinking their coffee and enjoying the silence. Finally Nolan spoke, in a soft tone that their guest in the outer room wasn't likely to pick up, "Kid, you did all right out there."

"Yeah, well I hope I didn't screw things up for you with that Family lawyer."

"I can handle Felix. He ought to know better than to send the likes of that around."

"How was your friend?"

"Wagner? Okay for a guy whose hobby is heart attacks."

"Oh?"

"Yeah. He's one of those guys who pushes himself all the time. Runs all day, then goes home and runs in place. He owns that restaurant downtown, that Elks Club they converted."

"I hear it's really something. Seafood restaurant, isn't it?"

"Haven't been in there myself." Nolan sipped his coffee. "He asked me in."

"He asked you in? He asked you to *buy* in, you mean, as a partner?"

"Yeah."

"Well?"

"Well what."

"You going to do it?"

"Don't know. Might be hard. You know where I stand with the Family."

Jon lowered his voice even further. "You mean that if they

found out about Detroit they might get pissed off? Is that what you mean?"

"That's what I mean."

"But don't you want out of the Tropical? Aren't you getting bored with that?"

"The word is numb."

Out in the other room, Cotter said, "A cab's pulling in. Felix is getting out."

By the time Nolan got downstairs and outside, Felix was sitting in the back seat of the Continental, waiting with the door open for Nolan to join him. The plush interior seemed large even for a Continental, but perhaps the diminutive Felix just made it seem that way. The lawyer was wearing a gray suit, so perfectly in style he might have picked it up at the tailor's that afternoon; his shirt was deep blue and his tie light blue. He had a Miami suntan, and a face so ordinary, so bland, if you looked away for a second you forgot it. His hair was prematurely gray and cut in a sculpted sort of way that made it look like an expensive wig. Felix was older than thirty and younger than fifty, but Nolan wouldn't lay odds where exactly.

Nolan leaned into the car and said, "So we're out of the motel and into the back seat. You really think that's an improvement, Felix?"

"Nolan, please," Felix said, his annoyance from the inconvenience Nolan had caused him showing around the edges of his voice. "Can't you set aside your perverse sense of humor for the moment so we can get on to business at hand?"

Felix was right.

Nolan got in, shut the door, settled back to listen.

Felix cleared his throat, folded his hands like a minister counseling one of his congregation. "I'm here to make a proposition, Nolan. I'm going to have to be vague at first, and I hope you'll bear with me. The Family is facing a, well, sensitive situation, and I can't go into detail until I feel reasonably sure you'll be along for the ride."

Vague is right, Nolan thought, but he didn't say anything.

"Once we get into the...problem at hand, I think you'll understand my caution. Before I do, may I ask a question? May I ask what your financial situation is currently?" Nolan hesitated. Could it be Felix knew about the Detroit heist, and that this meeting was a pronouncement to the effect that Nolan was once again in the bad graces of the Chicago Family? *No*, Nolan thought, *that couldn't be it; otherwise, what was that bullshit about wanting Nolan "along for the ride"?*

"You know my situation, Felix," he said.

"Yes, I do," Felix said. "If you'll excuse my bluntness, it can be stated this simply: You're broke."

Good, Nolan thought. *They don't know about Detroit; this has nothing to do with that.*

"If not 'broke' exactly," Felix continued, "your savings from these few months at the Tropical can't be much to write home about, eh, Nolan?" And he laughed at his little joke.

Nolan didn't; he just nodded.

"You've shown a great capability at the Tropical, Nolan. Which was of course no surprise to anyone in the Family. As you know, before, when you were more financially solvent, the Family was anxious to have your participation in a more important, more rewarding operation. But then you had some money troubles and—well, I don't have to go into that, do I? Nolan...are you familiar with the Hacienda outside of Joliet?"

"Sure."

The Hacienda was a resort purporting to be a slice of "old Mexico," with such rustic old Mexican features as two golf courses, three swimming pools, and a dinner theater with name performers. The decor had a rich, Spanish look to it, and the most expensive of the resort's four expensive restaurants was a glorified taco stand where patrons were served Americanized Mexican dinners at lobster prices, and nobody seemed to mind. Nobody seemed to mind, either, that you could've gone to Mexico itself on a three-week vacation for the cost of a week at the Hacienda. And Nolan, who had been there before, knew why: the Hacienda was just the sort of elaborate, glossy hokum the rich widows and the honeymooners and the rest of the tourist trade eat up. It was a fantastic piece of work, and he'd have done anything to have a shot at running it.

"How would you like to run the Hacienda, Nolan?"

"Now who's got a perverse sense of humor, Felix?"

"The present manager is being moved into a similar operation at Lake Geneva. The opening at the Hacienda is there to be filled. By you, if you say the word."

Felix had a "Let's Make a Deal" tone in his voice: Which door will you take, Nolan, one, two, or three?

"What do you want me to say, Felix? The Tropical bores my ass off. You know that. Of course I want something bigger. Of course I want the Hacienda."

"You'd have to buy in, naturally."

"Well, no problem. You can have my watch as down payment."

"One hundred thousand dollars would buy you a considerable block of stock, with options to buy more. Your salary would start at sixty thousand a year and climb. How does that sound to you?"

It sounded fine, but Nolan was starting to wonder if Felix did know about the Detroit haul. One hundred thousand bucks was, after all, Nolan's split, prior to the loss of thirty grand or so he'd take fencing the hot money.

"You see, Nolan, the Family has…an assignment, you could

call it, for you that wouldn't take much of your time and effort. But it's an assignment that you are uniquely qualified to carry out. And it's an assignment that would pay one hundred thousand dollars."

Nolan thought for a moment, shrugged. "My mother's already dead. Who else is there I could kill for you?"

And Felix laughed, nervousness cracking his voice in a way that told Nolan he was perhaps not far wrong.

Three:
Friday Morning

8

Carl Reed's study was an afterthought, a cubbyhole that in the architect's original house plan was a storage room, just an oversize closet, really. But in the ten years Carl and his family had been living in their ranch-style home on the outskirts of West Lake, Iowa (a village just west of Lake Ahquabi, just south of Des Moines), the cubicle-size study had provided an invaluable sanctuary from evenings disrupted by the sounds of two teenagers growing up. Of course there was only one teenager around the house these days. Len was twenty-one now and taking prelaw at the U of I, while Len's wife (a pretty little brunette girl from Des Moines who was a year older than him, with her B.A. degree behind her) taught second grade and took the burden off Dad as far as paying the kid's bills was concerned. Which was nice for a change. Carl's daughter Amy was seventeen, a high-school senior, a cheerleader and student council member and, with her 3.9 grade average, a potential class salutatorian. She was also a potential political radical, or so she liked to say; anyway, she was to the left of her liberal dad. Amy would be living at home next year (commuting to Drake in Des Moines) where her old man, thank the Lord, could still keep an eye on her. You'd think growing up in a little flyspeck town in the middle of Middle America would serve to isolate or at least protect a child somewhat; but apparently it didn't. Perhaps that was because Des Moines was so close by. Whatever the reason, the kids around here were as wild and disrespectful as anywhere else, and maybe that was the way it should be: Carl wasn't sure. But he was sure that growing up in a vacuum wasn't good for a child, as he'd once thought it might be, and was glad his daughter had a mind, even if it didn't necessarily mirror his own.

And that was typical of the sort of decisions Carl made in his little study: quiet, perhaps not particularly important decisions. They were the leisurely reflections of a man who grabs leisurely reflection where he can, in the midst of a life full of the wearing of various hats: politician, banker, father, husband and lover (both of those hats being worn in the presence of his wife Margaret who seemed as lovely to him today as twenty-seven years ago when they'd met on the Drake campus after the war, and thank God for Margaret's sustaining beauty, because Carl just didn't have the time to fool around).

There was a couch in the study, and a desk with chair and not much else. There were books and an occasional keepsake (such as the dime store loving cup inscribed "World's Greatest Golfer" from his kids a couple of Christmases ago) in the ceiling-to-floor bookcase behind the desk. The other walls were cluttered with framed letters (the one from Robert Kennedy, particularly, he treasured) and photographs of him with various state and national political leaders (shaking hands with then-Governor Harold Hughes on the steps of the Capitol building). Sometimes he wondered whether his private sanctuary being decorated with the mementoes of his political life was a sign of idealistic dedication to public service or just overblown feelings of self-importance. Not that those two traits were necessarily contradictory. It was possible, he supposed, for a man to be both an idealist and a pompous ass. He just hoped he didn't fit the description himself.

This study, then, was his private, self-confessional booth, a place for the sort of soul-searching everyone must go through, now and then, to retain sanity in a chaotic universe. But tonight (or this morning, as it was nearly one-thirty already; he'd been sitting here for hours now) his usual run of the soul-searching mill was set aside for more practical concerns. And first priority was the sorting out of the events of the day—or, rather, yesterday—to try and make some coherent meaning out of them, to try and find the proper response for Carl H. Reed to make to these events.

The shooting at the country club, on the heels of Joey DiPreta's bribery attempt, seemed to have happened years ago, rather than mere hours. The events seemed to recede in his memory like a nightmare that, while vividly realistic as it runs its course, begins to fade immediately on waking. They were the stuff of madness, and his subconscious was trying desperately to protect his psyche, but Carl wouldn't let it; he sat at his desk and set those events out before himself and examined them one by one.

Perhaps the most confusing of all was the only event he himself had controlled: his conduct at the police station. The station was on the East Side, across from the old post office and near the bridge, an ancient, rambling stone building he had driven by daily but had never really seen before, not before today, when he found himself in the company of two detectives, who ushered him into a gray-walled cubicle about the size of this study but hardly as pleasant and asked him questions about the shooting.

And he hadn't told them.

Why? Even now he wasn't sure. Oh, he'd told them about the shooting itself, of course. What was there to tell? The eerie experience of seeing the bullet tear through DiPreta *followed* by the sound of gunfire. He'd told them that, and they'd nodded.

But when one of them—the hatchet-faced, pockmarked guy with the short-cropped gray hair—Cummins his name was—began to ask questions (such as "Were you aware of Joseph DiPreta's alleged connections to organized crime?") Carl had held back. Held back the conversation leading up to the shooting.

Held back DiPreta's offer of fifty thousand dollars "hush money."

And it certainly wasn't because he'd had second thoughts about the offer; it wasn't that Carl was waiting for another DiPreta to come around so he could accept this time. Quite the reverse was true. Every time he thought about Joey DiPreta's offer he got indignant all over again.

So what had it been? Why hadn't he said anything?

"Carl?"

He turned in his chair. It was Margaret, peeking in the door behind him. She was in an old blue dressing gown and her hair was in curlers and she wore no makeup and she was beautiful.

"Dear?" he said.

"I thought you might like a drink." And she handed him a Scotch on the rocks.

Margaret didn't approve of drinking, and Carl had long ago had to put aside his college-days habit of two-fisted drinking, at home anyway. The liquor cabinet was stocked strictly for social affairs, and a before-dinner or before-bedtime cocktail was not the habit around this household. So for Margaret to fix and bring him a drink was an occasion. He was suitably impressed.

"Thank you, Maggie. What have I done to deserve this?"

She came over and sat on the edge of the desk. She smiled in mock irritation. "You've stayed up close to two in the morning, worrying me half to death with your brooding, is what you've done."

"Is Amy off to bed?"

"Yes. You shouldn't have told her she could stay up for that late movie. It just got over a few minutes ago, can you imagine? And on a school night."

"She's a young woman, Maggie. If she wants to trade sleep for some silly movie, that's up to her."

"The Great Liberal. If I had my way, the girl would have some discipline."

"The Great Conservative. If you had your way, she'd be in petticoats."

And they laughed. It was a running argument/joke that came out of one of the better kept secrets in the state: Maggie Reed was a conservative Republican who canceled her husband's vote every time they went to the polls—with one obvious exception.

"Carl..."

"Maggie?"

"Did...did what happened this afternoon upset you terribly? Does it bother you terribly, what you saw?"

Carl sipped the Scotch. He nodded. "That's part of what's on my mind, I guess. Come on. Let's go over and sit on the couch. What's it like outside? Kind of stuffy in here."

"There's a nice breeze. I'll open the window."

Maggie opened the window by the couch and they sat together and he told her about Joey DiPreta and the offer he'd made. He hadn't been able to tell the police, but Maggie he could tell. She listened with rapt interest and with an indignation similar to his own. The very idea of someone even considering her husband corruptible got up the Irish in her.

"What did the police say when you told them about this?"

"That's just it, Maggie. That's what I'm sitting here mulling over. You see, I didn't tell the police what I've just told you."

"Carl...why not?"

"I'm not sure, exactly. Have you ever been inside the police station?"

"Just downstairs. To pay parking tickets."

"Well, then you know the atmosphere, at least."

"You mean the halls seem so cold and clammy."

"That's it. And there's an antiseptic odor, like a public restroom that's just been cleaned. I can't explain it, but that atmosphere got to me, somehow, and I found myself hesitating when that detective, Cummins, began asking questions."

"*Are* you going to tell them?"

"I don't know. There was something about that fella Cummins that...I don't know."

"What was it about the detective that made you lie to him, Carl?"

"Dear, I didn't lie. I just didn't tell the truth."

"Now you do sound like a politician."

"Please. That's hitting below the belt. If you want to talk about *that* kind of politician, talk about my predecessor, Grayson—one of your Republicans, incidentally—who was on the DiPreta payroll and raked in God knows how much money."

"You must've had a reason, Carl, for holding back when that detective questioned you."

"Well, I did have a reason. Or not a reason, really...a feeling. Instinct. Something about that man Cummins. I just didn't feel comfortable with him. Didn't trust him is what it boils down to, I guess."

"Didn't trust him?"

"I guess not, or I would have told him what I knew. It was just that his voice stayed so flat, so controlled, while his eyes... shifting around all the time, narrowing, nervous...God, Maggie, the damn eagerness in those eyes. Lord."

"Could he be on the DiPreta payroll himself, Carl?"

"That thought occurred to me. Of course. And why not? If the DiPretas can buy a state highway commissioner, they can buy a lowly damn detective on the Des Moines police force. Sure."

"Then I think you did the right thing. Holding back, I mean. But where do you go now?"

"I don't know. I have to admit the whole thing's got me a little bit scared, Maggie. Maybe more than a little bit. Suppose I had talked freely to Cummins. When word of my refusing Joey DiPreta's offer got back to the surviving DiPretas, that and my telling of that offer to the police, well, I might not have made it home tonight. I might have had a mysterious accident of some sort, got run off the road by a drunken driver, something of that sort."

"My God, Carl, now you're starting to get *me* scared, too."

"You should be. Because the DiPretas are going to make their offer again. I don't know when or how, but they will. My business meeting with Joey DiPreta was interrupted, but as soon as the smoke clears, the rest of the family will be there to take up where Joey left off. Since I said nothing to the police, the DiPretas will assume Joey either didn't get a chance to make his offer or that he did and I accepted. Either way, they'll be wanting to see me."

"What can you do? Couldn't you go to the newspapers?"

"Telling the press isn't a bad idea, Maggie, but I have no evidence. Just my word about what a dead man told me. I've been thinking it over. Carefully. I've been examining what I've seen today, and heard. I've been thinking about what options are open to me. And I've decided to amass evidence on my own. DiPreta said that as soon as I begin to delve into the highway commission records it'll become apparent enough what was going on during Grayson's administration. So I'll begin that examination, tomorrow. Today. As a full-time project. And I'll keep the lid on, too. Minimum of secretarial help, and then only in a way that could not make clear what I was up to. It'll be a tough, time-consuming job, but it shouldn't take me long, if I get at it, and when I have the evidence amassed, *then* I will talk to the press. I'll hold a press conference and tell the damn *world*. But not till then."

"Finish your drink and come to bed."

"You think it's a good idea?"

"Yes. Know what else I think?"

"No."

"I think my husband is a great man. Even if he is a damn liberal. Now come to bed."

"I'll be in in a few minutes. I think I'll go out on the back stoop and finish my drink and get some air first."

"Carl..."

"Just for a couple of minutes. Then I'll be in."

"Okay. I'll read till you join me."

"You don't have to do that...unless you want to."

"I want to. That is, I want to if there's a chance of this dowdy old housewife in curlers and robe seducing her brilliant and handsome husband."

"There's more than a chance. I'll guarantee it. And you're not dowdy, Mag. You're beautiful."

"I know, but it sounds better when you say it." She smooched his cheek. "Go out and get your air and finish your drink. I'll give you five minutes and then I'm starting without you."

He laughed and patted her fanny as he followed her out of the study. She turned off toward the bedroom and he went on out the back way and sat on the cement stoop and sipped the Scotch and thought some more. There was a nice breeze, but it wasn't cold. The night was dark, moonless, but there were stars. Very pleasant out, really, and he felt good...about the pleasant night...about the decisions he'd made...about his wife, his beautiful wife of almost three decades waiting in the bedroom for him.

Someone touched his shoulder. "Maggie?" Carl said and started to turn.

He felt something cold touch his neck. He knew almost

immediately, though he didn't know how, that the something cold was the tip of the barrel of a gun.

"Who is it?" Carl whispered.

"That's right," a voice whispered back. "Speak softly. We don't want to attract the attention of anyone in your house. Your wife or your daughter, for instance.

"I'm not here to hurt you. I'm a friend. I know you may find that hard to believe, but it's the truth."

"I have a lot of friends, my friend," Carl said, hoping his fear would not be apparent, hoping he could put a tough edge in his voice. "None of them holds a gun to my neck when they want to talk to me."

The coldness of the gun barrel went away.

"Maybe that was unnecessary," the voice said, "but my situation's kind of precarious. I hope you can understand that. I hope you'll excuse me."

The voice was deep but young-sounding, and there was a tone of—what? Respect? Carl wasn't sure exactly. But whatever it was, he wasn't afraid anymore, or at least not as much as perhaps he should have been in the presence of an intruder with a gun.

"Is it all right if I turn around?" Carl asked.

"Please don't. I'll be sitting here right behind you, next to you on the stoop, while we talk a moment. But it'd be better for us both if you didn't see me."

"Then I shouldn't ask who you are."

"You won't have to. I've already told you I'm a friend. Do you always stay up so late, Mr. Reed?"

"Do I what?" The question caught Carl off guard, and he almost laughed, despite the gun and overall strangeness of the situation.

"Do you always stay up so late? I've been waiting for you to go to bed for several hours now. My intention, frankly, was to enter your house after you were asleep so I could look through your papers in your study."

"Why would you want to do that?"

"To see if my judgment of you today was correct."

"Your judgment? When did you see me today?"

"On the golf course."

"On the…oh. Oh my Lord. You…?"

"That's right. I shot Joseph DiPreta this afternoon."

"My Lord. My God."

"I hope you'll forgive me, but I'm afraid I was listening outside your study while you were speaking with your wife. I found what you said encouraging. I'm glad you're taking a stand against the DiPretas and what they represent. We have that in common." The man paused, breathed in some of the fresh night air. "The breeze feels nice, doesn't it? There was a breeze like this this afternoon, remember? I was watching you through the telescopic sight of a rifle. You were arguing with DiPreta. I'm not a lip reader, but it was clear you were having some sort of disagreement. And then at the end of your argument the wind carried DiPreta's voice to the high grass where I was watching. If I heard correct, DiPreta threatened you because you would not accept money to keep quiet. But I couldn't be sure. I had to come here tonight to try to see if I could find out where you really stood. And I think I've found an ally."

Carl's mind stuttered. The boy seemed lucid enough, not at all the madman he must be, but then madmen often seem lucid; their illogic is often most seductive.

"You may be wondering why, if I learned what I needed to know by eavesdropping earlier, I would risk coming out in the open now to contact you. Because you obviously won't approve of my methods, even if our goals are similar. But I have something important to tell you. I have this certain body of data you will be interested in."

Carl found the ability to speak again, somehow, asking, "Data? What sort of data?"

"Tapes. Of conversations in motel rooms, both private and meeting rooms. Of phone calls. Also photographs, other documentary material. Pertaining to the DiPretas and their family businesses and their connections to organized crime, specifically to Chicago. A lot of the material, in fact, pertains directly to Chicago. I hesitate to call this body of data evidence because I'm no lawyer. I don't know what a court would do with this stuff. But if nothing else, it can serve as a sort of blueprint to the DiPretas and everything they have done, are doing, and are likely to do."

Carl spoke with all the urgency he could muster. "If you do have such a collection of data—and, damn it, I believe you do, Lord knows why—you must turn it over to me. You were listening to my wife and me, you know that I'll be mounting a personal, intensive investigation of the DiPretas and their activities, and it's my intention to expose them and the people they deal with for what they are. To tell anyone who's interested that the Mafia is alive and well and living in Des Moines."

"I may do that. Eventually."

"Eventually? And until then?"

"I'll use the...blueprint...to serve my own methods of dealing with the DiPretas."

"You mean...killing them."

"Yes."

"My Lord, man. That makes you no better than they are."

"Mr. Reed, war is amoral. There is no morality in war, just winners and losers."

"War? Is that what you imagine yourself to be doing? Waging

war? Launching a one-man campaign, one-man war against the DiPretas? How old are you? You're just a boy, aren't you. Twenty-five? Thirty? Were you in Vietnam? Is that it?"

"I was in Vietnam, yes, but that's not 'it.' Please don't use that as an easy answer, Mr. Reed."

"Turn your information, your data—turn it over to me at once. This course of action you're charting is not only dangerous, it's—forgive me—but it's psychopathic. Good intentions or not, you're charting the course of a madman."

"Mr. Reed, I thank you for your concern."

"Listen to me, I beg you.... You can't go on trying to...wage this crazy war or whatever it is you picture yourself doing."

"I don't expect your approval, sir."

"What do you expect of me then?"

"Your silence."

"What makes you think I won't go to the police and tell them about this conversation tomorrow? Or call them right now, for that matter?"

"Because of your suspicions about Detective Cummins. Which are correct. He is on the DiPreta payroll. To the tune of five hundred dollars a month."

A sick feeling was crawling into Carl's stomach.

"I'll make arrangements so that if anything should happen to me...if I am a casualty in my own war...then the body of data I mentioned will be turned over to you. Good night, Mr. Reed."

"Please! What can I say to change your mind!"

"Nothing."

When Carl entered the bedroom, his wife was asleep. He went out to the liquor cabinet, refilled his glass of Scotch, and went back to the study.

9

Frank DiPreta buttered his hot Danish roll. Even before Frank had begun stroking the butter on, the pastry was dripping calories, sugary frosting melting down into cherry-filled crevices. But Frank had been born thin and would die the same; nothing in the world put weight on him. He bit into the sweet circular slab and chewed, in a bored, fuel-consuming way that could make a fat man weep.

He was sitting in the back booth of the Traveler's Inn coffee shop. Alone. Elsewhere in the shop, strangers were sharing booths and relatively cheerfully, too, but not Frank. He was in a rounded corner booth that could have seated six, and this was the busiest time of morning—it was seven-thirty now, the peak of the seven-to-nine rush—but Frank seemed blissfully unaware that the rest of the rectangular shop was a sardine can crammed with people as hungry for room to breathe as food. The regulars knew better than to say anything, however, and most of the non-regulars were too busy just trying to get some food and get it down to bother complaining. Complaints, of course, came on occasion, and to take care of that a sign was placed in front of the back booth: THIS SECTION CLOSED, SORRY. This was all part of a routine that dated back to the day the motel and its coffee shop first opened, eleven or so years ago.

The coffee shop was aqua blue: the booths, the counter and stools, the mosaic tile floor, the wallpaper, the waitresses' uniforms; even the windows that ran along the side wall by the booths were tinted aqua blue. It was like eating in a fish tank. Nobody seemed to mind; nobody seemed to notice. The food was not particularly reasonably priced, but it was good and attracted an almost exclusively white-collar clientele; and then there were the guests at the motel who mistakenly wandered in for a leisurely breakfast and became a part of this morning madhouse instead. It was this latter group who most often expressed displeasure about the man in the big back booth who was sitting all by himself, eating a buttery Danish roll. And Frank ate three or four of the Danish every morning, and he took his time.

It would have been hard to guess, looking at this calm, self-absorbed man, that very recently he had suffered a great personal loss; the death of his brother Joey did not show through the mask that was Frank DiPreta's face. His eyes were not red. His appetite was certainly unhampered; he was now engaged in the consumption of his second Danish and looking forward to his third. He was not wearing black; in fact, the tie he wore with his tailored powder-blue suit was colorful: red and white speckles on a blue background, like an American flag exploding. There was no apparent tension in him either—no tapping foot, no drumming fingers. No, the only way to know the condition of this man, to understand the extent of grief he felt and his desire for revenge and the depth of that desire, would be to look into his mind; and no one could look into the mind of Frank DiPreta. Frank DiPreta was a private man, with private thoughts, needs. Even his late wife, Rosie, had never been really close to him and had known it. His daughter, Francine, thought she was close to him, but she wasn't really.

Cummins came in at seven-thirty. Fifteen minutes late. He was a tall man with a skinny man's frame and a fat man's belly. He was dark-haired, dark-complexioned, wore a rumpled brown suit and looked like a cop, which is what he was. As he joined Frank in the back booth, a waitress put Cummins's usual breakfast down in front of him. The Friday morning meeting between Cummins and Frank was a ritual, and the necessity of placing an order had long since passed. Cummins mumbled an apology about his tardiness, then dug into the double order of waffles and ham.

"You're late," Frank said. With people in the booth behind him, Frank naturally kept his voice down. But his words were anything but soft-spoken.

"I'm sorry, Frank."

"You're sorry."

"Look, I almost didn't come."

"You *what*?"

"I sort of forgot."

"You forgot Friday, Cummins? I never knew you to forget Friday before."

"I just didn't think you'd be here, because of—I thought you'd be making funeral arrangements and things."

"I made those last night. Tomorrow is the funeral. Today is business as usual."

Cummins looked up from his waffles and ham. "Well, that's fine. I think that's the way it should be. You got to order your priorities, you know?"

"I know," Frank said. He handed the envelope under the table to Cummins who took it and stuffed it casually inside his suitcoat.

"You going to want anything special on this thing, Frank?"

"Not really. Keep me informed. You're on the case?"

"Yeah."

"So there should be no problem, right?"

"Right."

"Only thing special I want from you is I want this guy personally."

"You want him how?"

"I want him. When you find him, I want him."

"Frank, uh, if you mean what I think you mean..."

The booth was large enough, and the racket in the room loud enough, for Frank to say anything he wanted without fear of being overheard. But just the same he leaned across the table and whispered harshly, "You know what I mean, Cummins. These last few years not much has been asked of you. We're goddamn businessmen now, thanks to Vince, and maybe he's got the right idea. But this time we're doing it the old way. This one time you're going to earn your goddamn money."

And Cummins said, in a whisper that was little more than a moving of the lips, "You're going to kill him."

"I'm not going to fuck him. Fuck him up, yes. Hell, you may not ever find the son of a bitch's body. I might lay some goddamn state highway over him and let the trucks and cars make their tire tracks on his goddamn grave."

"What...what am I supposed to do, Frank?"

"Give him to me. Find him and give him to me. And then cover for me. Shut up for me. That's what you're paid for, mostly. Shutting up." He leaned back.

"Whatever you say, Frank," Cummins said and returned to his waffles and ham.

"Now," Frank said. "What do you have to tell me?"

"Just what I said on the phone last night. Empty shell casing in the high weeds, the rough. Four-sixty Mag."

"That's old. Nothing new? Anybody see the guy?"

"No. Nobody at the country club saw a thing. 'Course there wasn't anybody else on the golf course, being so late in the season and all. Back of the rough is a blacktop road with a farmhouse across the way, but the damn farmhouse is set back from the road maybe two hundred yards and nobody there saw a thing, didn't even notice if a car was parked out front or anything, which it probably wasn't. He probably parked it up around the turn, where there's no houses around."

"How do you read it?"

"Except for the size of the gun, which is weird, I'm telling you, I'd say it was a pro did it. I mean it was very smooth, very professional. No hitches at all. Only I can't see why some hit man would use a big-game rifle. That's—I don't know—silly, or strange, or some damn thing."

"Somebody's trying to scare us," Frank said, meaning the DiPreta family itself. "Somebody's trying to scare shit out of us."

"Who's got a reason?"

"I don't know. Nobody. Lots of people. Vince has been bitching with Chicago over some things. Talking about cutting some of our ties with 'em, which is part of his wanting to go even more legit than we are already."

"Would that be smart?"

"Going legit? Well, we could cut some of the dead weight off our payroll, that's for sure."

"Frank, that's not fair."

"Take it easy, Cummins, I'm just kidding. Me, I don't mind taking a few chances, if that's where the money's at. My brother Vince, he's older, more conservative, that's all. But this, this is just a business thing. I can't see Chicago shooting anybody over it. That's just not done anymore. At least not on our kind of level. The DiPretas are a family, just like Chicago is a family. Nowhere near the same level, sure, I'll admit we're not, but we're a family just the same, which is something that carries respect; *that* at least is left over from the old days. When *that* is gone we'll know the businessmen and politicians have took over. No, not Chicago, not likely. That four-sixty Mag, though, you know what that sounds like to me? That sounds like revenge."

"I talked to Vince about the playing-card thing."

"See? That fits in. Revenge. Some personal thing, somebody trying to scare us sort of thing."

"Yeah, well, I was talking to Brown, you know, my partner?"

"The nigger?"

"Look, Frank, I happen to like Brown, I don't see any reason calling him a nigger."

"He's a nigger, isn't he?"

"Yeah, he is, but you don't have to call him that. Anyway, he was in Vietnam."

"Who was in Vietnam?"

"You know, Brown, the nig, he was in Vietnam and he was telling me about the playing card deal. I mean, I told him about Vince getting that card in the mail, just like his brother Joey did, and Brown said in Vietnam they used to distribute whole damn packs of the ace of spades. Whole fuckin' damn decks of nothing but aces of spades, and the Americans, after they wasted a bunch of slants, they'd spread 'em around like confetti on the slant corpses, 'cause these slants, they're superstitious bastards, and the ace of spades, it stands for death, you know, so the Americans would leave ace of spades all over the ground, on and around the dead bodies, to spook the V.C."

"So what?"

"So maybe somebody's doing the same thing to you. Trying to spook you with the ace of spades. Like I said, it stands for death."

"Yeah, I know it stands for death, you dumbass, I know that's what somebody's trying to do is spook us with the goddamn ace of spades. I mean, it wouldn't make much sense sending the deuce of hearts, would it, dumbass?"

"No, Frank, you don't follow me. I mean maybe the guy who shot Joey is out of Vietnam. Maybe that's where he picked up on shooting, too. Sniping. If he was a soldier, I mean. In Vietnam."

"Wait a minute," Frank said. Something was starting to click in the back of his head somewhere. Something was starting to click together. "Wait a minute."

"What, Frank?"

"Nothing yet. Let me think a second."

Cummins shrugged and returned to his waffles and ham, which were cold now, though that didn't seem to cool his enthusiasm any.

A few minutes passed, and suddenly somebody rapped on the window right by their booth. Both Frank and Cummins looked up and saw, through the aqua-blue-tinted glass, a figure in jeans and khaki jacket. The most striking thing about the figure was that he was wearing a woolen ski mask. The ski mask was dark blue with red and white trim around the eye holes and was out of place. The morning was a little bit chilly, yes, but a ski mask certainly wasn't called for.

Then the man in the ski mask held up his right hand to show Frank and Cummins why he'd rapped on the window for their attention.

In the man's hand was a grenade.

The pin had been pulled, and only the pressure the man was applying to the lever was delaying the triggering of the hand grenade.

Both Frank and Cummins froze for a moment, not yet fully comprehending what was going on. During that moment they watched as the man in the ski mask jogged backward a couple of steps and brought his arm back and then forward, like a major-league pitcher, and the grenade was hurtling toward the window before either man had realized what was happening.

The aqua-blue window shattered, letting in the white light

of the sun and the grenade, which bounced once on the booth's tabletop and landed on the floor, where Frank and Cummins already had gone to escape the oncoming missile. The two men were on their knees and the grenade was on the floor between them. They looked at each other like two of the Three Stooges doing a take and then scrambled off in opposite directions.

"Jesus Christ, a grenade!" somebody hollered (not Frank, or Cummins, either, both men having their priorities in order, as usual, namely saving their own asses).

People got up from booths, stools, bumped into each other, doing the panic dance. Some of them, the ones close to the door, even managed to get out of the building.

Frank was praying when the grenade exploded; Cummins was crying. The explosion was loud enough to be terrifying, but only momentarily.

There was smoke, but not much, and when it cleared, the grenade was revealed as a lump of metal sitting on the floor of the coffee shop, looking like an oversize walnut with a cracked shell and just about as dangerous.

"A dud," Cummins said, getting out a handkerchief and hastily drying his eyes. It wouldn't do, after all, for the detective on the scene to be in tears.

"Not a dud," Frank said. "Whoever packed it with powder packed it with just enough to make a big bang and scare shit out of everybody."

The grenade's shell casing was cracked, but the explosion hadn't been enough to break it into the destructive splinters that do the damage.

"Like I said before," Frank said, "somebody's trying to scare us. Somebody's playing goddamn games with us."

"In Vietnam," Cummins said, "they called it psychological warfare."

Frank nodded.

Cummins turned to the confused, relieved, but badly shaken group of people, who were standing around the rectangular coffee shop like passengers in a surrealistic subway car, and began to speak in loud, reassuring, authoritarian tones. Pretty good for a guy who a few seconds ago was bawling, Frank thought.

Frank walked back over to the booth, where the broken window gaped; shards of glass filled the seats and littered the table. He went on to the adjacent booth—whoever'd been sitting there before was making no move to reclaim it—and sat down.

On the table was a playing card.

10

Francine DiPreta was sitting on her bed, which was shaped like a valentine and soft as custard. The spread was fluffy, ruffly pink. The room around the bed was pink, also: pink wallpaper, pink colonial-style dresser with mirror; even a pink stuffed animal—a poodle—peeked out behind pink pillows resting against the bed's pink headboard. When Frank, Rosie, and little Francine had moved into the house some ten years before, the little girl had loved the pink room. But Francine was a big girl now and kept in check her intense dislike for the room in all its nauseating pinkness only because it held for her father too many memories of Francine's childhood and those happy years when Mother was alive. Besides, next year, the year after maybe, she'd be moving out. She was, after all, nineteen years old and a college freshman. Living in this child's room was a beautiful young woman, with platinum blonde hair and China blue eyes and a trim, shapely figure. As she looked around, she shook her head and thought of the line from that Carly Simon song—

"Daddy, I'm no virgin"—but knew that particular sentiment was one she'd never find nerve to express to her own Daddy.

This morning, she sat on the pink elephant of a bed, wearing a pastel-blue cashmere sweater dress, and no pantyhose (her summer tan was holding up nicely, her legs looked nice and dark) and thought about the death of her Uncle Joe and wondered what it meant. She'd heard the whisperings, of course, from grade school on up, of how the DiPreta family was supposed to be part of the Mafia, which seemed so silly to her she'd never really got upset about it. Once, though, when she'd asked her father about it, he'd laughed and said, "Everybody who's got an Italian name, somebody's gonna think they're the Mafia…too much stupid TV, honey."

But every now and then there were indications that maybe her father was into something—well—shady, or something. He did, after all, carry a gun at times, but he had his reasons ("I carry a lot of cash, 'cause of the business, honey. There's lots of crooked people who would take a man's money if he let them") and she'd long ago dismissed that. And then there were the occasional men who would come around, the sort of men her father would stand outside on the porch and talk to, or hustle into the study and shut the door. Big men, with odd faces—faces that seemed somehow different from a normal person's face, colder or harder or something; she didn't know what. And when she would confront her father with these men, accidentally bump into him while he was talking with one of them, or burst into his study while he was conferring with one or more of them, he would never introduce her. Oh, sometimes he would say to the men in an explaining way, "This is my daughter." But never would he say, "Mr. So-and-so, this is my daughter, Francine. Francine, this is Mr. So-and-so."

And now Uncle Joe getting shot. Why would anybody want

to shoot Uncle Joe? Everybody in the family regarded Joe as the baby. Even Francine, his niece, less than half Joe's age, thought of him as the spoiled kid of the clan, the genial loafer, the golf bum, a practical joker, a kidder—but somebody who somebody else would want to shoot? That was crazy.

But then so were the rumors about DiPreta Mafia connections. So crazy Francine didn't take them seriously, even found them laughable. Look at Uncle Vince, for example. Chairman of half the charities in town, one of the all-time biggest contributors to the Church, besides. Uncle Vince was one of the most socially concerned citizens in all Des Moines. And her father, Frank, who like all the DiPretas belonged to the swankiest country club in town, counted among his close friends men in city, state, and national government, senators, judges, the highest men in the highest and most respected places. Were these the friends of a "gangster"?

Her father was a gentle man, a kind man, although he did keep his emotions in and might seem cold to, say, some of the people he did business with. Even Francine had considered her father somewhat remote, aloof, until she finally got a glimpse of the sensitive inner man when her mother died six years ago. Her mother had been killed by a drunken driver one rainy, slippery night, just two miles from home. (The road in front of their house in the country was then narrow and treacherous, and only recently—partly through her father's pulling of political strings—had that road been widened and improved and watched over diligently by highway patrol officers.) Francine, crushed, stunned and (perhaps most important) confused over her mother's death, had wondered why her father didn't show his grief more openly, why he seemed almost callous about the loss of his wife; and, as a child will do—and she'd been a child then, just having entered junior high and loving that pink room of hers—she had asked him straight out, "Why, Daddy? Why don't you cry for Mommy?" And the tears had flowed. The dam had burst, and for several minutes Frank DiPreta had sobbed into his daughter's arms. She had cried, too, and had felt very close to her father then for perhaps the first time. There had been no words spoken, just an almost momentary show of mutual grief; but it was the beginning of her father's transference of worship for his wife to his daughter, and thereafter anything she'd asked of him, he'd given. She had tried not to take advantage, but it hadn't been easy.

He was a remarkable man, though. What with all the silly Mafia rumors and all, you might think of him as the kind of man who would harbor thoughts of violence and revenge where his wife's killer was concerned. But Francine had never heard her father say even one word about that man who'd run his car over the center line, in a drunken stupor, forcing Rose DiPreta off the road and killing her. Francine remembered saying, "I could kill that man, Daddy. I could just take him and kill him." And her father had said, "You mustn't say that, honey. It won't bring Mommy back." He had seemed content to let the courts handle the man, who'd been arrested at the scene of the accident. Of course poetic justice or fate or whoever had taken care of things, ultimately. Before the man could be brought to trial, he himself was, ironically enough, run down and killed by a hit-and-run driver.

And now, with Uncle Joe's death, her father was again reacting in a subdued manner, though she could tell—or at least guess—that he was very much moved by the loss of his brother. The DiPreta men were a dying breed anyway, this branch of the family at any rate. Joe had been a bachelor; Frank had only one child, Francine herself; and Vince's only son had died of leukemia a few years back. Uncle Vince seemed more visibly shaken by his brother's death than her father, but then ever since Vince's son had died he'd been walking around under a cloud. That was the bad thing about Uncle Vince, sweet as he was: You could get depressed just thinking about him.

She didn't like being depressed. When her father had asked her to go down to the funeral home where Aunt Anna and the other relatives were greeting friends and such, she told him she wasn't up to it; she just couldn't take all the mourning and tears. And, of course, her father hadn't insisted she go; he never insisted she do anything, really.

She got up from the bed and grabbed her schoolbooks and sketch pad from off the dresser, having made the decision to get out of the house, to drive into Des Moines to the Drake campus and attend the rest of the day's classes, death in the family or not. She'd go downstairs and tell Daddy and that would be that. Life goes on; that's the best way to handle tragedy, right?

Francine found her father with her uncle in the study. They were talking to a tall, gaunt man with shaggy dark hair and a droopy mustache and a sort of Indian look to him around the cheekbones and eyes. Though the man was nicely dressed, in an obviously expensive tailor-made suit, he had that vaguely sinister aura of so many of the men Francine had seen in this house over the years.

"My daughter," her father explained to his guest and took her by the arm and stepped outside the study with her. "What is it, honey?"

"I'm going on ahead to school, Daddy. I don't see any reason missing any more classes. Unless you want me to stay and fix you lunch or something."

"Baby, I don't care about lunch, but don't you think you ought to be helping your aunt at the funeral home? People are coming from out of town, friends of the family. Lot of important people will be expecting to see you there."

"Come on, Daddy. It's a funeral home, not my coming-out party. I won't be missed. Besides, it's just too much of a downer, Daddy, please."

"Downer? What kind of word is that?"

"Please, Daddy."

"You should help out."

"Maybe tonight."

"For sure tonight?"

"Maybe for sure."

She kissed him on the cheek and he pushed her away gently, with a teasing get-outta-here-you look on his face.

The white Mustang she'd gotten for high-school graduation was parked in the graveled area next to the house. The house was a red brick two-story with a large red tile sloping roof, brick chimney, and cute little windows whose woodwork was painted white, as was an awning arched over the front door. The house sat on a huge lawn, a lake of grass turning brown now, though the shrubs hugging the house, and the occasional trees all around the big yard, were evergreen. It was the dream cottage every couple would like to while the years away in, right down to the picket fence, but on a larger scale than most would dare dream. Immediately after Mother's death, her father had put the house up for sale; soon after, though, he'd relented, and had since treated the house like a museum, keeping everything just the same as when Mother was alive—Daddy's-little-girl pink bedroom included.

At first she didn't notice the other car parked on the gravel on the other side of her Mustang. But it was hard to miss for long, a bright gold Cadillac that was finding light to reflect even on an overcast day like this one. A young guy was standing beside the car, leaning against it. He was cute. Curly hair, pug nose, nice eyes and altogether pleasant, boyish face. He was probably around twenty or twenty-one, kind of small, not a whole lot taller than she, and looking very uncomfortable in light blue shirt and dark blue pullover sweater and denim slacks. Looking as though he wasn't used to wearing anything but T-shirts and worn out jeans and no shoes.

"Hi," she said, when she was within a foot or so of him.

"Hi yourself."

"Are you a relative?"

He grinned. "I'm somebody's relative, I guess."

"But not mine?"

"I hope not."

"You hope not?"

"If I was too close a relative of yours, it would spoil the plans I've been making, ever since I saw you come out that door over there."

This time she grinned. "You're a shy little thing, aren't you?"

"Normally. It's just that sometimes I come right out and introduce myself to pretty girls. It's a sickness. I'll just all of a sudden blurt out my name. Which is Jon, by the way."

"Hi, Jon. I'm Francine."

"Hi, Francine. We said hi before, seems like."

"But we didn't know each other then."

"Now that we do, can I ask you something personal? What the hell made you think I was your relative? Because we both got blue eyes?"

"My uncle died yesterday. People are coming in for the funeral by the busload."

"Oh...hey, I'm sorry. I didn't mean any offense, I mean I guess I picked a poor time to make with the snappy patter."

"Don't worry about it. My uncle was a nice man, but he's dead, and I can't see crying'll do any good. So, listen, if you aren't here for my uncle's funeral, I mean if you aren't my cousin or something, what are you doing leaning against a Cadillac in my driveway?"

"I'm here with the guy who's inside talking to some people who probably *are* relatives of yours."

"You mean the guy with the mustache? Sour looking guy?"

Jon grinned again. "That's him. Brought me along for company and then didn't say word one the whole way."

"How far did you come?"

"Iowa City. Left this morning. What time is it now?"

"Getting close to noon, I suppose. Maybe noon already. When did you leave Iowa City?"

"Around seven. We had some business in Des Moines first, then we drove out here. My friend didn't say why, though. Didn't know he was paying last respects, though I should've figured it."

"Why? Should you have figured it, I mean."

"Well, this friend of mine usually dresses pretty casual for a guy his age…sport shirt, slacks. Today, we're setting out on a fairly long drive, and he shows up in a gray suit and tie and shined shoes, the works. And tells me to lose my T-shirt and get into something respectable, which is something he's hardly ever done before."

She smirked.

"And just what are you smirking about?"

"Just that I guessed right, that's all. The way you're squirming in those clothes you'd think you were wearing a tux."

"Is it that obvious? Hey, is that a sketch pad?"

"Yeah. I'm taking an art course at Drake. I was on my way to class, before you sidetracked me."

"Let me see."

She shrugged, said okay, and handed him the pad.

"Pretty good," he said, thumbing through. "That's a nice horse, right there."

"We own a farm with some horses down the road. I do some riding sometimes."

"Why is it girls always draw horses?"

"I don't know. Never thought about it."

"Must be something sexual."

"Probably," she said, laughing.

"Shit," Jon said.

"Why shit?"

"Shit because you are one terrific girl and I'm meeting you in the worst possible situation. Why didn't I meet you in goddamn high school? Why didn't I meet you in a bar in Iowa City? Why do I meet you during the warm-up for your uncle's funeral, while my friend's in the house talking to somebody for a minute?"

"I think they call it fate. How long you going to be in Des Moines?"

"Don't know. Today and tonight, reading between the lines."

"Your friend doesn't tell you much."

"What I don't know can't hurt me."

"That's your friend's philosophy, huh?"

"Christ, I don't know. He's never even told me that much."

"Jon?"

"Yeah?"

"I like you."

"You like me. Okay. Sounds good. I like you, too, then. The back of the Caddy's nice and roomy. Wanna wrestle or something?"

"Tell you the truth, I wouldn't mind it. My father, however, just might. Could you leave for a while? How long's your friend going to be inside?"

"I don't know. He never—"

"—tells you anything."

"Right."

"Right. So leave a note. Here, tear a corner off one of the sketch pad pages. I'll get a pen out of my purse."

They did all that, and Jon said, "Swell. Now. What do I write?"

"Did you see a sleazy little joint called Chuck's on the way here? Just outside of town?"

"Weird Mexican or Spanish-type architecture? Yeah. I mentioned it to my friend as we passed by."

"And what did your friend say?"

"He grunted."

"Does that mean he did or didn't notice the place?"

"Where my friend's concerned, one grunt's worth a thousand words. He noticed it." Jon scribbled a note and left it on the dash of the Cadillac.

Chuck's was a white brick and cement block building with a yellow wooden porchlike affair overhanging from the upper of the two stories. There was black trim on the yellow porch-thing and around windows and doors, and it looked vaguely Spanish as Jon had said. On the door to Chuck's was the following greeting:

NO SHOES NO SHIRT NO SERVICE

"No shit," Jon said.

Francine laughed, and they went in. The place, which was appropriately dark and clean, provided lots of privacy for Francine and Jon, as they were the only customers in the place right now. They chose a booth.

"I'm glad I didn't meet you in high school," Jon said. "I take back what I said before."

The barman came over and said, "What'll you have?" and they ordered draw beers. The barman went away, and she said, "Why do you take back what you said?"

"Why do I take back what I said about what?"

"About wishing you'd met me in high school."

"Oh! Well. If I'd met you in high school, I couldn't have got near you."

"Don't be silly."

"Silly, huh? Let me remind you about high school. You are president of the student council. I am hall monitor. You are Representative Senior Girl. I am left out of the class will. You are cutest and most popular of all the cheerleaders. I am assistant statistician for the basketball team. You go steady with the captain of the basketball team. I play with myself in the corner and get pimples. You are a vision of loveliness. I am a lowly wretch who…What you laughing at? This is serious stuff I'm layin' on you. This is the story of our lives. Am I right?"

"I plead guilty to a couple of those charges. But I'm not a high-school kid anymore, Jon. I hope I'm not that shallow anymore."

"There's nothing wrong with being shallow. I'm not saying you are, but keep in mind how boring most deep people usually are. Let's be shallow together, you and me. We can go wading together or something. Wonder where those beers are? Say, uh, I hate to ask this, but are you going with anybody or anything?"

"Broke up. You?"

"Breaking up, I think."

"Let's not bore each other with any of the details, Jon, what d'you say?"

"Fine with me."

The beers came.

"Hey," she said, sipping. "Why were you so interested in my sketch pad back at the house?"

"I'm an art major myself. Or was till I dropped out."

"Dropped out, or…?"

"No, I didn't flunk out. One thing I left out of my soliloquy before was 'You're rich, I'm poor.' No money."

"What about a scholarship?"

"Well, I did have good grades, yes, I did, but I didn't see eye to eye with the art professors, so recommendations for scholarships were kind of scarce where I was concerned."

"Why didn't you and the profs see eye to eye?"

"Because I want to draw comic books when I grow up."

"You what?"

And he repeated what he'd said and told her in fascinating detail of his aspirations to be a cartoonist, of his massive collection of comic art, of the projects he was currently working on in that field, in trying desperately to break in. Despite what he'd said about the merits of being shallow, he was a very intense and sincere young man, so enthusiastic about his chosen profession that she had no doubt he would eventually make it. To find out she handed him her sketch pad and pencil and told him to draw, and while he continued to talk, and while they put away three beers each (or was it four?) he drew her picture, at her request.

"Make it cartoon style," she told him, and he nodded and went on talking.

He didn't let her see the page as he sketched, and he hardly seemed to be looking at her; he seemed to be concentrating on talking to her, telling her of his hopes and dreams and such until she finally began to doubt he was drawing her at all. It certainly had to be a big sketch because he was all over the damn page, and it was a big page at that.

"Here," he said at last and handed the sketch pad to her.

There was not a single sketch on the page.

There were five.

In one Francine looked remarkably like Daisy Mae of *Li'l Abner*, though still recognizably Francine. In another she looked like one of those exotic girls Steve Canyon used to run around with before he got married: it was a full-figure pose of Francine in a slinky, low-cut gown, with a flower behind one ear. And in another she had Little Orphan Annie's big vacant eyes and, as it was another full-figure pose, a couple of things Annie doesn't have at all. In the fourth sketch Jon had drawn her as underground artist R. Crumb might have, with undersize breasts and exaggerated thighs, truckin' on down the street. The final sketch was fine-line style, a realistic drawing that showed her how very beautiful the artist must consider her to be.

"Is this your own style, this one here, Jon?"

"I wish it was. That's in the style of Everett Raymond Kinstler, a portrait painter who worked in the comics in the fifties. He did *Zorro*. One of the greats, but not as well known as he should be."

She was sitting, staring at the page.

"Jon."

"Yeah?"

"This is beautiful. It's wonderful. I mean it. I'm going to frame this, so help me. You're good, Jon. Terrific."

"Yeah, well, my problem is all I can do is imitate. I can do everybody's style, but I don't have one of my own."

She leaned across the table and kissed him. On the mouth. It started quick and casual but developed into something slower, longer.

The barman cleared his throat. He was standing by the booth. "Excuse me. I hate to bust up a beautiful romance."

Jon got a little flushed. "Then don't."

"Cool off, kid. Your name Jon?"

"Yes, my name's Jon. What of it?"

"Jesus, I said cool off. I don't care if you kiss her, hump her under the table if you want to. Jesus. There's a phone call for you."

"Nolan," Jon said.

"Who?" Francine said.

The barman was gone already.

"My friend," Jon said.

He got up and came back a minute later.

"He's got some things to do," Jon said, "and said if I can hook a ride back to the motel with you, he can go it alone for the time being. What say?"

"Sure."

"Okay. I'll go back and tell him." Jon did, came back, sat down again.

"Jon?"

"Yeah?"

"Would you like me to take you back to the motel?"

"Yeah. I thought we already agreed to that."

"I know. But I wonder if you'd think I was out of line if I asked to go back to the motel with you."

"With me?"

"That's right. I mean, I looked under the table, and it's kind of dirty under there."

"Kind of dirty under there."

"I prefer sheets."

"You prefer sheets."

"Yes."

"You prefer sheets. Let me see if I got this straight. You're beautiful, you met me forty-five minutes ago, and you want to go to the motel with me?"

Later, in the motel room, in his arms, she would offer a possible explanation for her impulsive outburst of promiscuity: "Maybe my uncle's death is getting to me more than I thought. I was trying not to think about him dying, and I was trying so hard I wanted to get my mind completely off it and just have some fun. And you came along and that was that. You know, there's something about making love that makes you feel protected from death and closer to it at the same time."

And Jon would tell her his uncle, too, had died recently, a couple of months ago, and she would say she was sorry, and he would go on to say he had loved the guy, that his uncle had been the closest relative he'd ever had, closer, even, "than my goddamn mother." And she would comment that life was sad sometimes, and he would agree, but go on to say that sometimes it isn't, and they would make love again.

But that was later, in the motel room.

For right now, Francine just said, "Yes," and let it go at that.

Four:
Friday Afternoon and Night

11

Nolan didn't hear the shot, but he did hear Vincent DiPreta let out a gush of air and smack against the side of the house. He turned around and saw that DiPreta, hit in the chest—through the heart or so near it, it didn't make much difference—had slid down to where the house and gravel met and was sitting there, staring at his lap, only his eyes weren't seeing anything.

If Nolan had left the DiPreta place when he first started to a few minutes before, he would have missed the shooting. But he'd gone out to the car, found Jon's note and had gone back into the house for a moment, to use the phone and call the kid, who understandably had gotten bored and had hitched a ride down the road to a bar for a drink. Nolan had decided to tell Jon to call a cab and go back to the motel or go over on the East Side for the afternoon and hunt through the moldy old shops for moldy old funny books; the rest of the day's activities, Nolan had decided, were perhaps better handled alone. The kid would just get in the way and would be all the time wanting to know what was going on. Later, if it proved he needed some backup, he'd call Jon in off the bench.

He hadn't spent much time at the DiPretas. He'd known that if he was going to be nosing around Des Moines, as Felix wanted him to, he'd better let the DiPretas know he was in town, even if he didn't tell them the real reason why. Felix hadn't told him to talk to the DiPretas, but then Felix hadn't told him much at all about how to handle the situation, probably because Felix knew it wouldn't do any good. Nolan would handle things his own way or say piss on it.

Vincent DiPreta had answered the door, though it was the Frank DiPreta residence. Nolan remembered Vince as a fat man, but he wasn't anymore; he looked skinny, sick, and sad. And old. More than anything, old, as if his brother's death had aged him overnight.

He didn't recognize Nolan and said, "Who are you?" But not surly, as you might think.

"My name's Nolan. We did business years ago."

"Nolan. Ten, eleven years ago, was it?"

"That's right."

"Come in."

Nolan followed DiPreta through a room with a gently winding, almost feminine staircase and walls papered in a blue and yellow floral pattern that didn't fit the foundation the house had been built on. They went to the study, which was more like it, a big, cold dark-paneled room with one wall a built-in bookcase full of expensive, unread books, another wall with a heavy oak desk up against it, and high on that wall an oil painting of Papa DiPreta. Papa had been dead four or five years now, Nolan believed. In the painting Papa was white-haired and saintly; in real life he was white-haired. Another wall had framed family pictures, studio photographs, scattered around a rack of antique guns like trophies. There was a couch. They sat.

"It's thoughtful of you to call, Mr. Nolan. We're doing our receiving of friends and relatives at the funeral home, not here, to tell you the truth, but you're welcome just the same. Would you care for something to drink?"

"Thank you, no. Too early."

"And too early for me. Also too late. I don't drink anymore, you know. Or at least not often. Damn diet."

"You've lost weight. Looks good."

"Well, it doesn't, I lost too much weight, but it's kind of you to say so. Did you make a special trip? I hope not."

"No. I was in town for business reasons and heard about your tragedy. I'm sorry. Joey was a nice guy."

"Yes, he was. You haven't done business with us for some time, have you?"

Nolan nodded. "I'm in another line of work now."

"What are you doing these days?"

"I manage a motel, Near Chicago."

Something flickered in DiPreta's eyes. "For the Family?"

"Yes," Nolan said.

The door opened, slapped open by Frank DiPreta, who walked in and said, "Vince, I...who the hell are you? Uh...Nolan, isn't it? What the hell are you doing here?"

"He came to pay his respects," Vince said.

"That's fine," Frank said, "but that's being done at the funeral parlor. Our home we like kept private."

Nolan rose. "I'll be going then."

"No," Frank said. "Sit down."

Nolan did.

Frank sat on the nearby big desk so that he could look down at Nolan, just as his father was looking down in the painting behind him. This was supposed to make him feel intimidated, Nolan supposed, but it didn't particularly. These were old men, older than he was, and he could take them apart if need be.

"Nolan," Frank said, smiling warily, narrowing his eyes. "Nolan. Haven't seen you in years."

For a period of several months, eleven years ago, Nolan had led a small group of men (three, including himself) who hijacked truckloads of merchandise that were then sold to the DiPretas for distribution and sale to various stores in the chain of discount houses the DiPretas owned and operated throughout the Midwest. Truckloads of appliances, for the most part, penny-ante stuff, really. A stupid racket to be into, Nolan eventually decided, especially at the cheap-ass money the DiPretas paid;

and when he discovered the DiPretas were loosely affiliated with the Family (who at the time wanted Nolan's ass) he abandoned the operation *right now* and left the DiPretas up in the air. His present claim of calling to pay his respects to the bereaved family wouldn't hold up so well if Frank DiPreta's memory was good.

"In fact," Frank was saying, "you sort of disappeared on us, didn't you, Nolan? I hear you were pissed off at Joey and Vince and me for paying you so shitty. You quit us, is what you did, right?"

Nolan shrugged. "I was mad at the time. But Joey and me got back together a couple times after that, when I was passing through, several years later. Didn't he tell you? Played some golf together. Patched up our differences." He smiled and watched the faces of the two men, trying to tell how well his lie had fared.

"I see. What about the Family? Not so long ago I heard stories about you having problems with the Family. You patch up your differences with them, too?"

"There was a change of regime. You know that. You're tied in with the Family yourselves, aren't you? The people I had problems with are gone."

"So what are you doing?"

"Running a motel for them."

"No, I mean, what are you doing in town? Besides paying respects."

Nolan grinned. "Running a motel doesn't pay so good, and sometimes you got to do a little work on the side. I brought some money in to sell Goldman."

That was plausible. That was something they could check on if they wanted to. It was also true. In the Midwest the place to sell hot money was Goldman, who ran three pawnshops and paid a higher percentage on marked bills than even the best guys back east. Having the Detroit money to unload in Des Moines had proved a blessing, because it provided a perfect cover.

But Frank still wasn't satisfied. "So what sort of job did that money come from?" he wanted to know.

"Rather not say."

Vince said, "It's none of our business, Frank. He was in town, heard about Joey, stopped by to pay his respects." He turned to Nolan. "You have to excuse my brother, Mr. Nolan. He's still upset about Joey."

"Bullshit," Frank said. "I think the Family sent this son of a bitch in to check on us. To see why we haven't called them and asked for help. To handle this them fuckin' selves. Well, we don't want the goddamn Family's help, understand? Like when they fucked up the McCracken thing that time, which is maybe the cause of all this, too."

For the first time Vince DiPreta perked up, seemed almost alive. "What do you mean, Frank?"

"I'll tell you later."

"Look," Nolan said, "I'm not into that side of the Family's affairs. If you know anything at all about my past history with the Family, you know that's the truth."

Frank thought for a moment, finally nodded. "That's right. When you quit, you quit because you didn't want any part of the Family, outside of club work and the like. Yeah, I did hear that. Okay, Nolan. Maybe I misjudged you. Maybe not. If you came to pay condolences, fine. If not, well..."

"Daddy?"

A blonde girl of nineteen or twenty came in. She was a sexy-looking little thing and didn't look like a DiPreta, though she obviously was, as Frank introduced her as his daughter and went over to her and took her outside the study and talked to her for a while.

"Change your mind about that drink, Mr. Nolan?"

"Scotch would be fine."

Vince DiPreta got the drinks and they sat on the couch and drank them while Frank talked to his daughter.

Frank came back in, saying, "Kids," shaking his head, but his mood seemed somehow mellowed.

"Fine looking girl," Nolan said.

"Takes after her mother. Okay, Nolan. So maybe I'm being paranoid or something, but I got call to be suspicious. And I'm going to tell you what's going down 'round here, so that if you're an innocent bystander like Vince seems to think you are, then you can get your damn ass out of the way, and if you're some damn idiot the Family sent in to troubleshoot and spy on us, then it's best you know the score and know what you're in for. Somebody's trying to wipe us out. The DiPreta family, I mean. I got an idea who, but that much I'm not going to tell you. So far Joe's been killed, and I about got killed this morning, and…"

"Wait," Nolan said. "Somebody tried to kill you?"

"Threw a goddamn hand grenade through the window right on the fuckin' table. In the coffee shop where I was eating breakfast, for Christ's sake. Do you believe it? But he wasn't really trying to kill me. Just throw a scare into me for now. The grenade had just enough powder to go boom and make everybody pee his pants. And I was about that scared myself, I'll tell you. Here, take a look at this. This is something he left me to remember him by." He took a card from his sports-coat pocket. "An ace of spades. Vince was sent one yesterday. Joey was, the day before yesterday. The day before he got it. Now me."

"Why?"

"I'm not sure. But if you're smart, Nolan, you'll get your ass out of Des Moines. Because the shooting's just started."

"You think you know who's doing it?"

"Maybe. You going to be in town long?"

"Just tonight, I figure."

"Good. Give my regards to the Family. Vince, I'm going upstairs, sack out awhile. Wake me in an hour, will you? Got some things to take care of later."

Frank DiPreta left the room.

Vincent DiPreta sat and stared at the door his brother had gone out; his face was sagging, heavily lined, tired, like a basset hound's. He turned to Nolan and said, "Did the Family send you, Mr. Nolan?"

"No."

"Another drink?"

"Please."

After a third drink and some idle conversation, about pro football mostly, Nolan had gone out to the car, where he'd found the note from Jon and had gone back in to use the phone. DiPreta had gone out the door with Nolan as Nolan went out to the Cadillac for the second time.

And Vince DiPreta had been shot, by a silenced rifle, apparently, and Nolan, who didn't intend to be next in line of fire, dove for the ground.

12

Nolan hit the gravel hard and rolled, kept rolling till he bumped against the side of the Cadillac. The shot had come from the other side of the Cad, beyond the huge lawn and white picket fence, from somewhere in the gray thickness of trees covering the section of land adjacent to the DiPreta place. He reached up and opened the door of the Cadillac, then carefully crawled inside the car, like a retreating soldier climbing into the security of his foxhole. He kept well below window level, lying on his belly while he fumbled under the seat for the holstered .38. He withdrew the gun, left the holster, got into a modified sitting position, leaning to the side toward the seat and still below window level, started the car, and began backing out.

The rearview mirror gave him a good view of the drive, which went straight back to the highway; but there was a gate, and since he couldn't afford to get out and play sitting duck opening the thing, he built up some speed, butted the picket fence open, and swung out sharply onto the shoulder of the road and a semi whizzed past and almost blew him into the ditch. For once he was grateful for the bulk of the Cad.

With the semi out of the way, the four-lane was free of traffic, or anyway the two lanes of it closest to Nolan were, the ones heading back to town. Over across a dividing gully the other two lanes were entertaining brisk traffic. He decided not to wait for it to let up and pulled out into what for public safety was the wrong direction but for his purpose the right one; his purpose being to head toward where the shooting had come from. He pushed the gas pedal to the floor.

He met only two cars: a Corvette whose driver didn't blink an eye, just curved around Nolan and headed on toward Des Moines; and another Cadillac, like Nolan's but blue, and this driver too had sense to get the hell out of Nolan's way. The driver in the Corvette had been a young kid and could have been Steve McCracken, but Nolan knew catching the Vette would have been an impossibility, even if he'd had room to make a U-turn and give it a try.

He found what he was looking for soon enough: a gravel side

road, bisecting the four-lane and running along the edge of the grove from which the sniping had been done. Nolan pulled in. The air was full of dust. The gravel had been stirred up just recently, by the assassin's car, no doubt, on its way home after a successful mission.

Nolan drove till the dust in the air began to dissipate, and it did so at a point roughly parallel to the DiPreta place across the grove. He slowed, figuring this was approximately where the assassin's car had been parked. It proved a good theory, as on the side of the road opposite the grove was a cornfield, and an access inlet to the cornfield was apparently where the assassin had left his car while entering the grove to do his sniping.

Nolan pulled into the inlet, got out of his car, crossed the road, the ditch, then walked up a slight incline to stare out over the October-barren grove. The trees were gray, as was the sky, their fallen leaves had been picked up and borne away, leaving the ground bare around them, but for the browning grass. It was a naked and uninviting landscape, a perfect backdrop for dealing out death, and Nolan noticed for the first time it was kind of cold today.

He also noticed for the first time, on his way back to the Cadillac, that he was filthy from rolling around in the gravel. He started brushing himself off and noticed he'd torn his suit-coat under the right sleeve, and that the crotch was ripped out of his pants. Shit, he thought, two hundred goddamn dollars shot to shit. Somebody was going to answer. Well, he'd have to go back to the motel and change. He got back in the car, re-turned the .38 to its holster under the seat, and headed back to Des Moines. He had a lot to do, and he really couldn't spare the time, but he didn't figure he better go running around town with the crotch hanging out of his pants.

He did not stop at the DiPreta place. Vince was dead; nothing he could do would help Vince now. Frank was probably still upstairs sleeping, and Nolan didn't want to be the one to wake him with the latest war bulletin. Hopefully Frank would assume the shooting had taken place after Nolan had left, though the possibility remained that Frank might assume Nolan was in some way a part of the shooting, an accomplice perhaps. Especially if that gate had been conspicuously damaged when Nolan butted it open with the tail of the Cadillac. Even so, that would have to be taken care of later. Nolan had more important things to do presently, such as getting into pants with the crotch sewn in them, and he just didn't have time to fool around with the DiPretas right now.

It took longer getting back to the motel than Nolan would have liked. He worked the key in the door with some impatience; but when he went to push it open, the door caught: night-latched.

"Jon," Nolan said.

Noise from within; bedsprings.

"Jon, for Christ's sake, shake your ass."

Which from the sound of the bedsprings was exactly what the kid was doing.

Finally Jon peeked out. He looked a little wild-eyed. His hair was all haywire, even more so than usual. He wasn't wearing a shirt; even with as little of him as was showing, that was evident.

"Hey," Nolan said. "I live here. Remember?"

"Nolan, uh, Nolan…"

"What are you doing, sleeping? Didn't you sleep enough in the damn car on the way up this morning?"

"Uh, Nolan, uh…"

"What?"

He whispered out of the side of his mouth, "I got a girl in here."

"Congratulations," Nolan said. "I'm glad the day is going right for somebody. Now let me in."

"Well, you kind of interrupted us."

"I'll wait out here while you finish. Don't be long."

"Jesus, Nolan!"

"Look. We got something in common right now, you and me. We're both in kind of sticky situations. I got no crotch in my pants, for one thing, but I don't have time to explain at the moment. I'm just here to make a pit stop, you know? Change my clothes, say hello, and I'm off."

"Yeah, you do look messed up. What you been doing, rolling around in gravel or something?"

"Jon."

"Yes?"

"You and your girlfriend go over to the coffee shop for five minutes so I can come in and change my clothes. Okay? I mean, I am paying for the room, you know."

"No kidding?" Jon said, genuinely surprised. "I figured we'd be going Dutch, like usual."

"Jon."

"Okay, okay. One second."

It was more like two minutes, and Nolan was somehow uncomfortable, hanging around outside a motel run by the DiPretas—or rather the DiPreta, as Frank was about the only one left, he guessed.

Jon came out in T-shirt and jeans, with the girl in tow. She was a pretty young blonde, stunning in fact: white blonde hair and a real shape to her. She looked familiar in some funny way, but maybe that was just wishful thinking. She seemed embarrassed, almost blushing, and Nolan smiled at her to put her at ease.

"So you're Jon's friend," she said.

"So you're Jon's friend," Nolan said.

Jon said, "Why don't you go on and order, Francine. I got to talk to Nolan a minute."

She said okay and both Nolan and Jon took time out to study the nice things going on under the blue sweater-dress as she walked away.

Then Jon said, "Nolan, I'm sorry about this, I didn't figure it would do any harm to…"

"No harm done. I'm glad you found a way to amuse yourself. But listen, don't call me Nolan. I'm registered Ryan."

"Oh. Sorry. What's going on, anyway?"

"You and me are getting screwed in Des Moines. We're just going about it two different ways. Now go away and eat and let me change."

Jon did.

Nolan was pleased to find that the war between the sexes had been fought on only one of the twin beds, and sat on the unused one and stripped off coat and tie and shirt and sat for a moment pressing the heels of his hands to his eyes. Things were happening fast. He wanted to catch his breath a second.

But just a second.

He rose, got out of the pants and took out a pair of dark, comfortable slacks, a lightweight black turtleneck sweater, and a green corduroy sports coat from his suitcase and put them on. He walked into the bathroom and splashed some water on his face and remembered who the girl was.

Christ!

He all but ran over to the coffee shop. It was a long, narrow aqua-blue fish tank of a room, and toward the rear of the place was the window that earlier today had been broken out by the tossing of a grenade; the window was covered over now with cardboard. Jon and the girl were sitting one booth away. As he approached them Nolan tried to convince himself that the girl with Jon was not Frank DiPreta's daughter, but when he got up close to the horny little bastard and bitch, that's who she was, all right.

Nolan cleared his throat, smiled. It was a smile that Jon understood. It was a smile that didn't have much to do with smiling, and Jon excused himself, and he and Nolan headed for the restroom, which Nolan locked, turning to Jon and saying, "Where did you pick her up, Jon?"

"At that place this morning."

"The DiPreta place, you mean."

"Yeah, right. That's her name, Francine DiPreta. And she picked me up, if you must know. Right there at that place we drove to this morning, where you went in and—"

"She's the daughter of the guy I went to see, in other words. You're banging the daughter of the guy I went to see."

"Well, I didn't figure that made her off limits or anything. Come on, Nolan, you saw her. Would you turn that down?"

"It would depend on the statutory rape charge in this state, I suppose."

"That's right. You got no call to get all of a sudden moral or something, Nolan."

"Fuck, kid, I'm not talking morality. I'm talking common sense. Okay, do you know who her father is? Besides somebody I went to see today."

"No. I don't know who her father is. Some rich guy, I assume."

"Yeah, he's rich. For one thing, he owns this motel."

"This, uh, motel?"

"Right. You're screwing the girl in her father's motel."

"Gee."

"Gee? Gee? Do people still say that? Do they say that in the funny papers or what?"

"I'll take her right home."

"No. Don't do that."

"Why not?"

"Because her uncle just got killed."

"I thought her uncle died yesterday."

"Not died, got killed. And this is another uncle. Two uncles in two days, killed. And did you notice that broken window out in the coffee shop?"

Jon nodded.

"Somebody threw a grenade through that window this morning at your girlfriend's old man."

"What's it all mean, Nolan?"

"Think about it. He's a rich guy. He's a rich guy I have dealings with. He's a rich guy I have dealings with who has had two brothers killed in the last two days and a grenade tossed in his lap this morning."

"He's a mob guy."

"He's a mob guy. You're screwing a mob guy's daughter in a mob guy's motel. There you have it."

Jon swallowed. "Are you mad at me, Nolan?"

"Mad? No. Hell, I admire you. You got balls, kid."

"What should I do, Nolan?"

"Have fun, I guess. That's a nice looking piece of ass you lined yourself up with. Maybe it'll have been worth it."

"Okay, so I fucked up. I admit it. But how was I to know? You bring me along and don't tell me a damn thing…"

Nolan slapped the toilet lid down and sat. His tone softened. "I know. It is my fault. If I'm going to bring you into these things, if I'm going to trust you to be capable of helping me out, I shouldn't keep you in the dark all the time. It's my fault. But Christ, kid, think with your head, not your dick. A grade-school kid could put two and two together and come up with four, right? You should have put me and that girl's father together and come up with hands-off-the-daughter."

Jon nodded. "I was an asshole."

"You and me both. We're doing our talking in the right room."

Jon grinned. "They say all the assholes hang out here."

Nolan grinned back, said, "Go out and have something to eat with your girlfriend. Take her back to the room soon as possible and make sure none of the help sees you going in."

"I shouldn't take her home, huh? And I shouldn't mention knowing who she is and all?"

"What do you think?"

"I think I shouldn't mention knowing who she is."

"Look, lad, she probably doesn't even know who she is herself. She probably figures Daddy is in the motel business and leaves it go at that."

"What's going on, anyway?"

"I can't tell you."

"Bullshit! You just got through saying how—"

"I know, but it's complicated and there isn't time. But listen. If somebody should come looking for me, which I doubt, because I don't see anybody in Des Moines linking the Ryan name to me, but if somebody does, just play it straight. Just say you're a friend of mine and I'm out handling some personal business. Got that?"

"Nolan, what the hell else could I tell anybody? You haven't told me shit about what's coming off around here."

"That's so when your girlfriend's father starts pulling out your toenails with pliers to make you talk, you won't have a thing to say. Now get going."

13

Nolan didn't expect anybody to be home. He'd gotten the credit card out of his wallet to open the door, looked around the apartment-house hall to make sure no one was watching him, and then, as he was about to slide the card between door and jamb, decided maybe he'd better ring the bell, just to be sure. And now he was looking into the very pretty, very blue eyes of Steve McCracken's sister, Diane.

"Yes?" she said.

She was wearing a white floor-length terry robe, and her platinum hair was tousled; she'd obviously been sleeping, her face a little puffy, her eyes half-lidded, but she was still a good-looking young woman. Not alert at the moment, but good-looking.

"Diane?" Nolan said, palming the credit card, slipping it into his suitcoat pocket.

She had opened the door all the way initially, but now, her grogginess receding, her lack of recognition apparent, she stepped back inside and closed the door to a crack and peeked out at Nolan, giving him a properly wary look, saying "Yes?" like, who the hell are you and what the hell do you want?

"I'm Nolan. Remember me?"

The wary look remained, but seemed to soften.

"Chicago," he said. "A long time ago."

The door opened wider, just a shade.

He smiled. "Make believe the mustache isn't there."

And she smiled, too, suddenly.

"Nolan?" she said.

"Nolan."

"Good God, Nolan…it is you, isn't it? I haven't seen you since I was a kid, haven't even thought of you in years. Nolan." She hugged him. She had a musky, bedroom smell about her, which jarred him, as his memories of her were of a child, and a homely one at that.

"Come in, come in," she was saying.

He did.

It was a nice enough apartment, as the new assembly-line types go: pastel-yellow plaster-pebbled walls; fluffy dark-blue carpeting; kitchenette off to the left. There was a light blue couch upholstered in velvetlike material, and matching armchairs, only bright yellow, across the way. Over the couch was a big abstract painting (squares of dark blue and squares of light yellow) picked to complement the colors in the room, he supposed, but succeeding only in overkill. He didn't know why exactly, but the room seemed kind of chilly. Maybe it was the emotionless, meaningless abstract painting. Maybe it was nothing. He didn't know.

"Excuse the way I look," she said, sitting on the couch, nodding for him to join her. "But I stayed home from work today. Not really sick, just felt a little punk, little tired. Nothing contagious, I'm sure, so you don't have to worry."

Nolan didn't have to be told she'd stayed home from work: he'd known she would—or rather should—be at work, and had hoped to avoid an old-home-week confrontation with McCracken's sister by simply searching her apartment when she wasn't there. But here she was, in the way of his reason for being here, which was to locate her brother's address or phone number or some other damn thing that might lead Nolan to him.

"What brings you to Des Moines, Nolan? God, I can't get over it. All these years."

"I was in town on business," Nolan said, "and it occurred to me I should look you up and say how sorry I am about you losing your folks. We were good friends, your father and mother and I. I was real close with your dad especially, as you know."

She didn't say anything right away. Her face tightened. Her eyes got kind of glazed. She seemed to tense up all over. Then she said, "It's been over a year since he died. He and mother. They were getting back together, you know."

"I didn't know," Nolan said. "I didn't even know they'd broken up." Which was untrue, but might prompt an interesting response.

"They were divorced ten years ago, shortly after we moved to Des Moines, in fact. I never really knew the reason why. It didn't make sense to me as a kid and it doesn't now. Mom had been unhappy in Chicago, didn't like what Daddy was doing there, with that nightclub and everything, and she seemed so happy when he said we'd be going to Des Moines, that he'd be getting out of the nightclub business and was going to manage a motel in Des Moines. But then we got here and a few months later, poof. Funny, isn't it? They both loved each other. They saw each other all the time, were welcome in each other's homes. But for some reason Mother refused to remarry and live with him again."

"And your mother never said why?"

"No. And I don't know why she relented toward the end there, either."

"They were sure in love when I knew them."

"You were out of touch a long time, Nolan. How come?"

"Didn't your father ever tell you?"

"No."

"I had a falling-out with the people who employed your father and me."

Years ago, in Chicago, Jack McCracken had run a club across from Nolan's on Rush Street; both clubs belonged to the Family. Nolan and McCracken were best of friends but had parted company out of necessity when Nolan made his abrupt, violent departure from the Family circle. It would have been dangerous to the point of stupidity for Nolan to associate with anyone linked with the Family, and vice versa, so he hadn't talked to McCracken for more than a decade and a half, hadn't even heard of his old friend's death until last night, when Felix told him.

"But you didn't have a falling out with Daddy, did you? Just the people you two worked for."

"That's right."

"I don't understand, Nolan. Just because you didn't get along with your employers, yours and Daddy's, doesn't mean the two of you couldn't still be friends."

That answered a big question. Unless she was playing it cute, Diane had no idea her father had worked for the Family in Chicago, and that his later employers, the DiPretas, were also mob-related.

"We just ended up in different parts of the country, Diane. Drifted apart. Happens to friends all the time. You know how it is. I didn't hear about your parents dying till just recently or I'd have got in touch with you sooner. So what have you been up to, for fifteen years? Your braces are off, you aren't flat-chested anymore. What else?"

She sighed and grinned crookedly. "I'm still a little flat-chested, now that you mention it. Say, what time is it?"

"It's after one."

"Have you had lunch yet?"

"No."

"So far today I haven't felt like eating, but seeing you after so long kind of perks me up. I got some good lasagna left over from dinner last night. If I heat it up, will you help me finish it off?"

He wished he could have avoided all this. She was pleasant company, sure, but he didn't want to sit around chatting all afternoon. He had to find Steve McCracken and soon: Frank DiPreta clearly had theories about the assassin which included McCracken as a possibility; and what with the tossing of a grenade this morning and the sniping of Vince early this afternoon, things were happening too fast to be wasting time in idle chatter.

But he did like her. And she could, most probably, lead him to her brother.

So for forty minutes they talked and ate and got along well. She fed him salad and lasagna, he fed her a terse, imaginary tale of working on the West Coast as a salesman, then finally ended on a note of partial truth, saying how he'd recently been trying to get back into the nightclub business, and was in Des Moines working on that. Then she went on to an equally terse account of going to college for a couple of years at Drake, getting married, having a child, getting divorced. She told it all with very little enthusiasm, and when she spoke of her ex-husband, Jerry, it was as if she were encased in a sheet of ice. Only when she talked about her six-year-old daughter Joni did she come to life again.

Eventually they were back sitting on the couch and he got around to it: "Listen, Diane, how's your brother, anyway? I'd like to see him while I'm in town."

She paled.

She touched a lower lip that had begun trembling and said, "Uh, Stevie…well, uh Stevie, he's just fine."

"What's wrong, Diane?"

"Wrong?"

"Yes. What's wrong?"

"Nothing at all."

And she broke down.

He went to her and gathered her in his arms. Let her cry into his shoulder. He let her cry for several minutes without asking any more questions.

And he didn't need to. She began telling him what he wanted to know on her own.

"Nolan, I don't know how the hell it happened you showed up today, after all those years, but thank God you did. I need somebody right now. I need Daddy, is who I need, but he's dead—goddamnit, he's dead. And Stevie's acting crazy. I…I wasn't sick today, you know, not really. I was emotionally…I don't know, overwrought, or disturbed, or something. Depressed, upset, scared, you name it. Last night Stevie came for dinner, and he just acted so crazy. He's been a little strange since he got home from service a few weeks ago. He got an apartment but then told me not to come over. I mean I know where he lives, but he said a condition of the landlord's was no visitors. I just don't believe that—it's silly, crazy—but Stevie was coming over here often enough that I didn't mind, didn't ever question what he'd told me about the landlord's silly rule. He did give me a phone number—it came with the apartment—but then last night he came over and said not to call him anymore unless it was an absolute emergency. He'd get in touch with me now and then, he said, but not to call him and not to give his phone number or address to *anybody* under any circumstances. He made me promise that. And then he said he wouldn't be able to see us for a while, Joni and me. Wouldn't be coming over anymore. He said there was a good reason but that he couldn't tell me. He would still be in town, still be around, but he couldn't see us. I…I almost got hysterical. I sent Joni downstairs to her friend Sally's, and I pleaded with Stevie, begged him to tell me what was going on. I even got to where I was screaming at him after a while. Then I got mad, furious with him, and that didn't do any good either. And he left. He just left, Nolan, and said he'd call now and then. I…I just don't know what to think."

She was confused and rightfully so, Nolan thought. Her brother's "wartime" precautions (and they were half-assed, insufficient precautions, at that) meant nothing to her.

"Nolan, do you think maybe you could talk to Stevie? Do you think maybe you could find out what's going on?"

"Yes." He stroked her hair. It was incredibly blonde.

"But right now just take it easy, Diane. Take it nice and easy."

"Nolan."

"What."

They were whispering. She was in his arms, and they were whispering.

"Nolan, I was in love with you when I was thirteen."

"I know you were. But you had braces, remember?"

"And I was flat-chested, too." She took his hand and put it under her robe. "Do you think there's been any improvement?"

"I think so."

"I haven't made love in a long time. I haven't been able to. After my parents died, I…I was dead inside too. That's…part of why the divorce happened."

"I see."

"That feels good. Keep doing that."

"I intend to."

"Nolan."

"Hmmm?"

"Could you make love to me?"

"I could."

"You'd have to make it gentle. I'm…I'm not sure what I'm doing. I mean I'm kind of mixed up."

"I could be gentle."

"Why don't you kiss me and see what happens?"

He did.

"Yes," she said. "I think it would be good."

"I do too."

"Where?"

It was dim there in the living room. The day outside was overcast, and once he'd gone over and drawn the curtains the room was very dark.

"Here on the couch?" he asked.

"Here on the couch'll be fine."

She slipped the terry robe down over her shoulders. Underneath she wore sheer beige panties and lots of pale, pale flesh; even her nipples were pale, which added to the platinum blonde hair bouncing around her shoulders and peeking through her sheer panties gave her an almost ghostly beauty. Nolan stood and undressed and looked down at the girl, studied her delicate, softly curved body, watched her slip out of the panties and open herself to him, like a flower, and for just a moment he felt like a child molester.

But only for a moment.

14

Nolan got in easy enough. He simply told the landlady, Mrs. Parker, that he was Steven's favorite uncle, and that he wanted to surprise the boy, and she smiled and led him downstairs, through the laundry room, to the doorway of the basement apartment.

"There's no lock on the door," she whispered. "You can go on in." She was a plump, middle-aged woman with prematurely white hair and a motherly attitude that irritated Nolan. He didn't like being mothered by a broad so close to his own age.

He thanked her, but did not "go on in" just yet. Instead he waited several long awkward moments for Mrs. Parker to leave, which she finally did, and the smile of thanks frozen on his face like the expression on a figure in a wax museum melted away. He didn't think the landlady would've understood why Steven's favorite uncle might find it necessary to enter his nephew's chambers with .38 in hand.

But it turned out the .38 wasn't necessary after all.

McCracken wasn't home.

Nolan returned the gun to the underarm holster but left his coat unbuttoned. He looked around the room. It didn't take long.

The large basement room McCracken lived in was sparsely furnished: just a big, basically empty room, which made sense. A soldier lived here. Or anyway somebody who fancied himself a soldier, Nolan thought, fancied himself engaged in a personal, private war. This wasn't an apartment; it was a barracks, a billet.

It didn't take long to find the soldier's arsenal, either. Nolan eased open the doors of a tall wardrobe, and there in the bottom of the cabinet were the weapons of the McCracken assault team: Weatherby with scope, .357 Mag Colt, 9-millimeter Browning and a Thompson sub, no less. There was ammo, of course, and about half a dozen grenades.

He went over and sat on the couch, put his feet on the coffee table. He folded his arms so he could sit and wait without getting the .38 out but still have fast access to the gun. He figured McCracken might freak at the sight of the drawn revolver, might pull a gun himself and the shooting would begin before talking had a chance to. Steve had seemed stable as a kid, but a lot of years had gone by since then; sometimes a seemingly normal child developed into a psychopath. Maybe Steve McCracken wasn't a psychopath, but he'd sure been showing violent tendencies these past twenty-four hours or so.

In a way, Nolan couldn't blame the boy. McCracken was a soldier trained in an unpopular, perhaps meaningless war. Why should it surprise anybody if the boy should put that training to personal, practical use? From Steve McCracken's point of view, Nolan realized, his reasoning behind the destruction of the DiPreta family seemed valid as hell. After being a part of the military jacking itself off in Vietnam, why shouldn't the boy seek a crusade for a change? A holy goddamn war?

McCracken was inside and had the door locked behind him and still hadn't seen Nolan.

"How you been, Steve?" Nolan said.

Steve turned around fast, got into a crouch that spoke of training in at least one of the Eastern martial arts.

But Nolan was well-versed in the major American martial art and calmly withdrew the primary instrument of that art from his shoulder holster. He showed the gun to Steve McCracken, said, "Sit down, Steve. On the floor. Over there on the floor just this side of the middle of the room."

And the boy did as he was told. "Who the hell are you?" he said, sitting Indian-style. His voice was deep, but it sounded young, like a voice that had just changed.

"I guess I don't look the same," Nolan said. "Your sister didn't recognize me at first, either. I think it's the mustache."

"Mustache my ass, I've never seen you before in my life. And what's this about my sister...?"

"I wouldn't have recognized you, either. You've grown."

Grown was right: Steve McCracken was more than a foot taller than the last time Nolan had seen him. Of course, then Steve was ten or twelve years old. Now he was in his mid-to-late-twenties and a massively built kid, whose whitish blonde hair and skimpy mustache made him look more like a muscle-bound California surf bum than a one-man army.

"If you're here to shoot me," Steve said, "get on with it."

"Christ, you're a melodramatic little prick. I guess it figures. You used to love those damn cowboy movies you and your dad used to drag me to. Randolph Scott. Christ, how you loved Randolph Scott."

"Who...who are you?"

"I'm the guy who used to sit between you and your dad, when we went to Comiskey Park to watch the Sox on Sunday afternoons."

"Nolan?"

Nolan nodded.

"I haven't seen you since I was a kid," Steve said. He seemed confused.

"You're still a kid. And a screwed-up kid at that, and since your dad isn't around anymore, I guess I'm all that's left to get you straight again."

"What do you mean?"

"I mean somebody's got to put a stop to what you're doing before you get your ass shot off."

"You go to hell."

Nolan grinned. "Good. I like that. It'll save time if we can skip the pretense and get right down to it. You been killing and generally terrorizing members of the DiPreta family. It's crazy and it's got to stop."

"Go fuck yourself."

"Will you listen to me? Will you hear me out?"

"Why should I?"

"Because I got a gun on you."

"Well, that is a good reason."

"I know it is. But I'd like it better if we could forget the goddamn guns for a minute and go over and sit at that table and have some beer and just talk. What do you say?"

He shrugged. "Sure."

Nolan rose from the couch. Steve got up off the floor, headed for the refrigerator. Nolan put the .38 away. Steve got the beers. Nolan approached the table. Steve handed him one beer, kept the other. They sat.

"Let me ask you a question, Nolan."

"All right. I may not answer, but all right."

"What makes you think you can trust me? How do you know I won't hit you in the eye with a can of beer or something?"

"You might," Nolan conceded, nodding. "You might even take my gun away from me. I don't think you're that good, really, but it's possible."

"Suppose I did. Suppose I took your gun away from you. What's to prevent me from using it on you?"

"Your own inflated damn idea of yourself."

"My what?"

"You're a man with a cause. You make up your own rules, but you stick to them. This morning, for instance. You wouldn't really toss a live grenade into a room full of mostly innocent bystanders. Oh, you don't mind throwing a firecracker and scaring folks a little—that's part of unnerving the shit out of Frank and causing more general chaos in the DiPreta ranks. But you don't kill anybody but DiPretas, and maybe DiPreta people, and since you don't know whether or not I'm a DiPreta man yet, I figure I'm safe for the moment."

"That's a pretty thin supposition, Nolan."

"Not when you add it to my being an old friend of your father's. After all, you're in this because of your father, and you're not about to go killing off his friends unless you're sure they got it coming."

"I get the feeling you're making fun of me."

"Well, I do think you're something of an ass, if that's what you mean. But I don't mean to make light of this situation. I spent the afternoon with your sister, Steve. I like her. I understand she's got a nice little daughter."

"What's your point?"

"I was hoping you'd have seen it by now. Look, how do you think I found you? Your phone is unlisted, isn't even in your name, is it?"

"No, it isn't. How *did* you find me?"

"Diane gave me the address."

"But I told her not to give it out under any—"

"And yet here I am. I sweet-talked it out of her, but there are other, less pleasant ways of getting information out of people."

"They wouldn't dare—"

"They wouldn't? You mean the DiPretas wouldn't? Why? Because it's not nice? You shoot Joey DiPreta with a Weatherby four-sixty Mag, tear the fucking guts right out of the man, and you expect the DiPretas to play by some unspoken set of knightly rules? You're an ass."

Steve looked down at the table. "They don't have any idea it's me, anyway."

"They don't? I heard Frank DiPreta, just a few hours ago, say he had a good idea who was responsible for Joey's death. And I also know for a fact the Chicago Family has a line on you, has had for months."

"How is that possible, for God's sake?"

"It's possible because the rest of the world is not as stupid as you are. Everything you've done points not only to a Vietnam vet but a Vietnam vet with a hard-on for revenge besides—military-style sniping, the use of a weapon designed not only to kill but to mutilate the victim, the grenade hoax, the half-ass psychological warfare of that ace-of-spades bit....Christ, was *that* self-indulgent! And top it all off with an obvious inside knowledge of the DiPreta lifestyle. The kind of knowledge provided by those tapes you have, for example. The ones your father gave you."

Steve whitened. With his white-blond hair, he was the palest human Nolan had ever seen.

"The possibility of you having copies of those tapes occurred to the people in Chicago long ago. You've been in their sniper-scope ever since, friend. Not under actual surveillance maybe, but they were aware you were out of the service, aware you were back in Des Moines."

"Jesus," Steve said.

"And when Joey DiPreta was killed by a sniper, who do you suppose was the first suspect that came to everybody's mind?"

Steve was staring at the table again. His color still wasn't back completely. He looked young to Nolan, very young, his face smooth, almost unused. Finally he said quietly, "I thought they might figure it out, yes, but not so *soon.*" Then he picked up the can of beer, swigged at it, slammed it back down and said, "But what the hell. I knew the odds sucked when I got into this."

"What about your sister, Steve? Did she know the odds would suck?"

"She doesn't know anything about it. You know that. This... this has nothing to do with her, other than it's her parents, too, whose score I'm settling."

"Score you're settling. I see. Do me a favor, Steve, will you? Tell me about the score you're settling."

"Why? You know as well as I do."

"I just got a feeling your version and mine might be a little different. Let's hear yours."

Steve shrugged. Sipped at the can of beer. Looked at Nolan. Shrugged again. Said, "I came home on leave a couple of years ago. Dad and I were always close, even though I was living with Mom, and he would confide in me more than anybody in the world, I suppose. I'd known for a long time about his...Mafia connections, I guess you'd call them. I knew that was the real reason for the trouble between Mom and him—that she wanted him to get out, to break all his ties with those people, and when we came to Des Moines, that was what she thought he was doing. But then she found out about the DiPretas, that they owned the motel Dad was managing and were no different from the bosses Dad had had in Chicago, and that was the end for her. She divorced him after that. Dad was crazy about her, but he liked the life, the money. I think you know that Dad gambled—that was a problem even in Chicago. And without the sort of money he could make with the DiPretas and people like them, he couldn't support his habit, like a damn junkie or something. Then when I came home on that leave, couple years ago, he told me he was through gambling, that he hadn't gambled in a year and wanted out of his position with the DiPretas. But he was scared, Nolan. He was scared for his life. He knew too much. It sounds cornball—he even kind of laughed as he said it—but it was true. He just knew too much and they'd kill him before they let him out. I thought he was exaggerating at the time and encouraged him to go ahead and quit. Screw the DiPretas, I said. He wanted to know if I thought Mom would take him back if he cut his ties with the DiPretas, and I said sure she would. And she did. They were going to get back together. He wrote me about it. In fact they both wrote me, Mom and Dad both. Two happiest letters I ever got from them."

Steve hesitated. His eyes were clouded over. He took a moment and finished his beer, got up for another one, came back and resumed his story.

"Dad had to find a way out. That's where the tapes you mentioned come in. Dad installed listening devices in some of the rooms at the motel, and so on. Then he offered the tapes to the DiPretas in exchange for some money and a chance for a clean start, fresh start. They didn't believe that was all he wanted. They thought he was going to try and milk them, so they tried to get the tapes from him, without holding up their end of the bargain. Dad sent one set of the tapes to me for safekeeping. He left another set with Mom. The DiPretas must've known about Mom and Dad being on friendly terms again, because somebody broke into her house, when she wasn't supposed to be home, to search for the tapes. But Mom came home early and…and got killed for it. The next day Dad hanged himself at the motel."

And Steve covered his face with one hand and wept silently.

Nolan waited for the boy to regain control. Then he said, "It's a touching story, Steve. But it's just a story."

"What the hell do you mean?"

"You put most of it together yourself, didn't you? From the pieces of the story you knew."

"No! I talked to Dad when I came home on leave that time, and he sent a letter with the tapes, and—"

"I guess maybe it's just a matter of interpretation and ordering of events. You say your father was afraid for his life. I believe that. But he wouldn't have cause to be afraid until after he'd begun recording tapes and collecting the various other dirt he was using to blackmail the DiPretas."

"Blackmailing..."

"Your father didn't want out, Steve. He was happy where he was. The DiPretas were considering firing him because his gambling habit was out of control."

"That's a goddamn lie!"

"It isn't. I listened to your version, now listen to mine. Your father bugged certain rooms in the motel, used the information he gathered to try and blackmail the DiPretas and the Chicago Family as well. Part of it was to blackmail his way out of certain gambling debts he owed his bosses. Part of it was to hopefully *retain* his position, not leave it."

"No!"

"By giving your mother those tapes to keep for him, he was putting her in mortal danger. He hanged himself because he felt responsible for your mother's death, Steve."

And Steve lurched across the table and swung at Nolan.

Nolan swung back.

Steve sat on the floor and leaned against the refrigerator and touched the trickle of blood running out of his mouth where Nolan had hit him.

Nolan had remained seated through all of it but half rose for a moment to say, "Get off the floor and listen to me, goddamnit. There are more things you don't know, and need to."

"I'll listen, Nolan," Steve said, getting back up, sitting back at the table. "I'll be glad to listen. I won't believe a word of your shit, but I'll listen."

"Christ, man, don't you want to hear about the DiPretas? Don't you want to hear about the object of your crusade? The DiPretas are not Mafia people, as you put it. Oh, they have connections to the Chicago Family, they sure do. And they do have a family background that includes a good deal of mob activity, prior to the last fifteen years or so. But more than anything they are businessmen. Crooked businessmen, yes, with connections to what you call the Mafia. But if you want to kill all the businessmen in America who fall into that category, you got a busy season ahead of you."

"That's bullshit! Vince and Frank DiPreta are gangsters, they're—"

"Vince used to be a gangster, of sorts. Vince the Burner, he was called, but even then he treated arson like a business. Lately Vince's been the conservative DiPreta, wanting to shy away from illegal business interests and associations. Frank? Frank likes to carry guns around. Frank likes to play mobster, but he isn't one, not really. Not in the sense you're thinking of. Income tax evasion and stock swindles and graft, sure. Should be plenty of that on those tapes of yours. But cement overshoes and Tommy guns and dope-running? Come on. The DiPretas are restaurateurs, motel and finance company owners, discount-store proprietors, highway and building contractors. Shady ones. But nothing more. Your first victim? Joey DiPreta never did anything more vicious than swing a golf club at a ball. Like all the DiPretas, he liked to play the Mafioso role, to a degree, anyway. It was his heritage. But he was no gangster."

Steve had the stunned look of a man struck solidly in the stomach. He said, "Then…then who sent the man who killed my mother?"

"Chicago. The Family wasn't satisfied the DiPretas could handle the situation, and they sent a man in, and that's who killed your mother. The DiPretas were incensed and have since been considering severing their ties with the Family."

"Nolan, Jesus, stop, Nolan. Is this true? Is what you've been saying true?"

"Every word."

"Then I've been…"

"Killing the wrong people."

"I don't believe it."

"I don't blame you. If I were you, I wouldn't want to believe it either. It would make everything I'd done without meaning."

"How do I know you're telling the truth?"

"How do you know I'm not? Haven't I at least established the possibility you're tilting at goddamn windmills? And the wrong windmills, at that."

"I got to have time to think, Nolan. I got to have time to think this through."

"There isn't any time to think. Frank DiPreta's closing in on you, friend, you and your sister both."

"What happened to the song and dance about how harmless Frank DiPreta is?"

"I didn't say he's harmless. I said he's a crooked businessman who likes to think of himself as some mob tough guy. And another thing: he's got this funny quirk. He doesn't like it when members of his family get murdered. He wants revenge. Is that hard for you to understand, Steve?"

"I…I see what you mean."

"I hope to hell you do."

"But there is something I don't see."

"What?"

"I don't see where you figure into this, Nolan. I don't see you as a DiPreta man, and I don't see you being lined up with those Chicago people, either. I mean, I heard the story from Dad about how you bucked the Family, walked out on them when they wanted you to do their killing for them."

Nolan spread his palms. "Well, there's been a shake-up in Chicago, Steve. Most of the people I had my problems with are dead. The same is true of the ones who sent the guy into Des Moines who killed your mother. I won't say it's a whole new ball game, but I will say the lineup's changed considerably."

"You work for the Family, then?"

"In the same sense your father did…the very same, in fact: I run a motel for them, too. I was asked to come here and talk to you, to act as an intermediary, because I was 'uniquely qualified' for the role, they said. I got unique qualifications because for one thing I got a reputation for refusing to be involved in Family bloodletting. But mainly I was asked because I was a friend of your father's. And yours, too."

Steve looked at Nolan for a moment. A long moment. Then he held out his can of beer in the toasting gesture and said, "Comiskey Park."

"Comiskey Park," Nolan said, and touched his beer can to Steve's and they drank.

"What happens now?" Steve said.

"A lot of things could happen. More people could die, for instance. Or…the killing could stop."

"Suppose I think that's a good idea. Suppose I'm ready for a cease-fire, Dr. Kissinger. What then?"

And Nolan told Steve about the Family's offer, the one Felix had outlined to Nolan the night before in the back of the Lincoln Continental outside the antique shop.

The Family's offer was this: Steve was to leave town immediately and drop out of sight as completely as possible, not telling even his sister he was going and not contacting her after he was relocated, either. For traveling and living expenses the Family would give Steve $100,000, to be deposited in the bank of his choice. All he had to do was contact Nolan after relocation, and Nolan would see to it the money was routed to Steve. The Family would provide Steve a new identity, with Social Security number, personal background history, the works. Several years of cooling off would be necessary. While the official police investigation would most likely be relatively brief, Frank DiPreta's interest in the matter would continue indefinitely. The Family would keep an eye on Frank and make sure Steve's sister and her little girl were not bothered. Eventually Steve should be able to reunite, at least occasionally, clandestinely, with Diane and Joni. But for a while—a good while—precaution would be the rule. In return, the Family wanted one thing.

"The tapes," Steve said.

"The tapes," Nolan said.

Steve sat and stared, his face a blank. "Well?" Nolan said.

Steve stopped staring. Took a sip of his beer. "Okay, Nolan. You want the tapes? You can have 'em. You can have 'em right now." He got up, turned to the refrigerator and opened it. He pulled out a drawer in the bottom of the refrigerator crammed with packages wrapped in white meat-market-type paper. Steve yanked the whole damn drawer out and tossed it on the table.

"That's all of them," he said. "Tapes, pictures, transcriptions, etcetera. All of it."

"Are these the only copies?"

"No. I made another set. They're in a locker at the bus station. I left the key with a lawyer with instructions that should anything happen to me, he was to give the key to this man." And he dug in his back pocket for his billfold, got out a piece of paper, handed it to Nolan.

"Carl H. Reed," Nolan said. "Isn't he the guy who was on the golf course with Joey DiPreta?"

"Yes. He's planning an investigation of the DiPretas. They tried to bribe him and it didn't take."

Nolan nodded. "He's the new highway commissioner. Just took office. One of the honest ones?"

"Apparently. He sure wants those tapes."

"Give them to him if you want, Steve. But you're on your own if you do."

"I know. I kind of wish I could help the guy out, though. But I guess that's not possible."

"Guess not. Can you get hold of that lawyer and get the key from him? Right away?"

"I don't know, Nolan. It must be after six-thirty."

"It's quarter to seven, but call him anyway. Maybe he stays late and screws his secretary."

Steve went to the phone, tried the lawyer's office, had no luck. He tried him at home, got him there, and the lawyer said he was going out for the evening but could meet Steve at the office at eight if it absolutely could not wait and if it absolutely would not take more than a minute or two.

"Fine," Nolan said. "You can leave tonight, then."

"I…guess so," Steve said. He seemed sort of punchy. "Nolan, I'm confused. It's all coming down on me so fast."

"Frank DiPreta is what's coming down on you fast. You got no time to be confused. You maybe got time to pack."

"Hey, what about the guns?"

"Better drive out in the country and ditch them. Probably should take the Weatherby and Thompson apart and dump them in pieces, different places. It's dark out, find some back roads, shouldn't be a problem. You got time to do it before you meet that lawyer if you shake it. What about those grenades? Any of them live?"

"Some of them."

"Well, disarm the fucking things before you go littering the countryside with 'em."

Steve nodded and went after some newspapers in the laundry room to spread on the floor and catch the powder he'd be emptying out of the grenades.

Nolan sat on the couch. He felt good. He felt proud of himself. He'd just done the impossible—taken a decent kid turned close-to-psychopathic murderer and turned him back into a decent kid again. Anyone else the Family might have sent would have botched it for sure, would have come down hard on the $100,000 payoff offer, when it was the psychological kid-glove treatment leading up to the offer that had made the sale. It was something only Nolan could have done, a bomb only Nolan could have defused. He was a goddamn combination diplomat, social worker, and magician, and was proud of himself.

The phone rang.

Steve came in with newspapers and started spreading them down, saying, "There's that damn scatterbrain Di bothering me after all I went through telling her not to. Get it for me, will you, Nolan?"

Nolan picked up the receiver.

And a voice that wasn't Diane's but a voice Nolan did recognize said, "If you want to see your sister and her little girl again, soldier boy, you're going to have to come see me first." The voice, which belonged to Frank DiPreta, repeated an East Side address twice, and the line clicked dead.

Nolan put the receiver back.

"What was that all about?" Steve said, getting the grenades out of the wardrobe. "That was Diane, wasn't it?"

"No," Nolan said. "Nothing. Just a crank."

"What, an obscene phone call, you mean?"

"Yeah. That's it exactly."

15

Basking in a soft-focus halo of light, golden dome glowing, the Capitol building sat aloof, looking out over the East Side like a fat, wealthy, disinterested spectator out slumming for the evening. Down the street a few blocks was a rundown three-story building whose CONDEMNED sign was no surprise. The only surprising thing, really, was that none of the other buildings in this sleazy neighborhood had been similarly judged. Some of the East Side's sleaziness was of a gaudy and garish sort: singles bars and porno movie houses and strip-joint nightclubs, entire blocks covered in cheap glitter like a quarter Christmas card; but this section was sleaziness at its dreary, poorly lit worst, with only the neons of the scattering of cheap bars to remind you this was a street and not a back alley. The buildings here ran mostly to third-rate secondhand stores; this building was no exception, though its storefront was empty now, showcase windows and all others broken out and boarded up. It stood next to a cinder parking lot, where another such building had been, apparently, till being torn down or burned down or otherwise eliminated, and now this building, the support of its neighbor gone, was going swayback, had cracked down its side several places and was in danger of falling on its ass like the winos tottering along the sidewalk out front.

Nolan leaned against the leaning building, waiting in the

cinder lot for Jon to get there. Less than twenty minutes had passed since he'd accidentally intercepted Frank DiPreta's phone call at McCracken's. If he hadn't been so pissed off by the turn of events he might have blessed his luck being the one to receive that call. His painstakingly careful handling of the boy this afternoon wouldn't have counted for much had Steve been the one to answer the phone and get Frank's unpleasant message. Nolan's description of the DiPretas as businessmen, not gangsters, would have looked like a big fat fucking shuck to the boy, in the face of Frank grabbing Diane and her little girl and holding them under threat of death, and Steve would have reescalated his war immediately. The cease-fire would have ended. Nolan would have failed.

But Steve was safely away from the scene, thankfully, out in the country somewhere, dumping the disassembled guns and disarmed grenades. (The boy had asked Nolan if he could hang onto the two handguns, since neither had been used in his "war," and Nolan had said okay.) Nolan had realized that if he tried to leave directly after that phone call, he'd raise Steve's suspicions; so for fifteen agonizingly slow minutes Nolan sat and watched Steve empty the grenades, take apart the Weatherby and Thompson, and when Steve finally left to get rid of the weapons, Nolan (tapes and documents in tow) followed the boy out the door, saying he'd meet him back at the basement apartment at nine-thirty.

Nolan had taken time to stop at a pay phone and make two calls: first, to Jon, at the motel; and second, to Felix, long distance, collect, to inform him of the successful bargaining for the tapes but telling him nothing more. Then he'd driven to the address Frank had given him, and now here he was, standing by the Cadillac in a cinder lot on the East Side of Des Moines, waiting for Jon.

A white Mustang pulled in. The blonde girl, Francine, was behind the wheel. Jon hopped out of the car.

"What's this all about?" he wanted to know.

"I don't have time for explanations," Nolan said. "Just listen and do exactly as I say."

Two minutes later Nolan was behind the building, in the alley; earlier he'd tried all the doors and this one in back was the only non-boarded-up, unlocked entrance. A garage door was adjacent, and Nolan reflected that this dimly lit block and deserted building, whose garage had made simple the moving of hostages inconspicuously inside, could not have been more perfect for Frank's purposes. There was an element of warped but careful planning here that bothered Nolan. Frank was out for blood, yes, out to milk the situation for all the sadistic satisfaction it was worth; otherwise he would have gone straight to McCracken's apartment and killed the boy outright, since having managed to get the phone number out of Diane the address itself would be no trick. But DiPreta was not berserk, was rather in complete control, having devised a methodical scenario for the destruction of the murderer of his brothers. Like Steve McCracken, Frank DiPreta was a man who would go to elaborate lengths to settle a score.

He went in. Pitch-black. He felt the wall for a light switch, found one, flicked it. Nothing. He fumbled until he found the railing and then began his way up the stairs, his night vision coming to him gradually and making things a little easier. The railing was shaky, and Nolan tried not to depend on it, as it might be rigged to give way at some point. Nolan was more than aware that he was walking into a trap, and just because he wasn't the man the trap was set for didn't matter much. It was like walking through a minefield: a mine doesn't ask what side you're on, it just goes off when you step on it.

At the top of the second-floor landing was a door. He tried it. Locked. He knocked, got no answer. He went on, climbing slowly to the third, final landing, where an identical door waited for him. Identical except for one thing: it was not locked. It was, in fact, ajar.

No noise came from within, but Nolan could feel them in there; body heat, tension in the air, something. He didn't know how, but Nolan knew. Frank was in there. So was Diane, and her daughter.

He pushed the door open.

It was a large room, the full floor of the building, a storage room or attic of sorts, empty now, except for three people down at the far end, by the boarded-up windows, where reddish glow pulsed in from the neons of the bars on the street below. Dust floated like smoke. Frank DiPreta, white shirt cut by the dark band of a shoulder holster, his coat wadded up and tossed on the floor, loomed over the other two people in the room, who had been wadded up and tossed there in much the same way, Nolan supposed. Diane was still in the white terry robe she'd been wearing when Nolan last saw her a few hours before, but the robe wasn't really white anymore, having been dirtied from her lying here on the filthy floor, hands tied behind her, legs tied at the ankles, white slash of tape across her lips. At first glance Nolan thought she was dead, but she was only unconscious, he guessed, doped or knocked out but not dead. The little girl, a small pathetic afterthought to this unfortunate tableau, huddled around her mother's waist, not tied up, not even gagged, but frightened into silent submission, clinging to her mother's robe in wide-eyed, uncomprehending fear, whimpering, face dirty, perhaps bruised. Nolan had never seen the child before and felt an uncustomary emotional surge. She was a delicate little reflection of her mother, the same white-blonde hair the whole family seemed to have, a pretty China doll of a child who deserved much better than the traumatic experience she was presently caught in the middle of. Nolan forced the emotional response out of himself, remembered, or tried to, anyway, that Frank DiPreta was a man driven to this point, that Frank was not an entirely rational person right now.

"Frank," Nolan said. "Let them go. They aren't part of this, a couple of innocent girls. Let them go."

"What are you doing here?" Frank said, for the moment more puzzled than angry at seeing Nolan. Not that the silenced .45 in his hand wasn't leveled at Nolan with all due intensity. A .45 is a big gun anyway, but this one, with its oversize silencer, looked so big it seemed unreal, like a ray gun in one of Jon's comic books.

"You were right this morning, Frank," Nolan said. "The Family did send me. To check the lay of the land. To…to negotiate a peace."

"I'm going to blow you away, Nolan. He's here with you, isn't he? Where? Outside the door? Downstairs waiting for your signal? You're in this with him. You were there with the soldier boy when Vince got it, weren't you? You set Vince up, you son of a bitch. You won't do the same to me. I'm going to blow the goddamn guts out of you, Nolan, and then I'm going to do the same to the soldier boy, just like he did Joey, only it's going to take me longer to get around to it. First he's going to have to suffer awhile, like I been suffering."

"It's too late, Frank. McCracken's gone. He left the city half an hour ago. He doesn't even know you've got his sister and her daughter."

"Don't feed me that bullshit. It hasn't been half an hour ago I talked to him."

"I answered the phone. I was there at his place. I'd just sent him away, put him in his car and sent him away."

"This is bullshit. I don't believe any of it."

"It's true."

"No!"

"Let them go, Frank. It's over."

Frank leaned down and grabbed the little girl, Joni, by her thin white arm, heaved her up off the floor. She hung rag-doll limp, not making a sound, having found out earlier, evidently, that this man would hurt her if she did. There was as much confusion as terror in the child's face; she simply did not understand what was going on. She looked at the huge gun-thing the strange man was shoving at her and did not understand.

"Frank..."

"I'm going to kill this kid, Nolan. He's downstairs, isn't he? Go get him, or so help me I kill this kid right now."

"A little girl, Frank. Five, six years old? You'd kill her?"

"She's one of his people, isn't she? He's murdered my whole goddamn family out from under me. There's none of us left. I'm the only goddamn DiPreta left, and I'm going to do the fuckin' same to his people. I don't give a goddamn who they are or how old they are or what they got between their legs. He's got to suffer like I suffer."

But Frank wasn't the only DiPreta left, and Nolan knew it. It was time to play the trump card.

"Jon!" Nolan called. "Come on up!"

"What's going on?" Frank demanded. "So help me, Nolan..."

And suddenly, Francine DiPreta was standing in the doorway. Her look of confusion mirrored that of the small child across the length of the room, who was presently dangling from Frank DiPreta's grasp like a damaged puppet. When Francine recognized this man as her father, the confusion did not lift but if anything increased. She said, "Daddy?"

Frank DiPreta tilted his head sideways, trying to figure out himself what was happening. His face turned rubbery. He lowered the child to the floor, gently; looked at the gun in his hand and held it behind him, trying to hide it, perhaps as much from himself as from his daughter, who approached him now.

"Daddy…what's going on here?"

"Baby," he said.

"Daddy, is that a gun?"

"Honey," he said.

"What are you doing with that gun? What's this little girl doing here? And is this…her mother? Tied up? What are you doing to these people, Daddy?"

He said nothing. He lowered his head. The gun clunked to the floor behind him.

"Is it true, then?" she said. "What they say about you? About us? The DiPretas? Are we…the Mafia, Daddy? Is that who you are? Is that who I am?"

Nolan and Jon watched all of this from the other end of the room. DiPreta's daughter and Diane and the child, with their blonde hair and pretty features, could have been sisters.

"Daddy," she said, "you're going to let these people go now, aren't you?"

He put his hands on his knees. His mouth was open. He lowered himself to the floor and sat there.

"I'm going to let these people go, Daddy, and then we're going home."

Francine DiPreta untied Diane, who had been coming around for several minutes now, and carefully removed the strip of tape from the woman's mouth. She asked Diane, "Are you all right?"

Diane, groggy, could only nod and then, realizing she was free, clutched her daughter to her, got to her feet shakily and somehow joined Nolan and Jon at the other end of the room.

Nolan said to Jon, "Help me get them down to the car."

Jon, who still had no idea what the hell was going on but knew better than to ask, did as he was told.

At the other end of the room, Francine DiPreta was on her knees, holding her father in her arms, comforting him, rocking him.

16

Nolan sat on the couch and waited while Diane put her daughter to bed. He could hear the little girl asking questions, which her mother dodged with soothing nonanswers. That went on for ten minutes, and then Diane came out into the living room, still wearing the dirty once-white robe; she looked haggard as hell, her hair awry, her face a pale mask, but somehow she remained attractive through it all. She sat next to Nolan.

"Is she asleep?" he asked.

"Yes, thank God. Don't ask me how. I guess her exhaustion overcame everything else. But she did have a lot of questions."

"So I gathered."

"I didn't have many answers, though."

"I gathered that too."

"How about you? You got any answers, Nolan? Can you tell me what this was all about tonight? Is Stevie really a…murderer?"

"Steve's a soldier, Diane. He's been trained as a soldier. Killing is part of that. Sometimes soldiers have trouble readjusting to civilian life, that's all. Steve will be all right."

"You mean he…he did kill the two DiPreta brothers? I…I don't believe it. And I…I don't believe you're sitting there and talking about his…his killing people as if it's some kind of stage he's going through, a little readjustment thing he has to work out now that he's back home again."

"Diane, you're tired. You're upset. Get some sleep."

"I won't be getting any sleep at all tonight, Nolan, unless you tell me just what the hell is going on, goddamnit!" She caught herself shouting and lowered her voice immediately, glancing back over her shoulder toward her daughter's room. "You've got to tell me, Nolan, tell me all of it, or I'll go out of my mind wondering, worrying."

"All right," Nolan said, and he told her—all of it, or as much of it as was necessary, anyway. She stopped him now and again with questions, and he answered them as truthfully as possible. But he kept this version consistent with what he'd told Frank DiPreta. He told Diane her brother had already left, that Steve would be well on his way out of Des Moines by now.

"Will he…he call me or anything? Will I hear from him at all?"

"Not for a while, probably. But maybe sooner than we thought at first. After what happened tonight, Frank DiPreta may not be the same man. I can't say in what way Frank'll be different …maybe he'll be a reformed, nonviolent type from here on out, maybe he'll end up in a padded cell, I don't know. But he is going to be different, and that'll affect how long Steve has to stay in hiding."

"Nolan."

"Yeah?"

"I…I don't know how to react to all this. It's just too…too much to digest at once, too overwhelming."

"Give yourself some time."

"You know, Nolan, my…my emotions have been all dammed up inside me for a real long time…you know, ever since the folks died. For better or worse, you've changed that, coming to Des Moines today, coming out of my past, a memory walking in the goddamn door. I guess I have something in common with that awful Frank DiPreta....It's going to take a while to see what person I turn out to be, who I am now. I'll be different, too, after today, and you're the cause of it, or part of the cause, at least. And you know what the hell of it is?"

"No. What."

"I don't know whether to thank you for it or kick you in the ass."

Nolan grinned. "I'll bend over if you want."

"No, that's okay."

"Come here a minute."

"You're...you're going to kiss me goodbye now, aren't you, Nolan?"

"I think so."

"But that's all."

"Yeah. I think you've had enough emotional nonsense for one day. We can do more next time, if you want."

"I think that's a good idea. Nolan?"

"Yeah?"

"You can go ahead and kiss me now."

Nolan got back in the car and Jon said, "That took long enough. We must be on an expense account or you wouldn't let me sit out here with the car running all this time."

"Well, it was kind of a sensitive thing, you know. People who get kidnapped require sensitive treatment."

"You want me to drive?"

"Yeah, go ahead."

Jon backed out of the parking stall, drove out of the apartment house lot and got back onto East 14th. He said, "How about when your old archenemy Charlie kidnapped me, not so long ago? I don't recall you treating *me* sensitive."

"You're not six years old, either."

"That mother's not six years old. That mother's older than I am. You give her sensitive treatment, too?"

"Damn right I did. Wouldn't you?"

Jon guessed he would. "Where do I turn?"

"Not for a while yet. I'll tell you when." They drove.

Pretty soon Nolan pointed and said, "Second side street down. Walnut."

A Cadillac pulled out in front of them. "Hey, Nolan, did you see who that was?"

"See who what was?"

"That guy in the Caddy. I'd swear it was that guy what's-his-name."

"You don't say."

"No, really, that guy Cotter, Nolan, don't you remember?"

"Felix's bodyguard, you mean?"

"Yeah, the guy I gave the bloody nose to."

"Couldn't be. Here, turn here. You're going to miss it." Jon cornered fast and the big car lumbered onto Walnut. Nolan checked his watch: quarter to nine.

He'd said he'd be back by nine-thirty and had made it easy, despite the DiPreta diversion.

"Hey, what's that?" Jon said, slowing. "Is that guy sick?" A green Sunbird was parked in front of Steve's apartment. The trunk lid was open, and a figure was slumped inside, sprawled, sort of.

"Stop the car," Nolan said, and hopped out.

Nolan walked toward the Sunbird. The quiet residential street was unlit, with no one in sight but the figure bent over in half inside the trunk of the car.

He drew his .38.

And recognized the figure. "Steve?" he said.

He ran the rest of the way.

When he touched Steve's shoulder, he knew.

He gently lifted the body, looked at the dime-size hole in Steve's temple, where the bullet had gone in. The boy's eyes were open. There was an expression frozen onto the boy's face, which seemed to Nolan an expression of disappointment.

Steve's last thought, apparently, had been that Nolan betrayed him.

He lowered Steve back into the trunk, which was filled with luggage and other personal belongings. Steve had been loading up the trunk, evidently when it happened. Since there was no milling crowd, it was apparent a silenced gun had been used. Nolan noticed an envelope in Steve's breast pocket, when he lowered the boy; he looked inside the envelope, pocketed it.

He put the .38 away. He knew who'd killed Steve, and why, and knew also that the killer was no longer around.

He walked back to the Cadillac.

Before he got in, he struck the side of the car with his fist, leaving a dent.

Five:
Saturday Morning

17

Nolan broke the egg on the side of the skillet.

Jon, yawning, came into the kitchen. "Oh, Nolan…are you up already?"

"No." He broke a second egg. A third.

"No?"

"Haven't been to bed yet."

"Oh. I never saw you cook before. I didn't know you could cook."

"I'm fifty years old and a bachelor. I can cook. You want some eggs?"

"Sure. Sunny side up."

"Scrambled."

"Yeah, well, scrambled, then. What are you cooking for, Nolan?"

"Practice. I'm out of shape scrambling eggs and want to make sure I haven't lost my touch."

Jon yawned. "Why didn't you sleep?"

"I had some thinking to do."

"What kind of thinking?"

"Figuring some things out."

"Such as?"

"Such as whether or not to kill some people."

"Oh. What did you decide?"

"I'm still thinking."

"You want me to fix some toast?"

"Why don't you."

It was seven o'clock in the morning. Nolan didn't have to ask Jon why he was up. The kid always got up at seven on Saturday to watch old Bugs Bunny and Daffy Duck cartoons; Nolan had learned that the time he was healing up from some bullet wounds here at Planner's.

Nolan stirred the eggs. Added a touch of milk. He was coming down now, coming down from an anger that had swelled in him all the way home from Des Moines, building through the night as he sat in the front room in the living quarters above the antique shop. The anger was beginning to taper off now, after peaking half an hour ago or so; he was beginning to see the way all the pieces fit and that a single piece remained, a piece that was in his control.

Jon got out some bread and put it in the toaster and came over to Nolan and said, "What's on your mind? You want to talk now? It has something to do with that young guy that was shot in Des Moines before we left, doesn't it?"

They hadn't talked about it yet, any of it. The drive back to Iowa City had been a silent one. Nolan hadn't been in a mood to discuss anything.

"Yeah," Nolan said, stirring the eggs. "It does. I'm the one who killed that boy."

"What?"

"The Family used me to set him up."

"Oh. I see."

"I fingered him. I didn't do it knowingly, but that doesn't make him any less dead."

"What are you going to do?"

"I'm thinking about it."

"Deciding whether or not to kill some people."

"That's one option."

"That other time, years ago, you killed a guy in the Family over something like this. Isn't that kind of, well, inconsistent? You don't want to kill people, so as a protest you kill somebody?"

Nolan shrugged. "It was the principle of the thing."

"I see. Are you going to handle it the same way now?"

"I don't know. I'm older than I was then. Young guys do… crazy things sometimes. Maybe I'm smart enough now to find something better to do than go around shooting people, some better way to…settle a score."

"I thought things were different in Chicago now."

"So did I." He'd thought the change of regime meant something. That times had changed, that the businessmen had taken over, public relations men and computers taking the place of strongarms and Tommy guns. Which was true, he supposed, to a point. Past that point, however, underneath the glossy corporate image, the Family was the same bunch of ruthless bastards they'd always been, always would be. Faces might change with the style of the clothes, and the polish on the front men, like Felix, just got smoother all the time. But adding in computers and P.R. men didn't change the nature of the Family. Fact was it made the killing all the more cold-blooded impersonal. He stirred the eggs. "I'll be going to the Tropical this afternoon. You can come along and help me move out if you want, kid."

"You're quitting them, then? What are you going to do, go in business with that friend of yours?"

"Maybe. Maybe I'll throw in with Wagner. Can you put me up for a while?"

"You can stay as long as you want, Nolan, you know that." Jon got a funny grin going. "So you're breaking with the Family. I guess I can't say I blame you, but…"

"But what?"

"I just don't see that working for them, managing a restaurant or motel, is any, you know, big deal. No worse than working for the government or something."

Nolan laughed. "Shit, lad, I wouldn't work for those sons of bitches either. Get a couple plates before I burn these things."

They sat at the table and ate.

Jon said, "That guy Cotter…when I spotted him pulling out in front of us…he'd just killed that kid, hadn't he?"

"Yeah."

"You think you'll, uh, do something to Cotter?"

"Probably not. He's just a finger that pulls triggers."

They ate in silence a few moments.

"Nolan?"

"What."

"Is it all right if I get in touch with Francine?"

Nolan thought for a moment. Then he said, "I don't see why not."

"Good. I hate the way we had to get out of Des Moines so damn fast, without a word or anything. I hate to think she thinks I was…using her. I mean I didn't get to talk to her at all, after you brought her in to cool her old man off."

"I don't care what you do, kid, but I wouldn't be calling her long distance this morning."

"How come?"

"She's got a funeral to attend."

A double funeral: Joey DiPreta, killed by Steve McCracken, and Vince DiPreta, killed by somebody else.

Somebody else being the Family, in the form of a guy named Cotter.

When he thought back, Nolan realized he'd never directly mentioned Vince's death to Steve, thinking it was unspoken common knowledge between them. But he saw now that Steve had known nothing about Vince's murder. For one thing, the boy had registered surprise and non-recognition when first facing Nolan, whereas Vince's killer had already seen Nolan plainly through a sniperscope; and Steve's arsenal had not included a silencer, whereas Vince had been brought down by a silenced rifle dispensing a bullet of a caliber far less than one that could have come from Steve's bone-crushing Weatherby.

And Nolan had seen two cars driving away from the shooting scene, one of them a Corvette, which Nolan had assumed was Steve's, only to discover too late that the boy drove something else. The other car, the one Nolan ignored, was a Cadillac. The Family liked its people to travel first class: Lincolns, Cadillacs. Nolan drove a Family Cad. So did Cotter.

It was a power play, pure and simple: Vince was the conservative DiPreta who wanted to cut the cord with the Family, and so the Family, not wanting the cord cut, took advantage of Steve McCracken's "war" to get rid of Vince, making him look like just another casualty. The younger, more strongly mob-oriented Frank would be the sole surviving DiPreta brother and could be easily manipulated into staying within the Family fold.

Steve had been killed because once the tapes were in Family hands—in Nolan's hands—the boy was completely and desirably expendable. He died taking the blame for Vince's murder with him. He died saving the Family the expense of paying him $100,000. His murder would be explained to Frank DiPreta as a show of support by the Family. Hey, Frank, look, we tracked down the guy who shot your brothers and killed him for you, *paisan*. His murder would be explained to Nolan as having been the work of Frank DiPreta; the Family would deny any involvement, via Felix's usual line of bullshit.

"So what are you going to do?" Jon asked. "Tell that Felix guy to stick that fat Family job up his ass and break it off? Is that how you're going to handle it?"

"No," Nolan said, shaking his head. "I'll just quit. Acting pissed off won't do me any good. And I'm too old to wage war. Of course they expect me to put the money they're paying me back into the Family, and they'll bitch when I want to take it with me, but they'll hand it over. And they'll let me quit. I'm not important to them."

"What about the score you said you had to settle?"

"I'm thinking about it."

Jon was finished with breakfast. He got up and said, "Well, while you're thinking, I'm going in the other room and write Francine. That okay?"

"Why not."

Nolan got himself some coffee, sat and drank and thought.

The only loose end was Diane. He wondered how she was reacting to her brother's death. She'd made some ground yesterday in overcoming some pretty bad hangups. Would she regress now? And would she blame Nolan, in any way, for the death of her brother? He couldn't have risked staying last night to tell her about Steve, and he couldn't risk contacting her now, not with all the police that would be hanging around. Somehow, sometime, he would explain it to her. Whether or not she'd understand was another question.

This afternoon he would go to the Tropical, hand the tapes over to Felix, collect his money, quit. With no fanfare. No harsh words. If he got a chance to catch Cotter some place dark, that would be fine. But that was a luxury he could only indulge in if the opportunity presented itself; he wouldn't seek it out.

Oh, and he would mention to Felix that it was unfortunate that the Family (or Frank DiPreta or whoever) had decided to kill Steve McCracken, because there was no way, really, to know whether or not McCracken had had an insurance policy—that is, someone holding copies of the tapes and related documents for forwarding to certain authorities, should anything happen to the boy. Felix would moan and groan, but Nolan would disclaim responsibility. He'd been told the boy would be left alone; it wasn't Nolan's fault if somebody chose to kill McCracken and thereby set in motion the release of the tapes.

And the tapes, apparently, could do some real damage to the Family. Not put them out of business, of course—that would never happen—but cripple them for a time, cause them considerable grief. Especially if somebody should happen to inform Frank DiPreta that the Family was behind brother Vince's murder, in which case Frank just might turn up in court as a key prosecution witness, getting revenge and limited immunity as a sort of package deal.

Maybe you can't destroy the Family, Nolan thought. But you sure as hell can kick 'em in the balls now and then.

He dug in his pocket for the envelope he'd taken from Steve's pocket when he'd found the boy's body slumped over in the trunk of that car. The envelope contained an address on a slip of paper and a key. The key was to a bus station locker, and in the locker was the duplicate set of tapes and related documents.

He found a small cardboard box under the sink and brown wrapping paper and string in the cupboard. He put the key, with a terse explanatory note, in the box, which he wrapped and tied. He copied the address from the slip of paper onto the package, and signed as a return address: "R. Scott, Comiskey Park, Chicago."

Then he went into the front room, where Jon was watching Elmer Fudd shooting Bugs Bunny with a shotgun and getting nowhere. He said, "I thought you were going to write a letter."

"When this is over."

"Do me a favor." He tossed the package to Jon. "Mail that. First class."

"Sure." Jon looked at the address. "Carl H. Reed. Who the hell is he?"

"Never mind," Nolan said. "Just mail it."

THE
END